THOMAS WILLIAMS

TOWN BURNING

ANCHOR PRESS
Doubleday
NEW YORK
1988

PUBLISHED BY ARRANGEMENT WITH RANDOM HOUSE, INC.

Library of Congress Cataloging in Publication Data

Williams, Thomas, 1926—
Town burning.

I. Title.
PS3573.T456T6 1988 813'.54 87-17123
ISBN: 0-385-24250-6

PRINTED IN THE UNITED STATES OF AMERICA

Man hath still either toys or care,
He hath no root, nor to one place is tied,
But ever restless and irregular
About this earth doth run and ride;
He knows he hath a home, but scarce knows where,
He says it is so far
That he hath quite forgot how to go there.

—HENRY VAUGHAN

TOWN BURNING

CHAPTER 1

John Cotter stopped beneath the maple trees and turned to look back down the hill at the spruces, dark green and almost black in the shadow. The sun came just over their tops, and crows, gigantic, too loud in the quiet air, circled trembling and crying up into the light and down into the darkness. Under the hill the first shade of dusk had begun to settle in, but here on the height of the land the level sun veined bright maple leaves and made the dark trunks gold. Even from this low hill the long convolutions of the earth were visible and still; the wind had died just at evening, and his home town lay neat and quiet along the riverbank.

In August the town of Leah was mostly hidden beneath pillaring elms and more angular dark maples; all but the red-brick prison of a woolen mill, the white Gothic steeples of the churches and a white clapboard house here and there. The Connecticut River came down from the north, meandering through the narrow valley, highway following it, the black ribbon of the Boston and Maine Railroad straighter, on the far side in Vermont. The train that had brought him home had long since gone, toward the north and Canada.

In two months or so the leaves would turn red and yellow and orange in the sudden frosts, give out their own fiery inner light for a week or two before falling to the yards and streets, leaving Leah bare except for the brittle crosshatchings of branches, open to the wind and the eye. Then from this hill, if he were still in Leah, he would be able to see everything—leaning unpainted back sheds, the mill tenements of Poverty Street, the rusty bodies of cars in Shapiro's junkyard behind the high school, the summer-end gardens full of stalks and rotting squash—all ignored or forgotten things come to light in the season of truth. But now the leaves were kind, and Leah in its little valley was set, cozy and permanent. Leah waited for him below, seeming to have a solid, strict reality about it, as if in Leah, more than in any other place in the world, everything counted. Just by coming back (unwillingly) after so long a time, it seemed to him that some of the vulnerable, oversharp senses of childhood had been restored in him. Here houses were square and sensible, chimneys wide, shutters green against dignified high walls—windows always seemed to look down at him—trees were broader at the base, the earth's basalt protruded and led the mind back down to the core. Leah stood on no transitory alluvial plain, but on granite scarred by ice.

The top of the hill, pasture for one straggly cow, was clear of brush except for patches of dark juniper, in spreading flat circles ten feet across. Around the tumbled stone walls tall pines and maples held off an advancing army of small gray birch. At one side, by the bouldery path that had once been a town road, a little family graveyard lay on slightly tilted ground. A deer trail ran right through it, bright and twisting between the slate stones, and a birch had fallen and rotted out of its bark, leaving a print like a white hand.

John Cotter sat on a familiar granite cornerstone and watched the warm light cross his town and stop against the eastern hills.

He was a small man, neat and dark, thirty years old, with a precise, quiet way of moving, even of disappearing, that occasionally made people extremely angry. He would watch them as he now watched the dying light, blue eyes deep in his head below brows that grew together across his nose, as if he were watching beneath a hedge, in ambush and unseen. His body was square, tense; yet unless he was deliberately in motion—going from one place to another, or manipulating some necessary object—he remained absolutely still, a characteristic so rare, so shocking to see in an animal obviously human, that most people were irritated by it. He was quite aware of this habit of immobility; and since the original purpose of it, he believed, had been a desire for invisibility, he had tried to imitate the little movements, the ear pullings, the head tiltings of his fellow men. But he was no actor. His imitations always struck him as false, as poor camouflage. When he did move he was quick. His feet landed where he wanted them to, and he was very gentle with physical objects, rarely breaking anything. Now he turned away from the light on the scattered fields toward the little graveyard.

HUCKINS

—carved deep on the center stone: a name that had disappeared from Leah. Around the granite center stone thin slate markers leaned according to the patterns of the ground frosts of many winters: *Florrie, Zacharia, Mary, Abraham, Ezekiel* and *Seth.* It was Florrie's stone that always drew him—the only one with a verse, with the youngest age of death except for the babies and for the child Ezekiel, who died at six years. Her stone was straighter, too, mainly because several years before he had straightened it, feeling at the time guilty, remembering the rather unjust fate of the man who tried to support the falling Ark of the Covenant. There'd been no sense of righteousness or of good deed about the act—he remembered the thin edges of the stone in his hands, and the wet earth moving beneath his feet as the stone straightened, then the soft, fleshy feel of the sod as he stamped it tight along the stone's edge. He hadn't thought of Florrie Stonebridge's possibly being grateful, either, but only of the silence of the Huckinses.

One of his own damaging ideas about himself had to do with the fact that he would certainly have died at birth if it hadn't been for some medical inventions fairly recent in terms of the age of Leah—the incubator was one. And it seemed to him that he was somehow artificial, out of the stream of evolution and survival, as if he really belonged here with the babies under their little stones all in a row in back: John, aet. 5 days; Mary, aet. 1 day; Nathaniel, aet. 1 month, 17 days. They had to take their chances and he had not.

Florrie had lived to be 25 years, 7 months and 3 days old, and died on the nineteenth of February, 1806. The verse beneath the carved skull and wings was startling on the grim slate:

Her load was heavy.
Her back was slim.
Her heart was merry.
Rest her with Him.

Zacharia Calvin Huckins lay at the right of his three wives. His stone, the size of a brick, bore only three letters, Z. C. H. His full name appeared on the center, granite stone, but over him only the little one rode the frost heaves. The little stone—John had pulled it up one time with a gooseberry bush, the plant's roots having grasped it loosely, and had been a little shocked at the ease with which he kicked it back into its depression in the earth—it should have been turned under by frost and roots long ago. He was always impressed by Zacharia—the man had evidently chosen his own marker, after a lifetime of rolling and carrying the cragged monsters to the walls. Well knowing the weight of stone, he probably didn't want to have a big one pressing down on him. Or maybe his children deliberately chose the small marker—but this didn't follow, hadn't at least in the case of his own grandfather, that frightening man who lay encased securely in an expensive cement vault in the town cemetery, below the ground in a casket, the casket in the vault so that the ground would not slump in when the casket rusted through. They had planted him expensively and finally. No, Zacharia had probably said, "By God, I'm sick of stones," being a New Hampshire farmer. But was he responsible for the verse on Florrie's slate? She had been his second wife, and he had outlived three wives and several children, according to the carved date, and had lived until 1843, seventy-eight years of fighting behind him. Such discipline might easily have tried the sentiment out of Zacharia, but John had seen old hill farmers who had some small touch of humanity left—not much, but some, when there was time for it.

But even in his own lifetime, in the time he could remember, the hill farms had mostly all gone back to dark, the farmers dead or gone South and West or gone to the mills. This farm had long since gone, except for the pasture on the town side of the hill, where the juniper and birch were slyly creeping in. In a few years it would be jungle like the rest.

A chipmunk had been watching him, and suddenly it jerked up straight, then ran, clattering dry grass and leaves. It stopped on the wall, quivering, tail snapping just at the tip, and looked beyond John to the pines. Something had come up behind, and he turned his head slowly, not really startled, but still feeling himself to be a stranger here. He had been away from Leah and the woods for two years.

At first he saw nothing but the shadows growing toward him, edges long and broken by the disappearing sun. As the sun went down, the wind came on again and the pine boughs sighed and moved. Something watched him, he knew, and he would stay motionless and carefully cover the area with his eyes, up and down, then on a few feet, then up and down again until he had marked each tangle of bush—then back again—and he would perhaps see what it was. If it were a man he would see him soon enough when he moved. If it were an animal he could only wait and hope to see it. In the woods again where there were no straight lines and no arbitrary edges and squares, where every leaf and twig waited to be crushed or to catch and crackle, he sat still and continued his examination of each shape, feeling himself to be invisible as long as he moved nothing but his eyes.

Then he saw the tall man standing in the darkness under the pines, very near, as motionless as he was himself. A long gun partly hidden beside his leg, the man stared straight into John's eyes. Knowing at once that he had been seen, an uncontrollable smile suddenly appeared across the man's long, narrow face, shortening the face by inches. It seemed to turn from its original dark oval to a circle, and John saw long yellow teeth. The shotgun swiveled up and over his shoulder as he came out of the shadow, and the brush under his feet crackled and zipped across his overalls.

"Hi, John!" he said. "Didn't know who it was, straight off." He came and stood, grinning at John and then at the chipmunk, who still snapped his tail. "You seen that striped squirrel when he seen me!"

"You gave me a start, there, Billy," John said.

"Not so as you'd notice. Anyways, so did you me. I figured you looked kind of natural, except for them clothes you got on. I knew you weren't no game warden, anyways, and I got a couple pa'tridges hung in my crotch. Didn't know as it might be somebody'd tell on me." He twisted the visor of his cap that had once been white and that now, molded greasily to his head, the words *Duco Enamel* barely legible across the front of it, was the indistinct woods color of animals. He grinned, his large brown eyes sinking back among red wrinkles, blackheads and stray hairs on his dark cheeks, deep wrinkles black across his forehead. His lips thinned and shrank back away from his gums as he grinned, so that the long teeth were as bare as those of a grinning dog that might be snarling except for the slim evidence of a wagging tail. Billy Muldrow's grin had frightened people in Leah, as had the strangling, paroxysmal laugh that usually accompanied it. A big man, somewhere in his forties, he was known for his great strength.

"Everybody knows you half live off the woods, Billy."

"Cheaper than the town feeding me!" Billy yelled, and let his head fall back to laugh, a piercing clatter. Then he shook his head, pretending to be out of breath. "How come you ain't been up to see me, Johnny? You used to like my brand of cider, as I remember."

"I've been away."

"Now, that's right! Seems I heard that. How long you been away, now?"

"Two years."

"Two years! What'd you do, Johnny, go back in the Army?"

"No, I've been traveling around, going to school some."

"Seems you're a little old to be going to school, ain't you?"

"I know it, Billy. I'm too lazy to go to work."

"You and me both! I don't suppose you been home yet," Billy said, looking at John's clothes. When he turned around to listen to something in the woods, his overalls followed just a little behind, and then fell swinging to catch up. "Nothing," he said. "How about having a snort—won't keep you long, Johnny. I got a new house now. Come up and see it."

He waited for John to decide, and as he waited his face, that seemed to have been beaten and weathered by the same forces that had acted upon a gnarled pine bole behind him, grew nervous to the point of fright. Billy Muldrow, on the edge of Leah's containing, demanding grasp of everyone who lived in Leah's valley, had always, and with reason, feared the answer to any question. Impatience was entirely unconvincing in him; now he tried to be sternly disapproving, and achieved a poor parody of Leah's common attitude toward himself. "Seems to me you been away for two years you can wait fifteen more minutes."

"All right, Billy." John had his own reasons for waiting. He might have gone straight home from the station instead of taking this procrastinating long walk—a scouting trip—up Pike Hill and around in back of Leah, where he could see everything at once, and from a safe distance.

He turned his back upon Leah and followed Billy through the pines to a small clapboard building, surprisingly neat, painted bright yellow. On the side, stenciled in black, were the words NEW HAMPSHIRE HIGHWAY DEPARTMENT.

"How do you like my new house?" Billy asked.

"Fine. Do they know you've got it?"

"Sure do. It's one of them traveling offices, like. Washed into the river this spring and I paid twenty dollars for it, put her back together and hauled her up here behind my truck. Now I got two houses."

The other house lay on its side in the brush where Billy had rolled it, silvery boards nail-shot and bent, large red hens hopping in and out of it.

Billy, with a proud and proprietary flair, pulled out his key ring and selected, from a pound of brass keys strung like a sunburst upon it, the right one for the little door's padlock.

"My new house!" he said, and showed John in. In the dusty brownness, in the old-clothes stink—an odor hardly human and therefore not too sharply unpleasant, as if Billy Muldrow were as inoffensive in his filth as a hooved animal—he pulled out his only chair for John, tucked his shotgun into the spindly, dust-icicled rafters and lit an oil lamp. The two windows, under the dark pines, let in very little of the dying light.

As the warm lamplight grew in the glass, Billy's furniture, moved from the slightly bigger and draftier shack John remembered, came to view: black woodstove, oilcloth-covered table covered again from edge to edge with nuts, bolts, pipes, dishes, wrenches, interesting steel, brass and copper things that were angled, bent, joined, worn—

Billy's collection to be gleefully explained: "That's a sliding spline and a Spicer U-joint from a GMC 1950 three-ton truck. That's a needle valve from a thirty-gallon water heater." Billy's truck was smaller and older, and he hadn't running water, but he knew the names and uses of all his metal pieces. "Sometimes they come in handy." They never did. No handier than the treasures of a lepidopterist, they were no less accurately and lovingly designated.

In the corners of the shack, stacked and hung, were the supplies and tools of the woods—rifles, cant dog, a pyramid of turnips, a five-gallon can of kerosene, the immense links of a rust-brown logging chain, great rubber boots polka-dotted with cold-patches.

Billy turned to John and spread his arms. "A mite smaller than my old house, Johnny, but it's tight's a drum, and cozy. Don't take nothing to heat." He sat on his brown hammocky bed and lit his pipe, his long face thinning to a V as he sucked. Then he jumped up. "Jesus!" he shouted, feeling his pants, "I forgot them pa'tridges!" The wild laugh clattered as his body bent backward—a banshee fit, scattered tears and explosive hisses, screams beyond mirth. Then it all stopped short. He leaned toward John, who watched calmly, remembering that no response was necessary, and blew his cheeks into chipmunk balloons; a moment of silence to commemorate the fantastic humor of forgetfulness.

The moment over, he undid his overall straps, reached into his pants and pulled out the partridges. "One's pretty fat," he said, and squeezed it delicately with huge thumb and forefinger. "Pretty little bastards, ain't they?" The birds lay ruffled upon the nuts and bolts, brown and black, plump breasts and skinny necks.

"A lot of good meat there." John made the required, remembered comment upon edible game.

Billy suddenly braced, mock-serious, his stare barely belied by a smile withheld, and tore his cap from his head as if he were going to throw it like a gage into John's face. "Cider!" he shouted. "Hard stuff!"

"You did mention it," John said.

"I did mention it, by God, Johnny. I did! Well!" He kicked a floorboard, and it jumped up far enough so that he could get his hand under it and pull it up, and with it came a trapdoor. He climbed down out of sight.

The lamp gave a silent, smooth light. In the cellar a jug clinked and a wooden spigot squeaked.

He was nearly home, and as if Billy Muldrow's place—on the very edge of Leah—were a kind of compression chamber, he waited for the possibly suffocating plunge into the greater pressure of town and family below; into the involvement he had evaded for so long. Leah, this little nub of activity among the low New Hampshire mountains, in spite of all experience was to him the hard center of the world. The center, even though it had always seemed to him that one of the main reasons for growing older had been to escape—and he was not the only one who had tried and been unsuccessful. He had been to all the cities of the common dream of freedom and found them unreal—therefore delightful. He did not want to come home. Leah, however, was the place where life began, where death called and struck. His brother was in the hospital, and it was serious, and they had called him back to the place where everything began.

He heard a furtive, immediately inhuman scratching in the dark beneath the table, and reacted with uncharacteristic nervousness. He jumped up and away as shyly as a girl, then received the scornful glance of a large raccoon who swaggered out into the light, coughed warningly and picked his nose with a black, spidery hand. The dark eyes, secure and knowing, planted like jewels in the fine mask of his face, took care to examine his possible enemy before he turned to climb upon the table. He found no reason for fear, evidently, and let his glossy fur settle down again along his shoulders. He then sat down upon a plate, picked up the fatter partridge by the neck, and looked into the bird's dead and gummy eyes.

"Hey, Billy," John called softly.

"Yo! Just a minute, boy, I'm filling a jug!"

The raccoon looked accusingly at John, and his fur rose a bit.

"There's a raccoon on the table."

A gallon jug of amber cider appeared upon the floor, and Billy followed. "Oh, that's old Jake," Billy said. "He's all right."

The raccoon watched with great interest as Billy filled two tumblers. His nose was twitchy, his little tongue furtive upon his furry chops.

The cider was light, slightly bitter, with something of the aftertaste of old yellow cheese about it. John thought of the cellars of old houses—white clapboard houses and black earth basements, late fall and the odors of old wooden rain barrels: that wind in the nose was cool and damp.

"Have some more," Billy said, and tapped the jug with his palm.

John reached for the jug, but the raccoon's sharp teeth got in the way, white and grinding.

"Ain't he the cussedest animal?" Billy said, then turned and, without pause or transition from his calm, conversational tone, raged: "God damn it, Jake! This is my house and that's my cider and I'll do what I want with it!" The raccoon held his ground, and snarled back. When Billy raised a threatening hand the raccoon backed off a few inches, but with little loss of face. "Here, Johnny, I'll pour it myself," Billy said. He scowled at Jake and filled John's glass full to the brim. "Ain't no goddam critter going to tell me what to do!"

Jake sat on the table and watched them drink.

"Enough people in this town trying to tell me what to do as it is. You know, Johnny, they got me black-listed in Leah."

"They got you what?"

"They got me on the black list. I can't buy no beer in no grocery store. I can't 'enter' the goddam liquor store. How do you like that?"

"Is that legal? What did you do, Billy? You haven't got any dependents."

"I don't know if it's legal, but Chief Atmon wrote it out on this paper and stuck it up in all the stores. Says 'blacklist' on it and my name right next Susie Tercotte and Eightball, Sam Wells, Wallace Widdicomb—all them drunks and a couple old bags live down on River Street. Enough to make a man git mad."

"You're no drunk, Billy."

"I know it! I *git* drunk, but I ain't no souse, Johnny. You know that." Billy took a drink and looked over John's head into the dark corner where a dusty ham hung on a thong. He cleared his throat. "They just don't like me. They just don't like me, that's all. Shot my dog. Shot Daisy. I lived here all my life and never did no harm to nobody." He took the jug and poured Jake a drink, first dumping a pile of nuts and bolts out of a soup bowl. The raccoon lowered his delicate black nose into the cider, shivered and began to lap.

"I never did like this town," John said.

"You and me both. I lived here all my life and I never did like the goddam town of Leah. It can wash on down the Connecticut goddam River like it almost did in Thirty-eight, blow away, burn up—wouldn't bother me none. Like to have one of them big adam-bombs, I'd roll her down Pike Hill bumpity bang bump right down the center of Maple Street, smoking and hissing and all like that. Wouldn't them little farts run and jump? BOOM! They can have their lousy store-bought beer."

"Why did Atmon do it?"

"It ain't that I'm poor—I got nobody depending on me. I eat good, don't charge nothing at the store, make good money in the woods when I feel like it. I got a truck. I register it every time and git it inspected like everybody. Don't none of them people like me, is all—Atmon don't like nobody ain't got bucks up the chute. Them old biddies this side of Bank Street—now I don't mean your maw, Johnny, she ain't as bad as the rest—but them big society big-ass biddies with their Women's Club and all. You know what I mean? Sometimes I wish I'd of stayed in the Army; they want a man to kiss their ass like that. They don't like the way I smell, they don't have to talk to me. Nobody's going to tell me what to do. I had enough of that in the Army. Now I got to drive across the river to git a quart of beer."

John shook his head.

"Now I hear Atmon's going to try to git me black-listed over in Wentworth Junction, too. Then I'll have to go clear to Northlee."

"What started it with Atmon?"

"Johnny, I don't know. Seems they won't let a man live his own life any more. I'm my own boss and Atmon ain't. I don't feel like working, I lay abed or go fishing. Atmon's got to suck up to them old biddies run this town, the high bloody muckymuck sixty-nine-degree Masons, Rot'ry Club, Elks, Lions, Owls, Mooses, Gooses, Skunks and all that goddam zoo. They won't leave me be, is all I know."

"If you ever want any beer I'll get it for you," John said.

"They can keep their beer, Johnny. But I want to thank you, Johnny. You never was one of them people. You never was a lousy Junior Stevens nor Keith Joubert nor one of them used to pick on me."

"They used to pick on me, too."

"Latest thing, they sawed out the cross brace on my outhouse seat, hoping I'd fall in. Course I saw it. I seen them going down the hill. I told Junior Stevens next day if I ever caught him in the woods he'd wish to God he never was born."

"He and my brother used to make me wish that," John said.

"If you'll pardon my saying it, Johnny, I never could like your brother Bruce."

"Neither could I."

"Not that I ain't sorry he's in the hospital. I don't like to see no man in the hospital, Johnny. I guess that's why you come home. Ain't that right?"

John put his glass on the table. "I hate to go down," he said.

"It ain't your fault, Johnny. It's the goddam town of Leah. It's our misfortune we was born here. It's funny about a little town can be good or bad. You take Wentworth Junction, for instance. Now, that ain't a bad town. I always did like Wentworth Junction. Nobody never done me no dirt in Wentworth Junction."

John poured himself half a glass. "I hate to go back, Billy. I don't think I ever would've come back at all, ever, if it wasn't for this happening."

"Where was you, anyway?"

"Paris."

"Paris, France? Well, by God, Johnny, I don't blame you none!"

"I mean I'd of had to come back to the States, anyway. No money. But I wouldn't have stopped by at Leah."

"Your ma and dad wouldn't like that, though—not coming to see 'em." Billy looked him straight in the eye—disapprovingly.

"I know they'd want to see me. But Bruce always got so upset whenever I was around. They said in the telegram he wanted to see me, but they always say that anyway." He got up and finished his cider standing. "Thanks for the hooch, anyway."

"That's right!" Billy said, laughing. "Ain't that batch strong, though! Jake won't drink of the other barrel, but by God he loves that one!" He looked around. "Where'd that critter go, now, anyways." The raccoon was gone, but both partridges were still on the table. "Now, you come up anytime you want, Johnny. Anytime. If you want, bring me a case of beer sometime. I'll pay you for it."

"I will. And I'll find out why Atmon shut you off."

"Yeah, sure, Johnny." He didn't seem too interested in that. "But you be sure to come and see me, now. You do that."

John was at the door, and opened it.

"Misery loves company, you know," Billy said. "You can find the way."

John left Billy standing in the little door against the lamplight, filling the door and stooping over in it, chinks of yellow light coming out around him.

And still he didn't want to go home. He should never have stopped, should have let the momentum of the thousands of miles take him straight into Leah. He walked forward, letting his feet in the thin city shoes slip on the pine needles, toward the Huckins graveyard. The west still had color; the sky was bright as day, but the ground was dark. The stones in the little square graveyard tilted darkly against high pale grass, and the birchbark hand lay phosphorescent against the swallowing ground. Florrie Stonebridge Huckins lay in her moldering bed, her bury-hole. *My* back is strong, he thought, but how do I know it?

When he was a little boy and first saw the stones, they meant graveyard, to stay out of, to be afraid of, and later on he could read the verses and the dates. Then it didn't seem too bad that Florrie Stonebridge had died at the old age of twenty-five. But she had grown younger every year. Now he had lived five years longer than Florrie, and she had died too young. *Her heart was merry*—they loved her. *Her back was slim*—they pitied her—old Zacharia did, anyway, with his stiff spine and horny hands and a sea of stones to carry from the fields, the dwarfish apple trees to keep alive.

The pine boughs sighed. Nearer, a single dry leaf clicked. Suddenly it seemed possible that Florrie Stonebridge, whose slim back wasted among the stones and roots, might come swaying up as a ghost, like thin cloth pulled under water. Or a moldered hand might reach out and feel his ankle. He walked stiffly to the wall, deliberately slow, stiffly moving each foot as if cold bones would touch him if he ran.

He could see the neglected road he must go down, vague among the advancing birch, and at the bottom houses, visible as warm yellow windows among trees. Maple Street, a tunnel under elms, led to his home.

As he walked slowly down Pike Hill, the town came up to meet him. He could not escape its enfolding arms and a warmth that seemed to flow out of the houses and touch his skin. Lamps shone from windows onto lawns and lilac bushes. Thick tree trunks led up into the dark over his head, arching out to form the ceiling of a cave. A smudge of random August leaves smoldered in the gutter—leaves from the maples and one great beech he remembered as if it were a resident person on this street. He could tell the odor of the beech leaves from all the others. Beside the smudge, a wooden wheelbarrow and a wooden rake caught the light as the red hole in the middle of the pile grew bright and faded. He knew the names of the people who lived in the houses, even remembered the bulges and cracks in the sidewalk where roots passed beneath, could name the tranquil faces inside in the light of bridge lamps, in rooms he had been in himself. He remembered evenings after supper on Maple Street, and could hear, eerily as if through an old radio, the cries of children—*Aing going in aing tell maing mama! 'Fraidy cat! You don't play fair, you don't play fair!* And the last cry was probably his own as he once again found out how unfair things could be. And yet the town held him close, folded itself around him. He remembered this tunnel of a street in all seasons, in all weather—spring days of warm air above melting snow, the first odor of thawing earth; sweet, entirely new and strange after winter, late fall and a horizontal sun at four o'clock; red against the red clapboards of an old square house, the dusty umbrella of a tall elm in bonfire smoke, the same elm upside down in a summer rain puddle; down, down as it climbed to a summer sky and white clouds, lilacs around the kitchen doors, springy and sweet, dog days, mosquito days, the hours after supper when it was getting dark and blue and the children ran smack through the hedges to get away, calling to each other around the corners that were new and dangerous in the dark. The tunnel shut softly behind him. He was home, and sober as a child. He passed the Baptist Church, all dark. The town hall bell rang eight o'clock, each *dang* of the bell wavering on the wind.

He stopped across the street from his own house, still not wanting to go in. But now the windows were all dark and the garage doors were hooked open. I can't get in, he thought, knowing at the same time that there were several ways he could get in the house, even if it were locked, and it never was. The dark windows looked down at him, the house solid among thick bushes, framed by two blue spruce, the lawn barely green in the streetlight. Above the broad wooden panels of the front door the fanlight's narrow triangles of glass winked in the streetlight; shadows of leaves moved up and down across the white boards. The house was clean, the paint spotless flat white that seemed to be slightly fluorescent against the dark shutters and small windowpanes. The house neither pulled him toward it nor rejected him, but sat there on its own ground with a solidity, an everlasting solid reality that made him suddenly shy, nearly afraid. He had no protection, none of the objectivity that he had been able to depend upon in foreign places. He wished for another tumbler of Billy Muldrow's hard cider, then turned toward the town square, having decided quickly and, he thought, rather clinically that he had better get a drink.

Bruce must have had a car, and since there were no cars at all in the double garage, his father and mother had gone separate ways—most likely his mother to the hospital in Northlee and his father to the office. He would go to the office and see his father, but first to Futzie's Tavern, if Futzie's was still there, if anything outside of Maple Street was still there as it used to be.

He came out into the Town Square, store windows and neon shining across the green below the tall elms, and walked along the dark side where the great old houses stood. On two sides of the square were gaunt Victorian blocks with Roman arches for windows: *Tuttle Block 1901, Masonic Hall 1893, Cascom Savings Bank Bldg 1907.* On the other two sides of the square the houses of the wealthy, the little round library, the Congregational Church and the colonial-style post office (1937) gave the square a settled, cozy New England look. On the business side the ground floors of the red-brick blocks contained F. W. Woolworth, the familiar red and gold sign hung against brick arches, Follansbee's Hardware, Strand Theater, Fire Station, Trotevale's Department Store—shoes on the left, dry goods on the right, plumbing and mistakes in the basement. People were just coming out of the first show at the Strand, and he circled the dark side, walking among the trees and vacant wooden benches so that he would meet no one. Lights were on in the tourist information booth beneath the wooden bandstand, and inside he saw one of his high-school teachers, Miss Colchester, stacking folders and sharpening pencils, making things neat, fussing busily as she always did.

He managed to reach the comparative darkness of River Street without speaking to anyone, knowing that he had been seen and noted by three people, knowing also that the three were aware of his having seen them and of his deliberate avoidance of their eyes. He approached Futzie's carefully, then walked quickly past, trying to see who was in the dim room below the bluish television set. He saw enough—a broad black leather jacket and the back of a familiar head. Junior Stevens, who would most likely not be there without some of his friends. Although no motorcycles leaned against the building, he decided not to take a chance on it, and continued down the crooked little street toward the railroad spur and his father's office.

The lights were on, and the yard light shone on the familiar black-and-white sign:

Wm. Cotter & Son, Building Contractors
Bldg. Materials, Paint, Lumber
Cement & Cinder Blocks
Lehigh Coal

His father's Buick was parked beside the low clapboard office. Paint cracked and peeled on the office trim and on the sign; weather had warped and separated some of the clapboards, shooting the nails. Frost and rain had gullied the cinder driveway, and the old storage buildings sagged. But the huge padlock on the main gate was shiny, as were the tracks of the railroad siding that entered the yard beside the gate. All wood touched by hands was smooth and clean on gates and railings.

Still scouting, although he had nothing to fear from his father, he went to the office window. His father sat at Bruce's desk in the outer office, his large head cocked sideways in order to keep the smoke from his cigarette out of his eyes, staring with a puzzled, humorous expression at a sheaf of forms. In his brightly checked sport jacket, striped shirt and bow tie, his gray slacks with their thin and elegant folds, he seemed the personification of the adorned male—the pheasant cock, the bright strutter of his glaring virility. He was, John sadly knew, afraid, as any cock would be, of the two sons he must consider, alien as they were to his open nature, dark and silent weasels.

At that moment his father looked up and saw him at the window. An expression of fear quickly crossed his father's face—so quickly he could barely tell that it had been there before a huge grin shone like a light. The big man stood up and waved John around to the front door.

"Come on in, Johnny, for God's sake!" His voice was deep and strong. "Jesus H. Christ you gave me a turn! For a minute I thought it was your brother."

"How is Bruce?" John asked.

"Well, Johnny, we don't know yet. How was Paris, anyway? You could write us a postcard once in a while." His father's eyes watched him warily, worried as they always were when he met his son again. "You didn't rot your gut out with that red wine, did you? Did I send you enough to get home on all right? I guess so. You're here, aren't you? I sure am glad to see you back, Johnny. Your mother's damn' near crazy with this hospital business." His voice trailed off at the end. Any expression of doubt or pain was terrible on his father's face.

"They don't know what's wrong with Bruce?"

"There's something wrong with his head, Johnny. In his head."

"His head?" John said.

"I mean he's not mental, or anything like that." He put his hands up over his ears and shakily pushed them up over his head to form a steeple. Then he took them down quickly. "He's been having these terrible, God-awful headaches. His eyes get bloodshot, and water. You know him. He wouldn't go to the doctor nor say anything, but we sat at dinner and watched him. He got mad at first if we mentioned it—you know, like he always did get mad. But he's been acting funny lately, for him. He was tired, and sometimes he didn't even get up in the morning. He was—ah—sort of different —to get along with. He was easier to get along with, to tell you the truth, Johnny."

His father looked down at the sheaf of forms lying on the desk, and let himself down into Bruce's creaky swivel chair. He picked up the forms and weighed them in both hands, moving his hands up and down, and then tossed them into a corner of the cluttered desk.

"Well, I can't make head nor tail of those," he said.

"Is it a brain tumor?" John asked.

"I guess so, Johnny. I guess so. But don't say that in front of your mother. She don't like the word. I don't blame her. Cigarette?"

John took one and sat on the secretary's desk. His father swiveled around.

"You mean they have to operate?" John asked.

"That's what Bruce is deciding now. The doctors figure they better, because it got worse so quick. Two months ago he was O.K. It came on all of a sudden." His father's face softened into a look of wonder. "Johnny, you wouldn't have known Bruce in the last couple of months. He was sort of gentle. I mean he'd sit and visit with people. He'd even make jokes—you know what I mean—jokes so people could laugh *with* him. You know what he said when they gave him this test at the hospital? He said he was going to have his brains waved. They were testing his brain waves, or something like that. That's not *like* Bruce."

His father poked his cigarette at the butts in the ash tray, turning them over, making a neat little pile in one corner. John could not see Bruce making that joke. For a second he wondered, startled, at the possibility that it might not be true. But his father would never make up such a thing. It might have been one of his mother's little plots to bring John back into the family, into her lovely dream of a family, like her habit of telling him in letters that Bruce missed him. No, his father had at least learned never to get mixed up in his mother's little plots. If Bruce *had* changed that much under the weird pressure of his disease, he didn't want to think about it. He didn't know if he could stand to think about such a thing.

His father had been watching him, and turned away shyly. "It took you a long time to get home, Johnny." He could hear no trace of blame, no trace of opinion in his father's voice. "I was worried I didn't send you enough money for the plane ticket."

"Things were a little mixed up then," John said.

"Mixed up how?"

"Well, I owed some money around and I had to use some of the money and take a ship back."

"Same old Johnny," his father said, still no trace of blame in his voice. "I guess we better be getting home before your mother gets back from Northlee. You got your bags?"

"Over in the station."

While his father turned off the office lights and locked the door, John went out and got into the big Buick. It was new, and when his father came he mentioned it, thinking at the time that this was a conscious act of kindness toward his father, who then proudly pushed buttons and said, "See?" as some goo appeared on the windshield and the wipers efficiently wiped it off. The radio tuned itself; the seats whirred and moved up and down; the windows whirred and did the same. The car floated over the bumpy cinders. As they turned out of the yard driveway he saw the mountain of sawdust by the sawmill, partly damming the little Cascom River that had once powered the sawmill and the woolen mill and even the paper mill farther down toward the Connecticut. The double peak of the sawdust mountain had grown considerably in two years. The pile had always seemed huge to him—the dust of a full century of trees. The pile was crusty and hard; big chips, really, torn out by the great circular saw, full of splinters and unpleasant to slide in. There were supposed to be pockets down deep in it—traps for boys—and he had often been pulled, slivery and itching, from the slopes of it, spanked, and sent home, knowing all the time that he would slide on it again even though it was an unpleasant thing to do.

They crossed the Connecticut through the long wooden covered bridge that was full of little hills and dips, the bridge making the same rhythmical tune, *flimp flamp flump flimp,* the Buick floating over all the little dips, diving forward softly at the last big one.

They got out of the car and went into the little yellow and brown station together. John's trunk and suitcase were still where he'd left them by the ticket window, and he took them out to the car. He could hear his father and the stationmaster yelling greetings and laughing.

"That's right, William," he heard the stationmaster say. "It ain't as bad as you'd think!"

"At your age, you old goat!" his father called back as he came out of the station.

"So long, William. Take it easy, William," the stationmaster said.

It seemed to John that the stationmaster's voice had changed too quickly at the end, as if he had shut off his amusement instantly and was now seriously back at work. His father came back chuckling and smiling—for too long a time, as if he were starved for banter. Thus his overjoy; the sign of inequality, the mark of the clown. Still, John could not really know—never having entered easily into Leah's amusements—what sort of man his father was supposed to be. With his head of brilliant white hair, his handsome face that always seemed to be expensively tanned, he did seem larger than life, and vivid, as if he were an actor (or a clown) just off the stage and still part god, part paint.

They drove back over the river into Leah. "Your mother won't be home yet," his father said. He parked next to the kitchen and insisted upon carrying John's trunk and suitcase inside. "How about a cold beer, Johnny?"

As he took his suitcase up the back stairs to his room he heard the familiar noises of his father opening the refrigerator for the beer. His room was the same except that his mother had changed the wallpaper. Huge, feminine flowers bloomed behind the squat black desk and the old leather chair. It was typical of his mother that she had carefully rehung his gunrack and stuffed partridge against the flowers.

He started down. The steps slanted pleasantly to the left, old and worn in the middle to a shallow scoop, as if they had been the steps of a waterfall instead of stairs. The house was old, for America, and yet made of wood. Compared to his hotel in Paris this house was young. In this house the mice had only to cut through wood, but in his hotel in Paris the mouseholes ran through solid stone. All the original wood had long since been replaced, there, bit by bit. The only original part left was the stone hull, and it leaned heavily against the next building. Here the walls were dry, at least. In Paris he had to scrape white mold off the inside of his typewriter case. Here clothes were dry and clean, and the bathroom was as neat and clean as a field. Hot water, plumbing—symbols of materialistic decadence, he had been told by his French friends. He smiled. But would the regular fellers welcome him home? Rotary, Elks, Kiwanis, Odd Fellows, Moose, Grange, Lions, Masons, Knights of Columbus, Knights of Pythias, DeMolay, Rainbow Girls, Eastern Star, Shrine,

Boy Scouts, American Legion, Veterans of Foreign Wars—would they all welcome home a fellow materialist? The Junior Chamber of Plumbing, the Legion Drum and Bugle Corps—how about them? He remembered phrases from clean, materialistic rooms: *R.O.T.A.R.Y. spells Rotary! We stick together! Brothers, the degree which you are about to receive represents the tragic climax of the career of Jacques DeMolay, the hero and martyr who was the founder of our order. No giggling. This sign means, brother, that a brother's sister is in need of assistance. Step forward and kiss the book!*

His father stood by the electric stove, waiting for him, a can of beer in each hand.

In the living room they sat back in the comfortable chairs. For a minute they were silent, and John looked, remembering, around the colonial room. The fireplace, original brick mellowed and dulled; faded by time and his mother's antiquing, the woodwork; scraped, treated, warm old wood, the cobbler's bench, the hooked and braided rugs, the painted trays; stenciled in old patterns—that had been a Women's Club project years ago and had lasted until all the old tinware in town was painted black, stenciled and bordered with flowers—the bright wallpaper of old design, the polished brass of the fire irons: it seemed to him that in this room, cheerful and slightly cluttered, every object had been oversmoothed, rubbed, sanded, waxed, varnished, linseed-oiled until, as in a padded cell, there were no sharp edges on anything.

"Your mother ought to be home by now," his father said.

John hoped he would be able to have at least one more beer before she returned.

"Is she taking it O.K.?" he asked.

"Like a soldier. She's taking it like a soldier."

Maybe she was taking it like a soldier, but another beer would help. The idea of his mother being any kind of soldier was too upsetting. He finished his beer and went to the kitchen to get two more. When he came back his father was smiling at him.

"Now don't get worried, Johnny," his father said. "She's taking it very quietly. You don't have to get worried."

John was suddenly ashamed of himself.

"I don't blame you, though," his father said.

"There's Bruce, lying up in that bed in Northlee," John said slowly, "worrying about getting a hole drilled in his head, and I worry about a scene. I won't take off this time, though. Don't worry about that."

"You and me both, Johnny. This time we both have to face it. You can't take off to Timbuctoo, and I can't go fishing."

They both listened tensely, not moving, as a car came crunching up the gravel driveway and stopped beside the kitchen door.

CHAPTER 2

Jane lay dry and alone upon the wide white bed in the high room. From one window came the sound of the elm branch that gently touched the house, aimless yet gentle, as if old fingers absent-mindedly leafed the familiar clapboards. High above, the wind passed clear and steady over the roofs of Leah, and in the whisking of the leaves she felt stronger forces working upon the great trunk of the elm—the torque in the supple body, all forces in balance deep in the hard and twisting wood.

Streetlight, scattered by the tree's movement, glanced across the high ceiling, and her open eyes followed the cold patterns as if, like a drowning mouth struggling for air, they struggled for light. Michael Spinelli, her husband of ten years and a man of thirty, supposedly mature, would now be riding the black and windy road back from Concord. Drunk on wind and beer, deafened and exhilarated by the exploding engine between his legs, he would be moving up in deadly curves to try to lead the pack. He must show the rest of the fools —the cautious fools—the white death's head stenciled upon his black jacket. The Riders would follow him northward into Leah.

She moved carefully, arching her spine, keeping within the outline of her body's warmth upon the sheet. She could shut her eyes temporarily, but they seemed sprung open, and shutting them was to force down little springs. Then the question would come back, carefully inserting itself into her mind in different ways. Sometimes it came disguised as a recent memory, sometimes as a memory of herself as a young girl in grammar school. Who was that girl? What did she want to be when she grew up? And then the question: Why did that girl marry Michael Spinelli? She fought against answering the questions, and could not go to sleep. Not go to sleep. How did it happen? How could it have happened? But you know, she told herself. After the war everyone decided to get married, that's what happened. That's clear enough. And when the heroes came home they didn't look like high-school boys any more. They were supposed to be grim, serious men who might wake up in the night crying out, caught back in the fire and pain of war and the deaths of friends. And the women would have to be so gentle and understanding—so carefully natural and understanding in order to cure them of the wounds of war. How long had it been since Michael Spinelli had stopped being a grim, sensitive hero with a sudden bright smile? The glory of the submarines had worn off so easily. The sour smell of the woolen mill replaced it. Now he had his motorcycle, and tattoos on his arms, and a black leather jacket with chrome studs.

"I don't want him to get hurt," she said aloud in the dark.

"No, Janie." A black shape moved by the door, and Jane could see it from the corners of her eyes. "He'll be all right, now. He'll be coming home. Don't you worry." Her mother-in-law moved quietly toward the bed. The springs squeaked, and the surface of the bed tilted slightly.

"Don't turn on the light, Janie." Mrs. Spinelli's hands moved quickly in a gesture of restraint, and Jane heard the click of beads.

"You shouldn't have to go through all this, Janie," Mrs. Spinelli said. Her voice was too soft and gentle, with hysteria too obvious beneath the breathy lowness of it. She went on, trying to be calm: "He's just trying to be like he was. He's sick of the mill."

Jane thought, He's too lazy to get out of the mill.

"You don't answer me. I was just talking. I don't know what's the matter with him." The voice skittered on the edge. Jane knew that if she showed sympathy to Mrs. Spinelli the voice would break and the horrible noise of crying would start. She couldn't stand that again.

"Now you go to bed, Mother," she said in a practical, daytime voice. "He'll be back soon now." She would have to be very careful in order to get Mrs. Spinelli back to bed, or Mrs. Spinelli would feel that the strangeness of her wandering through the dark house deserved something special in crying fits.

"He'll be ashamed of himself," Jane said. "He won't run off again." For a week, she thought. She reached for the light beside the bed.

The light ticked on and caught Mrs. Spinelli by surprise, bending over her strong hands, the rosary knotted through her fingers. Tears had squeezed themselves out. She looked up at Jane, resenting the bright light. Her face was smooth between fine wrinkles, burnished like an Indian's, and her black eyes looked out at Jane reproachfully. Her hair was not all caught in the net she wore at night, and it was as black as her eyes. She looked like a young woman until she stood up beside the bed and turned away. Her shoulders pulled forward, her hips spread against her nightdress. Her waist, no longer a waist, filled out against the rayon

"That's right, Janie. I'll go back to bed," she said, and moved hesitatingly toward the door. The backs of her slippers were crushed down flat, and on the backs of her legs were fine black hairs.

"Mother!" Jane called, the old woman suddenly too pitiful.

"I'm going to bed, Janie." Still resentful.

Damn her.

Someone rapped softly, hardly loud enough to be heard, and then spoke loudly behind the door.

"Anybody up in there? I see the lights on!"

"Come in, Papa," Mrs. Spinelli said. The door opened quickly and Mr. Spinelli marched in.

"You ought to be in bed, Mama, dammit! Mikey ain't home yet?" He bowed quickly as if to look under the bed, and then looked behind the door, a thin little man in baggy long winter underwear.

"Whatsamatter you can't sleep? Dammit I ought to—Janie, he got you worried again? That lousy Mikey! You go to sleep, Janie. Now I talk to him in the morning." He took his wife by the arm. "Come to bed, Mama. Good night, Janie."

The door closed behind them. Mrs. Spinelli's voice, higher but not quite shrill, closed behind another bedroom door.

Silence. Jane turned off the light to wait for morning. The elm branch rubbed the house softly, and in the colder air the leaves made a brittle noise like the crushing of thin paper.

She thought she might have been asleep, and must have been, when she heard the low roaring in the town at four o'clock, echoing down the empty streets and across the river and back. Many motors in rhythm and out, in rhythm and out, like a pulse. They did not come closer, but slowly faded northward. The Riders were back from Concord. With this knowledge she was suddenly overcome by the tiredness she had been holding off, and fell asleep.

In half an hour the phone began to ring in the downstairs hallway. One ring, muffled by a door; two rings, clearer, insistent. Had there been three? She looked for Mike on the bed and could not find him. The phone began again, after a pause. One, two, three rings. The third made it too real, too much directed at her alone: Cesare Spinelli's number at half-past four in the morning. She felt that she must beat Mrs. Spinelli to the phone. The stairs creaked in the morning cold as she went down in her bare feet. She reached out quickly and took the receiver off the hook to keep it from ringing again, then stood holding it in her hand. The receiver spoke in a tiny voice, like a djinn in a bottle. She put it to her ear. It was as cold as a piece of ice.

"Hello," the phone said.

"Hello," she said into the phone.

"Janie? This is Charlotte. This is Charlotte Paquette at the hospital."

"In Northlee?" Jane asked stupidly. Sounds came from upstairs. A door opened, and the floor squeaked.

"I'm on night duty now," Charlotte said from the phone.

"Yes." The upstairs listened.

"Janie, they brought Mike here. He had an accident."

"Yes."

"Now don't worry, Janie. Don't get upset. Are you still there?"

"Yes." Dully, not wanting to let the upstairs know, she could ask no questions.

"It's pretty bad, Janie, but they're taking care of him now. Are you coming up here?"

"Yes, Charlotte. Thank you." She put the phone back together, knowing what would come from upstairs.

"Jane! What was it? Mikey?" Mr. Spinelli said from above. He came running down into the hall.

"He's at the hospital. He had an accident," Jane said.

"Oh, Jesus," Mr. Spinelli said, looking anxiously up the stairs. "Oh, Jesus. Mama's gonna go nuts. Is he O.K.? Is he hurt bad?" He took Jane's hand. "We'll go right now, Janie. Take it easy. Is he hurt bad?"

"I think so," Jane said. She looked at her father-in-law, and he looked into her face. He needed a shave, his little eyes were tired, sunken, surrounded by circles that were red, wet and shiny. His neck was red as a turkey's comb down to the place where his shirt came, and below that line his chest was bony and fragile, fish-pale except for delicate blue veins that seemed to be barely submerged in the skin. His large, gray-callused hands, the knuckles huge dabs of callus from the toggling racks of the tannery, rose as if detached from his body and settled on her shoulders.

"Are you O.K., Janie?"

"Yes, I'm all right," she said, knowing that she would have to go to Northlee anyway. She didn't want to go; this journey to see Mike wounded by his own stupidity had been taken in her imagination too many times. Now it hardly retained the pull of emergency, and as far as love was concerned, he had divorced her in favor of the machine too long ago. Who had done the deserting? She thought, perhaps, she had loved Michael Spinelli once; really she had loved the man she thought he might become.

Cesare Spinelli turned her toward the stairs, gently, and started her forward. "You get ready, now. It won't take me no time at all. I'll get the car out and wait in the driveway." He followed her upstairs and opened the door of her room for her. He whispered, "If you want we won't make Mama come, huh?" then patted her shoulder and trotted down the hall.

She faced the empty bed.

As she dressed, she thought of the coming scene, and it, too, had happened before in her mind. The Riders would be there, with her brother, Junior, and they would have to face her in whatever guilt they could assume for themselves. Junior would feel especially responsible, and the sight of her would give him pain. Junior would then lash out, in his poor brutal fashion, at himself, at anyone, at the world in general. It would be a scene more damaging to Cesare Spinelli than to anyone else, because he would blame no one but his own beloved son.

She dressed, combed her hair, put on lipstick and looked again in the mirror to see nothing but the way her hair lay against her head and the way the lipstick turned out. Between and around these two things a white face flashed and was gone.

Mr. Spinelli's old Plymouth idled in the driveway, the white exhaust curling up around the back in the morning air. The door opened for her.

"All set?" Mr. Spinelli asked. He reached across and shut the door carefully, then eased the old car down the driveway into the street, turning north, shifting as silently as possible. "I told Mama not to worry," he said.

The town was still asleep under the black sky. They went around the empty square and took the river road to Northlee, Mr. Spinelli driving the five miles slowly on the winding road. They met no other cars until they came into the larger town and passed the all-night taxi stand, the silent campus and square. Summer session was nearly over, a few lights were on in the college dormitories, solitary and lonesome in the large banks of darkened windows.

The old red-brick hospital seemed to be alive, crouched among its elm trees. The hall lights were all on, showing at the ends of the wings, and steam puffed regularly from a vent near the ambulance entrance. The parking lot was an island floodlighted, surrounded by large whitewashed stones. The bright machines of the Riders waited precisely in formation, leaning on identical kickstands, boondoggle and coontails hanging down from their handlebars.

Jane and Mr. Spinelli got out of the car, shut the doors quietly, and walked nervously and carefully to the front entrance, up to the round porch and through the large, thick-windowed doors. The Riders, in black leather, sat awkwardly in the old wicker chairs of the lobby, looking at magazines. They all watched Jane and Mr. Spinelli as they came toward the reception desk. Junior Stevens got up and followed, but would not look directly at his sister. Charlotte Paquette came around the desk and reached for Jane's hand.

"We'll have to wait for a while, Janie," Charlotte said. She looked down, dark and sympathetic, her white uniform binding and stiff.

"Is he all right now?" Jane asked.

"As soon as the doctor is finished I'll have him talk to you. I just called." Charlotte looked from Jane to Mr. Spinelli, including him. He had worn a necktie to the hospital, a formal place.

"They're doing everything they can," Charlotte said.

Jane had heard those words before, on the night her father died in this same hospital. Her mother had died here, too.

"Why don't we sit down?" Charlotte asked, motioning toward the tired wicker chairs.

Junior picked up a copy of *Look* magazine and hid behind it. His face was the face of the biggest boy—red, somewhat brutal in its shape, uncontrollable; and like the biggest and most awkward boy in school he kept his face set in a knowing, immature expression which excluded both interest and sympathy from the feelings of anyone who looked at him. He was thirty-two years old, unmarried, and worked as a laborer for Cotter & Son.

"It was an accident," Junior said from behind his magazine.

"I know it was an accident," Jane said.

Mr. Spinelli looked disgustedly at the *Journal of American Nursing*.

"It was windy as hell above Grafton, and he slued into a mailbox," Junior said. "It kind of stuck out on a pole, almost right into the road. They shouldn't stick mailboxes out like that."

"It was his own fault!" Mr. Spinelli said fiercely.

"His bike went on almost a hundred yards, but that mailbox scraped him right off of it. He was way ahead of us, going like hell on wheels," Junior said. He let the magazine come down for a moment and looked quickly at his sister. He started to put the magazine back to his face, but then threw it on top of the others on the table.

It isn't your fault, Junior, she wanted to say, but don't you and all your Riders look so heroic, as if this were war and this casualty were sad but inevitable. Don't brag about how fast Mike was going to show how brave and reckless you are or how drunk you were!

But then she looked at the Riders across the room—four girls and six men—boys. They were not enjoying themselves. They looked, aside from the trim bodies, pale and unhealthy. She knew all of them: the girls with the narrow hips and big breasts and pretty but now pallid faces, the boys with narrow hips and broad-shouldered uniforms. They were not bragging now. They did not want to die, or to be brushed as closely by death as they were now.

An orange light went on and off behind the desk, and a low buzzer gently kept time with it.

"I have to go, Janie," Charlotte said. "I'll come back as soon as the doctor is ready."

"Thanks, Charlotte," Jane said.

Mr. Spinelli's hand shook as he turned the pages of the *Journal of American Nursing*. On Jane's other side her big brother sat on his spine, his long legs in riding pants, his feet, in expensive Western boots, extending too far out into the room. She smelled the gasoline that had sloshed on the Riders, and she smelled Junior's fear as bitter sweat. The Riders looked into the distance or at magazines, occasionally glancing at their leader and his sister, the mourner.

"Why don't you go on home, Junior?" Jane asked.

". . . Wait and see how Mike's coming," Junior mumbled.

"You can't help now. They're doing all they can in there. Look how *they're* suffering." Jane pointed toward the Riders, who stared back at her, shocked by this gesture from the mourner.

"Can't do that," Junior said, slowly beginning to be indignant, then becoming terribly indignant. "Our friend!" he shouted, then went on in an angry whisper: "Mike was one of us. Don't get so damn' superior like all the rest! One of us, too, not all yours, God damn it, you! So damned superior! We'll wait all night and tomorrow, so shut up!" His hands crushed the brittle wicker arms of his chair, and he smiled. The Riders heard all this, and went fiercely back to their magazines, embarrassed, but with a principle to uphold.

Jane knew them well; the lobby was too quiet and too bright. Within half an hour of whispers and creakings they had left with Junior, truculent and ashamed, giving as their last word the deep roar of their machines in the silent town.

When Charlotte came back with the doctor they followed him down the long hall and into a little room. The doctor smiled at them and put his stethoscope firmly into his side pocket. He wore a clean white jacket he had obviously just put on, and his forehead was still red-lined from his surgical cap. He looked extremely tired.

"Janie, this is Dr. Karmis. This is Mrs. Spinelli, Doctor, and Mr. Spinelli, his father," Charlotte said.

"I think I should tell you first," the doctor said, rubbing the red line on his forehead, "that his condition is very serious. I understand that he hit a telephone pole. . . ."

"A mailbox," Jane heard herself say. The doctor looked at her closely, as if he were trying to look through a fog.

"A mailbox," he said. "His chest is very badly crushed. Fortunately he didn't hit his head. His lungs are punctured badly. The only thing we can do now is wait and see if he improves within the next few hours. If he improves, he may recover rapidly. I don't want to get your hopes up, though. I want you to know we've done everything possible. Everything we can for him. A nurse is with him now and will stay with him." The doctor paused, looking from one to the other.

Finally Charlotte spoke. "Thank you, Doctor."

"Thank you, Doctor," Jane said, turning toward the door.

Mr. Spinelli put his hand out and the doctor took it, surprised, and smiled warmly.

"We're doing everything we can for your son," he said. "Everything."

Mr. Spinelli nodded, without expression, and followed Jane out the door and up the long hall.

In the car, going very slowly toward Leah in the morning light, Jane watched the new sun light up the tops of Vermont hills across the river. A bright, beautiful day. In Cascom, to the east, her grandfather, Sam Stevens, would have finished the chores and would now be having his second breakfast, telling his hired men what had to be done today. In Leah, people would be getting up to go to work. Mrs. Spinelli would be waiting in her kitchen. Waiting . . .

CHAPTER 3

John Cotter lay in bed in his bright room, the morning sun flashing on the new wallpaper, the air still cool although the dry wind that came rolling down from the open window to his bed would soon blow hot. His watch, that had told the time in dingy stations, in bars, in his mildewed room in Paris, here told the hour of a fresh morning at home. Seven o'clock, and the house was about to wake up. He sat up in bed and looked at the back yard. The lawn had been cut recently, and this was one of the years the Cotters did not have a garden. The garden grew weeds on its uneven surface, and near the garage tough rhubarb had gone to seed. A dusty pile of kindling leaned against his father's outdoor grill.

Trying to remember other times he had looked out this window—other specific times: in Leah, memory tended to become one hazy scene stretching, without system, back to nothing—he thought the rock maple had grown perceptibly. Nothing else had changed very much. The birdhouse in the first fork of the tree was about to fall down, as it was always about to fall down. He had put it up himself fifteen years ago, tying it with half-inch rope which even then showed signs of rot.

That was the day he shot the red-shouldered hawk, and the bird-house was a kind of payment to all birds, necessary to help absolve him of the sin of the hawk's murder. It *was* murder; murder pure and simple, with all of murder's thick feeling of pleasure and power. He knew that boys must do this. Boys step on caterpillars and shoot English sparrows with their BB guns because the little birds are unprotected by law and because boys like to kill. Was there ever a boy who *never* pulled the wings from a fly? He had known this at the age of fifteen, known then that among his friends he, at least, found this weird joy mixed with pity and guilt.

He found the hawk sitting on the branch of a white birch, on Pike Hill, sitting erect and motionless, bemused for some bird-reason by the bright day. It would not fly even when he shook the tree. He ran home and got his .22, ran back and shot the hawk through the breast. He heard the *thunk* when the little bullet pushed through feathers and bone, and the hawk slowly raised its wings and flew down, losing altitude quickly, half gliding. One leg dangled. It hit the road and twirled around on the one good leg, wide wings raising a cloud of dust as they supported the bird in place of the useless leg. He ran up to the hawk, but the expression in the bright eyes kept him back. The hawk hissed and snapped his beak, ready to fight. Fearfully, John watched the brave animal arrange what weapons he had left—one talon, beak, and most of all his pure and fearless hate. John fired the rest of his ammunition directly into the breast, the feathers shredding, bullets digging up the dirt behind. Finally the hawk fell to its side and died.

At least he did not hate forever afterward the objects of his cruelty. Bruce did that. Whatever Bruce hurt he hated. John remembered very well the time Bruce had sealed his hatred for toads. He had been there on the beach at Lake Cascom with Bruce. John was five and Bruce was twelve, and that year there were toads of all sizes around the beach; little toads as big as a fingernail and toads bigger than a fist. Under every piece of driftwood, in every clump of grass, beneath every root of the shore trees there were toads, and Bruce killed them. He had an anchor, a tin coffee can filled with cement, and he dropped it on the toads. John followed him excitedly as he found more and more toads to squash. Finally Bruce found the granddaddy toad of them all and kicked him, rolling and ugly, covered with sand, out into the middle of the narrow beach. Like a fat old man, very dignified, the toad righted himself and looked around. He saw no way of escape—just the two boys above him. Then he put his hands over his head. Squatting there alone and in the open he didn't try to get away; he just covered his head with his stubby hands and waited. Bruce held the anchor high.

"Look," John said. "He's got his hands—"

And the anchor fell on the toad, blotting him out. Bruce went back to the cabin and didn't come out all afternoon. John was allowed to go fishing with his father, who even let him hold the tiller of the outboard motor for a while, and in all that excitement he forgot about the toads. Two years later, when he was seven, he remembered them because of the thing Bruce did when he found the toad on the lawn. Bruce got into a lot of trouble over that, because he took his father's deer rifle out of the upstairs closet and the ammunition out of the bureau drawer and shot the toad, point-blank, on the lawn, right in town. Nothing was left of the toad but some odd gore in a smoking hole six inches wide. Miss Colchester, the high-school teacher, was going by, and she called the police. What a time that was! That was the summer, too, when Bruce took the car and went for a drive—two years before he could get a license and hardly knowing how to shift gears. He got his behind warmed for that, too, although he didn't run into anything and probably wouldn't have been caught at all if he hadn't driven downstreet right through the middle of town. Seven or eight people saw him and called up to tell his mother. That had been a bad summer for Bruce.

The house began to come awake. The first sounds were floorboards creaking down the hall, then the bathroom door closing, then the toilet flushing. Another door opened. The bathroom cupboard closed with its glassy jingle and his father's electric razor started its bee-buzz. They were not going to wake the returned traveler. All the necessary morning noises that he knew so well were a little hushed, as they used to be when he was a child and sick in bed.

He did not worry this morning about seeing his mother. She hadn't been as bad as he expected the night before. No crying, no noises, except he suspected a certain artificial, brave look about her as if she had heard someone say that she was taking it like a soldier. No, she was too upset to put on an act. She really was worried and afraid for Bruce. She really loved him, if it were possible to love Bruce. Or perhaps it was now possible to love Bruce, because of the threat to his life. If there was anyone in the world who wanted to love, it was his mother. For some reason—perhaps because of this too obvious surplusage of love—he continually held her off. At least *he* did. Maybe Bruce never did. It was a mistake to credit Bruce with his own feelings—he'd learned that early—because no matter what he expected Bruce to do, Bruce probably wouldn't do it. It was as if Bruce looked coldly upon each experience and only then figured out how he would react. He seemed not to carry anything over from the past. Nobody ever figured Bruce, and he could think of no one who really liked Bruce. Perhaps it was because Bruce never got away from this town and the ton of known things it made him carry, like a heavy pack: not horrible things, or even very shameful things; things people might have completely forgotten. But these were his own, not Bruce's feelings. Did anyone remember, for instance, the time he, John, at the age of four, went down the schoolyard slide after he had filled his pants? Did they remember the expression on the face of the second-grader who followed him? He did, and he remembered who the second-grader was—Junior Stevens. The expressions that passed so quickly over Junior Stevens' face: wonder, as he felt his behind, guilty fear for a second, and then the remorseless, inevitable logic that led to John. Accusation, disgust, loud and detailed derision. Perhaps it had been forgotten—that and all the other things—or maybe the doings of a four-year-old were not held against a grown man. That might be worse. In Paris he'd had a clean slate, and that made all the difference in the world. Maybe if Bruce had been able to get away from Leah he could have started over on a different tack. Maybe . . .

The doorknob turned slowly and his door opened wide enough to admit his mother's head. She saw that he was awake.

"Good morning, Johnny," she said, coming in. The flowers on her rumpled, quilted housecoat matched the flowers on the wallpaper. She was tall—taller than both her sons, and her long face was coy and girlish. Her gray hair, pulled taut to her head by painful-looking curlers, was partly covered by the top of an old nylon stocking.

"A beautiful day for your first day at home," she said, sitting on his bed. She put out her hand to touch his forehead, and he involuntarily pulled back.

"I haven't got a temperature," he said. She looked at him fondly. "What's for breakfast?" he asked.

"Anything you want. Ham and eggs? Pancakes? Waffles? You look thin, Johnny. Have you been eating well in France?"

"Sure, but they don't eat good breakfasts in France. They more or less drink their breakfasts."

"I hope you didn't do that," she said, smiling.

"I drank my lunch and dinner," he said.

"Oh, don't try to fool me, Johnnykins!" She got up and did an awkward pirouette as she went to the door.

"Ham and eggs?" she asked. He nodded. "Get right up now, and you'll get a good breakfast for a change."

She went down the back stairs to the kitchen, leaving his door open. This was to make him get up. She seemed always to do little things like leaving the door open, as if she realized that a simple request was not enough, and people had to be forced to do what she wanted. He could never ask her what time it was: if she wanted him to hurry she would add fifteen minutes to the time, and if she didn't want him to hurry she would say it was fifteen minutes earlier than it was. At least she was consistently fifteen minutes off, and if her wants were known to him he could make a fairly good guess. One always had to know her motives.

He rolled over and looked out the window, seeing the leaves of the rock maple bright against a brighter blue sky. He was thirty years old and she called him Johnnykins. Oh, well.

His father came in, washed and shining, tying his necktie.

"Welcome home!" he said. He sat in John's old leather chair and looked seriously at his son.

"You know, we all have to go and see Bruce this morning. They may have to operate right away. That is, if Bruce gives them the go-ahead. When did you start smoking before breakfast?"

"I don't know exactly when. Don't they have visiting hours?"

"Not in Bruce's case. It's too serious, I guess, Johnny. I guess they think we may not have much more time to see Bruce. You know, he made out his will the other day."

"Jesus!" John said.

"You said it."

They both stared at the flowered wall. Finally William Cotter got up.

"I smell ham and eggs," he said. "How about you?"

They ate breakfast in his mother's specially constructed breakfast nook, cramped into a corner of the big kitchen.

"We'll eat a good breakfast and then we'll go and see Bruce," she said. John and his father went on eating.

"He wants to see you, Johnny," she said.

"He wants to see me?"

"Of course he does! What's the matter with you?" She suddenly started to cry as she bent over the toaster. The toast popped up and made her jump. "What's the matter with this family? What's the matter with it?"

John and his father looked at each other quickly and went on eating.

"He's your own brother! I don't understand any of you people!" She left the toast unbuttered and worked her long legs out of the breakfast nook, then went to the window and stood with her back toward them.

"It's O.K., Glad," William Cotter said, "Of course he wants to see Johnny. And Johnny wants to see him. Don't you, Johnny?"

"Sure I do," John said. "I haven't seen Bruce for two years now. Got to see how the old boy's getting along."

This was the lie she wanted. Now one of them, John or his father, would have to think of something to do to get her back to the table. John put two pieces of bread in the toaster and pushed down the lever. A little bell inside tinkled and attracted his mother's attention.

"I'll attend to that," she said. "You two finish your breakfast." She buttered toast and poured coffee, her long fingers expert at it.

They took the river road, William Cotter driving. John watched the sluggish river, low and dead between high mudbanks and mud-encrusted stones. He had never seen the river so low. Twisted tree trunks lay half covered, stubby branches reaching out of the muck. Even the hills were different; a lighter, dustier green. The fields along the river flats were overdue for the second cutting, but the sparse stalks of hay would not be much meat for a cutterbar.

"It's been cold, nights," William Cotter said, "but no rain and this everlasting wind . . ." He easily passed a pickup truck and swung back into his own lane. "I'm going to drop you two off and head back to the office for a minute. Got to get things going. Then I'll come back."

"It seems to me they can get along for a while without you this morning," his wife said.

"No, I'd better be there. Nobody knows what to do now Bruce is gone—in the hospital. Got to start things going," he said, looking straight ahead.

"I don't understand you," his wife said, waving away the office. "This morning! Your own son!" Her voice turned ragged.

John decided not to take sides.

"Now, Glad. I'll come right back as soon as I can! Bruce wouldn't want things all messed up. Now, would he?"

"I can't understand you. You know the decision he has to make about operating! And you want to get out of it! Oh, *goodness!*" She lost control of her voice and put her head down to cry. John put his arm around her and patted her shoulder, but this didn't seem to help. William Cotter, his forehead beginning to sweat, finally reached over and patted her.

"All right, Glad. All right, Gladdie. Take it easy now. Of course I'll stay if you feel that way about it. It's just that business . . ."

"Business!" she said, sobbing.

"I'm sorry, now. Everything'll turn out O.K. You wait and see. We'll have him back before hunting season, you wait and see. Of course I'll stay!"

She raised her head and took a Kleenex out of her purse.

"I'm sorry," she said, "but today . . ." She started to cry again, but braced herself against it and this time managed to stop. "There!" she said. She reached up and tilted the rear-view mirror so she could see her face in it, and got to work with the Kleenex.

They came into Northlee and went around the square, past the college buildings. John noticed that the palms of his hands were wet. He felt that he was in a mild state of shock. His face, in the still-tilted rear-view mirror, was pale and unhealthy, and he had to go to the toilet. His father didn't look very good, either.

They parked in the parking lot beside the ambulance entrance and walked in line around to the front, John's father and mother slightly ahead, walking as people walk to see the very sick—carefully picking their steps, aware of the fragility of their own bodies. He felt stiff, yet tired, as if he had run a long race and had his wind back, but not his strength. The doors were ahead, up stone steps. It was the first time he had gone to the hospital for such a reason. Before, he had always entered the place in strength and youth—even with his broken ankle the visit meant youth and vigor; the ankle had been broken skiing. But now his brother lay rotting, weakened by his disease, out of shape, in the hospital because of some internal corruption.

"Hello, Johnny," said a girl whom he had seen in his preoccupation only as a flash of white. Her name. In the neighborhood of Leah he must remember names.

"Hello, Charlotte." It was Charlotte Paquette. He looked at her out of his nervousness and saw that she had become less pretty, remembered that she had been in nursing school a long time ago.

"You look different," he said.

"Well, I'm older."

"Are you married yet?"

She blushed a little. That hadn't changed, but where was the quick answer she always had for such questions? Her five brothers had asked many embarrassing questions, and she always had an answer.

"No, not yet. Maybe I look tired. I've been on duty all night." She straightened her uniform. "Mike Spinelli got hurt on his motorcycle—very bad. They brought him in last night."

"That's too bad," he said. Mike Spinelli had sat next to him in home room one year. That was the year Mike had managed to be kicked out of school three times in one week. "He married Jane Stevens, didn't he?"

"You know that, Johnny."

"I know. I never could figure out why she married him. She didn't have to. They don't have any kids, do they?"

"No, thank God." Charlotte looked back toward the desk, then to the door. "He'll probably die. He crushed his chest. On a mailbox. The damn' fool!"

This startled him. Charlotte, among her five profane brothers, never used to swear at all.

"I'm glad to see you back, Johnny. Are you going to stay for a while this time?"

"I guess so."

"You'll be out to see us," she said. She had gone before he realized that she hadn't mentioned Bruce.

His mother and father had gone ahead. He asked at the desk and followed the directions to his brother's room, down cream-colored halls, past trays on stands and sudden views of people in bed, past an old man in a bathrobe walking stooped and slow. Bruce's door was open, and they all looked up as John entered.

"So he did come," Bruce said. His bed was tilted so that he could sit up, and his round face, pale, with the eyes dark and burning in it, and the blue of his shaven beard below, turned, after he had spoken, toward his father. John looked away, out the curtained window.

"How are you, Bruce?" he managed to say, and then realized what he had said. He waited for Bruce's sarcastic answer. But it didn't come. A man moaned down the corridor, long and windy, then moaned again.

"He always does that," Gladys Cotter said. "The nurse says she's disgusted with him."

"It must hurt bad," William Cotter said. His forehead was wet. He sat in a deep chair with his knees together and his hat and coat ready on his lap.

Bruce smiled, and as they furtively looked toward him he carefully lit a cigarette. John stood at the window and saw his brother reign over the room as he had always tried to dominate any room; strong, this time, in his sickness. A nurse came in with a tray of medications, picked out a jigger of colorless oil and fed it to Bruce.

"Agh!" Bruce said loudly. She tried to smile. "Would you have somebody bring a chair for my brother?" he said, pointing at John. Her smile became professionally fixed.

"Surely," she said, and as she left Bruce called to her.

"Hey, Miss Pease! Hey, Peasy! When are you going to give me a back rub?"

"You just had one," she said. "My, you're spoiled!"

"I like your touch, Peasy. I love your lovely touch."

"Bruce!" Gladys Cotter said.

It was necessary to smile. John made his face smile until the old man's moan grew in the corridor again. Bruce didn't seem to hear it.

"Do you have any more of those headaches?" William Cotter asked shyly.

"They keep me doped up," Bruce said, and then went on quickly, turning to John. "Well, how's the prodigal son like it back in the sticks? Pretty dull after Paris?"

"Now, Bruce," Gladys Cotter said, "let's not start arguing now. Johnny just got home—came home to see you."

"Ran out of money, you mean. Just made it for the funeral." Bruce grinned at John, his eyes glaring—the old expression that asked for a fight.

"Same old Bruce," John said, trying again to smile. My brother, he thought, my brother.

Bruce seemed perplexed. His mad grin disappeared and he reached for his cigarette with a shaking hand.

"He's probably afraid the goose won't lay any more golden eggs, or something. . . ." But the effort was evidently too much. He leaned back, and the cigarette rolled out of his fingers and down the sheet. John stepped forward and picked it up.

"You'll burn youself up," he said.

"Who cares?" Bruce said, his eyes cramped shut.

"We do! We all do!" Gladys Cotter cried. "What's the matter with you?" She began to cry.

"Well, well," Bruce said, watching her carefully.

"Now don't be like that, Bruce," William Cotter said without looking up from his bundle of hat and coat. Bruce ignored him and turned to John.

"I suppose this is your chance to go whoring around in my car." But he began to look perplexed again, and John saw, amazed, that this time Bruce tried to grin and make a joke out of it. As he spoke he became more and more unsure of himself. "I'd give you a list, but I haven't had time." He turned his face away and reached for the ash tray on his bedside table, then turned back. "Well, we've decided to drill a hole in my head tomorrow."

"Bruce!" Gladys Cotter said. She could barely speak, and came toward him, her face in fragments. She made a sound like escaping steam and her teeth clicked together several times.

"For God's sake, Bruce!" John said. Bruce reached out and grabbed his coat, a quick, vicious jerk that turned him around.

"What do you care?" Bruce said. "It's not your head they're going to shave. They save the hair, did you know that? Then the undertaker can stick it back on again, did you know that? What did you do? What did I do to get this? You bastard! You son of a bitch!"

"Bruce, I never hurt you." He pulled away and went to the window. His eyes began to stream tears. Outside, across the green lawn, a woman walked with a little girl who limped. The sun shone on the little girl's brown hair as she pointed to a gray squirrel. She and the woman spoke to each other, their faces serious and serene.

The room behind him was silent. An English sparrow landed on the windowsill and flew away. John blinked away the tears, precariously balancing them on the edges of his eyes, hoping none would run down his face. The sparrow darted back, saw him and veered away jerkily on short wings.

Bruce, he knew, could not take it any more than he—take the fact of metal in his head, of cutting tools working at his own dear skin and skull. Bruce, who possibly with good reason never trusted anyone, had now to let himself be drugged and hacked. What would he do in Bruce's place? Call for help? There was no one to call. He might say to the doctors: "Well, thanks for everything. Thanks for your trouble and all, but I guess I won't have it just now." No, he must wait while the minutes go by, smoke another cigarette, think about the sound a saw makes on bone. (And what corruption will they find inside? Something is wrong and working in there.)

His father mumbled in the corner. My father, he thought, our father who sits afraid in the shadow, cuddling his hat and coat, his two passports to the freedom of outside. Our mother, whom for some odd reason we despise and love, who can help us? Love we cannot use at the moment. We're overstocked on it at the moment.

They were talking in the room behind him, and he knew he must turn around.

"Oh, Johnny will help you," his mother said. He turned, hoping his tears were dry.

"Sure," he said.

"He doesn't like to have the nurse," Gladys Cotter said.

"I would in other circumstances," Bruce said.

"Oh, *Bruce!*" she said coyly, happy at once.

Bruce slowly swung his legs over the side of the bed, then pulled his bathrobe around after.

"Here goes," he said, and stood unsteadily, holding the edge of the table. He arranged his slippers with an uncertain toe, then sighed as he worked his feet into them. He had gained weight, a soft white babyish padding. In spite of the dark blue shadow of his beard and the wiry hair on his chest and shoulders, he seemed too clean to be a man.

"One of my few remaining pleasures is my bath." He put his arm out and John took it, hardly able to believe this gesture of need. They had never touched each other except, as children, with the cruel hardness of fists, elbows and knees. And now his hand circled Bruce's arm above the elbow and found weakness in the soft flesh. The idea of touching Bruce had been to poke a snake with a stick to see the fearful, fascinating coil and strike, or even more to see in Bruce's eyes the same simple hatred he had seen in the eyes of a wounded hawk. But now he held his brother with a hand suddenly superior in all the mechanics and electronics of the body. The frightening machine needed help.

In the hall nurses and attendants passed, unaware of the miracle. Bruce's slippers shuffled. John took short steps, knowing that if he let Bruce go, Bruce would fall. For a terrible second he contemplated letting go: Bruce would stare up at him, unsurprised, perhaps, the hawk's eyes hating and understanding all that needed to be understood, and say, "Now you do it. Now in my weakness you do it."

In the busy heat of the corridor, his hand upon the sick flesh, he began to feel faint. A dented aluminum tray turned from dull silver to orange, and he let his head fall forward to bring back the blood. Bruce pulled weakly on, intent upon his bath. In the bathroom an old-fashioned deep-sided tub pushed its hollow belly above the floor on claw-and-ball feet. The narrow faucets dripped yellow stain on the porcelain. Bruce sat passively on a cane chair and watched John work the drain plug and faucets.

"Not too hot now," he said, a greedy look on his face. John helped pull his bathrobe off, then had to lift him over the high rim and sit him like a baby in the water. "Ah," Bruce said, leaning back against the cold porcelain.

"Isn't the back cold?" John asked.

"Don't feel it. They got me all doped up. A little hotter—got to feel it. More. There! That's good."

The water came around his plump stomach and over his belly-button. With limp white hands he splashed it up over his chest. His skin became pink beneath the black hair. He began to slip down, not noticing it; his stocky legs opened and his knees broke water until he lay completely relaxed and helpless. All tone gone from his muscles, he turned as limp as a dead, boneless water animal—like a squid in a tank of alcohol. After a while John woke him up and lifted him out. He had to do everything for him now; prop him in the chair, dry him, slide his arms through the bathrobe sleeves.

"Thanks," Bruce said. In the hall he began to walk a little bit, but he could barely support himself.

"You know the old man's kaput. Business no business with him. You know that, don't you?"

"We all know you do everything, Bruce."

Bruce smiled. "You going to give it a try? Or just let it go to hell and take off for Paris?"

"I'll help the old man until you get back."

"What? Don't kid me, sonny. They don't know how to unscramble brains yet. I'll be lucky if I know my own name after tomorrow." Bruce started to sink down, and John had to grab him with both hands. "Sorry," Bruce said.

"You'll come out of it. You wait and see. They've done a lot of work on stuff like that."

"Like what?"

"Like what you've got—tumors and stuff."

"Listen. They don't know asshole, those doctors. They don't even know what's wrong with me. When I first came over here they thought my ears needed cleaning. Then they thought I was working too hard—you know—lost my marbles. Now they got to knock a hole in my head and look at the cream-of-wheat."

In the room Gladys and William Cotter sat as if they hadn't moved.

"Oh, was it good, Bruce?" Gladys Cotter asked.

"Very good," Bruce said sharply. When he was settled in bed again he lit a cigarette. "You must be tired of sitting here," he said in a low voice.

"No! No, Bruce!" his mother said. "No! We want to stay with you!"

Bruce stared at his father, who would not look up, then at John.

"I'll stay as long as you want me," John said.

"Sure," William Cotter mumbled.

Bruce stared them down. "Sure," he said. "Now go home and get some air. Go home. I want to go to sleep."

"Oh, Bruce. We don't want to leave you!"

"Get the hell home," Bruce said.

"We'll be back at one," John said. Gladys Cotter stood against the doorframe, crying. John waited until his father and mother left the room. "Is there anything we can bring you, Bruce?" he asked.

Bruce wouldn't answer, wouldn't look at him. John saw the dark profile against the white window, steady and tense again as Bruce brought the cigarette up to his mouth.

CHAPTER 4

Jane waited alone in the Spinellis' living room beneath the terracotta Virgin and burning candle. Mrs. Spinelli had gone whimpering to bed, and her little husband ran up and down attending to her while they waited for the call from the hospital. The new television set stared blindly across the room. Michael Spinelli, tinted and in black and white, smiled here and there from framed photographs. He looked at her from across the room, his lips too red, his hair too black, his face too white, his Navy uniform too blue. On the sofa, tilted against a white crocheted doily, a rayon pillow in gold, red, white and blue:

M is for the Million things she gave me,
O means only that she's growing Old,
T is for the Tears she shed to save me,
H is for her Heart of purest gold,
E is for her Eyes with love light shining,
R means Right and right she'll always be—

Put them all together
They spell MOTHER,
A word that means
The world to me.

SAMPSON NAVAL TRAINING STATION

Mike's favorite pipe, in the shape of a toilet bowl, lay cleaned in a shining ash tray on a bookcase full of Encyclopædia Britannica. Above the glass-fronted bookcase hung the two discharges, Mike's from the Second World War and Mr. Spinelli's from the First. At Château-Thierry Mr. Spinelli had won several blue indentations in the flesh of his right arm, a collapsed lung and the Silver Star. He wore the miniature ribbon in the lapel of his good suit when he went to the Legion Hall.

Now he came downstairs and stood in the archway between the hall and the living room, his angular hands hanging slightly forward of his body.

"I got to call the shop and tell why I can't work," he said. He picked up the telephone twice before he asked for the paper mill. "I never called up before," he said, turning and smiling, "I don't even know the number, twenty-five years." Then back to the telephone, "Hello. Speak to Mr. Jarvis, please. What? Where? O.K. You tell Mr. Jarvis I can't work today. My son got in a accident. Hospital. Cesare Spinelli. You tell him. Thank you, thank you." He came over, stood in front of the Virgin in her corner and stared at the linoleum floor. "You feel O.K., Janie?"

"I guess so," Jane said.

"I'm sorry you got to worry like this, Janie." He sat down on the edge of the sofa and picked at a callus on the palm of his hand.

"It's all right," she said. She wanted at that moment to put her arms around him, but didn't know how to do it. She didn't even have a name for him. She had never called him Dad, or Cesare, or even Mr. Spinelli—had lived in the same house with him for ten years and never called him by name.

"You got a lousy deal, Janie. I know that. Mikey's a good boy, but he ain't—I don't know." He looked straight at her. "I'm sorry a nice girl like you had to get mixed up with him, that's all!" He jumped up and walked to the front window, breathing deeply and shrugging his shoulders. "I don't know what's wrong, but Mikey never was no good. They kick him out of school." He raised his hands above his head, palms up; then he went out of the room and Jane heard him climbing the stairs.

Before he reached the second floor the telephone rang three times. Jane heard him stop to listen, then run quickly back down the stairs. In a second he came into the living room.

"Janie? You answer it?"

"Mrs. Spinelli?" The telephone asked.

"Yes. Mrs. Spinelli," she said, but it didn't sound right. For a second she felt that she was impersonating Mike's mother.

"You'd better come to the hospital right away, Mrs. Spinelli. Your husband's condition is worse, now. This is Dr. Karmis. Are you there?"

"Yes, Doctor, we'll come now."

"We're doing everything we can, Mrs. Spinelli."

She went into the living room and up to Mr. Spinelli, who stood at the window looking out. She put her hands on his small shoulders. "We've got to go to the hospital right away," she said.

"O.K., Janie," he said, his eyes averted. She followed him into the hall.

Mr. Spinelli called upstairs, "Mama! We'll be back as soon as we can!" No answer from upstairs, but she had heard.

Mr. Spinelli drove fast, for him, but when they were let into Michael Spinelli's room they heard the last two or three of long, croupy breaths, and the time between them lengthened and stopped being important. All at once the doctors and nurses straightened up and began to make distinctly different, purposeful movements around the bed. They put away stethoscopes, folded the oxygen tent, gathered long tubes, pulled the sheet up over Michael Spinelli's head. Jane saw this before Dr. Karmis' worried face appeared before her. "I'm sorry, Mrs. Spinelli. We did everything we could." How could he stand to tell anyone this? She looked at him stupidly. Mr. Spinelli led her out into the hall.

"It's all right, Doctor," Mr. Spinelli said, "you done all you could. I'll take her home. I'll come right back. Is that O.K., Doctor?"

He took her to the car and helped her in, then drove through Northlee and took the river road to Leah. When they had gone a mile he pulled over to a wide shoulder where, in winter, the snowplows turned around. He stopped the car and began to get out, but he forgot to turn off the ignition and the car jerked forward and stalled.

"My boy," he said. His forehead hit the horn, which went *beep*. Jane let him cry but could not help him. Finally she went around to the other side of the car and helped him move over, then drove him home to Leah. By the time they turned into the driveway he had recovered. "I'll tell her, Janie," he said.

They found Mrs. Spinelli in the kitchen, and when she saw their faces she began to scream. Jane walked on through it, and it felt as it had once as a child when her brother put a whistle to her ear and blew as hard as he could—a nearby physical blow against the bones of her head. In her room the closed door did not stop the sound. It rose and fell, sometimes like a siren and sometimes watery, like surf.

Later the sound diminished. Neighbors and relatives talked in the kitchen in low voices, and only once in a while the siren rose and stopped, or a breaker crashed among the insistent murmurs of sympathy.

Her window was a hot white square upon the side of the cool room. She went to the window and looked at the street, up and down, bright and clear as childhood in the sun. She had rarely come to this street as a child. The school bus hadn't passed this street, although the red-brick parochial grammar school, an alien, nun-haunted building, stood on the corner. Mike went to the parochial school, and because of this she hadn't really known him until high school. She had never been interested in him, except that the continual excitement he caused in school kept him in the news—the girls' washroom news, the scandalous, whispered news. If someone turned his back on Mike at the wrong time, someone got goosed. It was Mike who started the bent-pin business with the rubber bands, and that ended with another one of his expulsions from school. He shot Miss Colchester, and the pin stuck into her leg. That was when they found out she wore men's garters with white bandages under them. The teachers always knew when Mike was guilty. How many times had he been expelled? And each time Mr. Spinelli brought him back again and talked to the principal. Nobody disliked Mike. Not the way they disliked Junior, who was nearly as bad, but lacked

Mike's good looks and utter cheerfulness. Mike had never been sneaky—he was always caught. But now he'd been caught and expelled from life, and Mr. Spinelli couldn't bring him back, apologize and make impossible promises.

Mike was the first in his class to go into service. All the boys wanted to go, or nearly all, and when they graduated in June, 1944, all but two or three did go. Most came back in 1946. Four were killed, but more came back just to say goodbye to Leah before going West, where most of Leah's sons went when they were old enough. Some stayed, but they were the ones whose parents owned businesses, or they were the ones who stayed because all they wanted to do was to go into the mill or whatever—the post office, a store, the tannery—and work and marry and get it regular, as Mike said once.

She had chosen one of these, although it hadn't been obvious at the time. Mike seemed to have so much energy left over, and she believed that the war had done something to him beyond making him put on the common grim act of the veteran, which sooner or later became old-fashioned as terminal leave pay ran out and time payments became more threatening than the memory of war. But she knew that she tended to plan sketchily, in visions and scenes: to her the constant excitement and energy of Michael Spinelli would somehow, through some maturing process, in time produce the home she saw vividly, as if she were looking in the window to see herself in a lovely scene of firelight and children.

But there had been ten years and another war since then, and another crop of young men come home only to say goodbye. The town seemed always to send away its best. The population of Leah hadn't changed in one hundred years, her grandfather said, and he once told her of the farms and hills that in his lifetime had turned from field and pasture back into woods. Even the woolen mill in the town had become obsolete. Last year it shut down for two months, and everybody was afraid that it would be for good. It was then that Mike started going with Junior and the Riders and cashed in his defense bonds to buy the new motorcycle. "It's a Harley-Davidson!" he kept saying, as if it were impossible that his father and mother and wife were not infected by the magic of the words. "Look at the spark plugs!" He made them look at the two cylinders, the big saddle of genuine cowhide, the big balloon-like fenders. He insisted that they come and look, as if the bright, dangerous meaning of the machine might convince them of his need of it. And when he saw their disapproval he answered with the boom of his engine at night, burned rubber on the driveway, lifted his front wheel in the air as a horse rears and turns before it gallops away.

She woke up in the middle of the afternoon, hearing a knock on her door. Mr. Spinelli looked in.

"Your grandfather is here, Janie. I thought maybe you want to wake up."

In the living room she found her grandfather sitting uneasily on the edge of a wooden chair, a huge old man in clean workshirt and overalls. His great head solid on his short pillar of neck, he sat and mauled his visored cap between fingers that looked like the arms and legs of brawny wrestlers. His face was ruddy, shiny in little squares between fine cracks and wrinkles that were nearly as regular as the grid lines on a map. Curly white hair came down over his collar in back and on the sides halfway over his ears. A faint, pleasant smell of horses drifted across the room. He stood up and watched her, his feet wide apart as if he thought the fragile house might fall apart beneath him—but if it did he would still land in the basement right side up and on his two feet amid the fragments.

"Hi, Grandpa," Jane said. As he came toward her the floor creaked under his feet. His expression seldom changed, and it didn't now. His eyes were bright and wide open; so blue it seemed that she looked right through his head into the sky. His eyebrows were raised as if he were slightly surprised and amused. He put one hand on her shoulder, lightly, yet she felt that if she were to fall the hand would hold her up as easily as if the old man held a rifle at arm's length to weigh it.

"I figured maybe you'd want to come home for a while," he said. His voice was soft and breathy, yet everything he said sounded at first too aggressive, almost accusing. The surprised, sweet expression on his face belied the tone of his voice, and one result of this difference between voice and meaning was that everyone felt compelled to look him straight in the eye.

"I could stay over tonight," she said.

Cesare Spinelli came into the room, harried and damp from his running through the house.

"Mr. Stevens, I heard," he said. "I think maybe that's good for Janie. She'd be happier out of this house for now. I think you got a good idea."

Sam Stevens nodded. "I'm terribly sorry about your son," he said. "I hope your wife feels better."

"Oh, I worry about Janie," the little man said. He looked at her closely. "She don't seem to be taking it too good."

She hadn't cried. If she cried, she was afraid she would be crying for Jane Stevens Spinelli and ten wasted years, not for a poor fool who had killed himself. She would not cry at all.

When she came downstairs with her suitcase—a wedding present she had never used before—the two men stood as she had left them: the huge farmer and the little father. Mr. Spinelli took her hand and said, "It's all right, Janie. You'll feel better after a while, now. You just wait and see."

Her grandfather backed the pickup truck carefully out into the street, then started slowly, as he always did, going deliberately through each gear, watching and not trusting other cars. They went around the Town Square and took the road to Cascom and the farm. When they turned off the asphalt onto the steep gravel road up the mountain, he spoke for the first time.

"He's a mighty funny feller, Spinelli." Jane didn't answer, and she saw him glance at her out of the corners of his eyes. "Seems to me he's a good man," he said, "although you never can tell about them people."

CHAPTER 5

John sat in his room in his old leather chair, a can of beer in his hand and four empties on the floor. His father had gone to the yard and his mother to a neighbor's. The old house was empty around him, brittle and too clean. He thought of his miserable cave of a room in Paris; mold, mice, cockroaches and all, and he wished himself back there again. There were roses on the walls of that room, too, in the places where the paper hadn't been turned back into brownish pulp by rot, the plaster absorbing, as if it were a sponge, the sweat of the ancient stone walls.

He sat staring at the sun-glittering leaves of the rock maple, then got up and took his .30-.30 carbine from the gunrack. He balanced the short rifle in his left hand and flicked down the lever. *Click clack;* the crisp sounds were lovely and satisfying. The square bolt slid back and then forward to lock, leaving the large hammer cocked. He let the hammer down slowly and worked the action again: after two years the rifle had regained, as beautiful objects do, a measure of its original freshness and wonder. He didn't want to put it to his shoulder just yet—he wanted to save that view of it—but he turned it over in his hands, discovering again the little planes and curves of it, from the slightly curved butt plate to the deep rifling visible at the muzzle.

Then, with the rifle in one hand, he took his beer and went out into the hall. Bruce's door was shut. He stood in front of it, convincing himself that Bruce was not there, could not be there, put his empty can on the banister post and turned the knob.

The room was as bare as it had always been when it was forbidden to him on pain of— On pain of what? he asked himself as the details of the room sorted themselves out: single bed, highboy, two windows, closet door, bedside lamp. He thought of death. On pain of death. On pain of something like that—something awful and frightening, compounded of more than physical hurt alone. The pain of his brother's screaming rage; the pain of his brother's hate.

The room had the cold, clean look of a guest room. Of course his mother had been through it, straightening and cleaning, but his mother could never have created such frigid order. In the closet a similar order governed the neatly hung clothes, the shoes lined up toes to the baseboard. Bruce's automatic shotgun leaned against the wall, a heavy, bruising, unlovely gun John didn't bother to examine. By the smell, it was well oiled and clean. As he closed the closet door a nearly unbearable twinge of guilt, of being caught, came over him. The feeling went away quickly, but not until a twisting, nervous shake traveled from his legs to his head. He brought his rifle up to his hip and stepped out into the empty hall, collected the empty beer can and went back to his room. Ten o'clock. In three hours he must be back in Bruce's room in the hospital.

His mother had given him the keys to Bruce's black Ford, and it was not necessary for them to make an agreement not to mention this to Bruce. A general rule in the family for many years—a symptom of their fear—was that what Bruce did not know and act upon hurt no one.

John parked in front of the Town Hall, the half colonial, half Victorian building on the square. The rear half was older, built of pale small brick, with severely geometrical high windows. The front half, the aesthetic addition of 1880, was built of darker brick, with heavily arched, Greco-Roman windows. He thought of the Town Hall as a pair of Siamese twins horribly fused at the navel, one cool and chaste, the other round and ripe.

Mr. Bemis, the town clerk, a little balding Yankee, stood behind his tall counter, his tight-skinned, almost miniature skull set with blue eyes. He peered straight and humorously at John over the maple counter.

"Well, well, if it ain't the town prodigal come back from the far and fancy places."

"Hi, Mr. B.," John said. At the moment he felt an expansive affection for the little man. "Mr. Bemis, that's the nicest thing anybody's said to me since I got back."

The town clerk's eyes wrinkled around the edges, but he held off smiling.

"You come in, I suppose, to pay your head and poll tax? No, you don't have to pay poll tax, seeing as you're a Democrat and it don't matter how you vote anyways." He let out a high laugh that brought his secretary to the door. "It's all right, Edna," he said, waving her back.

"You don't mean to tell me you're still a Republican?" John said.

"John Cotter. I swear! If some people heard you say that I'd lose my job come town meetin'!"

"It's enough to make a man turn Communist," John said. Mr. Bemis reared back and screeched his high laugh again. Edna put her head in the door.

"Now, it's all right, Edna," Mr. Bemis said, but she came on in.

"Hello, Johnny," she said.

"Hello, Mrs. Box. What do you hear from Walter?"

Her motherly instincts aroused, she rippled a little about the breasts. Walter was her successful son. "Why, Walter asked about you, Johnny. They have a new baby."

"How many is that, now?"

"Three. Two boys and a sweet little girl and he said in his letter, 'What's with old Johnny Cotter?' just like that. They live in Cleveland, you know. Walter sent me an airplane ticket and I'm to come out and visit, take the airplane from Concord and change in Boston and go right to Cleveland. It scares me so, but I've just got to see that baby! I've just got to get my hands on that baby!"

"Johnny's going to be a bachelor like me," Mr. Bemis said. "He ain't interested in babies, are you, Johnny?"

"Now, that's just what Walter said in his letter. He said, 'Old Johnny Cotter's the wise one,' just like that. I don't think so, though." She went out to answer the telephone.

"Now, John, what can the Town of Leah do for you?"

He had to pay a five-dollar head tax before he could send for a driving license. Being a veteran—"Isn't everybody?" John asked—he didn't have to pay a poll tax.

"It's that dang head tax ain't fair, Johnny," Mr. Bemis said. "Why, I just shudder to think what will happen some poor fella comes in with two heads and I have to charge him ten dollars!" He screeched and pounded the counter, then stopped suddenly and looked seriously at John. "Say, John, how is Bruce coming along up to Northlee?"

"They're going to operate, I guess."

"I'm sorry to hear it. Gory! That's too bad, John. Bruce and I never knew each other too well, but I hate to see a man down like that."

When John left, he drove around the square to the Post Office. Mr. Bemis saw him drive away and knew he didn't have a driving license, but John didn't worry about that. Mr. Bemis would consider it none of his business. The town police were just a little too eager to catch people out, had always been, and though this was considered to be bad taste on their part you couldn't tell a policeman not to do his duty. You could just dislike him, which had the effect of making him more dutiful. Chief Atmon and his one officer, Joe Beaupre, according to most people, saw too many TV shows. *Dragnet,* in particular, was considered a bad influence, since every suspect who was impolite to the police turned out to be guilty and all the laws concerning search and seizure were somehow violated. The only public outcry came when Atmon bought the submachine gun from Army surplus. He finally had to pay for it himself.

He knew he had beer on his breath, and, as everyone in Leah did habitually, he looked carefully around for the police. Atmon would be in his office in the Town Hall, but Joe Beaupre might want to talk. He made it to the Post Office all right and bought a money order from Donald Ramsey, the assistant postmaster, whom he had known in high school. Ramsey had been one of Junior Stevens' bully boys, but had become tame and respectable in Civil Service. Now he chose not to remember the time he and Junior and Keith Joubert had thrown John into the fountain in the square. As John watched him fussily stamp the money order, it did seem fantastic that this pale man in black arm elastics and green eyeshade could have helped at such an athletic prank.

"Is that right! Did we do that? Well, boys will be boys, won't they, John? I guess we had our times, didn't we?"

I guess we did, you yellow bastard, John thought. You and Keith Joubert and Stevens. And me in the water with the broken glass just before the DeMolay dance. He mailed his application for a driving license, and left.

He still had more than an hour before he had to be at the hospital, and he drove out of town on the winding road toward Lake Cascom, past the new drive-in theater that had been built in the time he'd been away. Very little else had changed. A pasture where he used to ski had grown up in little birch and poplar. Soon he was climbing the long hill below Cascom Mountain. The sky was a bright, luminous blue—bluer than any sky he had seen in Europe, bluer than any tropical sky, yet capable of changing even at noon into a night of black thunderheads. Now there were no clouds in the sky, just the hard bright shell of blue, smooth as an egg from hill to hill. The fields were too yellow, parched to the edges of the advancing jungle, dangerously tindery. A cigarette thrown from a car anywhere along any road could set it all off.

He circled the mountain, spruce-green to its granite ledges near the round top, and came down a winding hill above Lake Cascom, blue as the sky; a long knobby finger of a lake following Cascom's valley in a half-circle. At the head of the lake a few big houses and a white church stood among tall maples, and that was Cascom Center. The hills rising back of Cascom Center had once been cultivated fields, but now only small pastures kept the woods from dooryards. The people of Cascom Center were old, and lived in the high rooms of the old houses. They sat on narrow porches or puttered in kitchen gardens in the summer, and in winter they stayed indoors in hot, woodstove-heated rooms, coming out seldom and then only to push the snow from the sidewalk or to split kindling, bundled up and slow and careful of old bones.

He remembered one of the thick-based sugar maples very well for having seen a slight bark-bruise disappear slowly over the years. Just before the war a boy he knew hit the tree at eighty miles an hour and wrapped his 1936 Ford completely around the tree so that the front and rear bumpers locked together. The police cut through the top and part of the frame to get his body out. The old people of Cascom Center had emerged from their houses like careful ghosts, and slowly crossed the road to see if they could help.

Near the dam at the foot of the lake, where Cascom River started its winding course toward Leah, he turned the car around. Below the huge granite blocks of the dam a boy swung high over the river on a long chain. They called the swimming place there "the scrape" for all the skinned knees and elbows and banged heads that were the usual price for swinging out and dropping from the chain. The chain was fastened to a limb of a crooked rock maple that grew out of the foundation of an old mill long since washed downstream. All that was left was the granite foundation and some huge bolts, one of which protruded from the bole of the rock maple and served as a step up to the platform from which the swingers took off over the water.

John remembered when the chain had been a rotten rope, and when Bob Paquette fell from the highest point of the outward swing, turning over and over, pale gawky arms and legs in the sunlight—and hit a bellyflopper. They were thirteen or fourteen.

He could still feel the wonderful weightless fear of the long drop into the cold water, and the tightening of his skin. But there was something unpleasant about that memory—Jane Stevens had come along on her bicycle, in her bathing suit. He would never forget what happened, and wondered if Bob or Jane might remember. He could see her still, her bathing suit pale, faded red, made for a younger girl. The front part was too narrow, and when she moved in certain ways he could see the hard, beginning rise of her breasts. The suit was faded even more around the seat from sitting on rocks and sand, and it was made of a cottony material not used any more. At that time he had been committed to not liking Jane because of her brother, although there was between them a grave respect born of the seriousness of his feud with Junior. So it was a terrible shock to him when she swam up beside him—he saw the water running through her long pale hair and the hair flowing down over her skinny shoulders—and she said, "I love you."

He immediately submerged and stayed down until he couldn't stand it any longer. When he came up for air he saw a different girl. She sat on the bank throwing water out of her hair and watching him, having become something terribly shocking and wonderful in that underwater minute. He let his head come out of the water, stood there in the current and watched her, then dived and let the cold water move over his body. He came up again and watched her, seeing her straight, light hair, her ears that stuck out with the hair hooked behind them, a dinky little pimple on her forehead, wide dark eyes and little nose. Her eyes were suddenly deep and clear as she looked at him, and her lips were slightly blue from the cold water. The beauty of her! She was three inches taller than he, but the possibility that this might become important could exist only in dreams of body contact, and that ecstatic idea followed him in the deep water that brushed coolly along his ribs and between his legs. He came up again and looked at her. It was early summer and her arms and legs were untanned, raw-pale against the faded red suit. She stood up, conscious of his watching, and went to the diving stump. Her hips, just beginning to look like a woman's, moved sideways as she stepped up to the stump.

He had a sense of great responsibility, and was not ready to accept it. It was the same when he got his bicycle—he remembered looking at it, at the delicate bright spokes and gears, and thinking, I must be responsible for all of this, and for a second he did not want the bicycle at all. But that had quickly passed. This was more complicated. He wanted to hide, and yet he wanted to take off his trunks and swim as hard as he could through the cold water. There was also a great disbelief in him. How could she love him? He had run away crying from her own brother. Could a girl love a coward such as John Cotter? If so, and in a way he could believe it, it was not the kind of love the hero of his daydreams accepted and was worthy of.

Then she made a shallow dive and coasted toward him, bubbles trailing the ends of her hair. He looked quickly to see if Bob Paquette knew, but that was all right for the moment. Bob was climbing the tree to the swing platform. Jane came up right next to him, wiped the water from her face with both hands and opened her eyes. They looked directly, painfully into his, and he dived to the bottom, grabbed her ankles and dumped her over backward. She came up sputtering, water up her nose, and smiled at him. Smiled at him! He did it again, and this time held her under for a moment, his hand on her head. She put her hands lightly, coolly on his body below his arms.

He jerked away as if he'd had a shock, flailing his arms in the water uncontrollably, and then they both looked up to see Bob come turning down, his big feet out anywhere and his mouth open, the broken rope clutched in his hands. "Ow ow ow ow!" Bob yelled. He hit the water flat on his belly, and a thin sheet of spray shot out and over them. They dragged Bob to shore and waited for him to get back his wind. In a minute he was diving from the stump.

John took his towel and flicked it experimentally at Jane. She jumped back, smiling again immediately. She knew. "I saw you and Bob go by, so I came too," she said.

He snapped his towel again, this time against a flat rock, and the sharp, mean *crack* stopped her. The towel end flicked through the water and snapped again in the air, leaving a small burst of misty droplets floating.

"That's the only reason I came," Jane said.

"Let's duck her!" he yelled to Bob.

Bob came swimming over. "Huh?" he said.

"Let's duck her!" He ran at Jane and pushed her into the water. She was smiling. They went after her and grabbed her ankles, lifted her unresisting body out and dunked it in the water, again and again. At first she smiled, whenever she could, but it went on and on. They grabbed her legs, her waist, anything they could get hold of. One time she came over and John saw red fingermarks on her white buttocks. The old bathing suit had pulled tight, and her buttocks stuck out like little white balloons.

"Stop it!" she cried over and over, and finally, in a surprising burst of effort, broke loose and ran up the bank. John ran behind her and, taking his towel from the rock, caught up with her as she reached her bicycle. One flick—one sure, accurate flick and *crack,* he saw the dark red triangle on her buttock where the towel bit and burned. She turned, bawling, and looked at him once before she rode off.

Sitting now in Bruce's car above the scrape, he could still hear her hoarse bawling, see her red, injured face looking at him. Even now his hands shook as he lit a cigarette. Things like that could be explained, he knew, by saying that he was a child. But did he graduate from childhood on a certain day, receive a diploma that proved he was no longer a child? He could say that he was older, now, and a man. But when had it happened? Years were short and didn't seem to matter very much any more. He couldn't count on them to cure him or to change him.

He drove into the hospital parking lot at a quarter to one, before his father and mother arrived. He intended to sit in the car and wait for them, and then go in with them; their slight protection would help. At least Bruce's violent remarks would then be shared, scattered over a larger target. But he felt exposed to the windows of the hospital. Bruce's room was on the other side of the building, but still . . . No, Bruce could not walk through the long halls. But Bruce might just *feel* something about it. John got out of the car and started toward the entrance, feeling as if Bruce's eyes were on him. This must be conscience, he thought; a mixture of fear and duty. The word *duty* was a strange one, especially to him. Duty in the Army had been a particular job he had to do, like standing guard, or K.P. An officer once told him that because he would not go to Officer Candidate School he was not doing his duty. Even going to OCS seemed easier than seeing Bruce alone today. For a moment he felt quite heroic.

"Oh, it's too much," he said out loud, and then in a low voice, "It's too, too much for a delicate, sensitive flower like yourself, John Cotter, to have to see your only brother before they open up his head."

He could run away, as his father tried to do in the morning, but he'd never caught himself doing anything so obvious as that. When he ran away, he managed to create a fugue of wonderful and complicated motives, so that when he arrived at his safe, new destination he was fairly free of guilt. He could now go back to Leah, drop in at Futzie's Tavern and start creating, but he was afraid his talents were not up to it. His excuses would last no longer than the effects of Futzie's beer.

He found himself again in the long, cream-colored hall. He was afraid to look into the open doors that invited his eyes, afraid of the stark, sick people on the high beds. He walked toward Bruce: the horror at the end of the aisle in the dream. Bruce saw him at the open door and turned toward him, aggressive in his helplessness.

"You're early," he said. "Couldn't stay away?"

"You don't make it so pleasant."

"Oh, I don't? Why'd you come early? You want to leave early? Don't worry, you'll be rid of me soon enough."

"Bruce, if you want me to stay, I'll stay." His eyes filled with tears, and he knew and loathed the fact that it was self-pity made him cry. Here he was, volunteering his presence and being cruelly rejected.

"What are you crying for?" Bruce said, with a triumphant smile. "You got a lot to cry about. It's me ought to be crying. You're a weak, sniveling bastard of a brother, aren't you? I hurt your feelings? Tough shit!"

Bruce sat up straight, a certain joy evident in his expression; his eyes were opened wide, not at all sleepy from medication. He intently watched John's effort to calm himself.

"I'm your brother," John said.

"Jesus Christ! You a brother? You aren't even a man. You never did a lick of work in your life. What the hell good are you?"

"I've worked."

"Worked? You mean summers so you could have money to play with? Work? You don't know what it means to work. You couldn't *work*. That's hard! You'd rather bum around Paris with the queers, polishing your ass on a bar stool, pretending you're a hot-shot artist or some goddam thing. G.I. bill! You're a bum! What the hell have you ever done?"

"Nothing," John said, but this was a lie, or nearly a lie. He meant nothing he could tell at this moment to Bruce that might have meaning to Bruce, although he wondered at the same time if, perhaps, Bruce's methods of evaluating "something" were not the valid ones. He himself had never managed to define, although he seemed always to be trying, the meaning of "something."

He went to the low chair in the corner and sat far down in it. He felt that as long as he said nothing more, Bruce would not continue to jab and twist. Bruce was not very witty and needed a straight man. Anyway, Bruce looked very tired now with his eyes shut and the cigarette burning down toward his fingers.

All of John's bad memories (the persistent memories were always bad) concerned things he had done. Weren't these "something"? He had killed a man—but that was in the Army and didn't count because he had no alternative to that. It didn't count, so why should he have to remember it? It must have counted once, because he couldn't eat meat for several weeks afterward. Why go into that? he asked his uncontrollable memory. Don't go into that again. We've had that out. . . .

But there he was looking up at the statue of Quezon by the Chinese cemetery. It was so hot! The sky was gray-blue and hazy, a stifling blanket, and the seven men stood around waiting for him to do something—Ben Nakano the interpreter, Parsons, Iwashita, the others. He couldn't remember all the names, and that was good. Maybe someday the whole business would fade away as the names had. The men of his squad: he could still see their faces too well.

Parsons said, "Where the hell are the street signs? They ought to have street signs."

"We'll find the house O.K. There's no hurry," John said, and the others slouched around while he looked at the ridiculous map. "I guess it's over there," he said, and they followed him down the dusty street, looking around indifferently. It was all his responsibility, but what was so hard about finding a house in a city?

The number was still on the door of the four-story house. It stood alone, shored up by the rubble and occasional walls of the buildings that had stood on each side. The front door was partly open, and just as they were going up the front steps the old woman burst out and went through them, bumping and bouncing off one and then another with her head down as if she were a goat. She made the sidewalk and ran like hell in her long black dress and black shawl.

"Lookit her *go!*" Parsons said. "She must of broke the NCAA muh-fun mile!"

"Now they'll all be nervous in there," Nakano said. As he spoke, John pushed open the door. They all heard another door slam down the hall.

"Well," John said, "Parsons, you take Cummins and Johnson and go around back and up the back stairs."

Parsons and the other two ran around through the wreckage of the house on the side while John and the four others ran into the hall and stopped on the stairs to the second floor, where they could not be enfiladed. They had all run into doubtful buildings before. They could cover the hall from the stairs. John motioned to Nakano.

"Who the hell are they supposed to be?" Nakano asked.

"People from the Riken Company."

"Come on out!" John yelled down the empty hall. "We won't hurt you, but we've got to ask you some questions!"

Silence.

"Tell 'em in Tagalog," John said to Nakano, and Nakano shouted the strange syllables down.

Silence.

"Tell 'em in Japanese," John said, and Nakano shouted the Japanese. Still no answer.

"What the hell would they speak?" John asked. Parsons and the other two came up the back stairs.

"No other way out of the house," Parsons said.

Just then they heard the muffled, flat *pop,* and a narrow strip of the hall door just to the right of the stairs peeled down and swung like a reed in the wind. Across the hall a flake of plaster fell to the floor.

"They shot, by God!" Parsons said.

"Stop that!" John yelled at the door. The answer was another *pop.* A larger piece of plaster fell from the opposite wall.

"Don't be foolish!" John shouted down. He looked around at his men. At least four were wearing the hot, bulky pistol belts and holsters they had been issued. "Give me a gun," he said. One of them handed him the big pistol. He hadn't carried one because of the weight and because he didn't like the feel of the pistol. The service automatic wasn't a pistol; it was a cannon.

Nakano put his hand on John's shoulder. "Maybe they speak Spanish," he said.

"Naw. Hell, they'd know English," Parsons said.

But none of them knew enough Spanish, so John went down the stairs, close against the wall. When he came as near as he could to the door he stopped.

"Come on out, now," he said. "We don't want to hurt you." This time the gun inside the door was louder, and he looked at the door and saw three jagged holes in it. It was made of plywood and the outer layer of ply had split down in long strips. He reached around with the Colt in his left hand and put it to the door, then pulled the trigger four times. The Colt jumped around in his left hand and up, and the last hole was a foot higher than the others.

For a moment he let the sound die, and then a terrible screaming began behind the door. He kicked it open and rushed in.

The two women in black squatted screaming over the old man. Their mouths opened too wide and were red and black inside, and the screams blatted against his eardrums and whistled and blatted out again. Their black skirts were beaded with shiny blood, and the old man on the floor had taken all the slugs in his chest and neck and face. He looked a little like a wicker basket that had been full of strawberry jam, chopped by an ax; or like fresh red beef, chopped and cut. He had been peering through the bullet holes in the door, trying to see what was in the hall. An old nickel-plated revolver lay on the floor beside him, and in one corner of the room sat the reasons for his defiance of the law—four cartons of cigarettes and two one-gallon cans of Crisco. He and the women were not the people from Riken. They were awfully small-time black marketeers.

"What did you say?" Bruce asked, sitting up higher in order to see John in the low chair.

"Nothing," John said again, and then looked more closely at Bruce. Bruce smiled at him, and the smile had no hard malice in it. It did not seem to belong to Bruce—as if he were wearing a mask.

"I guess they're a little late," Bruce said.

Gladys and William Cotter came into the room, the tall woman first, hurrying to her son's bed. She stopped with both hands pressed upon his pillow.

"How do you feel?" she asked.

"O.K. I don't feel too bad," Bruce said, "but they're going easy on the dope today and tonight." He winced at the sound of the last word. His mother pulled a straight chair over to the bed and sat leaning toward him, her long hands making nervous circles upon the sheet beside his pillow.

She wants to touch him, John thought. She wants to hold him and cure him with those nervous hands, but he won't let her and never has. Neither of us ever has. I wonder why.

"How's the Miller house coming?" Bruce said to his father.

"O.K., Bruce. The architect got mad as hell this morning when he saw that tin drip-edge, though."

A moment of fearful expectancy.

"God damn it! I had that out with him before! Just because I'm not around, that sheeny son of a bitch! You tell him he agreed a month ago and if he don't like the looks of it he can paint it. This isn't Florida, for Christ's sake!"

"O.K., Bruce, I'll tell him." William Cotter didn't look up.

"Yeah, sure," Bruce said in a low voice, staring at the top of his father's head. "How's the Waters' house? How's the roofing going on?"

"Good weather for it," William Cotter said, "but a crazy thing happened the other day. Junior Stevens put the vent in upside down. I saw it before they had it boxed in." There was some hesitant pride in his voice. He looked up and smiled.

"Put him back sawing slabs," Bruce said. "He'll never make a carpenter. How the hell did we ever get such a dumb bunch down there? Cotter's playground for the mentally handicapped. We ought to get assistance from the state."

Bruce reached for a cigarette, but his mother found one first, put it in his mouth and lit it. She held the match up and he blew it out; then she smilled happily, turning around to John and William Cotter as if to say, "See? Did you see that?"

John shut his eyes. Baby tricks! When he was a child he thought that if he put his hands over his eyes his whole body was invisible.

And now Bruce, blowing out the held match. See? Baby blew out the match! It was too goddam perplexing to figure Bruce; and then he had the horrible thought that if Bruce really let himself go to his mother, all the way, he would end up a plump, unshaven babe-in-arms, sucking a bottle or his thumb. And his mother would look around just as fondly and proudly as she cuddled him. Perhaps he and Bruce both knew that their mother had no limits, at least that they had never seen her stop, and that such needful love must be brutally curbed.

Gladys Cotter sat at her son's bedside staring across the bed at the wall. Bruce smoked a cigarette and looked at the window. John smoked a cigarette that had no flavor, but a dry mechanical usefulness. His throat seemed like a flue and his teeth tasted like dry bones. His mother moved her hands, smoothing the sheet, and his father looked at a magazine with too much concentration, never looking up, never turning a page. The white window was hard to look at from the cool depths of the room.

Time moved, John knew, but he couldn't look at his watch. Bruce might see that. He let himself fall into a dry, almost rigid position of waiting, thinking that he would not move at all until the afternoon was over and he could leave. He tried to hypnotize himself by staring at the light switch on the wall, but nothing worked for him. Time moved, he knew, and at least he had to do nothing to make it move. He was not responsible for that.

"More words," Bruce said suddenly, "will be spoken at the funeral."

"What? Why, *Bruce!*" his mother said.

"I mean everybody is pretty quiet," Bruce said in an even voice. "But I can hear—well, look at *him* suffer!" He pointed at John. Gladys Cotter put a shy hand on Bruce's arm and he quickly pulled away from her. Her hand went back with the other, to smooth the sheet by his pillow. "But I can hear," he went on, "Reverend Bledsoe—the Reverend Mr. Bloody Bledsoe, the Reverend Mr. Bloody Bedsore—harping upon my wonderful qualities such as working my ass off and wondering how much the traffic can stand even at a funeral when he tries to say what a fine loving character I was. I can hear the old hypocrite now. I bet he's got the speech all written already."

"Oh, Bruce!"

"Bruce!" William Cotter said. He stood at the foot of the bed. "I'd think you'd have more . . . I'd think you'd not be so mean to your mother! What's the matter with you, anyway? You're damn' mean and nasty. You act like they were going to kill you, when all they're trying to do is help you and cure you!"

The big man stood tall and angry at the foot of the bed, and his smaller son stared back at him, half smiling. John had seen this happen before. In a second the fire went out of William Cotter, but it remained burning in Bruce's eyes, his face thrust forward out of his weakness, vicious and conquering. He stared his father down and broke him back into his chair and into his magazine.

The silence came on again, and John knew that they would not look to him for any help or strength. He was even weaker than his father. Hollow and weak and good only for running. His father had never run away so far: his father had to come back day after day.

The afternoon went on in small noises and the long tired moans of the old man down the hall, bedspring creaks and sharp heel clicks. The wind flicked an aerial wire against the window frame. John ran out of cigarettes and couldn't make himself borrow one from his father or Bruce. Outside, the cars ground in the gravel. The nurse came in and gave Bruce his mineral oil, but this time he said nothing to her, and she seemed to be in a hurry to pour it down his throat and leave. John rationed his trips to the bathroom, figuring that two and no more would not make Bruce think that he couldn't stand to sit in the room. When the intern wheeled in the napkin-covered stand he found himself moving his lips, saying over and over, "Please make us go home. Tell us we have to go home." He had no more feeling for Bruce; now it was self-preservation alone. He had to get out of the room. He had a headache and wondered in fear if he had a tumor. He could plainly see the tumor—it looked like a black walnut right in the back of his head, and he found his hand up there feeling around as if he might feel the bulge in his skull. My God! he thought. *What if it was me?* The intern spoke to Bruce in a low voice.

"I thought you might want them to go," the intern said.

"Yes," Bruce said, and then turned, smiling, to the others. "This is when I lose my hair, but don't worry, they'll save it for me."

The intern was embarrassed. He fiddled with his equipment, and wouldn't raise his head. Gladys Cotter stood up, and the intern said, "I'll be back in a little while," and left.

"We'll come back after supper," Gladys Cotter said.

"No. This is it," Bruce said.

"But they aren't going to operate *now!*"

"No. But they're going to get me ready for morning."

"What about your supper?"

"I don't know about that. Goodbye." Bruce smiled, his eyes triumphant, and John thought, *If only he can hold on until we get out!*

"Then we won't see you until . . . afterward?" Gladys Cotter's voice went high and out of control and she ran around the bed toward Bruce, but his eyes held her off.

"Goodbye," he said in a level, taut voice, and deliberately took her hand, holding her away from him.

"I'll see about the edging," William Cotter said, "and tell you how it comes out."

"Sure. Goodbye."

John and his father both shook Bruce's limp hand, so weak compared to the hard determination in his face.

John looked back, once the doorframe was past and Bruce's room was at least a room he had left, as if it were in another dimension. He saw Bruce's steady profile against the white window, one hand bringing a cigarette slowly up to the face. It was the face of the gut-shot hawk he had killed in the woods—cold, violent and brave.

The next morning they were summoned, with a certain amount of apology, to the hospital, where three neurosurgeons explained that the cancerous tissue in Bruce's brain was too widespread to be removed completely. The patient lived, and might recover consciousness for a while. They would just have to wait and see.

Gladys Cotter had to be helped from the room, from the hospital, and into the car. She didn't scream or cry, and after spending the day alone, in bed, she went back to the hospital to sit by Bruce's bed.

CHAPTER 6

Michael Spinelli had been dead a week. Because of the long dry spell his grave had not begun to heal; the replaced blanket of sod was brown around the cut, and the flowers in pots were wilted and dying. Jane went twice to the Catholic cemetery with the Spinellis, Mrs. Spinelli humped and older in shiny black dress and veil, Cesare Spinelli dried up and silent as the faded flowers.

Jane knew she would now see the Spinellis only by chance, in Leah. She had moved to the farm the few things ten years of marriage had brought her; wedding presents such as unused silver and dishes, linen and a little radio. Mike's motorcycle leaned against the wall in one of the farm sheds where Junior had put it after hauling it back from the accident.

Mrs. Pettibone, Sam Steven's housekeeper, washed dishes. Jane wiped, taking the thick white plates from Mrs. Pettibone's rough hand. Her grandfather and the two hired men were out behind the barn butchering an old horse for dog meat. She had heard the shot, an hour before, but had gone on wiping, glad that she had not seen the old gray gelding die. She had known the horse most of her life, had ridden the broad, warm back when he had been led out of his traces to his stable; a gentle, phlegmatic giant of an animal with great dignity and not too many brains. He had worked hard all his life pulling stoneboat and pulpwood, and in early spring the maple-sap sledge. But most things on the farm, animals included, were used completely—used in some way until nothing was left. Only dogs and people could die and have done with their usefulness.

Mrs. Pettibone scrubbed the dishes slowly, carefully, with the steady concentration she gave to all her work. In her small round face black eyes looked out of deep brown cavities. The color of her skin was pale ivory on forehead and cheekbones, turning to dark brown in all hollows and creases. Even the shallow concavities of her temples shaded perceptibly into unhealthy brown. Her few teeth were her own, but were widely separated and pointed almost straight out of her mouth. Although Jane could not remember a time when Mrs. Pettibone had been sick, she looked terribly unhealthy. Her black hair hung limply to her neck, and her back was slightly bent all the time. And yet she looked at her dishes now as she looked at all things and all people, with an eager, cheerful expression. She was always ready to say the pleasant, conciliatory words; to try to cure any pain, to end any disagreement. As she handed a gravy boat to Jane she smiled, keeping her mouth closed against the alarming flash of her malocclusion.

"Poor old Gray," Jane said.

"He was gitting old and lame," Mrs. Pettibone said. "He used to kind of sigh to himself all the time, for the pain."

"He always was so gentle. Wasn't he strong, though?" Jane said.

"He could pull!" Mrs. Pettibone said, her hands motionless in the dishwater for a second. Her face lighted up—proud for the horse. "He was a worker." She nodded and went on washing. "But he had to go, Janie. He was gitting awful old for a horse."

"But it seems a shame to go for dog food. A great big horse like Gray."

"Hm-mm?" Mrs. Pettibone said, sloshing water around.

"Well, it's too bad."

"He's happier now," Mrs. Pettibone said.

Jane went to the windows facing down the hill toward Lake Cascom. Between plastic curtains made to look like lace, plants in pots on saucers, the wide slopes of Cascom Mountain's foothills went down to the valley. Behind the farm and its back pasture the dark mountain rose wooded to the top, but could not be seen from the house because of a long series of sheds and outbuildings that had grown up between the house and barn. Down at the end of the farm hill's gravel road she saw the small black ribbon of the main road here and there between brush and trees. The hills to the east were blue-black in the shadow of evergreen, lighter green in the hardwood. The sky was deep and cloudless to the final hills.

"All done, Janie. I'll do them pots and frypans," Mrs. Pettibone said.

The men were coming through the connecting sheds, stamping and kicking the gore from their boots. Sam Stevens pushed the door open with an elbow, and gestured with a bloody hand.

"Git me that little hone, and the other one."

Mrs. Pettibone went to a drawer and got the stones. Behind Sam, Adolf and the old man, Aubrey, waited patiently, bloody knives in their hands.

"Don't want to blood up your floor," Sam said. They went back to the carcass of the horse.

In a few minutes Adolf came back, grinning and holding out one of the stones. He spoke little English but seemed to understand anything that had to do with the farm, having come from one, via war and prison, in Poland. Sam Stevens had hired him from a displaced-persons agency after the war. Jane never managed to find out exactly what his nationality was. He insisted that he was not Polish, and claimed that he could speak German, Polish, Russian and some other languages. Usually he grinned and made signs, as he did now with the stones. Jane rinsed them off and put them back in the drawer, while Adolf grinned and nodded. He was in his thirties, thin and wiry. He seemed awkward, yet never had accidents, never dropped anything. He wore his black hair combed straight back and long, and when he bent over, the whole top layer of it would fall down over his face to his chin. Then he would snap his head in such a way—an expert, unconscious motion—that the hair would whip up and exactly back into place. He must have done this fifty times a day.

"Are they through yet?" Jane asked.

"Huh?"

"Are they done?"

"Ah! *Done!*" Adolf said, grinning wider. "Done? No! No! Big horse! Meat!" He held his arms out as if over a big pile. Jane turned away. "Goodbye!" Adolf said, laughing, and shut the door behind him.

Mrs. Pettibone was already peeling potatoes for lunch. She looked shyly at Jane. "I think Adolf's got a crush on you, Janie."

"A crush?"

"That's what I think." Mrs. Pettibone grinned at her potatoes.

"Well, I haven't got a crush on him," Jane said, smiling at the excited Mrs. Pettibone, who dipped a potato several more times than was necessary in her pan of water. Her shoulders moved up and down as she worked, as if her back were stiff.

"I guess nothing much ever happens on the farm," Jane said, putting her hand gently on Mrs. Pettibone's moving shoulder. The shoulder kept twitching, and Mrs. Pettibone smiled without trying to hide her teeth.

"Why do you do that—that twitching?" Jane asked.

"I don't know, Janie. It don't hurt none. I don't know why I do it." Then she began to hum a song, occasionally singing the words when she remembered them. "Mm-mm—hm-mm—'my Honolulu bay-bee.' "

A black Ford, dust following, climbed the farm road and turned into the worn space by the dooryard. Mrs. Pettibone ran to the window, holding her wet hands and a potato in the air.

"Who could it be?" she said eagerly, hiding behind a potted fern and peering out from under its feathery branches.

The door of the car opened slowly; then the worried face of Bob Paquette turned to the blind windows. Jane knew why he had come—he wanted to buy Mike's motorcycle. Charlotte told her that, and also that Bob couldn't make himself say the words concerning money to her—it seemed too soon after Mike's death to mention price; to haggle (he would never do that, she knew) over the extent of the damages to the machine. It was hardly damaged at all, but it was not new and the paint was scraped. "He says he can't buy anything from a woman," Charlotte had told her, "but he'll be scouting around, mumbling and looking." Jane decided to be as helpful as she could, but knew she must preserve the appearance of mourning.

Then she was really surprised to see John Cotter get out of the other side of the car.

"Why, it's John Cotter!" Mrs. Pettibone said.

"Do you remember him?" Jane asked.

"Of course I do. He came for you!"

For a moment Jane was startled. He came for me? she thought, and then remembered how oddly selective and independent of time Mrs. Pettibone's memory was.

"Yes. The DeMolay dance. But that was over ten years ago. Fourteen years ago . . ."

"Such a nice boy. He looked so nice," Mrs. Pettibone said.

Did time never pass in Leah? Fifteen years, ten years, how many wars and seasons passed without dimming the memory of one event?

"He wore a bow tie with polka dots. He wore a fingertip coat. Wasn't that a funny kind of coat? You were so pretty, Janie!"

Yes; 1944, and she was sixteen, and she was pretty. Her hand shook when he took it on the dance floor, her hand was wet and she was afraid her breath smelled bad from nervousness. Yes.

"You were a Rainbow Girl, remember how nice it was?" Mrs. Pettibone gave up her position among the fern fronds and went back to the sink. A knock on the kitchen door.

Like all the Paquettes except Ma, Bob's face was round and red, and the black hair sprang straight out. Charlotte's face and hair were just the same, and Jane could never understand how Charlotte could look like her brothers and yet be pretty. Bob came into the kitchen and took a long time to wipe his feet on the mat inside the door. Behind him, John Cotter watched, his eyes strangely unfocused. She knew him to be a man who forgot nothing, as she did not, and carefully began to find what made him so noncommittal. She felt that if she ignored him at this moment he would go with Bob and it would be as if he had never been there, as if they had never known each other at all.

"You want to look at the motorcycle," she said to Bob. He gratefully acknowledged this, said, "I won't bother you none, Janie," brushed by John Cotter and headed for the shed. He had evidently been talking to Junior and knew where the machine was. John Cotter, left unshielded, could not turn his back on her. They stared into each other's eyes.

"What an ass I am," he said.

She thought: Yes, you are, and you would have gone off noncommittal, too. But out of your shyness come the unexpected, disconcerting things, and you are always and always the boy who when I was a girl put his hand *there* (in dreams only) and put his mouth *there*. Strange thoughts on a sunny afternoon!

"Are you interested in motorcycles?" she asked.

"No." If anything about his face had changed, perhaps he had become darker. It had always been this darkness, the black of his hair and the dark glow of his skin that had in her dreams been the perfect opposite to her lightness. Michael Spinelli was dark, too, but dark with a racial darkness that seemed sallow and flat, as if Mike's handsome darkness came of genes, but John Cotter's came of some romantic effusion of the mind and castles on mountains.

"It's awfully dumb," John said, "but I really couldn't say that I wanted to see you, not motorcycles. I damn' near didn't come at all."

"You'd just as soon not go look at the motorcycle?"

"Yes, I'd just as soon not," he said. She remembered that her brother and John had had some unpleasant times. She always thought of Junior as the insecure one, and John Cotter as the one perhaps victimized, but the one somehow superior. Now she saw that she was not the sole cause of John Cotter's hesitation.

"I want to make some coffee," she said. "Will you wait? Bob will be looking at the machine for a long time, I suppose. Charlotte told me how much he wants it."

Mrs. Pettibone said, "Coffee's made, Janie. Take it into the sitting room."

They took the coffee and sat in the front room beneath the stuffed heads of deer and bear. One of the deer heads was a rifle rack, its horns holding a rifle across each set of prongs. On the end wall a huge black bearskin was tacked head down. A mounted wildcat grinned from the top of the upright piano.

"I was sorry to hear about Mike," he said shyly; "I always liked Mike." He knows, she thought, in spite of his awkwardness, that I am not connected with Mike. And I should ask about his brother, Bruce, and then that whole business will be over.

"How is Bruce, Johnny?" she asked.

"Not very good. He hasn't come out of it yet. I guess we both have that in common, except that with me . . . I mean, with you and Mike it's different. . . ."

No. No difference. Was there supposed to be? She watched him closely, to see if the quality of his embarrassment had changed. He stopped everything about his expression, assumed his familiar stolid motionlessness, then reached for his coffee cup, drank a little, and set it down. She had seen him retire from a situation before, seen him become inhumanly quiet.

"You've been in Paris," she said.

"I've been using up the last of the G.I. bill. There's only so much mileage you can get out of a disability, and I'm afraid I've run out of gas."

"I guess you'll be going into your father's business now," she said.

"My father's? I guess it will be, now."

"I know. You know I know. Everyone knows in Leah."

"I hate this goddam town," he said.

"Maybe you don't want to do anything," she said.

"Maybe." He smiled at her. "You see, that's my disability. I don't want to do anything."

"I heard—you know—I only know what Leah knows—that you were shot in the war," she said.

"Yes, but I usually say that I got hit on the head by a crate of oranges, or something like that. Anyway, it wasn't in the war, it was afterward. I did get shot, yes. An old man shot me with an antique pistol, because he was afraid, and I shot him at the same time. That's the truth—what really happened."

"You say that you got hit on the head with a crate of oranges?"

"Sometimes I say that I had a duel with a Japanese soldier—one of those suicide types who wouldn't surrender. That's the usual story with people in the Pacific who didn't get there in time for the war. But this old man was a Filipino and he was scared to death."

"But he shot you," she said.

"Yes. I didn't notice that he had for an hour afterward. An old cartridge. The bullet hit me right in the knee, and I can still limp pretty good if I try."

"You shot him."

"Yes, I killed him."

"Do you want some more coffee?" she asked.

"When we came in, I wasn't even going to say hello to you, for Christ's sake!" he said. "Can you imagine that? That's what Leah does to me."

"You'd think your home town would be where you knew what to do," she said.

"It's the only place in the world where I don't know what to do."

"So you've been going to school all these years?" she said. She watched him, and thought she saw some embarrassment, or guilt, and wondered why this school-going needed an excuse. Evidently it did. Amazing, because in her family going to school had always been a reward deserved because of brilliance or talent. Everyone thought that she should have gone on to college because she was the valedictorian of her high-school class. Yes, such a wonderful address she gave: "Robert Frost and R. P. T. Coffin: Poets of Our Granite Land." Somehow it seemed a ridiculous title now, but she wasn't sure quite why.

"I heard that you wrote poetry," she said.

"I wrote every goddam thing," he said, "but believe me, Jane, I never used that as an excuse for goldbricking on the G.I. bill. I didn't."

"You're just another person from Leah who thinks he has to earn ten dollars a day," she said.

He laughed. "You're right! Only I don't earn ten dollars a day. I just don't excuse my lack of industry."

She saw him become immobile again, and waited, thinking of her experience in this. Although short, it was spread over many years: he was getting ready to say something difficult.

"Why did you marry Mike Spinelli?" he finally asked.

She thought: That's a good question. Because John Cotter wasn't in Leah when I needed him? No. At least that is not what I should say. Because I had no time and settled for what was here and looked possible? No. Like all young girls at the glorious end of a hysteria that convinced all of my country, I was sucker to movies and to that dream of warriors. She should ask him: Did you see *The Best Years of Our Lives?* You see, Mike was a legitimate hero. His submarine went into Tokyo Bay and waited for a carrier.

"I don't know," she said.

Bob Paquette came in on them, trim and taut in his boots and Levis.

"I saw it, Janie," he said, and then to John: "Come on out and see it." John meekly followed Bob out through the sheds.

It seemed as if the last ten years had never passed, except for a heaviness, a weight in the mind that meant time had passed as if she'd been asleep and woke up to know that time had passed. Coming back to the farm, leaving the Spinellis and their house—it was like having been in another room for a while and then coming back. She knew time had passed, ten years of time, but it could just as well have been three years, one year or just six months for all the change it made. The biggest change on the farm in all that time had been the death of old Gray, and that happened just today.

It must have been that way with John Cotter, too. He hadn't really done anything since the war. Other people had married and had kids and changed into parents and homeowners—at least they looked and acted older. John could have come home from the war yesterday—he looked no different. Perhaps he looked even younger. After the war all the boys had been so careful to look like veterans, but all that was over now. And so did she look the same, as far as she could tell. It was as if she had been in storage: loved but not *used.*

She went into the kitchen to help Mrs. Pettibone, but by then the table was all set. Mrs. Pettibone sat close to the radio, listening to polkas and tapping her feet. She looked up, smiled, and moved her feet around as if she were dancing. Jane sat in a straight chair by the window, not quite listening to the music but aware of the frantic electric guitar and the shuffling of Mrs. Pettibone's old black shoes on the new linoleum rug.

Adolf came in with a bushelbasket full of thick chunks of red meat, grinned and did a little dance on the mat, in time with the music, then crossed toward the cellar stairs. The old man, Aubrey, followed him, his undone overshoe buckles tinkling.

"All over my floor!" Mrs. Pettibone called cheerfully. Aubrey turned and shrugged his shoulders, perhaps smiling, perhaps not, then clumped down the cellar stairs after Adolf.

In a little while the two men came up from the cellar with their empty bushel baskets, and Adolf asked again for the sharpening stones. Aubrey waited stolidly, looking at the wall, and then followed Adolf out. The polka program was over and the radio turned off.

"Where's Aubrey from?" Jane asked. Mrs. Pettibone thought for a minute.

"Why, Aubrey's from Cascom. Least he's always been around Cascom, long's I remember. I believe Aubrey's father had a farm over toward Switches Corners. It's all gone, now. He's just one of them come out of the woods, Janie. He never had no home of his own, I know of."

"He must be awfully old," Jane said.

"Well, now. Aubrey ain't so terrible old. Not as old as your grandfather, but Aubrey acts pretty old for his age."

"Is he all alone?"

"No, Aubrey's got one married sister, anyways, in Leah. He never sees her, though."

"Never?"

"Nope, never." Mrs. Pettibone had the broom, sweeping up after the men, and as she swept the last of their dirt out the door she turned, ready to go on with the story.

"I don't know exactly why, but Aubrey just never goes to Leah. He just eats, works, sleeps and smokes his pipe and chews tobacco, that's all Aubrey does. Aubrey hasn't been, now, ten years, anyways, further off than Cascom Corners. I figure he and his sister must of had a argument."

When Bob Paquette and John came back from the motorcycle, Bob was too shy to ask about buying it. He wanted it badly, and she could see him wanting it almost the way Mike had, but she said nothing. She meant to. She never wanted to see the thing again. She felt about the machine as if it were somehow female, her competitor —his mistress. *La Belle Machine Sans Merci.* Perhaps it should be shot and dismembered as old Gray had been. Then it wouldn't lead Bob Paquette into some deadly mailbox.

Bob stood around trying, but he finally decided he couldn't bring it up and edged toward the door. She felt there must be something obscene, or perhaps just in bad taste, about her being a widow, and she was suddenly angry with him. Before she could say anything John touched her on the arm, so lightly she might not have known if she hadn't seen his hand there.

"I'd like to come and see you, Janie," he said, impassive as an Indian. He, of course, had seen her anger. His hand hovered upon her arm, motionless and yet there.

"All right, John."

"I will. I mean it. I've got Bruce's car to use now. We can go to a movie. Would you want to?"

"Yes, I would," she said, thinking, Isn't that pretty brave of you? And he could not at that moment say when, or say anything more, for that matter. She understood that. They said goodbye to Mrs. Pettibone, and left.

She watched them drive down the the long hill and go out of sight on the main road, then went into the living room and picked up the coffee cups.

"I guess I better git to serving," Mrs. Pettibone said. "Them hungry men are coming in."

This time the three men stamped to the door and took off their boots and rubbers before coming into the kitchen to eat. They had washed at the spigot by the watering trough, but finished off with soap at the big slate sink in the kitchen.

"Nearly done," Sam Stevens said as he sat down at his place at the head of the table. There was still some blood caked under his big fingernails. The men ate pot roast, boiled potatoes, pickles, cheese and macaroni, and drank coffee. No one talked until Sam leaned back and pulled out his pipe. Jane and Mrs. Pettibone walked back and forth, serving.

"I hear in Leah they're going to close the woods," Sam said.

Aubrey nodded, his full and toothless mouth folding around his food like a cow chewing cud. "Heard the raddio say so," he said finally.

"Hull state. I guess they know what they're doing," Sam said. Adolf nodded his head, too.

"No more of them cigarettes in the woods, Adolf," Sam said,

raising his voice to make Adolf understand, as if Adolf were deaf.

"O.K.," Adolf said, grinning.

They took about fifteen minutes to eat and to drink their coffee. Sam put his pipe out and stood up, the other two getting up with him.

"Too hot to let that meat alone," Sam said. "It'd best be froze up quick. Come on, boys."

They adjusted suspenders, tucked in flannel shirts and went out to put on their boots and rubbers. Mrs. Pettibone started to clear off the dishes again, as she had in the morning.

After Jane and Mrs. Pettibone had eaten they did the dishes and peeled potatoes for supper, set the big table again. The remainder of the long afternoon seemed to come into the kitchen and stop everything, as if the hot sun could stop time and all, as in a photograph. Later Jane went up into the attic and found her old leathertops she had worn on muddy days a long time ago. Because the leather was dry and dusty, she took them down to the kitchen and rubbed Vaseline into them. The woods were dry even in what had been swampy places, but the boots would protect her ankles.

She carefully skirted the place where old Gray had died, just once seeing the men bowed over as she climbed the back pasture toward the mountain. At the top of the pasture she turned to see Lake Cascom in its valley, parts of the little river leading to Leah in the west, and the thousand hills leading her eyes off into a whitish haze on the horizon. The farmhouse and the barn seemed far down and far away, held to the valley by the little hill road that was like a string going down. In back of the barn the men looked like bugs, and in the cropped grass she could barely see parts of the old horse strewn about.

She turned to the mountain on an old trail through maples and then deep in the spruce, climbed to Porcupine Ledges where she could see on this clear day Leah and Northlee and even part of the Connecticut River toward the green hills of Vermont.

As she sat on an angled outcrop of granite, there was a soft explosion of a partridge in the woods beside her. The big bird came sailing on stiff wings, then made whistling short strokes, then glided again across the trail into the thickest brush. She wanted a cigarette, but hadn't thought to bring any. The woods were too dry, anyway, even if they hadn't been officially closed yet. Instead she took long breaths of the air, of the constant hot wind so dry and clear it hurt her lungs. She felt that such breaths should hurt a little. It had been a long time since she'd done anything to make her breathe hard—a long time since she'd climbed any hill.

CHAPTER 7

Gladys Cotter came running back into the dining room and stopped short.

"I knew it before the phone stopped ringing," she said. "I just remembered that instant." John and William Cotter looked at her, waiting. "It was the Fresh Air lady." She turned and tapped a painted tray with her fingernail. William Cotter leaned back in his chair, letting his head fall back.

"No!" he said. "No! You said you'd call that off. Well, I hope you told her."

"I couldn't. I meant to send a letter when Bruce first— Oh, I don't know what to do!"

"You've got to call back and tell her what the situation is here, and that we can't take the kids. Next year, maybe, but not now." He watched his wife carefully as she turned back to the table.

"I never heard anything about this," John said.

"Your mother said she'd take a boy and a girl for two weeks— from the slums. The New York slums. You know, up here in the fresh air."

"Fresh air!" John said, wonderingly.

"We can't have them now," Gladys Cotter said, but she made no move toward the hall and the telephone.

"It'd be an awful strain right now. You couldn't do it," William Cotter said.

"I know it."

"I don't think the kids would have much fun in this house now," John said.

"I know it," Gladys Cotter said. She had her mind made up. John wondered just how he could get out of it. He'd have to take off. But he couldn't. He'd promised his father he wouldn't take off.

"Damn it! I'll call myself!" William Cotter said.

John tried to back him up. He let his voice rise, and stood up. William Cotter had to stand up, too, because of his threat to call the Fresh Air lady himself.

"Don't be foolish!" John said, "There's Bruce over there and we don't know whether he's dying or not! And you want to take on two kids you don't know what they're like, for God's sake! They're probably problem children anyway. Probably unhappy or something. Probably steal everything they get their hands on!"

"I didn't say I'd take them," Gladys Cotter said, her face beginning its familiar collapse.

She was getting the martyred, persecuted look. His father saw it and gave up. John sat down.

"I don't know what's wrong with you people!" Gladys Cotter said, crying.

John thought, For God's sake she's crying right *at* us, as if she were arguing that way. It was her way of arguing, in fact, not even putting her hands up to her face. And his father, used to being beaten down one way or another, looked away.

"You don't know what's wrong with *us*," John said. "Why don't you figure what's wrong with you for a change! Can't you see what a stupid thing this is?"

She cried harder.

"Johnny," his father said, admonishing him in a weak voice.

John went into the living room. He looked out to Maple Street as the dusk came over it slowly, softening, bluing everything. His mother sniffed and hiccuped in the dining room. One of them, his father, probably, was pouring more coffee. After that his father would go out to the kitchen and pour some bourbon into it. There he went—the cupboard door squeaked. His father came back through the dining room and stood beside him.

"You're being kind of cruel," his father said in a low voice.

Cruel?

"You don't want those kids to come, do you?" he whispered to his father. No answer. "You've got to help me, for once. You've got to do something, too. We can't take a bunch of kids around here now. You know that!" His mother had gone out to the kitchen.

"Haven't I ever helped you?" his father asked.

"I don't know," John said, angry at both of them. He sat down in a deep wingchair, out of sight in the darkening room.

"Maybe you're right," William Cotter said. He turned, carrying his cup, and went slowly out of the room and up the front stairs. One step, two steps, crunch, creak. John counted seventeen stairs, balcony and two more. The bedroom door shut, and above him the bed moved.

His mother came in and stood in the light from the dining room.

"Johnny . . ." she said.

"For Christ's sake I don't want a *conference!*" he said, and then he was ashamed. He went past her, almost running, out the back door to Bruce's car. He had to back onto the lawn to get by his father's Buick, and as he left the driveway one rear wheel thumped over the curb.

He drove down Maple Street to the square and turned down Water Street, stopping in front of a store with a sign in red neon over the front window: *Teach Your Dollars More Cents.* He had ten dollars he had borrowed from his father, and he went in and bought from Anna, the old Polish woman, a case of twenty-four bottles of beer. This left him five dollars and sixty cents—to last until he asked for more money from his mother or his father. Anna, sleepy and squat, with her blond-gray hair mussed up, didn't recognize him. She grudgingly gave him a bottle opener.

He drove toward Northlee until he remembered that Bruce lay unconscious there, then turned to take the wooden bridge across the river into Vermont. He opened a bottle of beer with one hand, pressing the bottle against the seat of the car for leverage and steering with the other. He followed an old asphalt road through the low hills, going slowly through the banked turns as he climbed, sipping his beer and watching the road in front of his headlights.

Now at home his mother would be doing the dishes, her face composed, almost frozen. His father would probably have come back downstairs, and would be sitting in the living room. The house, standing still and brittle over this mess, would be the same. *Home.*

And yet the word *home* did not mean, at least did not mean completely, the place of tension his own home had always been to him. He seemed to have another home, another family, God knew where. Perhaps the idea came from every legend about such a place—a place where love could be taken for granted and affection could be expressed without shame, where pride was not always afraid of wounds.

Bruce could not win in an exchange of sarcasm, and yet like a compulsive gambler played at it until John, forgetting, said the stupid, unanswerable words, "Don't get your water hot, Brucie." Bruce— "DON'T GET *YOUR* WATER HOT!" The mother trembled. The shrinking father, wary of stray shots, doused his coffee with bourbon.

"Now, you boys," Gladys Cotter would say.

"SHUT UP!"—one of the boys. And William Cotter rarely dared to chide.

He threw his empty bottle out of the window of the car, heard it bounce on the shoulder of the road and whick into the underbrush. In Vermont the fine for doing this was fifty dollars, but all along the road the bright bottoms of beer bottles and cans winked at him, like the eyes of animals.

He knew of real families who were not like his. The Paquettes, for instance, were not continually in crisis. They had their moments, and he had seen some quarrels among the Paquettes, but beneath the quarreling, even the violence, there seemed to run a calm stream of family. It did not matter. It was not deadly.

He thought of *Peter Pan,* or *The Wind in the Willows,* of *A Child's Garden of Verses,* or even of such things as *Mary Poppins* and *Winnie the Pooh.* Did his vision of love arise from such stuff? In his language group at the Sorbonne he had known an English girl, Muriel, who seemed to be the final product of softness and wonder.

She was seventeen, a large girl, and called her mother "Mummy." She was very sweet, very talky, and had lost her left hand when a very small child in the blitz. Her brother was killed by the same bomb. But in most ways it was as if this horror had never happened, as if she had just come fresh from the nursery, with her Teddy bear somewhere nearby, her rocking horse waiting with her dolls in that cozy place. She wanted to *live;* to go to the dark cave of his room with him and find out about things, and he took her there. One night on his bed that was always damp with the moisture of the stone walls he took off most of her clothes and found that her underpants were white knit cotton with a little blue ribbon woven around each leg and finished in a bow. Christopher Robin's wide blue eyes watched, Mary Poppins glared, Mummy wouldn't like it—though Muriel would—and that was that. He took her home to her respectable pension feeling quite noble and defeated; Muriel, he was sure, quite surprised.

The road led northward, up the river between hills, and after he had climbed the low mountains above Wentworth Junction, he turned around and started back. He nearly threw his cigarette out the window, then remembered in time the tindery brush. He put the butt in his empty bottle, held it to his ear to hear the hiss, then threw bottle and all out.

Then there was the Russian who always came to the Bar Vert—at least he was there whenever John went there—a well dressed, dark man with a thin face. He always smiled, joked, and eventually got the guitar player to play Russian songs. Then he sang. His voice was deep, resonant but out of control, and he sang with a painful, weepy smile on his face. His eyes filled and he cried as he sang, and his homesickness was so great even the French stopped talking and listened to him. John would find his own eyes burning for this stranger's grief, even though homesickness was one disease he thought he never had. Not for his own home; but didn't he have a Russian counterpart to his legend? Natasha's family, the Rostovs, in *War and Peace;* and he remembered, as if he had been there, one Christmas when they went visiting in sleighs over brittle, noisy snow, everybody warm and snug under fur robes, the horses farting sweet steam into the icy night, everybody loving each other and sleighing over the long plains toward other people they loved. The Russian's strange syllables, his breaking voice, meant this scene to John.

But he was no exile, like the Russian. Strange, that the memory of Leah contained so little nostalgia! If he remembered any period of his life with nostalgia it was not Leah, where he was always the little boy who dirtied either the playground slide or his own conscience, but the time when he first got away, when he was a young soldier.

And after the war there was the pleasant business of being a veteran, that easy crutch of the times, and the G.I. bill, another one: hippity hop from one university to another—Vermont, Chicago, Iowa, Paris—all of them far enough from Leah. He did catch certain enthusiasms in those years; became voluble and sometimes violent. He joined the American Veterans' Committee, stood frightened and aggressive before large groups of people. The Communists had wooed him for a time, until his inaccessibility enraged them and drove them to acts of complete alienation. He still believed in the importance of the issues that had so excited him, but somehow the energy of his beliefs had seeped away.

He drove back across the covered bridge into New Hampshire, avoided the Town Square and took the back road toward Cascom; a narrow, curving asphalt road similar to the one he'd taken in Vermont. As soon as he left Leah town proper, he opened another bottle of beer.

He knew the back road to Cascom well, having taken it often in the past to visit the Randolfs—Howard, Phoebe and their rather exotic daughter, Minetta. When, in high school, the romantic ideas of Miss Colchester began to lose their power—when Shelley and Byron no longer meant to him glorious freedom and rebellion, the Randolfs' more contemporary oddness fascinated him. They had migrated farther north than most of the returning exiles of the twenties, and somehow stuck. He suspected that the Randolfs stuck more because of lack of money than for the depth of their philosophy of old houses and the virtues of the soil. Howard Randolf had written two best-sellers in the early thirties, but it had been a long time since the early thirties. He had written many novels since, and John made it a point to read them. "Howard Randolf," one critic wrote, "is *one* bloodshot-eye boy who keeps up with the times. His heroes used to be either unbuttoning their flies or buttoning them up, but now they are either unzipping them or zipping them up."

The Randolfs owed Cotter & Son quite a sum of money for coal and roofing—or at least they had two years ago. Bruce had been fond of mentioning this. Though they had lived in Leah for twenty-five years or so, they were still "summer people"—but they did owe a lot of money here and there, and to many of the townspeople this fact seemed to entwine them sufficiently within the fortunes and history of Leah. A few more debts and they might be natives.

Suddenly the Randolfs' mailbox flew by, white with the lettering washed out, but he knew it well enough because of the huge maple stump it sat on. He let the car slow down, not putting on the brake but letting the motor slow it, his foot off the accelerator. No, he didn't want to see anybody. He wanted to drive around slowly and drink beer by himself. But the Randolfs would sure like it if he brought them a case of beer—what was left, anyway. He felt around in the case and decided he'd only had four. That left twenty, which was enough. Enough for what? His ambition had always been to get Randolf and the old lady drunk enough so that they would go to bed and leave him alone with Minetta, but the trouble was that nobody ever came to see them except Minetta's admirers and the Randolfs were starved for talk. They might go to bed and leave Bob Paquette, all right, but when John came they always wanted to talk. He'd gone nearly a mile when he decided to turn around and see the Randolfs anyway.

The road to the old farmhouse was still rutty from the spring thaw, and in the dry spell the ruts had dried hard and ridgy and had stayed that way all summer. The Randolfs had an old car, but they walked the half-mile to the mailbox and drove to Leah only once a week for supplies.

The old white house was surrounded by a grove of huge pines, and it looked under the roof of branches like a house within a house. Several brick chimneys, like tent poles, supported the tired roof. The house had been painted recently, and the old cedar shingles had been covered with modern mineral roofing. Across the road an old gray barn stood in a relaxed fashion, propped up here and there by the beams of another barn long since fallen into its foundation. One small window gleamed, high up under the purlins. It was there, warmed in winter by the heat of sheep and cows, that Howard Randolf worked. Rats chewed his manuscripts and sat beadily watching him as he wrote. Once he had introduced a rat to John, a long brown fellow with a white patch at his throat, as Aldridge H. Aldridge, a literary critic. "He feels," Howard had said, "that my work is too naïvely optimistic, and has invited me to follow him beneath the old hencoop, where reality exists."

John parked on the thick bed of pine needles that surrounded the house. The Randolfs did not have electricity, and the soft gleam of oil lamps shone in the downstairs windows.

Minetta and her mother had seen his headlights and were waiting for him on the side porch.

"John Cotter," he said as he walked toward them on the slippery pine needles.

"Oh!" they both said at once, surprised and glad to see him. He came into the circle of lamplight.

"The world traveler!" Mrs. Randolf said, smiling, her mouth nervous and jerky. Her voice was low and ragged, and now it suddenly burst through into a higher note. "Well! John Cotter, come to see us!" Her gray hair was straggly, always seeming to be a little damp with sweat, and strands of it stuck out at right angles to her head. She had become even plumper and waddlier in the past two years, and she waddled into the house, holding her lamp on a level with her eyes.

Minetta hadn't said anything after her first "Oh!" of surprise. The night was hot and she was barefoot, wearing only shorts and a halter that looked like the top of a two-piece bathing suit. As usual, she wore just a little too much lipstick, even out here where there were few visitors and no neighbors for three miles.

"What's new?" he asked. With Minetta he always reconnoitered carefully.

"Nothing," she said brightly, shaking her head. He thought he'd better try again.

"Bob Paquette told me you were here. He said you were going to stay the winter, too."

She turned her blue eyes directly on him; black hair surrounded her face. For some reason she held her long hair together under her chin, as if she were looking out of a black hood. "I know it, God damn it! Howard's got a loft in New York, but he sublet it for all year. Now we've got to hibernate."

"Why don't you take off?" he asked. They followed Mrs. Randolf into the living room.

"I did that last winter, but I ran out of money." She walked away from him, then turned around and put her foot up on a chair, leaning her elbow on her knee. The lamplight shone through a delicate fuzz of reddish little hairs along her thigh. Mrs. Randolf, who had been bending over the fireplace, stood back to let the bright flame of burning newspapers flood the room.

"Good God, Phoebe, isn't it hot enough?" Minetta said, moving away—always to a point directly across the room from John. He could never figure out whether she wanted to get away from him or wanted him to look at her, and this was another of her little inscrutabilities. He sat in an antique rocker, rather gingerly, and leaned slowly back to look at her some more. There was something a little too muscular and gross about her, but she made him think—or not think—thinking as such didn't enter into it—about taking off her clothes. Bob Paquette said once that Minetta Randolf was the most popular girl in wet dreams in Leah. John tried to imagine, but couldn't, a girl who was more sexy. There weren't any. No movie star, no Egyptian belly dancer; nobody. In grade school and in high school, when sex began to dominate the minds of boys in Leah, Minetta Randolf was mentioned quite often. "She's always turning up—I mean laying down, in the conversation," Bob said. And yet the rumor was that she was a virgin: a persistent rumor, as persistent as the opposite kind of rumor about one chaste, old-maidish girl in town. Now she sat down and hooked her arms over the back of her chair, making her breasts stick out. What other rumor than this unseemly one of virginity could be worth repeating about lush Minetta? He would like to investigate the situation carefully. The nearest he had ever come to finding out was the time she invited him to a Bennington prom. But then for some reason he ended up with her blonde, skinny roommate, the only girl he had ever met who drove a Nash because of the reclining seats.

Mrs. Randolf stood on tiptoe at the high, darkly gleaming sideboard, reaching for glasses. The sideboard stood on simple, gracefully carved legs, its strap hinges just slightly darker than the old wood of the doors. She put the wineglasses on a small table, then bent gruntingly at a low cupboard and brought out a gallon of white wine.

"I've got some beer in the car," John said.

"Why, John Cotter! I'd love some beer!"

"Good God, Phoebe! Are you going to mix?" Minetta said.

John went to get the beer. As he opened the car door a tall figure appeared beside him.

"Who is it?" The voice was loud and angry at first, then plaintive. "Well, who the hell *is* it?"

"John Cotter."

"Well, well, if it ain't! John Cotter come up to see us reecluses."

"Ayuh," John said.

"What? What? Beer?" Howard took the case out of John's hands. "I'll carry it! Ah, yes! You've just come back from France, and Phoebe's wine? Agh! The memory of the Beaujolais! No, her poison is now white—kerosene laced with grape juice, one dollar and four cents a gallon!"

Howard was really quite angry. John was not always able to tell, when Howard was angry, just what he was angry about. This time he felt that Howard resented his bringing the beer. And yet there was no doubt he was glad John had come.

As they came into the room and the lamplight, Howard's thin muscles were like taut snakes on his forearms. He was a big-jointed man, all bone and wire; very strong. His dark face seemed to be muscled, too, and resembled an anatomy chart of the facial articulations. His blue eyes gleamed out of dark hollows, rolling easily, protuberant and yet deep behind his brow, as if they were attached to his head by the optic nerves alone.

Minetta opened bottles. Mrs. Randolf decided to stick to the white wine. Howard said: "Phoebe, this lucky young fellow has been in France. Do you remember?"

"Do I remember?" she said, sipping wine and banging a package of cigarettes on the table at the same time, "Do I remember? God damn these cigarettes," she said mildly, a dreamy, reminiscent look on her face.

Minetta had carefully seated herself across the room from him again, and John had to look at her while trying to be unobtrusive about it. He suddenly realized how much he would hate, even fear, to have Howard Randolf discover his thoughts concerning Minetta, even though she must be twenty-seven or twenty-eight.

The Randolfs reminisced. John soon found that they were not interested in his more recent impressions of Europe, and that his little lecture, the property of all returned travelers, would remain unspoken. He listened instead to the Randolfs' sentimental journey into a time when such names as Ezra, Gertrude, and Tristan Tzara were fresh and meaningful. Their faces lighted up; they hugged themselves and chuckled delightedly. They lived in Montparnasse, sat at the Dôme, the Rotonde, the Closerie des Lilas. He didn't tell them what he had seen on his ceremonial visit to the place, with the now homeless whores so thick, so desperately grabby, and the flaccid, sodden faces of the American dreamers like cold moons above the round tables.

In spite of a beginning feeling of disappointment because they were not interested in what he had to say (after all, what could a local yokel like John Cotter have to say?), in their self-confident, stagy voices he found again, as he had in high school, a pretense to intellectualism he would never find in Leah. Even though he recognized the pretense, the show-off part of the Randolfs, he apologized for it by asking himself who in Leah was at all concerned with such exciting stuff? No matter that they vied with each other for the floor, cut in on each other's stories, became shrill and childish while trying to be knowing and wise—and all the time he wondered why one didn't haul off and hit the other in his eagerness for the center of attention—he listened and caught some of their sadness for time past.

John's attention began to wander. He sneaked occasional looks at Minetta's legs—she had crossed them and he found himself mentally putting one hand between the soft flesh above her knees, perhaps to lift a leg up and set it back down on the floor. A sudden silence startled him, and he remembered the last few words of a question.

". . . do you think?"

He hadn't any idea what the question had been, and tried to appear to think about it.

Minetta smiled. She knew why he hadn't been listening. Almost imperceptibly she shook her head.

"I think it's asinine," John guessed.

"Well, so do I!" Howard said, seeming to be amazed that they agreed. He continued, his sentences just slightly surer and more balanced, as if they had once been written. John thought that he recognized Howard's style:

"A book is like a tree: its vitality is determined by growth and by propagation. A tree rotten at the core may bear for a time beautiful fruit, but its future is certain, and its future is not the glorification of trees. . . ."

Howard recited on. John drank his beer and watched the lamplight's glow on Minetta's flesh. Then Howard stopped again, his eyes glittering, and drank his beer in one swallow. He brought the bottle down on the table, for emphasis, a little too hard. His wife, her face sagging below smooth and surprisingly shiny little cheeks, reached over and rubbed the dent in the table with the heel of her hand. Howard gave her a disgusted glance, as if to say that his argument was more important than a dent in the table. John was afraid he might say this to his wife, who was getting rather drunk and in no condition to bear it calmly.

"You mean a book should glorify the human race? And a tree glorifies trees?" John asked quickly.

"Now wait a minute!" Howard shouted. "Let's not get our goddam trees mixed up with our goddam books! That metaphor was accurate as far as it went. . . ." He raised his empty bottle, lipped off the last drop, and motioned in Minetta's direction. She went out to the kitchen to get more beer.

Mrs. Randolf took the opportunity to speak, her voice starting high and running down the scale to reach a shaky level after the first few words: "Nothing shakes them. If they are trapped into explaining what they do, which is seldom, they first describe themselves physically and then say that they are promoting the understanding of mankind!" She threw her head back and laughed. Her belly rumbled, her breasts fell into her armpits and seemed to knot themselves into fists, as if they were another pair of hands. It occurred to John that Minetta had come out of this thing, and that something of her mother's ugliness waited in Minetta.

"I don't mean just the queers!" Howard said. "They never amount to much anyway—come and go like a recurring disease. I mean these goddam crybabies who hate the whole bloody human race and still write books about it. *Long* books about it! Christ! I just finished one—three days it took me—and I got so disgusted I threw it across the room twice a day. Once I threw it out the door and it fell through a hole in the porch and I had to crawl under the goddam porch after it. I said by God I'd finish the damned thing if it killed me and it damn' near did. I'd rather read the Monkey-Ward catalogue. At least they know what they mean!" He stood up and turned convulsively, walked to a bookcase and violently jerked a large book out and into his hands, where it opened raggedly, looking like a dead white chicken with its feathers mussed. He turned pages by handfuls as he came back into the lamplight.

"*Listen* to this! '*He could see it in his mind, crawling from the greasy tumbrils, a reptile garland of dead hair, seaweed hair, writhing amid the warty excrescences of its bull shoulders—and the teeth; jagged, coin-colored, ripping, tearing (Oh, God! his mother saying, You'll be home by nine-sharp, won't you, Jolly Jimmy?). So sweet, so pure—and guilt; agony in a pretty afghan settled, sullied his eyes and made his brain turn in its white cave like lava and he smelled the lubricous oil of that dark hell in his dry nostrils along with lavender sachet. . . . A subway roared in its hole and passed. . . .*' "

"He sounds like he's in bad shape," John said.

Howard threw the book out into the porch, where it slid across the gritty boards and thumped against the railing. "Bad *shape!* There's five hundred pages of that! Five hundred solid pages of it! You can start that book from the back and it's just as clear—one solid supersaturated colloidal suspension. You know how much time passes? About five hours! The rest is flashbacks of flashbacks of flashbacks, and in each flashback of a bloody flashback there's a poor, mean, carping, sniveling, loaded-pantsed, rotten-souled rat of a human being doing that kind of interior stinking. And that book"—he raged silently for a moment, his arms twitching as he raised them—"that so-called novel is generally felt to be *important! Important! Ad puke!*"

Howard drank thirstily, coughed, drank some more, then went on: "I met one of these fellows in New York this spring. I asked him why he hated humanity—you know there wasn't a real man in any of his books, just mean little creeps and sadists. Anyway, I asked him what the hell good was it if man was such a shit? I said why the hell do you write? Or even go on living? He said he had to beat the hours. That's all: *Beat the hours*. I said you're not beating the hours, you're just beating your meat. You can write, but you'll have to get to be a man before you have anything to say. I said you're just mad, pouting mad because people have been nasty to you. He said I was naïve and outdated. I told him I went through and remembered his present attitude when I was ten years old and lost all my marbles, and if catching up to him meant I'd have to regress that far I guess I'd wait this cycle out."

Howard finished his bottle. Mrs. Randolf had fallen asleep during his diatribe, and now she sat back, her eyes open but slightly glazed. Minetta kept bringing in the beer, and John counted bottles. Howard had been hitting the beer pretty hard, in spite of his talking. Now he began again, his hands flailing, his eyes bloodshot. John found himself watching Howard with much interest, but not hearing the words at all. How sad, he thought as he watched Howard's passionate gestures. How sad and lonesome not to be heard! To be kind to Howard, to sympathize, would be to disagree, to get angry and argumentative himself. But here he was, watching and sometimes listening, but giving nothing at all.

The kerosene lamps were streaming. A fine tissue of smoke curled over the glass chimney of one and slowly deposited carbon on the scalloped edge. The beer bottles reflected amber light. Across the room Minetta's urgent thigh rounded into amber and into darkness.

More words from Howard: "Man is no longer the subject and the theme. Instead of the really great insights into the nature of man we have the cruel use of humanity to illustrate some sterile intellectual syllogism. Man isn't the subject; he's a kind of puppet!" He banged his empty bottle on the table and roused his wife. She stood up and said, "Come on Howard. We're going to bed."

He looked at her angrily. "You finish the goddam wine?"

She didn't answer, but pulled him out of his chair. He came up slowly, suddenly weak, willing to be guided.

"Say good night and thank John for the beer," she said. "Minetta, dear, will you clean up and take care of the lamps when you come to bed?"

Howard said nothing, but let himself be pulled toward the stairs.

"You're all upset and nervous and you drank too fast," his wife said. They climbed the stairs together, helping each other.

John and Minetta stared at each other over the beer bottles.

"He gets very tired when he talks like that. He'll be tired for days," Minetta said, and then she added as if she were talking to herself, "They insist upon calling his books that—'naïve and outdated.' " Then she spoke to him again, "There are a few bottles left, I think."

"We might as well finish the case," he said, and watched her as she passed him and went toward the kitchen, her hips swaying slightly, graceful in an overripe way. He thought of a ripe, yellow plum—an overripe plum, and the image of the plum dropped and squashed in his mind with an exciting plop. He walked unsteadily to the front porch and took a leak into a lilac bush.

Minetta waited for him in the living room. "It's so hot," she said. As she handed him the bottle their fingers touched. But that didn't mean anything. She had always done little things like that. She looked at him as if she were the seducer and he the reluctant virgin. She squeezed his arm above the elbow and led him out into the black shadows of the pines. White moonlight shafted down between the solid, bulky branches. At the car he turned and put his arms around her, feeling her narrow waist with one hand, his bottle in the other, her wide hips against his legs. Her arms came around him, but it seemed automatic. Nothing happened. She was a big, beautiful rubber statue. He took a drink over her shoulder, then kissed her. She was soft, pliable, but she seemed to be full of nothing but air—until he tried to get her down onto the ground. Then she was surprisingly strong; so strong he would have to use a serious wrestling hold on her. He tried it tentatively, but knew he would have to hurt her and gave it up. What did it matter?

"I hope I didn't break your back," he said. Some beer had sloshed out of the bottle, and he could feel it sticky under his wrist watch. Then he realized that she had been whispering.

"Not here, not here." Her black hair was a cloud across his eyes, and he began to shake. She moved quickly against him, then pulled him across the road into the moonlight and down a little slope into tall hay. She stood up straight and looked around, as if she were measuring the little field. They seemed to be in the exact center of it. Evidently satisfied, she undid her halter and let it drop. Her breasts were satellites of the moon, glaringly white against her tanned body, or great eyes, black-irised. She pulled off her tight trunks and stood with her arms down, letting the moonlight wash over her.

"Take off your clothes," she ordered.

Under her eyes and the moon's cold light, as his clothes dropped off he felt as if he were plunging into cool water—water full of the light touch of hands. She came against him and they rolled easily, almost in slow motion, onto the springy stems of the bent hay.

Later he raised himself up on his arms and looked at the sweating body beneath him. Hadn't he seen that black triangle before, and caused the same, always the same, urgent moans? But she hooked him down with her legs and the moaning began again.

They dressed. He found his beer where he had set it on a level place, and they walked, not touching each other, back to the car. She opened the door and got in.

"Hadn't you better . . ." he asked.

"Get in and don't worry about it," she said. He went around and got in behind the wheel. She leaned back against the door and looked at him, her long hair shadowy over her shoulders.

"I'm by nature cautious and sober," he said.

"Sure you are. You stink of it. You're pretty good, aren't you? Better than your brother."

"Bruce?" he said, startled.

"Oh, you're an expert, you are. What do you think about? Do you do addition in your head? Subtraction?" She spoke coldly, reached over and put her hand in his pants, then took her hand away. "Have you ever *loved* a girl? Would you be such an artist?" Her anger built up until her voice was choked—raging: "You're not a man! You're a lousy self-conscious gigolo! Bruce is a *man!* He does what he needs to do, what he *feels!* I need a man who needs and jabs and *does,* none of you fancy experts!"

He began to chuckle involuntarily, half horrified, half amused by her outburst. "Ram, bam, thank you, ma'am," he said.

"You goddam professional! Run off home and gloat how good you are and how you made me purr! How many times?" She got out of the car and shut the door, then put her head in the window.

"You and all the lousy honyaks in Leah. You think you're all so damn' good, but none of you is half the man he is. Murder him, hate him, live on his money!" She ran up to the house.

Bruce! He watched Minetta's shadow pass the windows. He was too vulnerable; all the starch was out of him—his laughter was cut short by a chilly wave of fear as the warm lamplight in the windows faded and snuffed out. He found himself desperately searching for the switch. A warm breath of wind came over the back of his neck and head like a hand, and he shivered. Did the hawk watch him? He feared that if he turned on the headlights Bruce himself might be standing immediately in front of the car, hawks' eyes in his head, waiting. . . .

CHAPTER 8

Junior rarely came to the farm. Jane had never seen his room in Leah above Futzie's Tavern. Now he came in his old Chevrolet and parked it at the far end of the driveway instead of the usual place in front of the kitchen. She watched him from the window as he walked toward the door. Though it was Saturday afternoon, he wore a suit and tie—his dark blue pin-stripe suit he had bought for his mother's funeral. The pants had always been too short, and his white socks flashed above his black Navy dress shoes. Mike had known how to dress—not like the other people, the Maple Street people like John Cotter and his brother in their sport jackets and argyle socks—not that way, but at least Mike had a certain style in a suit with too wide shoulders and pegged pants, and a yellow tie. Junior was too big and gawky; he was from the farm, and looked it.

"Hi, Janie," he said, his face composed, formal. "We're going to come and see you. We decided that we should come and see you, on account of Mike. Not just on account of Mike, Janie. The Club thought that was the thing we better do." He stood by the door with his hands clasped behind him. He was terribly worried. She had never seen him so worried, but she couldn't ask him to sit down in his own grandfather's house. He stood as if he were a stranger, frowned at her, and then turned to frown at Mrs. Pettibone, who just then came into the kitchen.

"Junior Stevens!" Mrs. Pettibone said. Keeping her eyes on him, she put a bowl of potatoes down on the table and went toward him quickly. She stopped suddenly and turned to Jane.

"What's the matter?" she asked, and then to Junior: "What are you all slicked up for, Junior? What's happened?"

"Nothing," Junior said. He motioned with his head toward Jane.

"The Riders are coming to offer their respects to the widow," Jane said.

"Oh, isn't that nice—" Mrs. Pettibone began.

Junior cut her off. "You don't make it any easier!" he yelled.

"Me?" Mrs. Pettibone asked in a quavering voice.

"No! Not you! Her!" His hands came from behind him for the first time and he pointed a big finger at Jane. The callused brown finger looked like a club.

"And you came first, so you could find out how I'd be," Jane said, " 'cause you were scared I might not act right."

"We're just trying to be nice to you!" Junior shouted.

Mrs. Pettibone had backed slowly and carefully out of the kitchen, shaking her head and looking sad. Now from the sitting room she called back with as much force as she could, "Junior! Is that nice?"

"Nice? You old bitch, you're always on her side!"

"You've got no call to say that," Jane said.

"I'm sorry!" he screamed at the top of his voice. Mrs. Pettibone hurried up the front stairs, sobbing.

Jane watched her brother and saw his neck swell and turn red.

"Oh, all right, Junior. I'll be nice during your ceremony. I'll be very nice."

"We're just trying to be nice to you! I don't see why you always have to be such a wisenheimer! You think you're the goddam Queen of Sheba, and what're the rest of us, goddam pigs or something?"

"Don't yell. I told you I'd be nice. When are they coming?"

"They ought to be here anytime now. Just coming to be nice to you."

"Before they come I think you ought to go up and apologize to Mrs. Pettibone. She's always been good to you and you know she's not what you called her at all. You've made her cry—" She began to lose control of her voice, and it rose a little higher than she wanted it to. "You called her a bitch. I don't care how upset you were. A *bitch!* She used to wash your diapers for you, and you're just as much of a baby now! You're a baby and a bully! Did you see how glad she was to see you? And when do you ever even come out here and see her? When you have to, that's when. She loves you and you come in here and call her a bitch! You want to ask me again if I think you're a pig?"

When he pouted he could have been the little boy she remembered in grade school. His lower lip pushed out, he frowned, he wiggled his shoulders; but the lower lip was coarse and cracked and the shoulders were thick under the suit coat. He went to the stove and looked at its bare surface.

"You going to make some coffee?" he asked.

"Mrs. Pettibone would love to make coffee for all of you, and you know it. She'd be hurt even more if you didn't ask her."

"All *right!*" He walked swiftly to the stairs and shouted up, "I'm sorry!" No answer. "I'm *sorry,* Mrs. Pettibone!"

"You'd better go up," Jane said.

He whispered at her, "You shut up and let me alone!" A car came into the dooryard, and when Junior heard it he shook his head, panicky. "It's always like this!" he said, and went upstairs.

Fortunately, the first one to come in was Bob Paquette. Mrs. Pettibone served coffee and cupcakes, but still hadn't fully recovered from being called a bad name. Bob was the only one to smile during the ceremonial hour, and the only one to say more than one or two words.

The Riders came in their old cars with the dirt caked up under the fenders and the metal salt-rotted through along the bottoms of the doors. They wore suit coats that crippled their arms and exposed long wrists, and they held coffee cups in awkward fingers, always by the dinky little handles. They wore ties on shirts that hadn't been used to wearing ties and their collar points were held down by heavy hardware clipped and skewered into the cloth. Their hands collided often with the hard knots of their neckties. The wives and girl friends of the Riders came too, and sat closer to Jane than the men, although they had just as little to say. Junior pretended that he was busy helping Mrs. Pettibone serve coffee and cupcakes. They were all as frightened and nervous as they had been the night at the hospital, and this time their machines didn't wait outside. Stifled in the strait-jackets of unfamiliar clothing, they were all present; Junior and Bob the oldest, the youngest nineteen-year-old Slugger Pinckney; blond crew cut, rosy baby cheeks and strangely old, lined folds under his eyes. His girl friend came, too, and she was his age—Wilma Berry—hard-faced, thin yet big breasted with narrow hips. She wore loafers and bobby socks, the high-school uniform. They all smoked constantly and tried not to rattle ash trays or cups. They were all so much alike—none were fat, or even plump—the women as well as the men. All had a scrubbed sheen to their skin and an insensitive, positive gleam in their eyes, even though they were embarrassed and ill at ease. And all were handsome. In each face Jane saw some of the traditional examples of good looks: good chins, wide jaws, thin lips—they were all put together right, and beneath the cheap clothes their bodies were spare and strong. Jane had never noticed before—perhaps thinking of them in a group only in their uniforms—how much alike they were. Gussie Contois she had known in high school, and Diane Rousseau, and Billy Frisch. They had all been silent people, never entering into school affairs, never raising their hands in class, never getting good marks—most of them had never finished high school. Bob Paquette was different, though; he was always open and friendly. But Junior, like them in some ways, had a certain mean streak she knew none of the others had. Mike had been a different kind of Rider, too, reckless without the silent control of these hard people, reckless as a child. He was a little like Junior, but with more courage and flair.

She had gone once with Mike and the Riders, but at the time she hadn't given up her own version of Mike's character. She could not enter into the group or find in the machines the Riders' bright excitement. She had always been an alien among them, and she was now.

When the hour was up they left, as silent and blank-faced as they had come. Bob Paquette stayed, and she knew he wanted to ask about the motorcycle in the shed. He almost asked, and she wondered how long he would have to wait before he thought it was time to talk money about it. He left in the last of the drab old cars.

She helped Mrs. Pettibone clear up the coffee cups. It had been difficult for the Riders, but they had done their duty.

CHAPTER 9

It was after closing time, and the secretary had gone. His father sat as he had when John first came back into Leah, smoke from his cigarette getting into his eyes, yet content to shake his head back and forth rather than move the ash tray. His long, ex-athlete's body bent over Bruce's desk, space cleared for his elbows in the piles of grimy circulars. When he saw John he smiled hesitantly, reached for his cigarette, and then saw that it was too short to bother with. It smoldered away among the butts and ashes.

"You wanted to see me?" John asked.

"Sit down, Johnny." He still smiled, but his eyes were worried, darting. "Johnny, I haven't asked you at all—in any way, you know, about coming down here and helping me. But since Bruce's operation things have been in a hell of a mess. You know how Bruce was! He had to run everything, take care of everything by himself or he wouldn't do it at all. You know how Bruce was."

"Sure, I know," John said. This is my father, he thought, who is afraid of me.

"So in the last few years—well, even during the war, too . . . for quite a long time! I mean Bruce sort of took over, and now Bruce is in the hospital I have to kind of learn everything over again, catch up on all the deals Bruce . . . you know he wouldn't tell anybody anything either." William Cotter reached in his pocket for a cigarette, then seemed to forget about it. He looked for a long time out the small window into the yard, the silly smile still half there on his face.

John remembered Bruce's saying once, right out loud at the dinner table, "God damn it, he's got to take some responsibility too. I can't do it *all!*" And "he" sat right across the table, looking big and strong but being weak and silent. That was during the war when John was home on furlough, and secure in his uniform he jumped up and pulled Bruce out of his chair. "He's your own father!" John screamed into Bruce's surprised face, and Bruce, for once not meeting him with a greater, louder rage, smirked and said, "You can't blame me for that," while William Cotter sat staring at his plate.

"You know how difficult Bruce was sometimes," his father now said to him. "He was a good boy underneath, but he had to run everything his own way."

John watched his father, knowing that by keeping silent he was hurting him, and not wanting to.

"I never saw what was underneath," he said. Then his father turned away from the window, hunched up his shoulders and held his face rigid, as if he were going to make a supreme effort.

"I don't blame Bruce for me. I mean you and I . . . well, I don't know about you, Johnny. You went to the war and did things—traveled, learned foreign languages. You've done a lot for your age, really. But me? What have I done but drift along and let Bruce take over? But I mean you and I are alike in lots of ways. I couldn't help liking you more than Bruce. I tried, but Bruce wouldn't let me, you know? He wouldn't let you *relax,* even for a minute. It was like an examination all the time. God knows when he was a little boy I never made him do that! *Why?* What made him do it to me all the time?" His hand had been tapping the desk, and now it moved up and down too fast, as if a nerve were doing it, out of control. "There was no *reason* for him to be like that! I've thought it over. I'll tell you, I've thought it over many, many times. You know what they say now, that it's really the parents' fault how the children are brought up. No, I mean when sometimes the child doesn't act right, like he should, it's because of something happened to him way back when he was a little boy, because they didn't love him or something." He looked straight at John. "Now you know that's a lot of crap, because if there ever were any people loved and wanted you boys it was your mother and me. Especially your mother. I know she's got her faults and all that, but you know damn' well, and I know and I'm not so dumb, that she always had more love to give you—both of you—than you ever wanted to take. Why that was —I mean your not taking it when it was freely given, *right out,* no strings attached—I don't know and I'll never know."

"I don't know," John said.

"I'll tell you what happened the other night. Your mother came up to me and she said she . . . 'I just don't feel like I ever had any babies!' She said that."

John winced.

"Oh, I know," his father said, waving his hand and trying to grin, "I know how that sounds, Johnny. I read *Generation of Vipers,* you know!" He looked at John, and the expression was an undecided one. John finally realized that his father wanted to know whether or not *A Generation of Vipers* should be admired.

"Oh, *that!*" he said. All right. Now his father knew it wasn't to be taken too seriously.

"I know mothers are out of style and all," his father said, "but when she said that about the babies it struck me pretty hard. You'd just been mean to her. I know you were mad and I don't blame you, but you know how easily you can hurt her."

"I was sorry about that. I apologized," John said.

"I know you did. And I respect you for it. But she's having an awful hard time with Bruce not knowing . . . their not knowing if Bruce is going to wake up or not." He paused and braced himself for a more horrible possibility. "Or if he comes to without everything up there." His big shoulders twitched and he placed his finger ends against his forehead. "He's all right physically, you know. They feed him with these tubes. I saw it this morning."

"Did the doctors say anything more?"

"No. Just that they don't know any more than you or I. They

can't tell what's going to happen, even whether he'll ever wake up or not or even live." He kept turning the old-fashioned inkbowl around in its grimy stand.

They were both aware of the constant wind. The creaky old building moved and complained. The clapboards shifted and a shingle flapped as a cloud of cindery dust whicked against the windows of the west side, swirled by and over and roiled the weeds along the railroad siding. Inside, in a ray of the afternoon sun, fine diamonds of dust moved back and forth above the desks, never seeming to settle. The glass of the front window bulged in and out with the gusts, yet behind the gusts the steady push of wind was constant, a low whine John never got used to. Day after day it rose in force, and the lulls of today were as strong as the gusts of yesterday. There seemed to be a malignant force in the long pushes of the wind, and they grew until he wanted to cry, "Stop!" And then always, seconds or a full minute afterward the push that seemed bent on breaking the building down would subside a little, play with his expectancy, grow just at the end insupportable before it died back down to a forceful, steady monotone. Now a gust stopped all at once, and the building audibly relaxed. William Cotter felt it too, and smiled.

"Won't it ever die down?"

"It makes you nervous," John said.

"It makes me more than that. It blew all—damn' near all, anyway, the fifteen pound felt off the Waters house before we got the roofing on and tarred down. It lifted—I mean *lifted*—the Miller house right up and the footing partly dropped out and it bent the stringers all to hell. Now that costs us money, Johnny." He looked right at John, who saw immediately that this could lead to the subject of his working.

"We just don't have a responsible man to watch things, Johnny. Madbury's too damned *confused* all the time, but I can't think of another yardman in the whole bunch. Maybe Bruce is right, and we've got a home for the aberrations here. What I mean is, if the carpenters go off and leave nothing but the felt on a roof in this wind, what can I do about it? I remember during the war thinking won't it be wonderful after it's over and the men won't give you any sass any more! And look what happened! I guess they just got sassy when labor was scarce and never got over it. Anyway, I've *got* to stay here and take care of the retail and the books."

"Yeah," John said. "I know. Sure." But the carpenters were the only ones who could be responsible for such things. You couldn't tell a carpenter anything about his job. His father couldn't and *he* certainly couldn't. Maybe Bruce could. In Leah only Bruce's frightening inner pressure could awe a carpenter. It was a habit in Leah not to take any sass from a superior.

"I don't know why it is," William Cotter said. "I've been working pretty hard ever since Bruce went to the hospital, but I just can't seem to get things going right. Back before the war I did all right, but I can't any more. I guess I'm getting old, Johnny."

"You're not too old," John said, and then they waited for the wind to let up a little.

"Not too old for what? I guess I'm old enough to see what I can do. I know me pretty well by now, Johnny."

"No!" John said involuntarily, then didn't want to go on. His father waited expectantly. He didn't want his father to say such a thing—to make such a final verdict. And it was not just because he didn't want to stay in Leah and work for Cotter & Son—now another son! He'd had the same opinion of his father for a long time, but for the man himself to say it, to see the end of his own life! Nobody should do that. As for himself, he'd always considered himself full of *potential,* and he firmly believed that one day everything would change and he would suddenly find himself in the midst of the future, happy and full of accomplishment. But he was thirty years old, and time was settling in. Would he ever have to make an admission like his father's, see himself one of the admitted mediocrities? For a moment he toyed with the idea of making such an admission, and saw with a chill how seductive, how peaceful it would be. The long years had once been his friends, when age itself was an accomplishment, but now they had turned into quick enemies.

"I don't want to push you, Johnny."

"I'll start to work tomorrow," John said. He would have to get used to this new feeling of mortality. If fate could strike so close as to take away his father's pride, to smash his only brother! He'd always been lucky in little things: he'd never had to be hungry for very long, money had always come from somewhere when he needed it, he was extremely lucky in poker, lucky with girls, lucky about catching trains. Maybe he'd been given this petty good fortune in place of happiness, or maybe some final tragedy would come along and smash him all at once.

He hadn't expected to see Jane at the Paquette farm. He hadn't expected to stay for supper, either, even though he knew that anyone who happened to be there after five-thirty had a difficult time refusing.

Bob had finally bought Mike's motorcycle, and he and two of his younger brothers were excitedly pushing it, starting it, running it down the driveway and back, burning their fingers on the hot cylinders as they probed in the grease for the carburetor adjustment screws. Any small damage to the machine was explained to him—the bent crashbar, the tiny licks of paint scratched off here and there. Oh, it was in wonderful shape, they told him, and a little red enamel would fix it right up. Before milking, John helped them clear a space for it in one of the sheds. They piled all scratchy, puncturing junk out of the way and led the machine inside.

"There!" Bob said, patting the saddle, "Ain't it pretty, John? I mean Jerome." They always called each other Jerome, for some reason.

"I guess so."

"You *guess* so! That's all my chicken money right there, Jerome. Worth it!"

He followed Bob to the barn. Bob walked ahead, impatient, springy on his feet.

"I'll get the hay," John said. He climbed the ladder into the great hayloft and walked along above the stanchions, throwing a forkful of hay to each cow. The heat and the heavy odor of the cows came up around him and mixed with the mown smell of the hay. The beams leaned together above him in gray clouds of cobwebs, and dusty rays of cathedral light shone from the gable-end ventilators. Bob came down the cement aisle below, followed by four milk-hungry cats.

"Hey, Bob," John said, and dropped a bunch of hay on his head.

"You'll give me the willyprickles, you horse's ass!" Bob went down beside a cow and shot a stream of milk six feet into the air, splattering John's shoes. The cats sat in a row and opened their mouths, presenting little pink targets. Bob sprayed them and they retreated to lick the milk out of their fur.

"That shaggy one can carry off a whole quart in his overcoat," Bob said. "Git yourself a bucket, you want anything to eat tonight, Jerome. We got twelve cows to milk."

John got a pail from the milkhouse and took the cow next to Bob's. She stopped eating long enough to turn her neck in the creaking wooden stanchion and look him over with one brown eye, then went back to chewing the thin hay. The milk sang into the pail, and the cats, hearing it, lined up for him, too. By the time he finished the one cow his hands were nearly paralyzed. Bob had finished two more and had moved on up the line of craggy rumps.

"You hear about old Prescott, Johnny? I mean Jerome?" he called above the zinging of the milk.

"Yuk, yuk," John said.

"Listen, Jerome. That old bastard, you know what he done? He got so rang-dang mad from being swatted on the head by his critters' tails while milking . . . Jesus! He took a hand ax and a block and chopped off every one of 'em's tail. The ASPCA preferred charges and it cost the old fool eleventeen bucks per whack! Hundred and fifty bucks he had to pay. You know what? He lost every damn' one of his cows come inspection. TB. How do you like that?"

"He always was a mean old bastard," John said.

"Cruel," Bob said thoughtfully, "awful cruel."

John managed to do four cows while Bob did eight. With aching hands he helped Bob lower the tall milk cans into the water tank in the milkhouse.

"Water's too low. We ain't going to just but scrape by this year," Bob said. "Spring's going dry. First time in my young life I ever seen that happen. They closed the woods yesterday, you hear about it?"

"My father told me today. Hey, Bob? I mean Jerome!"

"Huh?" Bob let the trapdoor down over the water tank.

"Did you know anything about Bruce going out with Minetta Randolf?"

"Bruce?"

"I mean it. She told me."

"Bruce *Cotter?* No, I guess you wouldn't joke right now. Don't that tear it? Bruce!"

"I guess so. I never knew Bruce to go out with any girl," John said.

Then Bob asked the inevitable question: "I wonder if he made out?" He looked shrewdly at John. "Old Minetta's one to speak right out, by God. I got a kind of natural feeling she and Bruce might of just hit it off."

"It was pretty strange. I brought a case of beer and old Howard and I drank it."

"You mean the old bag's on the wagon?"

"No, she stuck to her wine."

"She sure does, don't she?" Bob said.

"Wait a minute. Let me tell you how Minetta acted. Afterward we went down to the car—Minetta and I . . ."

"Yow!" Bob said, putting out his fist.

"No, wait a minute! Let me tell you! I started to neck with her—you know—same old story. Nothing. I was kind of lit."

"No gibroni," Bob said.

"God dammit, listen! I must have said something she didn't like, and she blew her stack."

"She did!"

"She said nobody in Leah was a man except Bruce. She said the rest of us were all honyaks. Stuff like that. Nobody was a man except Bruce."

"She never give me a chance to prove that, one way or the other," Bob said regretfully. "Well, I've more or less rang-dang had it! Bruce!" He continued to shake his head as they went toward the house.

They went through two dark connecting sheds and then a door opened into the bright, crowded kitchen, where the Paquettes seemed to do everything at once in a continuous roar. John said hello, shouting and being shouted at, to Ma, Pa, Dick, Paul, Jean, little Timmy, and Charlotte. It was then that he noticed Jane, sitting behind the huge kitchen table in a relatively calm, protected spot, talking to Charlotte. He started across the room toward her, but Timmy, who was seven, had spread a series of Montgomery-Ward catalogues, wooden blocks, little cars and a model road grader in and out among the table legs and out across the linoleum. John accidentally shifted one of the blocks, and Timmy's shrill voice came from under the table: "Dammit! Who done that?" He put his head out.

"Hush, now!" Ma said to him, a frown passing over her face. She poured water from a dishpan full of steaming boiled potatoes. In spite of the uproar she had to contend with all the time, she looked quite young, with a kind of French *chic* about her. Bob, the oldest, had been born when she was seventeen, and Bob was thirty. Pa was a good deal older than Ma; a wide, thick-featured man. All his children looked like Pa. His round face rarely showed any expression but one of serene amusement. He sat at the head of the table and said very little except, "Pass the picklelilly," but he did listen to the constant hubbub and seemed to get from it a certain infusion of contentment. The Paquettes set a loud, happy table.

John still tried to reach Jane, and found that in order to get there he would have to go underneath the table, where he moved another part of Timmy's highway system.

"Jesus, you're clumsy, John," Timmy said, but gently, to show there were no hard feelings.

Under the table John met Shep, who had been stepped on so often he had evidently decided not to worry about it. Shep knew him, nodded once, once flopped his much trodden-upon tail and went back to watching a cat who watched back from beneath the woodstove.

Jane raised the oilcloth to let him come out. For a second he looked up at her, seeing her arm above him, her face and silvery blonde hair, in a kind of shock. She smiled down at him, and she seemed terribly beautiful to him all at once. He had never before thought of her as anything but mildly pretty—in fact, rather funny-looking in a pleasing way, with her little puggish nose and crinkly eyes. Now she was clean and fresh, her summer dress crisp, her breasts small and firm, her narrow waist trim. There seemed to be a *tone* to her flesh; a healthy, spare, animal tone to it he had never seen in a girl before.

"Are you coming out?" Jane asked. Charlotte had been watching, smiling in a thoughtful way.

"You have a way of turning into a statue or something," Charlotte said to him. "Now, what could you have been thinking about?"

"Hey, John!" Bob called from the sink. He spread Boraxo up

and down his greasy arms and grinned. "Ain't you going to wash, John? We generally wash out here in the country." Pa smiled and Ma, passing, hit Bob on the back of the neck. He ducked and then said seriously, "Dirt ain't healthy. I been trying to make that clear to John, that's all."

John started under the table again. Jean, who was twelve, still blocked one side of the kitchen. He had his bicycle upside down on unsteady handlebars and seat. He had started to tighten spokes, but now turned the pedals by hand, as fast as he could.

"Look!" he yelled, "That's a gyroscope! Look at it? Look at it?" Ma looked and ordered him out to get some wood. Dick and Paul, twenty-six and twenty-four, were Indian wrestling.

"John don't seem to learn," Bob said. "Come here and clean your dirty self!"

Jean came back and dumped the wood into the woodbox. Ma told him to remove his bicycle. He turned it over, trying to hit somebody, missing Paul, and wheeled it into the living room.

"Jean!" Pa said. Jean and the bicycle came back into the kitchen. "Put that bike outside. It ain't new! You act like you want to eat with it!"

"Yeah, Pa," Jean said hopefully.

"You take it out."

"It's because of Bob's new motorcycle," Ma said, and then looked guiltily at Jane and away again. "Take it out, now!"

"Aw, hell!" Jean said, and banged the bike on the door.

Charlotte set the table while Timmy entertained Jane. He tried to ignore his mother, who wanted him to put away his highway system. John wanted to get back to Jane, but Dick challenged him to Indian wrestle. They put their right feet together and clasped right hands. The object was to force the other to move his front foot. To Dick's shame, John won easily. Then he won from Paul. It quickly became an affair of family honor. He beat Bob, and supper was forgotten for a time. They made Pa get up and try. Pa gripped John's hand with his great splayed fingers and set himself. They pushed and jerked sideways, trying to get each other off balance. John felt that he could tip Pa over anytime. It didn't seem to be a matter of pure strength, but of a certain rigidity in the upper arm and shoulder, and to John's surprise his shoulder was immovable, rigid—

he felt himself to be all of a piece, as if he were a statue. At the end he had Pa bent over and had his own wrist against Pa's foot. One sideways and upward jerk and he could have won. But he didn't make the move. After much grunting they called it a draw.

"You're strong, John," Pa said. The others nodded. Coming from Pa, it was a real compliment.

A little subdued, they sat themselves around the table. John sat on one side of Jane and Timmy on the other. Timmy probed the mustard pickles for pimento. Charlotte forcibly removed the mustard pickles, while he screamed, and put beet greens on his plate.

Pa was staring at John, frowning. Everybody noticed it, and even Timmy shut up.

"I got a feeling you held off, John," Pa said. "You could of beat me."

"No, Pa!" Dick said, horrified. Paul, Bob, Jean and even Timmy looked the same, their round Paquette faces, blue eyes and black hair, all seemed to flash and bristle with disbelief.

"Bob could beat me," Pa said.

"No, I couldn't!" Bob said, "I couldn't come nowhere near it, Pa!"

"And you beat Bob," Pa said to John. "You boys be quiet. What I want to know is why John held off."

They all turned silently toward John. He couldn't deny it—that would be calling Pa a liar. Silence. He heard for the first time that day sounds he hadn't been able to hear before—the old pendulum clock ticking, a drip of water at the sink, green wood hissing in the stove, and between gusts of the incessant wind the drone of the water pump out in the milkhouse.

"I don't know," he said.

"You must know something about it," Pa said, " 'cause right plumb in the middle of it you had a change of mind."

No one ate. They all looked at John until Jane said, "He didn't think it would be right to beat you, Pa."

"Hah!" Pa said, and then grinned, looking all around the table. "That's what I figured. Now, John, I don't mean to give you no third degree, nor nothing like it. But you been coming out here ever since you was kindygarden age and we always considered you as near a member of this family as a body could stand. You always called me Pa and Ma Ma, same as Janie, and you're both welcome.

But it don't strike me right you dasn't beat me if you could. I never wrestled with Bob, but if we did he wouldn't think nothing of beating me if he could."

"That's right," Bob said.

"If we try it again I'll do my best to beat you," John said.

"No, we ain't going to try it again," Pa said, and turned to the potatoes, obviously through talking.

Timmy had been listening carefully, and now his high voice cut across the clashing of forks on plates. "Did John do something wrong, Pa?"

"Eat your greens," Ma said.

His head bent over his plate, Timmy turned to John and whispered loudly, "What did you do, John?"

John was about to answer "I don't know" again, but caught himself in time.

"Timmy! You hush!" Ma said.

"He beat Paul and Dick and Bob and he could have beat Pa," Timmy said. Then a crafty look came over his face and he whispered again, holding a large forkful of beet greens in front of his face, like a screen, "Maybe he peed his pants."

"Timmy! You want to go to bed without your supper?" Ma said.

Bob choked and sprayed coffee over the table. Dick had to get up and wipe his face with the dishcloth, while Paul laughed and wiped the tears out of his eyes. Timmy sat pleased and smug—a comedian who didn't quite know whether to laugh or keep a straight face. Even Pa smiled.

"Did you, John?" Timmy asked.

"Now that's enough of that," Bob said, chuckling and sighing, "Don't milk it dry, Timmy. You got your point acrost."

John smiled, feeling absolutely helpless and stupid. He tried to keep his smile on, to keep it real, but was saved by the business of mashing potatoes. *Clink, clink, clink,* the forks went, in a surprisingly complicated and interesting rhythm. All faces, he gratefully saw, were turned toward plates; serious, concentrated upon the mashing. Pa held the gravy boat in one hand while he got his potatoes just right, then poured. After the mashing and pouring was finished, the less serious business of eating began. After the first helping Pa decided to speak.

"You was afraid I'd git mad," he said.

"Git mad!" Bob said wonderingly.

"Maybe that's right," John said. "I was wrong there. I never saw you get mad at anything like that, Pa."

"You're dang right!" Pa said, pleased.

"That doesn't mean you couldn't, sometimes," Charlotte said. Pa began to frown, thought for a second, and smiled.

"I reckon Dick was a little put out," he said. They all looked at Dick, who nodded seriously.

"I could beat him at something else," Dick said.

"What, for instance?" Bob said. "You just don't think a town boy ought to beat a country boy like you. You figure he ought to know more big words but you just naturally *got* to have big muscles. Well, that ain't always true." Dick turned red and scowled at his brother. Bob said, "What you need, Dickie-boy, is learning the facts of life."

Dick slammed his fork down. With a hard, lopsided expression on his face he glared at Bob.

"You want to ask me out to the woodshed?" Bob asked. "You want to git all lumpy again?"

Dick slid his chair back and jumped up. "God damn you!" he yelled, and headed for the door.

"Dick, you sit down!" Ma said. Pa sat back, grinning. "Pa! Tell them to stop it!"

"They ain't old enough to settle it?" Pa asked.

"You ought to be ashamed of yourself," Charlotte said to Bob.

"Me?" Bob said with exaggerated surprise. "Did I invite anybody out to the woodshed? Hell, no. I don't have no blood on my conscience."

"You coming, or are you yellow?" Dick said.

"Me, Dickie? Well, I got to tell you the horrible truth. I'm yellow! But seeing as it's only you." He got up from the table and followed Dick.

"I thought Dick was supposed to be fighting *John,*" Timmy said, pointing his fork first at Dick and then at John.

"Timmy, be quiet!" Charlotte said.

"After you, my dear Alphonse," Bob said, holding the door for Dick, who marched on through. "Lumpy will return in a moment, with his ass in a sling," Bob said, and followed after.

"It's Bob's fault. It's his doing. I hope he loses," Charlotte said.

"Dick's got to learn to keep his temper," Paul said. He had been on Bob's side all the way. John could easily see how the family lined up this time. Paul was for Bob, Charlotte and Jean were for Dick, Pa was impartial but maybe favored Bob a little, Ma was against the fight and Timmy was for it.

"Can I go watch, Ma?" Timmy asked.

"Eat your supper!" Ma was rattled. John wondered if the years were beginning to tell on her—she stirred her food around nervously, her hands shook. He thought she was about to break into tears. Paul had been noticing this, and now got up and walked swiftly to the door. He was gone before anyone spoke.

Then all three came back; solemn, no marks of battle on them. They sat down and began to eat.

"We're sorry, Ma," Dick finally said.

"My fault," Bob mumbled.

John expected Pa to disapprove of this truce, and was surprised when Pa looked back at him and winked.

"They're real good boys, though, ain't they, John?" Pa said. Identical slow, sheepish smiles appeared on Bob's and Dick's faces.

John could do nothing, although he knew that some signal from him was necessary. He even knew the mechanics of the needed remark and the attitude with which it should be given. It must be a little funny, and didn't have to be very funny—nearly anything would do to destroy the fading tension. It would go, anyway, but it was for John Cotter to hasten it along. But he could do nothing. Somewhere else—far away from Leah—he would not have had to think about it. He wanted to say to them, "Look, I'm not what you see here. I can be funny as hell too, and friendly. I like people."

But the noise reached its usual height quickly, and his chance was gone. Perhaps they hadn't noticed—but he knew they had, and now they would not be sure how he'd taken Timmy's remark. Because they wouldn't know he was less a part of them. No matter how carefully he watched, however, he could find no indication of this in their actions.

As Charlotte helped clear away the dishes he turned to Jane and tried unsuccessfully to get her away from Timmy, who was explaining the difficulties of second grade. Timmy said it was unfair, because he had to get up a whole hour earlier than the town kids and then wait around for the school bus. It was like having to go to school for an extra hour every day and it wasn't fair. He liked school, but he didn't like the bus driver.

"I like my new teacher. Everybody likes her," he said.

"That's nice," Jane said.

"She's pretty, like you," Timmy said, and put his head on her forearm and looked up at her, smiling as if he were doing something slightly wrong, but didn't care.

Bob looked up from the Montgomery-Ward catalogue. "My! Ain't he a little wolf, though!"

Timmy seemed a little embarrassed, but determinedly held Jane around the waist with both arms.

Paul came back from the shed and saw it. "Ain't he a little devil? It seems to me, Timmy, you're a little old to be sitting in laps."

"Little too young for anything else," Bob said.

Timmy smiled harder and blushed, but he didn't let go. It was worth it. Until the doorbell rang, at least. Then he jumped down impatiently and went under the table to wait and see who it was. Pa, Jean and Dick had gone out to the barn, so Ma answered it. The door opened to the jangled sound of Canadian French spoken simultaneously by three people—Uncle Albert, Aunt May and Ma, who was suddenly bright and active, leading them in, twirling chairs around, sweeping the last crumbs from the table, talking all the time in a language John could barely follow. It reminded him of his first days in Paris when the sense of any conversation was just out of reach.

Uncle Albert was a small, neat man who ran a little grocery store in Leah, and Aunt May was a smaller, neater woman who ran Uncle Albert. Their children had grown up and gone away, and now they lived in a small apartment over their store.

When Timmy saw that it was only Uncle Albert and Aunt May he headed back for Jane, but he never made it. Charlotte caught him from behind and picked him up.

"Hey!" he said.

"Hey yourself," Charlotte said firmly, "you're going to bed."

"Oh, Jesus!" he said, half resigned to it. Aunt May looked up, shook her head, and frowned. She was very religious, and when the organization of the store and Uncle Albert proved too unrewarding she organized Father Desmond and the church.

"Timmy, you got to stop that!" Charlotte said.

"He took the Lord's name in vain," Aunt May said in English.

"He knows that," Bob said. "He gits it from them goddam brothers of his."

"Bob!" Charlotte said. Aunt May had gone back into French, for protection, and spoke with quite a bit of heat to Ma, who shook her head hopelessly.

"Jesus," Timmy said experimentally. Charlotte whacked his bottom. "Jesus!" he said, getting mad. Charlotte carried him out of the room and started up the stairs.

"Jesus!" he yelled, and they heard another whack. *"Jesus! Jesus! Jesus!"* followed by three harder whacks. Aunt May was scandalized.

"He ain't cussin', he's *prayin'*," Bob said. But the whacks, the loss of dignity and the unfairness began to tell. Upstairs in the big house the next sounds were screams and hiccuping cries and bawling. A door shut off the noise. Aunt May and Ma went on talking French; Uncle Albert sat solidly and neatly, listening and nodding. Paul had gone out. Bob studied the catalogue and carefully filled out a mail-order form.

"I guess you made a conquest," John said to Jane.

"A what? Oh, Timmy," Jane said. She offered him a cigarette at the same time he offered her one, and then, confused, he lit his and forgot hers. He struck another match and held it out to her.

"I'm going to come up and see you," he said.

"Why don't you?"

"I've got to go to work tomorrow. I promised my father. Maybe I'll come up tomorrow after supper. Is that O.K.?"

"Sure, Johnny," she said, "come up anytime. I don't seem to do anything but sit around nowadays. I guess I'll get a job pretty soon, too. I can't stand it much longer just sitting around—that's why it feels so good to be with the Paquettes again."

"They do seem to keep ramming around every minute. Hey, Jane?"

She looked surprised. "Hey, what?"

"How about going to a movie tomorrow night? I don't know what it is. Maybe the drive-in."

"Sure, I'll go with you, Johnny."

"I'll pick you up around six-thirty, O.K.? I guess they start as soon as it gets dark."

Good. That had been handled all right. Now everything was settled, and he felt that he had done the right thing, for once. Charlotte came back and sat down, saying that Timmy must have been pretty tired. Bob asked where were the stamps, then where was an envelope, then where in hell was some ink? Ma found them, still talking French to Uncle Albert and Aunt May, and then Bob motioned to John to come outside.

"Look," he said. He had the catalogue with him, and he pointed to the picture of a set of saddlebags; black leather studded with reflectors, chrome stars and studs of various shapes and sizes. "What do you think of that?"

"They'll see you coming," John said.

"What? Why, goddam, John, they'll see me and hear me! But what do you think of 'em? Tell me, now!"

"I'm no arbiter of taste in saddlebags," John said.

"No whichiter? Don't kid me, Jerome!" He grinned and slapped John on the back, half pushing him through one shed, into the place they had cleared for the motorcycle.

"Look at her, boy!" He walked around the motorcycle, feeling it with one hand. "Let's take her out for a spin. I'll give you a ride."

"I don't know . . ." John began.

"Aw, come on." Bob wheeled the machine outside, turned on the switch and kicked down the starter. There was a metallic, chain-rattling, gear-teething sound and a mild pop from the motor. Then he turned the spark handle a little and kicked down the starter again. This time there was a terrible roar and the machine shook and tried to edge forward, then the noise turned into a vibrant, mounting hum of explosions. John thought it would blow up, until Bob straddled it and idled the engine down. "Get on!" he yelled, patting the back of the saddle. "Git on, boy!" He switched on the lights, and across the front yard in the dusk withered grass, two tires set with dirt and flower stalks, a broken toy truck of Timmy's, and then a huddled group of white mailboxes out at the road's edge stood out sharply. "Git on!" Bob yelled, turning around impatiently.

John swung his leg over the wide saddle and set his feet carefully behind Bob's on the narrow, hinged runningboards. Bob moved his wrist quickly on the rubber handlebar-accelerator and the motor roared higher; then he pushed in the clutch. John felt as if somebody had hold of him from behind. Gravel spurted out behind the rear wheel, the seat shifted to one side and pulled out from under him, leaving him stumbling dazedly on the driveway as Bob and the machine swerved on around the curve to the road. Bob continued on around and came up to him again—high laughter over the engine sound.

"You got to hold on, John! Now git on and stay on!"

"Well, take it easy!" John yelled back. This time he set himself firmly and took a firm grip on Bob's belt in back. "If I go, you go," he said, and the clutch went in, the wheel spun and they taxied around to the asphalt road, going through the gears quickly as the machine went faster, faster, and then was a projectile flying straight down the narrow road, the headlight bouncing and the motor screaming. In spite of the rushing air he smelled hot oil. The motor warmed his knees while cold air hit him in the face and at the same time climbed up his shirt in back and made him shake wildly from fear and cold. The road bent, snapped around and tilted as they passed a car. He looked over Bob's shoulder and made out the speedometer through his wind-watering eyes. The needle jiggled around sixty.

"Hey!" he yelled in Bob's ear, "slow down a little!" Bob looked around at him like an owl, his eyes staring and remote, his face fiercely set. He nodded slowly and just as slowly turned again to face the road and the bits of hurtling trees in the bright tunnel of his headlight's beam.

John recognized nothing along the road. He had no idea where they were or where they were going until a white sign flashed by: LEAH. Then in quick succession a golden Rotary gear, a Lions emblem, and mailboxes shot by. They hit a bump in the road and for one dreadful moment he flew along an inch above the seat, his feet lost the runningboards, his head began to pound. But soon the fear became strangely constant and bearable, and he didn't realize just how scared he had been until Bob idled down to go through the main part of town. He had never been so glad to see Leah. They stopped on the square by the Strand to be examined distantly by the young boys who were waiting for the first show to start and by the old men who would watch the people go by until the show started and then go home.

"How'd you like it?" Bob said, still stiff as he turned, with an inner excitement that amounted to intoxication visible in his eyes.

Now that it was over, the fright had gone, except for the hopeless realization that they had to go back to the farm the same way. He was left weak and cold—shivering—and found that he had sweat not only under his arms but all the way up his back to his collar. He got off the motorcycle and stood weakly on the sidewalk. He wanted to sit down. Bob looked at him expectantly.

"What do you want to do on that damn' machine, commit suicide?" he said.

"By God!" Bob said, zooming the motor for emphasis, "By God!"

"By God is right," John said, and walked around in a little circle, trying to shake some life back into himself. "Let's go down to Futzie's and get a beer or something. I lost my marbles riding that thing."

"Aw, you liked it," Bob said.

"Like hell I did!" He got back on the seat. "Now take it easy," he said. "I can't stand it. I mean it."

"You ain't got over the first thrill yet," Bob said. They went fairly slow and parked on the sidewalk in front of Futzie's Tavern on River Street. Bob leaned the motorcycle against a pole so he could keep an eye on it from inside.

River Street, one block of shabby frame buildings, staggered sootily to the railroad spur and a dead end at Cotter & Son's. Futzie's and the Army-Navy store were the only live businesses on the street—the rest of the buildings leaned sadly and emptily into each other, old clapboard fronts without decoration or pretension. Most of them had been residences, and Futzie's building was one of these, odd because of the large window in an aluminum frame next to the wooden Georgian door. A cool blue sign in the window said, *Petrosky's Tavern,* and below the sign several deer rifles and shotguns hung on a wire rack. Futzie traded guns and would accept nothing else as security against a loan or a drink.

John pulled the doorknob, and the weathered door came open. The front window was Futzie's only modern improvement. The floor was covered with odd ripped sections of linoleum, worn and faded in places, and in other places, where furniture had covered it in its previous home, bright and colorful. The ceiling was stamped metal in old-fashioned scroll-and-flower designs made hazy by many layers of cream paint. Two light bulbs hung down on long cords, shaded only by dust and grease, and along both sides of the room low brown benches and booths dissolved into a musty twilight. At the bar five silent old men held on to their glasses and stared without expression at television. Futzie leaned against the bar, his shrunken old monkey-face sharp and mean-looking. He never smiled and he never gave a free beer to anybody. When he saw Bob and John he reached for the tap and brought them two beers, standing silently until they put their money on the table. Then he took two dimes and went back behind the bar.

They sat at a booth, Bob facing toward the street so that he could watch his motorcycle. Across from him, John had to watch television. A fuzzy girl with a sharp, domineering voice kept opening and closing the door of a refrigerator, sliding the trays, opening the freezer door, smirking vaguely as if she were looking through a cloud and all the time saying, "See how handy! See how beautiful and economical . . . décor . . . modern, wonderful!" and the dark old men, completely absorbed, sipped their beer and watched.

John drank his beer quickly and put two fingers in the air. Futzie must have had an eye in his ear, he thought, because even though he had been half turned away he turned to the taps again and drew more beer.

"Slow down, John," Bob said.

"That's what I asked you to do on the way here."

The door at the right of the bar opened—the one that led to the rooms upstairs. Junior Stevens came into the room and slammed the door behind him. He was halfway to the street when he saw them and stopped in front of the booth.

"How do you like the bike?" he asked Bob.

"Fine," Bob said, and then looked from Junior to John and back. Junior hadn't recognized John. Now they looked at each other coolly and nodded.

"Sit down," Bob said. "You got time for a beer?"

"Why surely!" Junior said, too loudly, and John remembered

with a twinge of childhood that sudden change in Junior from curt silence to loud affability. It generally meant that he was about to hit somebody, or goose somebody, or trip somebody up. Now he watched Junior closely. He finished his beer and signaled to Futzie for three more.

John got up and put some money in the juke box, then sat back to listen, his eyes closed and a cigarette in his mouth.

"Well, hello, Mrs. Jones!" Junior said. John opened his eyes and saw Billy Muldrow, tall and wide shouldered in his dirty overalls, standing diffidently by the booth.

"Hello, Junior," Billy said coldly, and looked at John. "Hi, John!"

"Hi, Billy. Have a beer," John said. But Billy looked guiltily toward Futzie, whose cold eye seemed to chill him.

"I can't drink, John," Billy said.

"They got him shut off," Junior said to Bob. He wouldn't talk directly to John, not really having recognized him. Billy looked hurt. A chastened giant, he frowned and looked sideways at Junior.

"Yeah," Junior said, "they figure he ain't old enough to drink yet."

"You cut it out!" Billy said.

"Hey, leave him alone," Bob said, smiling. "Why did they shut you off, Billy?"

"Oh, he don't want to talk about that," Junior said, "does he, Bob?" Bob shook his head. Junior had hold and wouldn't let go. "Like this, Billy, warn't it? Let me see if I got it straight. You was in the movies one night, sucking on a bottle . . ."

"So what? You be quiet!" Billy shouted. He looked as if he were going to cry.

"Hey," Futzie said warningly. Even the five old men had turned around on their stools to see.

"Hey, what, Futzie?" Billy said plaintively.

"Don't make no trouble in my place," Futzie said.

"He's not making trouble," John said.

"Well, don't make none."

Billy stood facing Futzie and the old men as if it were a relief to turn away from Junior.

"You lousy . . . Futzie! If I had all the money I spent in your place I'd be rich! So what do you care? You got the money, ain't you? That's all you care for anybody!"

Futzie, even though he had often claimed to have been proud of exactly this philosophy, acted now as if his soul were in jeopardy. John watched his anger develop. Junior and Bob turned around to watch.

"I got a business!" Futzie began. "I don't lose my license for you or no bum!"

"I ain't no bum!" Billy yelled. "I pay my bills, you son of a bitch! I don't owe you nothing," he added in a lower voice.

"You ain't goin' to. Watch your mouth, too!"

"O.K., O.K.! Just don't call me no bum," Billy said. "You watch your own mouth."

Then it was over, and amazingly Futzie wasn't even going to kick Billy out. For Futzie it had been a big outburst, but evidently the remark about his coldheartedness had hit him. He was almost conciliatory.

"It ain't my fault Atmon black-listed you, but I got a business, and you come in here and start a trouble I lose my license. Ain't nobody in this town give me nothing if I go broke, so goddamit I ain't no charity, neither." He turned to washing glasses.

"Old Futzie must be going soft," Bob said.

"Ask him for a borrow of a dime," Junior said, "and watch him call his lawyer. Hey, Futz!"

"What you want," Futzie said, scowling.

"How about a couple on the house?"

"How about last week's rent you owe me?"

"See what I mean?" Junior said. "That Jew's got a heart cold's a nun's tit."

"He ain't no Jew; he's a Pollack," Bob said, "I seen him in Church."

Billy had tapped John lightly on the shoulder and motioned him over across the room. Now they sat across from each other in a booth, and Billy looked embarrassed.

"Remember what you said about coming up to see me, Johnny?" he said. "Well, I guess you got a lot on your mind, what with Bruce sick and all. It ain't more'n forty rod up Pike Hill to my place."

"I meant to come up, Billy."

Billy nodded. "Sure you did, Johnny. I ain't chiding you none. I was thinking maybe 'cause they went and closed the woods up maybe you thought it was against the law. It ain't, though. Pike Trail's a town road, though they don't fix it up. It's a town road right on the map. They can't keep nobody off it."

"It's not that, Billy."

"I know you got a lot on your mind," Billy said.

"Yeah, Billy."

"What I was wondering about, Johnny, was maybe you'd do me a little favor maybe, like if I was to drive you down around the corner of Anna's store you could go in—I'll give you the money—and git me a case of beer." He stopped and looked anxiously at John.

"Come on," John said, getting up. Billy followed quickly.

"Where you going?" Bob asked.

"Nowhere. I'll be right back," John said. Bob waved his hand and nodded, and Junior developed a sly smile, his eyes staring brightly, this time looking right at John.

"Goodbye, boys," Junior said in a simpering voice.

John froze. Billy fiddled with the doorknob, anxious to go. Junior still stared deliberately.

"What do you mean?" John asked, trying to keep his voice calm.

"It give me a start to see little Johnny Cotter in here. I didn't know he drank."

"Big Junior Stevens seems to have grown up to be pretty brave," John said. "It seems to me he never got impolite before to anyone who wasn't outnumbered."

"He did or didn't which to what to who?" Junior said, laughing loudly. Bob smiled.

"Maybe I better say something you can understand," John said.

"Oh, he knows a lot of fancy words! He's a goddam walking dictionary," Junior said, smiling but suddenly steady, his smile turning ferocious in a deliberately controlled way as if his patience with something small and crawly were really about to run out. "Now wait a minute. Look who's saying what to who." A momentary grin toward Bob, then he finished his glass of beer and raised two fingers in the air, signaling to Futzie. He looked ominously at John.

"Come on, Johnny," Billy said, "don't pay him no mind."

"Why don't Silly-Billy mind his own business?" Junior said.

"Come on, Johnny, that big blow-mouth won't work up to nothing.

Only reason he ain't scared is he knows if there's trouble Atmon'll blame me for it." Billy pulled his arm and John let himself be led out the door. Junior was grinning and nodding his head as the door closed.

"Ain't no use letting yourself git mad over him," Billy said.

"Me?" John said. He walked down the narrow sidewalk, Billy in the gutter but still towering over him.

"He didn't want to tangle with you, Johnny, you know that?"

"He started it," John said.

"Yeah, but he figured you wouldn't sass him back. If he was going to do something he had his chance."

John found himself trembling as he walked. Billy was flattering him. If he hadn't let Billy pull him out the door Junior might really have started something. He could see Junior's huge red hands tense upon the table—the way Junior grabbed his beer glass all the way around until the thumb and fingers met. The raw brutality in Junior's face, and that hardness all about Junior, as if he were a caged beast straining at the bars, looking for a way to get loose—the thought of it made him weak and unable, as he was unable in Futzie's, to say the straight words that would have forced Junior to get up. Instead he made the silly speech he had, half-knowing that Junior would make fun of it instead of getting angry about it. But what in hell was he scared of? It wasn't death, or anywhere near death to fight Junior, and he had never in his life been afraid of getting physically hurt. If the only way to deal with Junior was to stand up to him and get hurt, he ought to do it. He ought to turn right around now and go back and get done with it. But he was scared. He was *afraid* to turn around and do it.

"God damn it!" he said, and kicked a piece of cardboard, twirling it ahead to ride on an eddy of the wind.

"What's the matter?" Billy asked.

"That bastard's been picking on me all my life. You know when I was a little kid—even now, for God's sake—I always had to look around corners and watch ahead and behind me wherever I went so I wouldn't meet up with him and his friends? I remember having to stay home from swimming at the scrape because I knew he'd be out there. It was like there were Indians around ready to scalp me. I sure know how those poor bastards felt when they settled this country."

"Junior ain't no Indian."

"He's no Indian in the woods. I remember I met him out hunting —you never saw such a polite Indian. We even hunted together that day! Real buddy-buddy. And then the next day I had to fight one of his hammerhead friends outside the boys' entrance to the high school, and Junior and a couple of others tripping me up from behind."

"I ever catch Junior Stevens in the woods he'll wish to God he never was born!" Billy said, rubbing his hands together in anticipation.

At the end of River Street they turned and faced the west wind, a thick, dry torrent flowing up and over the town. John opened his mouth and the wind dried his lips. He could smell in it the faint, ominous, dry-leaf odor of a distant fire. It blew his clothes against his body, and the soiled heat of it was unnatural for a wind flowing out of a clear, starry sky.

They climbed into Billy's lopsided old truck and drove around to Water Street. Billy parked around the corner from Anna's and gave John the money. When John came back Billy hid the beer under some burlap bags in the back of the truck, but brought two bottles back to the cab, where they furtively drank them, Billy ready to hide them under the seat on the gas tank if Joe Beaupre or Atmon came along.

"I tell you what, Johnny. There ain't another man in Leah would do that for me. Not one son of a bitch in this whole lousy town would do that for me but you."

"That's a hell of a note," John said noncommitally.

"Not one no-good stinking friend I got in this whole town, excepting you, Johnny."

"You used to have friends, Billy," John said. "What happened to them?" He thought: Have you got any friends, John? You think so, but you don't owe them anything.

"I don't know, Johnny. Seems like they just kind of faded away since the war and they ain't my friends any more."

Billy let him off in front of Futzie's, made him promise to come and visit, then drove on up the lumpy street, the old truck clanking.

Bob was alone at the booth.

"Junior took off," Bob said. "He had to see a dame about a log."

"That's too bad," John said.

"Hell, Junior ain't such a bad guy, John, you git to know him. He ain't such a bad guy at heart."

"Forget it. What's the story on Billy?"

"Oh, Billy pulled a beaut. You never heard about it? I wish to hell I was there, only not down below! It reminds me of a dirty joke."

"Never mind the joke. What did he do?"

"Oh, you got to hear it!" Bob drank his beer and signaled for more. "Well, like Junior said, Billy was to the movies and he was nursing on a bottle. Had a bag of beer, too, I heard. He just come out of the woods and had some money. Well, you know how he always sits up in the balcony? That old bag Susie Tercotte was up there helping him on the bottle, and I guess old Billy was trying to help himself to Susie, only she wasn't having none of it. Pretty quick, the way I hear, they kind of forgot where they was. Talking it over, you might say. Anyway, by then nobody was watching the movie. Did I tell you what the movie was? Wow! All the mothers holding their hands over the kiddies' ears and screaming back! Billy couldn't of picked a better show. That Walt Disney picture about dogs! The *matinée*, by God! I sure wished I was there. Old Garwood runs down and gets Atmon, but while Garwood's on his way the fair majority of our fair matrons are hearing some words maybe they never heard before. They're all screaming for Billy and Susie to shut up. Billy goes stark raving *ape*, and hollers, 'Shut up, you Leah bitches!' He's hanging over the brass rail up there and hollering down, but of course they don't quiet down none, so Billy rares back and yells, 'By the Jesus if I can't shut you up I'll drown the whole bloody pack!' Good as his word, he damn' near proceeds to do it! Some say he only poured beer, but I heard different. Panic? Well, I guess! A fair considerable portion of the upper crust got soaked! Oh, *Jesus!* All them permanent waves! Oo-hoo! They say Atmon was a rang-dang demon that day. It took him and Joe Beaupre and half the Fire Department to git Billy downstreet to the police station. And even then Billy had this big piece of balcony rail in his hand and raised hell all night till he passed out whanging it up and down the cell bars. Nobody dasn't go in and take it off him, that's for certain! I'll say one thing, Billy Muldrow is a heller when he gits started."

"No wonder Atmon shut him off."

"Shut him *off!* Man, he spent six months in the rock factory, hard labor. They rammed it to old Billy. First offense and all that, too. But, Johnny, you ought to know you just can't have nobody acting so free with the Women's Club, Eastern Star—all the cream of our fair fat womanhood! Not to mention their dear little brats with their innocent minds! I'd given my . . . Well, I'd of given the little finger off my left hand just to of been there. I would!"

"I never knew Billy to act like that before."

"There was a lot of people mad at poor Billy. They even sent him down to Concord to the loony bin for a while. I guess Billy didn't take to being caged up like that."

"He told me he'd like to roll an atom bomb down Pike Hill and blow the whole town to hell," John said.

"When he gits ahold of one I hope I ain't in town," Bob said. He scraped his change off the table. "I guess we better be gitting home."

Out on River Street, John looked straight up past the pointed gables of the old houses, where the wind rushed by. In the hot pressure of the wind even the stars seemed to sway. He and Bob stood below in an eddying pool of warmth.

"To hell with Leah," John said. "I hope to hell you blow away!"

"Take some blowing," Bob said. He wheeled the motorcycle down off the sidewalk and jumped on the kickstarter. "You ready, boy?"

They came out of River Street into the square, around the tilting elms and roared out past the houses toward the road to the farm.

"To hell with Leah!" John yelled at a solid old lady. Her big face flashed by, unsurprised. The houses thinned out and he didn't mind the speed this time, nor the deadly mailboxes. The tree branches dipped overhead in graceful sweeping arcs, the stars tilted on curves and snapped back into place. Only the machine was solid—the world and Leah were left behind in fragments, blown apart by the roar of their passing.

CHAPTER 10

Bruce had taken a turn for the worse, they said, and his mother had to be at the hospital constantly. So the Fresh Air lady would be at the station and John would have to meet them. It was better than having to go there with his mother, and he would have had to, since she had taken the position that she couldn't drive because of nerves. She was distraught, she said. Well, who wasn't? So she took a taxi to Northlee in the morning and took the bus home at night.

In the yard washroom John washed nervously, the soap not sudsing at all in his impatience with the thin stream of warm water, so small and trickly each finger had to be rinsed separately and then the soap film was still sticky all over his face and between his fingers. The paper towels were all gone, as usual. Out in the yard he would have to walk, dressed up, past Junior Stevens, who had been demoted from rough carpenter to taking off the circular one-lunger saw. He had adopted an air of moral superiority because he thought John had been the cause of it.

"What do you call him?" Junior had said that morning, speaking of John's father. "What do you call him—'Daddy'?" They had seen William Cotter aimlessly fiddling with the truck scale next to the office, and everybody knew he couldn't fix it, didn't even know how it worked underneath the splintered platform. So what could he answer to that? He could, by way of answer, fire Junior. His father would back him up, all right—not just back him up, but do something even worse: the minute he started making decisions like that he would have to make all the decisions.

He put on the white shirt, so fragile and delicate in the yard washroom, so likely to get smudged, so somehow shameful to wear out past the lumber-stickers and the three men at the one-lunger. But this time they just smirked, turning their heads away as if they couldn't bear to smile at him, out of politeness' sake—even feeble-minded Freddie, who could do nothing but take away from a saw, whose dwarfed old body they had to turn so he would throw the wood in a new direction when one bin was filled. The whining *zing* of the saw stopped for a second as they politely turned away, and then continued as he passed them and turned the corner. He walked carefully so as not to get sawdust in his street shoes and tried to duck the waves of sawdust carried on the wind.

In Wentworth Junction the little station radiated heat, and the wind along the rails had little flecks of soot shot through it, blown from the long curving banks of cinders. The rails led to Concord and then to Manchester and then to Boston, where it was probably hotter than it was up here. The river below was sluggish, and showed high ugly mudbanks full of sticks and protruding metal among sickly weeds. There was Mrs. Rutherford in her straw hat and old stationwagon, seeing him and waving, full of life, as if she drew that awful red health out of the heat.

"The train's late, the stationmaster tells me. They had a hot rod or something. And how are you, John Cotter?" Smiling cleverly. "I thought it was terribly noble of your family in your trouble to take the children anyway. You know I offered to find another place, even take them myself, but your mother would have none of it. I can't tell you how much I appreciate it."

"Yes, thank you," John said.

"But I understand they are very nice children—little colored children, seven and ten. Brother and sister, and so bright, they say."

"Oh, yes. That's nice." One more thing his mother had neglected to mention. He was sure his father didn't know they were colored, either.

Mrs. Rutherford handed him a piece of paper, and he looked at it vaguely. First he saw large curlicues in pencil, then some names: Jenny Lou and Franklin Persons, 7 and 10. 338 W. 125th St., New York City. More curlicues underneath.

"Where *is* that train?" She swiveled her head around and her floppy hat nearly caught him across the nose. His feet made sharp, gritty sounds on the cinders. The wind forced soot into his skin, and little particles of it collected on Mrs. Rutherford's thick red arm as it rested on the car door.

"I'll bet they're little darlings, and such a long trip!" she said.

Nothing could stop the train, not even the wind and the heat; not even the fires they had been having to the west in Chaldee and to the south along the tracks at Summersville. The stationmaster leaned over his desk in the little bay window, a green eyeshade on his forehead, and a half-mile down the tracks a signal changed, hazy and wiggly on its pole.

"I offered to take the children over to Leah for your mother, but she said you'd come and get them yourself. So nice of you, John, and I've got four others to 'deliver,' so I appreciate that, too."

The train pulled in, stopping with many creaks and sighs, the Diesel engines zooming even though the train was stopped. Out came the children and their keeper, the only passengers to get off.

Mrs. Rutherford spoke to the travel-haggard woman with the shifting eyes, and between them they sorted a sheaf of papers. The six children for the moment stood gravely into the wind and looked stolidly at the yellow and brown station and the dirty tracks leading back to where they had come from, where John supposed they all wanted to be at that moment. They were stunned, and the haggard woman cast several glances their way as if to calculate just how long they would remain stunned. She probably depended a great deal upon such short periods of inaction. Only two of the children were colored, and they must be—he looked at the fancy handwriting again—Jenny Lou and Franklin Persons, aged seven and ten. But, God! They were black, black as night—so black he could, at ten feet, barely make out their expressions. The boy held his sister's hand and stared even more hopelessly than the rest back down the hazy roadbed toward the South. The little girl, in dungarees so new and stiff he wondered how she could bend the cloth to walk, hugged her brother's side and peered at the station eaves and the sky as if her brother were a roof protecting her from all this strangeness: she seemed to have to stoop and put her head forward a little to see out from under him.

John received the papers concerning Jenny Lou and Franklin Persons, and the haggard woman introduced them. Franklin nodded and said hello, but couldn't smile. With an almost painful surge of memory John recognized upon Franklin Person's shiny black face a constriction of nervousness and fear that he knew had once been his own. He, too, never smiled unless something was funny. He had always wondered how people could form those inevitable, easy, social smiles. Jenny Lou's face was impassive, although she still pushed against her brother's side. He had to lean to keep from being pushed off his feet, and it seemed as if she wanted to get right inside him. Finally Franklin, with firm, yet gentle hands, stood her on her own feet.

They followed him obediently to the car and waited, both sitting rigidly, without touching the seatback, while he went to get their suitcase. He found it in the pile by the Southbound mailbox, brand-new, made of brown-and-white-striped cardboard with their names carefully painted on it. He helped Mrs. Rutherford carry the other luggage to her car, where her four children were noisily recovering from the shock of leaving the train.

Back in Bruce's car Jenny Lou had pushed Franklin over against the door, where he must have felt the knobs rather painfully digging into his side. Once again he gently set her straight.

"Well!" John said. "It's hot, isn't it?" and immediately realized that he sounded like Mrs. Rutherford.

"Yes," Franklin said. Jenny Lou sneaked a quick look and turned back to watch the dashboard. There had been a certain rational, evaluating quality in Franklin's "Yes." Obviously it was hot. Feeling that he had somehow been squelched, John backed the car around and turned toward the covered bridge into New Hampshire.

Franklin looked curiously at the long bridge, at the great curved wooden arches along the inside of it, and held the door handle tightly as if he expected the old timbers to break. *Flimp flamp flump flimp* went the flexing boards beneath their wheels, and Franklin winced at each sound.

"It's all right," John said, glancing at him again.

"I've never seen a covered bridge before," Franklin said.

"Covered bridge!" Jenny Lou said, and hunched down harder.

"That's right, Jenny Lou," Franklin said tolerantly, then turned toward John. "Why do they put a roof on a bridge?" he asked, and John felt certain that Franklin knew why—that he now tried to make conversation for social purposes. For a moment John felt one up on the little boy.

"To keep the rain from rotting the wood, I suppose," he said, "and to keep the snow off in the winter."

"I see," Franklin said, and John knew at once that the question had not been a lie, but a kindness. They were now, in Franklin's estimation, supposed to be even for the remark about the heat. This time he did smile, and caught Franklin smiling too.

"Keep the rain off!" Jenny Lou said, and scrunched down again. As they entered Leah and turned around the square, she kept her eyes down and didn't see any of it.

"This is Leah," John said, and Franklin stared intently at the buildings and into the high elms, his eyes wide open, a slight smile on his lips. He nodded several times.

On Maple Street Jenny Lou raised her head and stared, her large eyes black and the whites so wide and clear John could see them flash from the corner of his eyes. She had been watching the high arches of the trees, and as he looked down at her for part of a second she looked right at him. He turned away first, having seen on her face an almost fierce, yet steady expression of inquiry. It was not the trees or the strange town she was thinking about; it was John Cotter, and he knew it. She was not shy, she was not afraid, she was not self-conscious—not in that small part of a second, anyway.

"Here we are," he said, turned into the driveway and stopped beside the kitchen door. Franklin opened the door and got out, Jenny Lou following him, and stood at the edge of the grass by the kitchen lilac bush. Sunlight moved, filtered by the tunnel of trees, and the wind rode above the street. Franklin took a few steps down the driveway, careful not to step on the grass, careful not to go too far. He looked up and down Maple Street and then turned Jenny Lou around and brought her back to the car.

"It's beautiful," he said, and waved his hand quickly at the row of white houses and neat lawns, the massive tree trunks reaching to the ceiling of the tunnel, "I never would've believed it. Like in *Penrod*."

"You read that?" John asked.

"Yes, I read it. I've got it in the suitcase." John had opened the rear door of the car, and Franklin went to it and pulled out the suitcase. "I'll show you," he said. He quickly undid the straps and opened the cardboard lid. There on top lay the light green, faded book, just like the one John had in the old bookcase in his closet.

"I've got that one, too," John said. "I've got some other books upstairs I read when I was around your age. Maybe you'd like some of them, too."

"I'd like to see them," Franklin said politely.

John picked up the suitcase, holding it together, and led them into the house. He understood Franklin's lack of interest in the other books, and he remembered himself when he was ten and everybody wanted him to read "other" books. You just barely began to enjoy a book when they wanted you to read another, entirely strange and different book all full of strangers you could hardly understand. You had a book and you read it all the time, backward and forward and in the middle, and you understood it and lived right in it. You had a book, so why did you want another one?

In the living room Franklin stopped in the middle of the braided rug. "It's just like I expected," he said.

"The house is?" John said.

"Just the same. Isn't it, Jenny Lou?"

"Like you said!" Jenny Lou shouted, then giggled and looked shy.

John took them on a tour of the house, showed them their towels on the bathroom rack. Their room was next to Bruce's—a guest room, but now cluttered by his mother with all the Teddy bears and Tinkertoys that had been in the attic. Flowers, old children's books, a wing-warped model airplane she had unskillfully patched with Scotch tape, jars of marbles—every bit of junk she could find, his mother had cleaned and set out. Jenny Lou went around the gaudy room and examined everything, touched nothing. Franklin stood in the door with John.

"Take anything you want," John said to Jenny Lou. He felt that he must apologize to Franklin. "They're nothing but old toys my mother got out of the attic. My brother and I wore them out a long time ago. I guess she thought Jenny Lou might like to play with them."

"Oh, I like toys," Franklin said. He picked up the airplane and began to wind the propeller. "I like airplanes."

Jenny Lou took Franklin's arm and shook it. She pointed to a newly laundered, one-eyed Teddy bear.

"Take it," Franklin said. "You heard what he said. He said you could." Jenny Lou looked at John, and he nodded.

"You call me John," he said.

"All right," Franklin said. He carefully put the airplane back on the bureau.

"O.K., John!" Jenny Lou said as if she were out of breath. She took the one-eyed Teddy bear and squeezed it roughly in both arms, putting its face to hers and staring into its one button eye. "I love this bear!" she said.

Jenny Lou had to go to the bathroom. She took the Teddy bear in with her, while John took Franklin into his room to see the stuffed partridge and the guns.

"You shot that?" Franklin asked. But his eyes were on the guns. When John handed him the carbine he took it as if it were terribly fragile and valuable, his long face tense, his small black hands smoothing the stock and the barrel—pink finger ends sliding gently over the rifle.

"It's the first real gun I ever held," he said. "It's heavier than I thought. Did you shoot the bird with this?"

"No. You use a shotgun on birds. This is a rifle—for deer and bear."

"You shot a deer and a *bear?*"

"I shot a deer once, but never a bear. My father shot a bear a few years ago."

"A *bear!*" Franklin looked eagerly out of the window, as if he might see a bear in the back yard.

"You won't see any bears out there. They stay up in the hills out of sight," John said. "I've never even seen one in the woods. I heard one once. I've heard them calling at night, too, but you don't see them very often—they usually see you first."

"They're afraid of you?"

"All the animals are afraid of you. They know man is the deadliest animal in the woods."

" 'Man is the deadliest animal,' " Franklin said thoughtfully. "I never thought of it like that. With this . . ." He held the rifle to his shoulder and said, with a note of pride in his voice, "man is the deadliest animal." He put the rifle back in the rack. "But without it, he's not much, is he?" He held out his small hands, pink palms up.

"Well, he's still pretty strong," John said, "but as far as the animals are concerned, maybe they think every man has a rifle built in. They run, anyway."

"I guess that's right!" He inspected the shotgun and the .22 pistol, and then they heard Jenny Lou come out of the bathroom.

"We're in here, Jenny Lou," Franklin called, and she came and stood in the door, still hugging the Teddy bear. "Once she takes to something she really *takes* to it," Franklin said.

Jenny Lou pretended not to hear this. She swung from side to side and hummed to the Teddy bear.

"She's like a kid with stuff like that," Franklin said.

John was about to take them downstairs when something in Franklin's attitude made him turn. Bookshelves were visible through the open closet door, and Franklin went toward them, a quizzical frown on his face. He pulled two faded green books into his hands, looked them over carefully and turned to John. John nodded, and Franklin opened *Penrod* in the middle, read a few lines and closed it, nodding. Then he opened *Penrod and Sam,* read a little of it, and turned his head around, his eyes perceptibly wider.

"More?" he asked.

"Didn't you know there were more?"

In Franklin's expression he saw first a desire to believe, perhaps much disbelief, increasing delight.

"Can I read it?"

"You can have it," John said, remembering the difference.

"I can *have* it?" Franklin seemed to give this offer serious consideration. He measured the thickness of the book.

"You'd like to read it right now," John said. Franklin smiled guiltily. "But you want to be polite. Isn't that right?"

The face changed completely. From long and narrow it turned round as Franklin grinned, and what seemed to be hundreds of little white teeth flashed across it.

"You read it, then. You don't have to be polite until my mother comes home."

"Thank you, John," Franklin said. He already had his finger in the first page, and he slowly let himself down into the leather chair, reading.

John and Jenny Lou went down the back stairs. Her black head bobbed below him, wiry pigtails bouncing and bending as she jumped from step to step.

He remembered Penrod's simple world with a clarity that was quite surprising. The streets of Penrod's adventures, from this nostalgic distance, might have been the shady streets of Leah. Part of his boyhood, certainly, existed only within the pages of the pale green book. His memories of Leah were darker—but then, he remembered, Penrod never laughed at himself.

CHAPTER 11

Sam Stevens sat next to the radio, and near him Aubrey, favoring his best ear. Sam worked the knobs but he kept the volume up for Aubrey. Adolf sat next to the sink and smoked his pipe, listening carefully even to the commercials, nodding his head when he understood something. Mrs. Pettibone stood at the drainboard carefully skinning out a red fox, the white rubbery underside of its skin turned outside, ballooned by the thick fur underneath. The body of the fox, naked and almost free of its skin, looked like a large rat. It would be thrown away, because even the dogs wouldn't eat it. After she had fleshed the skin Mrs. Pettibone would fit it, still inside out, over a wooden stretch-board to let it dry. Sam had shot the fox with a *.22* that morning as it came to examine the scraps of the old gray horse.

The two old men leaned toward the radio to hear the state news and the progress of the fires to the west, in Vermont. It was the new, local station in Northlee, and the announcer's voice was shallowly nasal and amateurish. He explained the great circulating high-pressure front that had settled over northern New England and would not move out to sea. The dry weather would continue and the wind would not change. One thousand acres of forest had burned in Summersville, to the southwest, and the water level was so low in ponds and rivers the fire-fighters could barely pump it out. Creeks had died altogether, and fires had crowned across fairly wide roads and highways. Houses and barns had burned to the ground while people watched helplessly.

"If that wind don't stop!" Sam said suddenly. Adolf nodded, but Aubrey leaned to the radio and concentrated on the announcer's voice.

"Tomorrow we're going to clear grass and brush all around the house and barn," Sam said, "as far as possible. Dry as tinder. Bad."

Jane sat still on a kitchen chair, waiting for John Cotter. Her grandfather was really worried, and for the first time she herself felt the danger of the dry weather as fear. In all her life she had never seen Sam Stevens clear the brush for fear of fire. He was not careless—far from it. Before anyone entered the barn he had to leave his pipe on a little rack outside, and that rule was never broken. But the farm spring on the hill above was nearly dry, even though it had been cleaned and cleared of mud. The spring had never failed before.

John Cotter's headlights flickered against the kitchen windows as his car turned in the dooryard, and in a minute he stood in the open door, looking neat almost to the point of frailty in his good clothes. Sam got up and shook his hand, smiling briefly before returning to the radio.

"There was a grass fire on the river flats today," John said, and even Aubrey looked up. "They got it out, though. They had about a hundred people out."

"They put it out?" Mrs. Pettibone said, holding her hands, dirtied with the fox's scent, up to, but not touching, her face. John nodded.

"They had brooms and shovels. It really flared up, right to the road. I guess the road stopped it. It's the wind."

"The God-damned wind!" Sam said. He turned the radio off and they all heard the wind around the windows. "It ain't natural for a wind to last so long."

"Hills ought to break it up and slow it down," Aubrey said, "if it's the wind you're cussin'."

Sam turned to him and spoke in a loud voice, "Aubrey, you recall the yellow day?"

"By God! I do. Ayuh. 'Way back, now."

"That was a freak," Sam said. "Scared the daylights out of everybody. I'll tell you what it was." He turned to Jane and John, who couldn't have known, and out of politeness to Adolf, who wouldn't understand. "The sky came all over yellow—no dusty yellow, neither—bright canary yellow. Nothing that warn't yellow: a man's face, his hands, the leaves on the trees was yellow, and the tree trunks was a darker shade of yellow. It near made a man sick to open his eyes. Nobody knew what it was. Air smelt good, like always, sun was up there, only yellower. I'll tell you what it was like—like looking through a piece of yellow cellophane. Only *everybody* saw it that way. Now we didn't have no raddios then. Nobody to tell us what was going on outside, so to speak, nor to git expert advice from Concord nor Boston. There was wind that day, too."

"Ayuh," Aubrey said.

"Hadn't been blowing for a month, like this, but it was the same kind of a wind—a mean, pushing hot wind. Some said it was the breath of hell, and believed it. Considerable thought it was the end of the world, and a hell of a lot more wouldn't have bet it warn't. No, sir! I was a young man then, and not given to fancying the end of the world, but I felt considerable better when the next day come clean and clear." He shook his head.

"What made it like that?" John said.

"We never knew for sure," Sam said. "Some was so ashamed about what they'd said they never asked, preferring to forgit it altogether. Some say 'twas yellow smoke, high in the sky, come from forest fires way out in New York State and further off even than that."

"No stink to it," Aubrey said.

"Some said 'twas smoke from a volcano blew its top 'way out in the Pacific Ocean. Some said 'twas God's warning we should mend our sinful ways. Nobody never knew for sure."

"No raddios in them days," Aubrey said. "A man had to make up his own mind." They were all silent for a minute, and then Sam turned on the radio again.

"We better go, Janie," John said. "It's getting pretty dark."

They said good night, and Mrs. Pettibone called to them to have a good time.

As she got into the car with John, it seemed like a dream of ten years ago, and wrong to be getting into a car to go on a date with a boy. But she wasn't married any more; she was a widow. A widow! It made her think of spiders, or anything black and in corners, chimney corners, spinning webs or knitting socks. She could remember going on dates and not being married to Michael Spinelli, but not very clearly. After they were married, they would get into Mr. Spinelli's old car and they would drive to Anna's or the Red and White, get the beer and then to the Drive-in and sit and look at the movie and when it was over without talking about it they would drive home, Mike a little irritable because the beer had given him a headache. At home if it wasn't too late Mr. and Mrs. Spinelli would be looking at television. Then they would all go to bed, and Mike would be asleep in one minute flat. The minute he put his head on the pillow he would be asleep. Or maybe if they went to the Legion Hall he would have talked the sleepiness out of himself, and when they got home they would go right upstairs after having come in, Mike laughing and his eyes bright. The old people would watch television longer and keep the volume up, knowing very well what was going on upstairs. Mike never seemed to mind that. "What's wrong with them knowing?" he would say. "They did it themselves." "Oh, it's not that," she would say. "Mike, I know they know and that's all right, but don't you ever want some privacy?" "Nobody's looking at us," he'd say. "The shades are pulled and they can't hear nothing over the television."

But she wanted to be in her own house where they could do it and nobody would know or have to know how often or when or under the influence of how much beer. "You act so proud of it, as if it were something only you could do," she would say, "and you want to do it and tell about it. I'll bet you'd do it out in the town square." "Nothing wrong with it, is there?" he'd say. Then there would be the business of preparation, because Mike didn't want to have children. "Let's wait a while," he'd say. "Wait till we git our house." And afterward he would draw away just a little bit when she didn't want him to and she would say: "No, there's nothing wrong with it. I love you. Put your arms around me." And for a while he would put his wiry arms, now weak when they had been so strong a few minutes before, around her and he would go to sleep like a puppy with his head against her neck.

They had driven for quite a while in silence, the headlights just able to compete with the fading brightness of the sky. Along the road beneath the trees it was already dark. In Cascom Center, John stopped in front of the filling station and general store.

"Do you want to get some beer?" he asked.

"If you do, John," she said.

"I mean, will you have one with me in the movies? I won't get any if you won't." He sat undecided until she said she would, then got out of the car and walked quickly up the wide steps to the store, almost too civilized-looking in his neat sport clothes. It seemed that he couldn't belong to her—be her date—dressed like that. His short, controlled body, wide shoulders and small feet were so different from the men she had had around her: Mike, Junior and their large friends, or Sam and the hired men. He seemed to be a kind of foreigner. She might call it also a kind of social gracefulness; he walked carefully, evenly, and when he stood still he was entirely still, not stooped and gangly-armed like Junior, for instance, who always cocked his elbows as if he were being crowded, or was about to be crowded. She did remember seeing John Cotter try to act that way, in high school. It never fitted him at all, and now he had evidently given it up. That was good. It was not for toughness she had always liked him. Wanted him? But what was the reason? It was not for weakness. She knew enough about herself to know she could never admire or desire weakness. She had seen too much of it, swaggering or otherwise.

She didn't consider him weak. Physically he was obviously not weak. In character, perhaps—yet even his ability to fade away and be gone was a kind of strength if it kept his personality intact. He left and he came back and then he left again, and he never seemed to change very much at all. She had never seen him drunk; he never got into trouble, never blew up or fought, just faded away, still clear-eyed and calm, politely saying goodbye.

He came out of the store with the beer, got into the car and reached across to lock the door on her side. His arm brushed hers, his face was close to hers, and suddenly she shivered and had to sneeze.

She began to recall the moves and hesitations of a code of action he had probably never stopped using. At least not for ten years, as she had. Now how must she act? Like a young virgin, the firm callow shell holding a treasure and a fear? Surprisingly enough, that would not be very difficult at all. She was at once uncomfortably and luxuriously aware of her body, of her hips and the smooth muscles along the insides of her thighs. She was aware of the hardness of his body and of his strength.

The movie turned out to be Abbott and Costello.

"I should have looked before we came out," John said.

"Why don't we just ride around?"

They took the road along the Cascom River, toward Leah.

"I seem to foul everything up," he said.

She thought of saying, And what have you ever done to foul up? But this was a strange projection of an idea not her own. She felt that John Cotter had done quite a lot of things, even if "things" were measured only in miles traveled, places seen. It was John who seemed to think that he had never done anything. Or maybe he had decided to give her this impression. No, one funny thing about John Cotter was that he was honest. What he *said* was true. It was the way he acted, the way he preserved himself, his immobility that was dishonest—as if he wanted to prove himself a liar by his gestures—or lack of gestures. He spoke like a man, and yet the man's voice came from that quiet, animal's body—a split personality? Perhaps the cleavage between the animal and the man was a little wider in him than in other people. In herself, she could not find the border, if there *was* a definite one, between the animal and the woman. Perhaps such a border was like the coast of Maine: as the crow flies, not so far, but following all indentations—hesitations—it might be a thousand miles long.

They followed the new directions for rotary traffic around the Town Square and crossed the covered bridge into Vermont.

"I feel almost as if I had to make things up to you," he said, "It's a long sort of thing. I mean when we were young we didn't really spend much time together. But to myself, in my mind, I spent a lot of time with you."

"You did?"

"When I thought about girls, I thought about you. Mostly about you. I used to have daydreams—only they were at night, just before I went to sleep. Funny damn' things. I remember one I used to think up pretty often. I'd be in a jungle, in a loincloth, and here you'd come along, stark naked, scared. You know. And then I'd be up in a tree above your head and I'd grab a vine and swing down beside you and put my arms around you. I could feel your skin sort of cool and bare. Some dream! Only the thing about the jungle was that it was mine. I invented it and *caused* you to be in it. Sometimes I had other girls kidnaped out of their beds and put into my jungle, but mostly it was you." He looked at her for a second, and she saw a glint of teeth in the semidarkness. "I had another one, too. In this one you and I were lying in a little hole, on the side of a mountain—sort of a little foxhole, with a small ridge of dirt in front, and I had a rifle. Somebody—Japs, Germans—some enemy of the time—sometimes it was the Ku Klux Klan, was attacking up the hill. I'd shoot them and you'd hand me ammunition. You always had one arm around me. I remember it was very comfortable and warm in the hole, and I'd keep picking off those attackers. It was always you in that one."

"Always me?"

"Yes. Believe me, it was. This was when I was fourteen or fifteen. But I'll never forget that feeling when we were in that foxhole. In a way it had everything that I wanted—everything all together and at the same time. Sex, comfort, danger. A little natural sadism mixed with honorable danger. What else is necessary?"

"Sadism? What do you mean, 'natural sadism'? I thought it wasn't very natural."

He drove slowly along the river, slowing down to let cars pass. "Of course it's natural. How else can you explain it? People are always cruel, and the ones who say they aren't are the cruelest. Did you ever know anybody who was never cruel? Wait a minute. The only people who aren't really sadistic are the ones who admit it in their natures. You know what I mean?" He turned toward her for a long moment—so long she began to worry about going off the road. She put her hand on the dashboard, and he immediately saw it, turned back to his driving and said, "Sorry."

"Mike's father," she said, and surprisingly a wave of pity came over her and tears came into her eyes. She saw the little man coping with his wife, and the word "gutted" occurred to her. Without his son he seemed as incomplete as a hung deer, and she could hear her grandfather say the words, *gutted and done.*

"Mr. Spinelli?" John said. "He has the Silver Star. He didn't kill twenty-seven Germans in self-defense. Listen. When you get the Silver Star it's not for doing something you actually *have* to do."

"Maybe he got rid of it then," she said, "because he's a good man." Tears again, and she distrusted easy tears. "I've never seen him do anything cruel. Never."

John put his hand on her arm. "Yes, I know," he said, "but he's a man who had to admit it. Can you *see* all those dead men? I can."

They came out from under the black branches of the elms as if from a tunnel. The moon was about to come up, and a red glow like a false sunrise shone above the Vermont hills. A tall pasture-pine with craggy branches like arms stood in a field, and as they rode along, it passed from the red glow back into darkness. She could smell fire in the night air, and as the black crown of a hill passed, the great red moon sailed out and followed them along.

"Haven't you ever done something mean?" he asked.

"Yes. I was mean to Junior when he brought the Riders to see me. I made him feel as bad as I could. I gave him an awfully hard time."

"Junior," he said.

"And once . . . maybe I shouldn't tell you this. It happened a long time ago, when we were pretty young. You were a freshman in high school."

"When we were kids. What difference does it make now?"

"These things aren't very funny to the kids," she said. "I sicked Junior on you once. Deliberately."

"He didn't have to be sicked," he said, a certain amount of bitterness in his voice.

"You see? It still isn't very funny, is it?"

"The funny thing is, I remember," he said, and now she heard a new emotion: he was ashamed of himself. "One of my many little shamefulnesses. I was thinking about it a while ago. I remember things very well—especially the things I don't want to remember."

"No, wait. This is *my* shameful piece," she said.

"Do you remember that time at the scrape? Sure you do. Whatever happened afterward I deserved it. You told me you loved me and I hurt you. Just kid stuff? Bob fell when the rope broke, and we ducked you—my idea entirely—and then I took my towel and snapped you raw and you went home bawling. Kid stuff? And Junior and Keith Joubert caught me that night at the Community House."

"I sicked him on you, but I never told him why."

"I knew you didn't. You don't know how much I admired you and how much worse I felt because you didn't tell him what I'd done."

"God! How mad I was!" she said, but then reconsidered: No, not angry. And it was very easy to remember. First his hands touching her, even though he grabbed her to duck her—the joy of that contact. And how it turned slowly, as the minutes went by, into desperation; into a real fear of drowning. The acid bite of water in her nose—she could feel that again—but most important was the terrible shame, the shame of her protruding buttocks, the shame of her breasts and the poor worn bathing suit that could not conceal them (but had, a short season before. It was as if her growth itself were a kind of shameful disease). Shame as when all the girls in school were afraid on their periods that their dresses would be spotted when the bell rang and they had to stand up; had to stand up and couldn't look.

"I know you didn't like getting ducked, Janie," he said in a soft, nervous voice. "It was childish and cruel of me. But when I snapped you with the towel, that was sadistic. It was a dirty thing to do."

"Maybe you were getting back at Junior."

"I don't know," he said. "I don't think so. I just couldn't take it when you said you loved me. I remember thinking what a tremendous responsibility it meant for me, and I got scared. I felt the same about you, you know, only I'd never dare say anything or do anything about it."

"It was a long time ago," she said, and began to laugh without quite knowing why.

"I'd like to think it was funny," he said, "but it wasn't really too long ago, Leah time."

"Yes. You can take one year and change it around with another and never know the difference. I know that."

"The rest of the country isn't like that, I'll tell you. You come back after a while and it's all changed. People have been walking all over it and building horrible things everywhere. Let me tell you. I always think of Leah as a center—no, a starting place, a calm starting place. Maybe it's more like the center of a whirlpool, where it's relatively quiet. But I never forget that the hole's right underneath. For me it would be safer out on the edge of it. I don't like Leah. I feel wounded here. I feel like a mental basket case. But everything means more here. Little things I'd forget, ignore, just laugh at; here in Leah they paralyze me. For some reason everything's *real* here."

"Weren't things real in Paris?"

"No, nothing's real in Paris. Nothing matters there. There are some things I can't imagine doing in Paris. I can't imagine doing *anything* worth while or serious in Paris."

"But you could in Leah?" she asked. He turned onto the bridge that led back across the river to Northlee. In the pale fluorescent light on the modern bridge his face was greenish and unhealthy looking. She was glad he didn't turn and look at her at that moment, and as she realized this she became terribly impatient with his self-consciousness.

"Yes, I'm afraid I could in Leah," he said.

"You're afraid," she said.

He turned toward her, and smiled. "I'm afraid of you, Janie. Always have been. Afraid of Junior, too. God knows why. If I met him anywhere else we'd get along. If I met you anywhere else I'd . . ." He stopped, then began to hum to himself.

"You'd what?"

"Well, you see, I didn't meet you anywhere else, or I'd tell you straight out."

She made an impatient noise.

"I'm sorry. I'm sorry," he said. "Look! It's stupid. You're more real to me. *Too* real to me."

Too real *for* you, she thought, and suddenly the picture of an old-fashioned can-opener came into her mind. John Cotter needed to be let out. At least she would then find if anything were inside. She kept silent as they went through Northlee and the campus, remembering a poem she'd written, or started to write, when she was a high-school senior and wanted to go to college:

> Across the college campus
> In the gloom of winter night,
> A thousand men are sitting
> In their rooms of yellow light.

Now that was a wonderful combination of yearnings: romance and higher education!

"Why didn't you go to Northlee?" she asked.

"Because I didn't want to commute. Things were crowded after the war. Number two: too close to Leah. But look, Janie, I don't want to go on with this business. I'm going to shut up about it for good and all. God knows what I'll talk about. No, let's see. I used to think what I'd do. . . ." He turned sharply onto a dirt road that led to Slocum Pond, Scrotum Pond to the students; a parking place.

"Oh!" he said. "Do you mind if we park by the pond?"

"No, I don't mind. I'm not scared of you," she said, and was immediately sorry. "What was it you used to think you'd do, Johnny?"

"Well, it was another dream—daydream. You and I were caught in a place where there was a huge forest fire. We knew we were going to be burned up. No chance of getting out. So what to do? Believe me it was worth it." He laughed and was embarrassed again.

"It's not too different now," she said. The air was heavy with the smell of fire. He parked beside the little pond beneath a tall pine whose broad branches made whisking noises in the wind. Summer session at the college was over, and they had the pond to themselves.

"You always seemed more *valuable* to me than Mike," he said hesitantly. "I don't know."

"Valuable?"

"Mike was just . . ."

"Mike just didn't care about school. He wasn't stupid. He just never *lit* anywhere." She was afraid that she sounded angry, and didn't want to give that impression.

"I used to envy him in high school," John said. "He was so damned free and easy. He was witty, in a kind of goosing way. How could he smile so damned easily?"

"And you were the strong, silent type," she said.

"The weak, silent type, you mean."

"Do you believe that, Johnny?"

"No, of course not. I'm not silent and I'm not weak. That's enough of that. Do you want a beer?"

"No, I don't think so, Johnny."

He picked up the carton of beer, opened the car door, ran down to the edge of the pond and threw it into the water. "There," he said as he came back, "what do you think of that? Wasn't that a non-John Cotter gesture?"

"It was," she said wonderingly.

"Some day I'll probably be diving for it. It'll keep cool, anyway. Why the hell do you always make me talk about myself? I don't like to talk about myself, Janie. I really don't. What have you been doing for the last ten years? Read any good books?"

I have, she thought, been the regular bed partner of an erratic but faithful husband. I read *Time* and *Life* and *Harper's* and *Atlantic;* I put my name on the waiting list at the library for the best-sellers; I have done exactly nothing for ten years. I read the Leah *Free Press* to keep up with what is going on in the world and in Cascom and Cascom Corners.

"I've done nothing," she said.

He was silent for a long time, then he put his arm around her shoulders and gently pulled her toward him. She was grateful that he didn't ask her if it was all right. His face was dry, like fine sandpaper against hers. She felt her lips become soft. Their teeth touched with a hard little click. Her nipples turned hard; the straps of her bra tightened over her shoulders. As she turned in his arms there was a moment of clear, rather cold wonder—she could never remember such immediate symptoms with Mike. He had not changed her body so much or so quickly. Never. She shut her eyes, and the hot wind ruffled over them, coming into the car with a push that seemed deliberate. She found herself thinking, If it were only real, if I could only know that he is going to stay this time. There was a tremor in his leg, and his toe tapped against the floor of the car.

"See that?" he said. "Hear that? I'm nervous as hell, for some reason. You'd think we hadn't known each other all our lives, wouldn't you?"

"It's because we have," she said. "You've never kissed me before. Now let me say something. I've been wondering what that kiss would be like for a long time."

"How is it?"

"Like I thought it would be."

"I only know how it is for me," he said, and tried to stop his leg from trembling. "I feel like a gawky virgin. It's like going back to the scrape."

She put her hands under his shirt, against his skin.

"Yes, you did that and nearly killed me on the spot. Yes," he whispered, his lips against her ear.

"All of a sudden I want to know if you are going away," she said.

"You feel that way?" he asked eagerly. "Do you, Janie?"

"Yes. I feel like a lawyer, or a miser. Right now I do. I want to know what's going to happen."

He moved his hands up her arms to her shoulders and neck, but kept them chastely away from her breasts. "I don't know what to do. It's the truth. I've never felt this way before. I mean it. It's brand new. I mean new for real, not for daydreams."

She had learned that reality had many definitions; that ten years, at least, could be unreal as a dream. To her, reality was progression, not stasis. She was quite sure it must include something she vaguely defined as "improvement."

John watched her, held her out at arms' length and watched her without moving. The red moonlight left black hollows beneath his eyebrows, and she could sense the eyes moving in the dark, and only the eyes. She wanted to move toward him, but would wait until he pulled her. Honest? she asked herself. Perhaps it meant too much to be honest; it was too late to be honest; perhaps honesty was not wanted. And yet John Cotter was honest. She could think of no one more honest.

Now his arms were steady; his foot had stopped tapping. The

short spasm of his hard muscles had ended completely, and he was again the immobile, watching animal.

"I love you. I only say what I know. You're not just my girl; you're the archtype, the essence, etcetera, etcetera, etcetera. That's the truth. Every girl I've ever had was you incomplete in some way. I don't like to get out on limbs, but I don't care what you think about me now. It's the first thing I've been able to say I *know* for an awfully long time."

"How do you know what I'm like?" she asked.

"I will know what you're like," he said, and pulled her toward him. As they kissed he began, with expert fingers, to undo her clothes. His hands moved surely and busily about her straps and plackets, doing what she wanted him to do—not tearing, not impatient, opening her skin to the hard touch of his hands, which moved down over her back and spine. Suddenly she shivered and there was a great, convulsive blunting of the mind—but then she began to plan again, asking herself how cold she might make herself become. She wanted his hands to press into her flesh itself, to bury themselves in her flesh, and yet she used all her strength to stop him. He knew when to recognize the strength she used against him, and when to really stop.

"I still love you," he said. "I am committed."

"I'm sorry. I almost . . ."

"Yes. Almost," he said.

"John, I was the first to declare myself, remember? At the scrape."

"Then what are you sorry about? I don't lie. No, I don't mean that. You're sorry for no reason. You think I'm in pain, or something. That's a myth, Janie. This isn't pain." He put his hand on the bulge in his pants. "If you love me it isn't pain. Pain is suffering. How can I suffer? For the first time in my life I know what I want, so I can wait. I felt you move toward me."

"Yes, I did," she said quickly, then put her mouth to his ear, wanting to be secret, as if to whisper in his ear kept the secret even from him. "I love you. It was the same for me. I didn't—maybe no one grows up just because glands start and all that. I grew up with you as the man I could receive when I changed and got big enough. I can feel your hand on my back as if I were burned there."

"Now we won't do anything," he said, "and I'll take you home, temporarily. Here, I'll help you fix all these things." He fastened up her dress.

The moon had climbed out of redness; the wind was still hot but did not push. An elation, a clearing of the eyes, a feeling of confidence and carelessness came over her and was strange. "Johnny, I'm so goddam happy," she said. And then she seemed to hear herself asking, *Yes, but for how long this time?*

CHAPTER 12

John drove carefully, yet with unusual speed down the gravel road from the Stevens farm. He decided that he would not think about Jane. "What a decision!" he said out loud in the enclosed, rocking privacy of the car. "I will not think about anything!"

He *had* kept his resolution—or was it Jane's resolution? And why was the resolution so important? Perhaps this new departure had brought them both back to adolescence, with all of adolescence's moral strictures. They would wait and take it slow. He remembered something Bob Paquette had said in high school: "If you ain't had it for two weeks, you're a virgin again." For his drunkenness and his fornication and his sin of casualness, he must somehow pay. The greatest sin he had committed was the sin of dissociation, of detachment. No risk: no reward. O.K.

Soon after he turned onto the hard-top road at the bottom of the hill he heard a roar behind him and for a moment thought he had lost his muffler. He turned around to see, and a bank of unsteady headlights came at him, swerved around the car and cut in sharply in front. On the Riders' black leather jackets white death's-heads grinned. One rider at the front of the column raised his hand and with military precision the column fanned out to block the road, then slowed down and made John stop. The head rider swung around and came back. It was Bob Paquette.

"Hi, John!" He yelled above his idling engine. "Where you going?"

"Home to bed!"

"Where you been? You're not going anyplace, then?"

"Home to bed!"

"Follow me!" Bob pointed back along the road, motioned the Riders to go along the way they were pointed, then motioned John to turn around. John reluctantly backed into an old logging road, turned around and followed Bob back toward Cascom, keeping Bob's elusive taillight barely in sight. In the driveway of the Paquette farm Bob slued around and parked his machine next to the kitchen door, hot cylinders creaking and smoking as they cooled.

"What's the idea?" John asked.

"Don't like to see nobody go to bed," Bob said. "Come on in and have a beer." He bent over his machine for a moment and patted the saddle. "Don't she go!"

"She goes, you ass. You'll kill yourself."

Bob grinned and nodded his head. He turned around so that John could see the death's-head on his back, then led him into the big kitchen. Dick looked up from a thick ledger, scowling.

"So you wrecked your bike already? I thought you was going on a wingding or some such. Hi, John. You bring him home?"

"That ain't a wingding, just going for a ride. A wingding is a kind of a way to flop," Bob said. He took three cans of beer out of the refrigerator.

"Don't mind if I do, seeing as it's your beer," Dick said. He took the beer and went back to his ledger.

"Dick's gitting married next week," Bob said.

"Congratulations," John said.

"Thank you, John."

"I offered to let him ride my old bike, but he's gitting chicken now he's going to be a family man."

"Amen," Dick said.

"Where were you headed when you came up on me?" John asked.

"To Billy Frisch's, then to Pinckney's on the flat. Old Slug says he's got a barrel of cider come out pink and hard. Beautiful! We was going to get a little of *that,* then take ourselves a little ride to Summersville and back. You take my old bike and come along!"

"Me?"

"Sure. What's the matter?"

Dick looked up. "It's been nice knowing you, John."

"Hell!" Bob said, "You can take her slow till you git the feel of it. You don't have to go no sixty, seventy miles per hour! Besides, you been on a bike before. I seen you ride that old Harley of Slugger's once."

"Around the block. I'm no daredevil, Bob."

"Aw, lay off that!" Bob said disgustedly. "Ever since you come home you been acting like a heart attact. Like you et something maybe would gag a maggot. What you need is a long ride, boy! Flush your glands out! Put some red in your cheeks!"

"Put some red all over the goddam road," Dick said.

"You shut up! Just 'cause you're gitting chicken and respectable in your old age."

"Don't start that again," John said. "Next thing you'll be out in the woodshed again." The brothers looked at each other cautiously and then smiled.

"I'll tell you what," Bob said. "You come on out and try my old bike, anyway. Won't hurt you none to try it. Maybe you'll git the bug." He stood up. "Come *on,* John. Bring your beer along."

He followed Bob through the sheds, reluctant but unable to do anything about it. He wanted to go home and think (not think) about Jane, to remember the way she moved involuntarily under his hands, to suffer his wait for her. And now this hard monster of a machine came in between with its oily weight. Bob kicked down the starter and the engine hissed, popped and roared in the shed, shook the discarded oil lamps on the walls and brought dust down from the rafters. A thin cloud of blue exhaust smoke rose to the bare bulb over their heads. Bob grinned and turned off the motor.

"Damn' good bike!"

"It's alive," John said.

"You damn' right! It ain't no car sitting on four legs like a lousy bathtub. Hell, John, a bike's right under your ass yelling bloody murder and let's git going! You got to *ride* a bike! You don't sit back like a sack of potatoes and steer with your pinkie! It takes your whole body to ride a bike. You can feel them old pistons humping between your legs. Man, you're out there in the air where a man ought to be." He kicked aside a cardboard box and wheeled the machine out onto the gravel. John took it by the handlebars and nearly let it fall. Stationary, it was tremendously heavy and awkward, wanting to jackknife.

"Go ahead. Take her for a spin," Bob said, standing well back.

"I can't remember how to start the damn' thing."

"Well, now, look. This here's an Indian, so everything's just about bass ackwards from a Harley. Here's your gas on the left, spark on the right. Push your clutch *in* to connect her up. That's all. You'll git the hang of her. O.K., retard your spark, turn switch, disconnect clutch, give a little gas—good, good! Kick her down. You can see how to shift. Three speeds forward. Let her rip!"

It seemed fairly simple, except that the machine wanted to fall over against his right leg, and when it had leaned far enough he had to exert an almost unbearable amount of strength to straighten it back up again. The engine started on his second try. He knew enough to adjust the spark, then sat precariously balanced, tentatively zooming the engine.

"Put her in low and let her go!" Bob yelled.

The little knob moved easily on its short post and the machine began to creep forward with a disconcerting, animal eagerness.

"Clutch!"

He pushed the clutch forward a little too fast. The back wheel spun and the machine surged out from under him. He held on, out of control for a second, but managed to keep his seat and to remember what to do. He rode slowly around the yard in low gear, surprised by the stability of the machine once it was in motion. He waved to Bob on the next cautious circuit of the driveway, shifted into second and shot into the darkness of the main road, clawing desperately for the light switch. He found it just in time, shifted into high, and as the panic drained out of him the chain noises smoothed into a high roar. The road and the trees together dipped and flashed toward him and past. He banked instinctively on the curves and let the world tilt—until he saw the glowing speedometer.

The needle pointed to 70. He felt for a moment as if he were falling, but held steady and let the engine slow him down. He made a pretty U-turn in the road and came back, each moment learning easily a new economy of control, a new bit of confidence in his speed. The machine seemed to become more and more a part of his body.

When he stopped in front of Bob he gunned the engine and turned off the switch. In the sudden silence he felt a draining weakness as that source of power died away, and the machine again became heavy and unbalanced.

"O.K., I'll go with you," he said.

Bob tilted his head and squinted at him.

"You liked it, huh?"

"I don't know whether I liked it or not, but I'll go. I hit seventy!"

"You want to take it easy at first. You got a lot to learn."

"You asking *me* to take it easy? Old Cautious John?"

They went back to the kitchen for more beer. Dick had gone to bed. "It's twelve o'clock," Bob said. "We better hump."

"Maybe I better not go, Bob. I've got to work in the morning."

"Who don't? You're young yet. You can stand it. Only time to ride is now. No cars on the road. Come *on!*" They went back to the machines, where Bob showed him how to jam the beer can into a special rack on the handlebars.

He knew what to do this time and they left the dooryard, bounced creakily until they hit the asphalt, then bored down on Leah against the air. Bob's taillight kept creeping away and disappearing on the corners, and in order to catch up John had to go just a little faster than he wanted to each time. Yet each increase in speed, each greater degree of list on a fast corner, once he had done it successfully, did not frighten him again. Fear became a matter of control and experiment, a twist of his left wrist increasing or barely decreasing it.

He looked up, startled to see the high elms and the darkened storefronts of Leah Town Square, then followed Bob through a power turn, his footrest sparking on the pavement, to shoot past the empty sidewalks toward the river flats and Pinckney's farm.

In the dooryard the shiny machines were lined up in formation, each leaning just so on its kickstand, each front wheel turned slightly and aligned perfectly with the others, coontails and boondoggle streamers hanging down. Light shone from the big kitchen which separated the barn and the house, and when he and Bob slued to a stop the door opened and a big man whooped at them, bending his head and trying to make them out.

"Hoo, boy!" It was Junior. "Who is it? Bob? Who else you got?" Then he saw who it was. "I be go to hell!" He turned back to the kitchen. "No wonder he was late," he said, and went inside. John and Bob followed him in.

The Riders and their women sat straight and neat in their uniforms, each holding a tumbler of hard cider. Slugger Pinckney went to a cupboard and got two more glasses, filled them from a pitcher and gravely handed them to John and Bob. John held his to the light and nodded, feeling quite sloppy in his civilian clothes. He felt that he had entered a highly select and formal club, and had a weird feeling that perhaps he should propose a toast, or at least bow and click his heels. He stood straighter under their scrutiny, took a sip and said, "Beautiful." It was. It was as good as Billy Muldrow's. The Riders seemed to approve of his formality. Billy Frisch, tall and rigid as a Prussian officer, nodded and let a tight smile cross his face. Wilma Berry, who was Slugger's girl, got two chairs from the entryway and without speaking motioned for them to sit down. Even Bob sat straighter. Junior was the only one who lolled back and looked gawky. Even the tight jacket and riding pants of their uniform could not Prussianize him. John had always thought of Junior as a leader of the Riders, and now began to realize that this was not true. They disapproved of Junior. It was evident in the way they ignored his sarcasm, even interrupted him—not to talk, because they rarely talked, but to get up, to pour more cider, to study a new piston and rod that lay on the table.

"Were you scared?" Junior said. "Did Robert scare your pants off?" The Riders listened, blank-faced, and then looked to John for his answer.

"When my footrest scraped in the square it scared me. I never did that before."

"*Your* footrest?" Junior asked, laughing.

"Sure, his footrest, whatever he wants to call it. You ought to slow down, Junior," Bob said.

Slugger Pinckney smiled and went for the pitcher. "Oh, Junior," he said, "you going blind? Seems to me I heard two bikes come in. Didn't you see 'em?" He looked disgustedly at Junior.

"You mean *he* rode over here?"

"Sure he did," Bob said. "You ought to slow down, Junior. Why don't you lay off? Give it a rest."

"I thought he rode behind on your bike."

"No!" Slugger said. Junior looked angry and confused, and the Riders smiled.

Billy Frisch took pity on him: "When you going to stick that piston in?"

"Tomorrow, maybe. The other'll do all right tonight," Junior mumbled. He poured himself some more cider and drew his chair a little farther away from the table. He would sulk a while.

But it was time to take off. The Riders began to zip up their pockets, straighten their pants and tuck them into their black riding boots. The women—John noticed one in particular and was startled that he hadn't recognized her. It was Dianne Rousseau, and he remembered her in high school as an awkward girl with acne. Now she stood tall and svelt with square shoulders and a trim waist. She stood proudly by Billy Frisch, evidently his girl. The acne had gone, leaving only a few discolored places on her cheeks. Her eyes were dark and wide apart.

The women stood up, carefully secured their hair beneath their caps and smoothed their clothes down with their hands. Gussie Contois, another girl, had been married after the war and had been pretty fat. Now she was as trim as the rest. She'd had a baby, too, he'd heard, and her husband had run off somewhere. Gussie was Joe Foss's girl—had been from high school, in spite of her marriage. Funny *they* never got married. Gussie had worked in Blakemore's drugstore for as long as he could remember her. They were all so much alike, except for Junior. Bob didn't quite fit, either, but he knew how to act with them. He kept his mouth shut longer, and his eyes open.

The Riders went out, each going to his bike, his girl waiting beside him until he started the engine. Then they lined up again, this time headed toward the road. One after another the bikes roared until the staccato sound of one was lost in the rumble of the fleet—a thunder blotting out the creak of stanchions in the barn, the hum of the wind, all the night sounds. John sat on his bike and felt the smooth rhythm of his engine. He retarded the spark for a second to hear the flat popping sound, then put the engine back in tune. The Riders began to peel off from the end and zoom past him, each girl posting slightly as a machine hit the edge of the hardtop, holding harder to her man for the pulling shift into second. Then Bob spun his back wheel and it was John's turn to follow. He turned his wrist, pushed in the clutch and his arms straightened out as the bike pulled beneath him straight into the cloud of yellow dust. His headlight beam shortened and then flicked out again as he came through the cloud. The little red lights ahead of him were the taillights of the Riders, and he had to go too fast to keep up with them, thinking: this is why they ride together, in the wash of all their explosions, and in formation. The whole world turned and faded in fragments. This was flight—not the slow motion of the airplane as it is insulated by distance from the ground and all obvious indications of speed, but close and in range of all the things that are hard and deadly. A mailbox, a patch of loose gravel, a barbed-wire fence, a fallen branch—ordinary things—all the ordinary things were remade by velocity into weapons directed against the Riders. At seventy-five miles an hour a corner turned the world into a hill. Leah traveled by, surely stunned and shaken by the sound of their passing.

They rode to Summersville, a hundred flat speedways, a thousand curves away, and he was numb, but not cold: numb as if his body ended below his shoulders and became the machine from there on down. The few cars they passed came at them backward and were lost behind. Loose gravel, in places where the road was being repaired, ripped away beneath his rear wheel, and he recovered only to remember later the fear-born reactions that saved his life. He followed the Riders all the way. They never lost him, and on the river flats again he came up among the leaders and was the first to see a steady ribbon of dark red flame streaming up from the gable of Pinckney's barn.

He passed them all then, and as they watched him, surprised at his speed, he held out his arm and pointed to the barn. This time they slued into the dooryard, still in formation, one after the other. They ran, in the first shock of it, across the road, where they could see the flame silently reaching high above the two silos. The flame turned brighter, to a Halloween orange, and yet no sound came from the house. No one in the house had noticed yet. Slugger ran apart from them, half toward the house, half toward a wide field, and raised his arms.

"The barn!" he yelled. Wilma Berry followed him, frantically imitating his gestures.

"The barn! The cows! The house! Christ! Git! Git!" They all ran to the house, yelling incoherently as the upstairs lights went on.

John went into the kitchen, where the lights had been left on, and there it was, just as they had left it; white, cream-painted and modern in the profitable farm. An electric clock above the sink said four o'clock in the morning. The metal and formica table, the new refrigerator, the chrome and enamel cabinets remained in their places bright and steady—and yet the barn attached to the kitchen was burning, and in it for fuel was dry hay and the grease of cattle. The black telephone sat calmly on its little stand. He picked it up and listened to it buzz.

"Operator," the girl said, and for a moment he wondered what to do, realizing that he had been about to give her his home number. "Operator," she said again. Well, he wouldn't want to wake them up at this hour. "Operator!" she said, and it seemed to him he could hear a slight crackling and a noise of rushing air.

"Fire," he said. "I'm calling from Pinckney's, on the flat. The barn's on fire." He could hear people running in the house, and the hoarse voice of Slugger's father, saying, "What? Where?"

"Give me the firehouse," he said calmly. And then he heard himself saying, "I don't know the number." The bright kitchen looked back at him calmly under fluorescent lights.

They burst into the kitchen, Slugger first, his father coming along behind, his mother in a blue nightgown among the Riders.

"The cows," Mr. Pinckney said. "Git them cows out!" It seemed a long time before the firehouse answered.

"O.K., O.K.," a voice said, "Do what you can. Git your cars off the road. We'll be right out."

With the door to the barn open the whoosh of wind was louder, a gigantic suction carrying with it dust and loose papers. He followed the Riders into the barn as the lights went on. Little straws were drawn up against the ceiling, found cracks and stuck there. Toward the rear of the long barn, down the rows of stanchions, cows were screaming under an orange light that came from above and was brighter than the electric bulbs. Two calves, their eyes rolling and insane, charged awkwardly on splayed hoofs down the manure-smeared cement. They were all forced to take cover beside the heaving cows, except for Slugger's father. His hairy legs wide apart below his nightshirt, bare feet gripping the slippery cement, he raised his big arms and grappled with the second calf.

"Open the doors!" he bellowed, strangely like the cows behind him, "God damn! Open the doors! Open them stalls! Git them goddam critters out!" He had the calf around the belly, and wrestled it down the aisle, the calf kicking out its hind legs while the front legs slid along. The first calf was hopelessly tangled between an upright and the end stanchion, and the end cow had pulled loose and speared it through the ribs with her horn. They both lay heaving, necks twisted, the cow trying to get a purchase on the cement with her hind legs. Her full udder flopped and squashed each time she tried to stand. The calf's mouth opened and closed, but no sound came out of it. Blood was black on the gray cement, and ran down into the urine trough.

The Riders ran down the aisle, John following, and began to open stanchions. The cows immediately backed out, still bellowing, and turned to crowd toward the front of the barn. Some fell to be trampled, to struggle up again, their hides steaming. The Riders stopped halfway down the aisle, raised their hands to their faces against the fire that fell in bonfire bunches down upon the backs of the screaming animals. The metal stanchions clanked and the stench of burning hair came in waves, lessening as the draft sucked it up into the hayloft.

"Leave them be! Git the ones you can git!" Mr. Pinckney came running heavily down to them, to fall as if he had been struck on the head, then slid into the drain trough. He got up and limped back, motioning them out of the barn. A panicked cow came back the wrong way and he stepped aside and smashed his fist into her belly. John found himself beside him and helped to twist the cow's neck back around, his fingers in her eye sockets. Under their combined strength she screamed and turned, a horn bruising John's chest as she swung back toward the front of the barn. They let her go and she crashed, horns hooking, into the side of another cow. Something held the cows back, near the doors, and John brushed away a handful of burning straw as he ran toward the crush. The Riders were climbing over the stanchions to find their way back through the kitchen, and he had time as he ran toward the cows to think, There won't be time.

He jumped up on the back of the cow he had helped turn, then scrambled straight over the angular ridges of their backs, half crawling, trying to avoid horns. A horn did thud against his knee before he managed to slide down on the far side. The end cow and the dying calf formed a barricade at the end of the aisle. The calf in a spasm had kicked its hind legs out to form a rigid fence against the upright. He tried to pull the legs away but they were like steel, only bending as the cows pushed from behind. He ran to the barn door and looked around. His eyes watered and he coughed in the stream of hay dust sucked up past him, but he found an ax in a chopping block. The draft helped pull him back into the bright hole, where he braced himself and brought the ax down on the calf's hock joint, knifing a cow across the nose. The cow screamed, and he was showered by a spurt of blood as the barrier gave way. The calf's other leg bent and broke and John ran limping on his hurt knee ahead of the stampede. He tripped on the chopping block beside the door and dropped the ax as two of the Riders grabbed him and pulled him out of the way. The cows streamed out and crossed the road, udders swinging, broke down a fence and rolled over in the grass, their backs smoking.

He stood in the dooryard, leaning against a young tree. The Riders were now carrying furniture out of the house. Every light in the house was on, and on the side toward the barn the white clapboards were orange in the light of the fire that streamed all along the ridgepole of the barn. The screams of the cows trapped below were higher, and as he tried to get his breath back, retching and spitting dust, the cows' screams melted into the high singing of the fire.

Junior was driving the motorcycles across the road into the field, and he yelled to John to start them up for him. John tried to do it, but his knee wouldn't work right. He found a hay fork and leaned on that, and managed to start the last two engines, then waited, once nearly fainting, until Junior moved them. Suddenly everything was a dirty brown—not just the fire along the roofpeak of the barn, but his hands, the lights of cars approaching from Leah, and Junior's face as he returned.

"For Christ sake!" he heard Junior say. Then he was being dragged along the ground.

"What the hell are you doing?" he said.

A constant stream of bureaus, chairs, clothing on hangers, and cardboard boxes was being carried by above him, and Dianne Rousseau and Gussie Contois bent over him. Junior stood aside, wiping his hands on his pants. "My God! Look at him!" Junior said.

"It's not all his," Dianne said.

"What isn't?" John said, wondering what he was doing on the ground.

"The blood," Junior said, backing away.

"Not mine, I hope," John said, and rubbed his hands over his face. They were covered with blood. "From the cow," he said.

"Are you all right?" Dianne asked.

He looked up at their faces, saw that he would not faint again, and stood up, favoring his knee. "I'm not good for much," he said. "You go and help. I better get out of the way."

He limped across the road, stepping painfully over the fire hose which had been spilled from the hose truck on its way to the river. Chief Atmon straddled the hose, bulky and red-faced, shouting, his dark police uniform wet with sweat.

"Git them cars off the road! What the hell have you got into?" he said to John.

"From the cows—getting the cows out," John said, and went past him. People were running toward the fire, some coming across the fields, their faces shining. A pile of furniture grew beside the motorcycles as more people joined the line to pass back chairs, boxes, and full bureau drawers. The cows ran all together to the far end of the field, then turned and gamboled as if they were playing, and came running back toward the barn.

"Keep them cattle out of the road!" Atmon screamed from his

commanding position astride the slack hoses. But the cattle stopped short next to the broken fence and stared white-eyed at the burning barn. People began to gather in little groups in the field with the cows. All faces pointed toward the fire; the flames were reflected by cheeks and foreheads as if each face were another small fire in the dark field.

John stood leaning on a motorcycle. The barn still stood straight and plumb, fire visible through every crack in the shrinking boards. At each end fire poured out and up, a thick river of pure flame. Even though he stood a hundred yards away the heat pushed against his face and hands and licked at his sweat. Then the ridgepole began to sink, and firemen scrambled off the kitchen roof, holding thick blankets of woven rope toward the fire and throwing down their little hoses. The tank truck backed away as the hoses reeled in, and the side of the house turned brown all at once. A flurry of running men, then a small group pushed their shields back again, as if they were climbing up a steep cliff toward the house, and managed to play the small hoses on the brown clapboards. The big hoses of the pumper still lay in dry folds down the road toward the river.

The ridgepole jackknifed all along its span as the purlins and the beams burned through. The barn folded in on itself like a huge flower closing, imploding down and then exploding upward again in an unbearable pillar of flame, as if the whole barn had turned into pure flame. The people all ran backward in the fields, not able to take their seared eyes away from the fire, but moving back. Nearer the house, a fireman danced in pain and rubbed his face. A shower of white ash began to fall like snow on the field and the people, twisting and billowing in the wind. The firemen crept back again, pulling the large hose. Finally the river water began to come through it in a thick, muddy fountain strong enough to reach the scorched house. Steam swirled along the gutters, and the windows cracked into nothing at the first touch of the water. The fire still rose and whistled in the red mound where the barn had been, but the house was saved. In the few seconds of the barn's collapse the house had not quite burst into flame, and the kitchen, a fuse leading to the house itself, as now being adequately doused with river water.

John began to realize how frightened he had been as the flame had climbed higher through the barn and into the sky over the flats, insatiable and violent. People were carefully examining the fields for sparks and Atmon had organized a patrol to guard the standing hay, sparse as it was, on the flats. No one had thought for a minute that the house could be saved, and yet immediately the big hose had begun to work they were carrying the furniture back inside again, slower this time, more careful of things, slack-armed and weary. He could not go and help them because of his knee, which refused to support him, and he was grateful for the thickening blood, like the campaign ribbons of a soldier, on his face and clothes. He could honorably wait and watch.

As the fire died down, the people began to go home. Firemen still sprayed the house and kitchen, and formed a ring around the barn to scrape a ditch clean against grass fires. The day came hot and hazy, and the wind still crossed the river from Vermont. The Riders straggled out of the house and came over to him. Their uniforms were dirty, torn and sweat-stained. Mr. Pinckney came with them, pale under the deep wrinkles of his face, sick with fatigue. He wore overalls over his nightshirt and his feet sloshed around in old overshoes.

They all turned to look at the farm, too tired to speak.

"You saved the house," John said.

"Saved the house," Mr. Pinckney said, breathing deeply and yet jerkily as if he were about to vomit. "We got insurance—some. Ain't too worried about that. Just hate to see that barn go."

"Damn' good barn," Bob Paquette said, he being the only farmer, beside Slugger, among the Riders.

"Straight, warn't it?" Mr. Pinckney said.

"Straight's a die," Bob said.

"No use crying over spilt milk," Mr. Pinckney said, and then looked around until he found John. "I want to thank you, John," he said in a low voice, as if he were embarrassed. "I mean what you done there, quick's a wink. Like as not you saved us twenty head of cattle. Now I ain't trying to overdo it nor underdo it. Maybe we would've got around in time, maybe no. Maybe none would have thought fast enough to take the ax to that calf and chop off her leg. We lost twenty head in the fire. We could've lost forty head. Insurance never come near covering that. You used your head and you done right. I want to thank you. How's your knee?"

"I can stand on it now," John said. "It's just stiff, that's all. It's O.K."

"The boy'll give you a lift home." He nodded to Slugger. "Sorry I can't offer all of you some breakfast, but the kitchen's all burnt up. Neighbors'll take care of us, but I can't invite you to somebody else's table. Howsomever, I mean to make it up to all of you."

He walked away from them, swinging back and forth, he was so tired, picked up a lace doily from the trampled grass and entered the house.

Bob told John he would take care of his old bike, and to take the ride home with Slugger in the farm pickup. One at a time the Riders left, their girls riding behind, dirty-faced but still erect on the buddy-seats. They drove slowly and carefully now they had been caught out in daylight; careful, too, because they were tired.

CHAPTER 13

After breakfast John took a bath and fell asleep in the tub, woke to hear his mother knocking on the bathroom door, then went to bed and slept until Franklin woke him up at two o'clock in the afternoon. His bruised knee seemed much better.

"You're sort of awake, aren't you, John?" Franklin asked cautiously.

"Sort of," John said, opening his eyes. Franklin stood in front of the gunrack, his hands behind his back.

"Go ahead and take them down, if you want," John said. "I showed you how to look in the breeches to see if they're loaded. They *aren't l*oaded, but look anyway."

Franklin carefully lifted the .30-.30 down, flicked the lever and looked in the chamber. "It's not loaded," he said, then held it awkwardly to his shoulder and sighted out the window.

"If the woods weren't closed we could take it out and shoot it," John said.

"We could?"

"You wouldn't be afraid of the kick, would you?"

"Well . . . Is it bad?"

"You've got enough muscle on you. It wouldn't hurt you, as long as you held it tight against your shoulder."

"I'd hold it good and tight," Franklin said eagerly.

"If we could get a little rain the woods would open again."

"Yeah," Franklin said. He put the rifle back in the rack and sat down in the big leather chair. "You going to get up, John?"

"Sure, in a minute."

Franklin said, "Do you remember Herman and Verman, in the book?"

"Yes. The two boys who moved in in back of Penrod's alley."

"You remember how they beat up on the big bully who was picking on Penrod?"

"They sure finished him off, didn't they, Frank?"

Franklin looked down at his sneakers, then tightened a loose bowknot in the laces. "I was Penrod up to then— You know what I mean? I wasn't really Penrod—you sort of stand off and laugh at him half the time, but still wish you were *him*. And then they call Herman and Verman 'colored' and it's hard not to think I'm maybe Herman or Verman. But I'm not! My aunt doesn't have a goiter, whatever that is! I wouldn't chop off my brother's finger, either, just because he said to do it!"

"That book was written a long time ago, Frank."

"I don't care about that!" Franklin was really upset about it. His mouth trembled, and he seemed to be about to say something more, but remained silent.

"There are other books, Frank," John said.

"I can forget it. That bothers me. Like I was laughing at Herman and Verman because they're black and funny. But I'm not too funny and I could never have beat up that bully. Never." Franklin looked up again and stopped, watching John with an odd, distant expression on his face. "I sure wish it would rain, John," he said.

John reached over to his desk for his cigarettes, not wanting to look Franklin in the eyes.

"You never forget, do you, John?" Franklin asked in an intense, emergency sort of voice, as if he must get the question out all at once and get it over with.

"What's the matter?" John asked, startled.

"I just asked."

"It isn't a question of forgetting, Frank. If you mean about you . . . you mean am I prejudiced? You ought to know I'm not. I don't think I am. What's bothering you, Frank? You tell me now!"

"Your mother said we should be nice to you because you got all upset when you found out we were coming!" The words came in a rush, with tears, and for a second John felt the familiar desire to retreat, even began to plan. Then he threw the cigarettes back onto the desk and sat on the edge of his bed. He took hold of Franklin's thin shoulders and shook him until he stopped.

"Frank, can you think of any other reason why I might have been upset? Think, now."

"I don't know."

"I didn't *know* you and Jenny Lou then. You know why I'm home? You know Bruce is in the hospital, probably dying, and that this isn't a very happy place. I didn't think you, or anybody, would have a good time here. That's why I got upset. Frank, I didn't know you and Jenny Lou were colored until I met you at the station. That didn't have anything to do with it! I thought you knew me better than that by now."

"You're not mad about it any more?" Franklin looked at him with a certain amount of suspicion, tears still shiny on his face.

"I'm glad you came." And he realized that he clearly *was* glad they had come, not just because Jenny Lou had taken over his mother completely. His feelings about Franklin were far from the resigned acceptance he had believed. A strange enlightenment, he thought, for John Cotter. "I really am glad you came. I really am glad about it, Frank."

Franklin smiled.

The door at the bottom of the kitchen stairs creaked, and Gladys Cotter called: "Johnny? Are you awake? Telephone!" She came running up the stairs and into the room. "Well, Franklin! Are you and Johnny having a nice talk?"

"Yes," Franklin said.

"Telephone, Johnny. You know, I think it's Billy Muldrow. I wonder what he wants with you, Johnny?"

"Tell him I'll be right down, Mother."

"I wonder what Billy Muldrow could want with you?"

"I'll tell you when I talk to him."

"I can't see what that old tramp could want with you."

"Look, Mother, will you please go down and tell him I'll be right down as soon as I can? I have to go to the bathroom first." Gladys went back downstairs.

"She sort of irks you, doesn't she?" Franklin said.

"She sort of does, sometimes."

"You know an old tramp?"

"Billy's not a tramp. He's not so old, either."

"How old is he?"

"Not more than forty, anyway."

"That's not *old?*"

When he picked up the phone, Billy's worried, apologetic voice began: "Johnny, I'm sorry to of woke you up. Your ma says you was up all night and I'm real sorry to of got you up."

"That's all right, Billy."

"Johnny, you recall I told you Atmon was going to git me blacklisted over in Wentworth Junction too? He done it."

"That bastard."

"I was just wondering if you'd git me a case of beer, Johnny. I'm downstreet now, calling from Futzie's. Futzie won't sell me no beer, neither. I'll give you the money, Johnny. I can meet you at the foot of Pike Hill and we'll go have a couple at my place. O.K., Johnny?"

"Sure, Billy. Give me time to get something to eat. I'll meet you at the bottom of the hill."

"I can't thank you good enough, Johnny. You're the only friend I got in this whole lousy goddam town. I mean that."

"It's no trouble, Billy. I'll see you later." He hung up.

"You want to come with me?" he said to Franklin.

"I don't know," Franklin said, "I guess so. . . ."

"Come on. It won't hurt you. . . ." He stopped, wondering why he wanted Franklin to come. Usually he spent a lot of time in like situations trying tactfully to keep people from going with him. "You aren't afraid of Billy, are you?"

"No." Franklin was obviously examining his feelings. He scowled and bit his finger. "I want to go, I guess," he said.

"You haven't gone out of the house very much since you've been here."

"But there's so much *in* the house."

Jenny Lou came in from the kitchen, her arms crossed, her face stern. "Gladys wants to know do you want some mustard on your lamb sandwich."

"Just a little bit," John said. Franklin grinned at him.

"He wants a little tiny bit of mustard," Jenny Lou called as she went back into the kitchen, "Pecky, isn't he, Gladys?"

"I'll go with you, John," Franklin said.

"You sure you want to? You don't have to if you don't want to."

"I'd tell you, John, I would. I'd tell you if I didn't want to go."

"You ought to get out of the house more, anyway. You know, Frank, you can see the whole of Leah from the top of Pike Hill. That's the funny thing about it. It doesn't look very high at all to look at it from the bottom, but when you get up there it seems high as a mountain. You can see far away from up there—Vermont, Cascom River, Connecticut River—just like being on a high mountain."

"I'd like to see that," Franklin said, then added in a hesitant voice, "About *Penrod* and all . . ."

"Yes, Frank?"

"I still love that book," Franklin said.

John was a sophomore in high school when he first met Billy Muldrow to know him at all. He went to Billy's old shack with Bob Paquette and Junior Stevens, Keith Goss and Keith's cousin, Merton Goss. Sometimes there would be one or two others. Of course, they were too young to buy beer then, and sometimes Billy would get it for them. Almost always he would give them beer or hard cider if they came to see him, and would talk to them as if they were men, not condescendingly. So they felt vastly superior to him, laughed at him behind his back and pulled tricks on him. They sawed out the braces of his outhouse seat fairly often, let the air out of his truck tires and wrote his name among the smut on the walls of the men's room in the Town Hall. John had done it along with the rest of them. There was no organized attack against Billy, but when they felt like writing dirty words on the walls of men's rooms, when they had to destroy something, this one older man with the simple-mindedness and bad taste to treat fifteen-year-old kids as equals became their target.

Stranger people than Billy lived in Leah, but Billy's strangeness was at least approachable. Others, like the pale, baby-faced old man who cooked at the diner and who asked the boys to come around the corner with him; the woman who dressed like a man and her companion, a young, almost pretty but huge, muscled girl who could have taken on nearly any man in town bare-knuckled; the laugher—a big man with an intelligent-seeming middle-aged face who suddenly and for no known reason would begin to laugh and continue to laugh all day long—these were just a little too frightening. Billy could be hurt more. They all realized it; not only realized it but discussed it and decided on Billy. They hadn't discussed why they wanted to hurt anyone. The fact of destruction—their unspoken need to destroy—they did not justify or even recognize. Yet the subject of their persecution they chose with lucid, frightening intelligence. There must be something to destroy—not an idiot like the laugher; not a queer like the old cook whose malady, though hysterically funny to them, opened dank, unsounded parts of the unknown; not the woman transvestite because they believed she might be something they called "morphadite," which was physical and freakish and thus not quite all her fault, and also because she was partly, or probably, a woman. Her companion was a woman too, and even more, a young woman who excited them and whose giant, muscled frame, severe dark hair and fierce eyes promised violence they did not dare unleash. Billy Muldrow was not too old, not too frightening, not too far beyond the bounds of society to be hurt: he was chosen.

No one, as far as John knew, had ever accused Billy of writing dirty words in public places. Everyone must have known that it had been done mostly by kids, and that Billy was not stupid enough to write his name under the primitive but terribly adequate drawings above the urinals. Yet if Mr. Bemis, the town clerk, every time he went to the toilet saw Billy's name as he smelled the disinfectant, the unclean dingy stink of the public latrine—if Chief Atmon, if any man of Leah were continually reminded in that place of Billy Muldrow—a connection with the sordid, born originally, perhaps, of the honest burgher's disapproval of Billy's independent life, would grow into more than a passive thing. Maybe this started Billy's feud with the town of Leah. More likely it had started long before John knew about it, out of Billy's character and Bemis' and Atmon's. No doubt the matrons of the town would never under any conditions have accepted Billy Muldrow, but that tolerance for the wild and different most men have in the face of their wives' disapproval had been broken down over the years. Billy no longer had even the status of town character. No amused forbearance, no tolerance at all toward Billy now. Even Mr. Bemis, whom John thought to be a tolerant and easy man, had no good word to say about Billy Muldrow. The riot at the movie matinée had turned their disapproval into a kind of hatred, had given Billy a prison record. Atmon needed no other reason for the black list.

Franklin stayed in the car while John went into Anna's to buy the beer. While Anna gruntingly hoisted the case out of the refrigerator and up to the counter, John watched through the grimy window. Franklin sat up straight, not quite looking at the people who walked by, the people not quite managing not to look at Franklin. He was so black, so glaringly black on the streets of Leah.

As they drove toward Pike Hill, Franklin said: "You're buying beer for this man because they won't let him buy it for himself. Is that right?"

"That's right. They black-listed him."

"Black-listed him," Franklin said.

"You're thinking of 'black.' "

"I always think of it," Franklin said.

"Black is bad and white is good—you know—like people were afraid of the dark."

"That's very interesting," Franklin said.

"I guess Billy'll be waiting at the bottom of the hill."

"John, you don't think this man deserves to be on the black list?"

"No, I don't. I don't believe in black lists, for one thing."

"Neither do I," Franklin said. "I believe the way you do, John."

"That's good," John said quickly, surprised at his sudden, almost paternal reaction. It was paternal. It must be. God knows he had never felt *that* before. For Franklin it was a declaration of friendship—almost of faith, and he had no real desire to dodge Franklin's claim. *I believe the way you do. . . .*

Billy waited in his old truck, parked carefully off the widened end of Maple Street on the edge of the brushy pasture that covered the town side of Pike Hill. He sat upright, the windows of the cab closed as if he were ill at ease so close to the houses, the lawns and hedges of the residential neighborhood. John pulled in behind the truck, and Billy watched through the rear window of the cab, a quizzical, disappointed expression on his face as he tried to make out who Franklin was. John walked over and opened the truck door.

"Hi, John," Billy said. "Who you got with you?"

"Just a friend of mine, Billy. You come and meet him."

Billy climbed out and saw Franklin, who stood hesitantly beside the car.

"Billy, this is Frank Persons. He's staying at our house."

"Well!" Billy said. "I says who in hell can that be with Johnny? How're you, Frank?" He seemed relieved to find that it was only a little boy he had to meet. They shook hands, Franklin trying to smile, his eyes going up and down as he tried to take in all of the tall, big-handed man. Billy grinned ferociously and let Franklin's hand go. Franklin flexed his fingers.

"You ain't got much of a handshake, Frank. Felt like a handfulla fishworms. Try her again! That's better. Didn't hurt none, did it? I never meant to squash you the first time, Frank."

Franklin nodded, smiling uncertainly, and put his hands in his pockets.

"You git the beer, Johnny? How much it cost you?" Billy took out four dollars and a fifty-cent piece and slapped the pile into John's hand.

"Wasn't that much, Billy."

"Near enough. Now we'll go up to my house and have a couple, O.K.? Best you ride up front next to me, Frank. You're liable to git throwed off the truck bed."

The truck ground and jumped ruts in low-low most of the way. John stood balanced behind the cab, which twisted back and forth, alarmingly independent of the truck bed. Leah flattened out below in its valley.

They passed the old Huckins graveyard on the height of the land and turned around into the tall pines near Billy's shack. The wind in the broad pines hissed steadily, audible even above the unmuffled coughing of the truck. Occasional hardwood leaves, blown a long way up the hill, flattened against the trunks and hung fluttering, meshed in the long needles of the pines.

A hundred yards from Billy's shack, the truck stopped. John looked in through the back window to see Billy pointing excitedly. Billy turned around and spoke in a high voice John could hear tinnily through the window: "See! See! See the deer!"

At first he saw nothing but the dark pines and a few red stalks of blackberry bushes, but then the deer appeared plain and whole through a clump of little birch. A doe, it lifted a big head, enormous ears veed, and watched them. The neck thinned almost to nothing below the head, then thickened toward the brisket. The whole body presented itself, then faded; then in a blink became vivid and enormous. The white along the belly of the deer and along the inside of the legs seemed the whitest white he had ever seen. It made the birches look gray, it was so white and clean. Big eyes were black and deep, the darkest points among the trees. Then the doe turned one ear halfway around, raised her head and flicked her white flag before taking one huge, graceful bound in which she seemed suspended in thick, slow air. When she came to the ground again she froze, this time completely in the open—even the black hooves and dewclaws were visible, even the thin whiskers along the face, small and black as spider legs. So much tension, such cocked, springing energy in that neck and along that sharp ear! John felt that if he were to touch the deer he would be electrocuted.

The doe looked quickly back into the murk of the brush, turned her head to examine the truck with her other eye, then moved her head again, ears turning and quivering slightly as the truck's engine creaked and cooled. John leaned tensely across the top of the cab, trying to breathe slowly, trying to keep his nostrils from moving as he breathed. One second the deer was plain and clear, the next only a pair of ears and a shaft of smooth brown neck faded to the grayness of the million-lined brush—one black eye at a great depth of grayness. Then a white flag bounded silently past trees. Two more flags appeared beside it, one much larger than the other two: a buck and another, smaller doe, perhaps one of this year's skippers, had been watching too.

The truck started and lurched forward. Billy parked next to his shack and jumped out, the case of beer in his arms.

"Did you see the buck? Oh, *Johnny!*"

"I just saw him at the end," John said.

"Oh, I seen him! You see the doe look around at him? Two, three times. Looked straight at him. I seen him clear. Eight pointer. Seen him before. Wasn't that something now, Johnny?"

"Was that a wild deer?" Franklin asked.

"Wild as wild," Billy said. "Frank, you saw something! Lot more'n most goddam hunters see. Warn't that doe nice and fat? Hundred, hundred-ten pounds dressed out. Buck'll go two hundred. I seen him around all summer. You see him, Frank?"

"I saw something run off after the first one went," Franklin said.

"Sure you did. You picked him out! Oh, *Jesus!* Johnny, you see him?"

"I'm glad Frank saw them too," John said.

"So am I," Franklin said.

"I *love* deer," Billy said. "I just *love* deer. There ain't *nothing* I love better than deer. I love to see, shoot and eat deer! There ain't nothing better than a deer. I love to gut 'em and skin 'em. Prettiest thing there is on earth. By far. Ain't *nothing* can match a deer! I see a deer, I feel good all day. Just to see it. Don't care if I shoot it or not, now or later. I love deer."

They went into Billy's little yellow house. Billy cleaned off the one chair and set a box on end for Franklin. "Sit down," he said. "By God! How about you, Frank? You like beer?"

"I never had any," Franklin said, looking at John as if to ask permission.

"Give him a little to try it," John said.

"Hell, here's a can, Frank. You don't finish it, I will. You don't care for it, don't drink it. I recall when Johnny, here, when he was a little older than you, he used to come up and see me once in a while with some of the boys. He couldn't stand beer, you could tell, but by the Jesus he'd stuff her down. Look like he'd rather suck woodpecker eggs. You got to learn to like it."

Billy settled back on his cot and loosened his overall suspenders, laughing and burping.

Franklin held his beer stiffly in front of him, smelled it but didn't drink until John did. Then he took a small sip.

"You like it?" Billy asked, about to grin.

"It's not as bad as it smells," Franklin said.

Billy leaned back to laugh. "You know, Johnny," he said finally, "it sure is funny, now, a boy about Frank's age. How old are you, Frank? About twelve?" He winked at John.

"Ten," Franklin said. "That's all."

"Well, now. Thought you was older than that." He winked at John again. "Anyways, you take your average, normal, regular boy of ten, twelve, fourteen. He just naturally don't care for beer. Give him a couple years and by the Jesus you got to watch him he don't drink anything'll run downhill!" He leaned back again and laughed and laughed. Franklin evidently thought that was pretty funny, too. He took a larger, longer pull at his can.

"That deer, though," Billy said. "Frank, you don't git to see a deer that close to, once a year. You can see them in the fields at night with your headlights, or early in the morning 'way far across, next the woods. You don't seldom come across deer like we done today. Johnny, you recall that fall you come home from service? We hunted some that year."

"I'll never forget that time, Billy."

"I guess not. Well, Frank, I met Johnny out in the woods—Cascom side of Pike Hill, it was. First day of the season, first of November. Warm day, wet and quiet—been raining for two days and everything was soaked clean through. Quiet. So quiet I seen Johnny 'fore I heard him, scratching right through all them blackberry bushes under the apple trees. . . ."

He had been particularly fed up with Bruce, with his mother and father and the town of Leah, and it was one of those times when he didn't have enough money to take off. His discharge hadn't come yet. He was on terminal leave, and somehow his pay and the few hundred dollars he'd saved were snafued up with his discharge. He'd spent his travel pay and he had nothing he could do but wait until the Army got around to straightening things out. Hunting licenses were free to servicemen, so he went hunting. He could have borrowed a few dollars from his father, but this time his own money was coming and he waited for it, too broke even to buy beer. Just to get away from the town he took his rifle and climbed Pike Hill, slowly worked his way through the abandoned, grown-over Huckins farm, not really trying to hunt, but going as slowly and silently as possible, out of habit.

Near some apple trees several partridges zoomed up and whistled through the branches, down across the bushes and out of sight before he got near enough to find them on the ground. The leaves underfoot were so quiet he began to suspect the birds had been jumped by something or somebody else. He searched carefully, trying to find one on the ground, trying to pick out one of the straggly little jack-in-the-box heads. There were many partridges that year; bunches of seven or eight fed together. Nearer the apple trees he saw one bird nervously walking and ducking around in the blackberries, and he waited for a clear shot at its head. A body-shot with the .30-.30 and the plump bird would explode into fragments of torn pink flesh and brown feathers. Yet the head, the size of a quarter on a neck thin as a pencil under the fluffed feathers, never came clearly in sight. The partridge strutted, skulked and bobbed along in its apparently aimless, idiotic fashion until it was securely out of sight in the brambles. A moment later he heard it flush out and skim away.

All this time Billy had been watching him, standing in plain sight, laughing silently. Finally, Billy sucked in air and let out a long, rolling belch. John moved his head slowly—something he was thankful for when he saw Billy. Instead of the kidding he expected, Billy nodded his head.

"Well, Johnny," he said, "maybe you'll make a hunter someday after all."

"I sure thought there was a deer made that noise," John said.

"Could of been. Sounded just like a deer. I got a deer to come to me once, making that same, identical noise." He tried it again. "Dang hard on the tonsils, though."

The sun came out in the fresh, washed air and the apples on one tree shone as red as the glass balls on a Christmas tree; on another they were waxy yellow, striped with pink. Billy threw a stick into the branches, and four yellow apples came bouncing down. He picked one up and snapped his fingernail on it. The frost had not softened it. It made a noise like a tight little drum.

"I got to pick them apples tomorrow," Billy said, tossing it to John. The apple was ice-cold, sweet and puckery, leaving a taste in John's mouth clean as spring water.

"Peach apple," Billy said. "Late, though. This here tree's always late." He took a bite, chewed out the juice and spat out the meat.

"You know, Johnny, sometimes I don't go hunting at all, just mosey around the woods from apple tree to apple tree, tasting. I'll bet you I know about every apple tree in the woods. Beech trees—when there's beechnuts sometimes I just grub around all afternoon eating beechnuts. Same in spring. I act just like a bear. First strawberries, then raspberries, blueberries, blackberries, cranberries, checkerberries—I even like juniper berries. I love buttnuts, too. Sometimes I act just like a bear."

"You eat ants and grubs?"

"Haw HAW *Hell* no!" Billy yelled, raring back, his eyes watering. Then he looked sham-thoughtful. "Though I got a mind to. I don't imagine grubs would be too bad, fried up nice." He nodded his head, mock-serious, then burst loose and roared for a while. Then he picked up his rifle and handed it to John.

"This here's Old Bungaloo, Johnny. You ever see her before?"

He had never seen the rifle in Billy's shack. He shook his head.

"You ding-dang right you never! I keep her out of sight in case somebody comes around I ain't home."

John put down his little .30-.30 and hefted the heavy rifle.

"It must weigh ten pounds," he said. It was an old Winchester '95 lever action, heavily breeched and rugged as a club. "Some piece," he said. "Old Bungaloo?"

"That's what my dad called her." Billy turned Old Bungaloo upside down and pointed to a line of little dents along the stock.

"Twenty-nine deer been shot with Old Bungaloo, and that don't count the ones I shot with her—ten, fifteen more. I never made no notches."

"Why not?"

"Tell the truth, I forgot the first couple times. Seemed afterward it warn't right to go notching in cold blood, so to speak. We going hunting?" Billy looked at the sun, watched the leaves for wind, and nodded his head. "You want to git a deer Johnny? You do what I say and maybe we can show you one. I ain't going to shoot it for you. *Now*. You go slow and easy back down to the crick. You know where that great big hemlock fell across?"

He did all that Billy told him to do, and late that afternoon he killed his first deer. He'd been walking some, standing still most of the time, or sitting. For once he was not impatient, not looking over the tops of rises or around the edges of thick brush tangles as if he could, by seeing more places, by covering more of the space of the woods, find the standing, clearly outlined deer the impatient hunter always sees in his mind.

This time he did not expect to see a deer at all. He followed Billy's instructions as he might have followed the steps of an old ritual, and the ritual itself occupied all of his attention; he hardly had time to look for deer, so carefully he moved and placed his feet.

Then came the time, a few seconds out of all the years of his life that he would always remember fully—a time made vivid and everlasting by an act perfect, instinctive and final. It seemed like love: he first saw a white flag flickering through the black trunks of a spruce grove, angling away from him, yet heading toward a small clearing open to him through a chance avenue of trees. The deer had seen him first and ran low to the ground, stealthy even in its long leaps, silent on the waterlogged spruce needles. As he saw the deer's long gray body his rifle came up and for once, still under the spell of the ritual of slowness, he did not begin firing through the trees. He waited, watching the brighter clearing through his sights, the black bar of his front sight waving at the level of a deer's chest. It seemed a miracle that the deer came on and crossed the space of daylight. He fired just ahead of the deer as it leaped for darkness and heard a rattle of aimless hoofs and a thud. His spent cartridge tinkled on the breach and fell brightly to the spruce needles. His hand flicked the lever and the action slid forward with a new shell in its teeth. It snapped shut loudly. As he ran forward he automatically put the hammer on half-cock—and the deer was there. A miracle again—so big, so obvious against the ground now that it was dead. He poked one large round bottomless eye with his rifle barrel. The deer was dead.

He saw now for the first time that the deer was a buck, with four perfect, beautiful tines on the left antler. On the right a strangely dwarfed single spike grew like a root. And then he thought it was too bad the buck had run into such bad luck in a single season—a dwarfed horn and a .30-.30 slug. He might have been a bachelor buck with his strange antler; a poor, frustrated fellow who ran into bad luck wherever he went. And yet he was a beautiful animal, strong and muscular, with a fine clean coat. And heavy.

John fired three shots in the air, counting slowly to five between each, then rolled up his sleeves and spread the linen-white belly, legs open, to the air. He was still trembling, still awed by the amazing, beautiful treasure the deer was to him then.

His knife drew through the hair easily, then through the skin and peritoneum. He was careful. The bullet had gone clean through the ribcage, and he was able to draw the stomach and entrails out unbroken and steaming, genitals attached. In the round, hot heap, peristalsis slowly, steadily worked. Billy came, and John borrowed Billy's big knife to chop through the pelvis and clean out the anus. The heart was smashed, but the kidneys and liver were whole and clean.

When the deer was gutted and ready, Billy crowed with joy and whacked John on the back.

"A buck! Johnny, ain't you happy?"

He was happy. He could only grin and rub his bloody hands together. The blood rolled off easily on the spruce needles. Much later he remembered and wondered why, with all the blood and matter he had probed with his hands, the image of the old Filipino had never come; the old women hadn't screamed in his head.

But they hadn't, thank God. It was too perfect. He sat down, shaking, leaned against a tree and took out a cigarette. Billy reached into the deer and took out another small handful of lung.

"Clean as a whistle. No sense dragging more than we have to. Let him bleed out a while, too. No hurry. We ain't got more than a couple hundred yards to drag. By God, Johnny, you done good!"

"He was running," John said. "I was right back—look right down there—I was right back there. Right back by that blowdown. Ash. See it? He was running."

Billy paced it off, counting out loud. "Seventy-five yards!" he called as he started back, counting again. "Seventy-five yards and a hair," he said.

"He was running," John said, "but he wasn't going out straight. He saw me first. I went slow like you told me." He found that he was out of breath. The cigarette had given him the hiccups. He tried to erase an inane grin from his face, but couldn't. His cheeks ached with it. He looked up through the trees to the sky, pale fall blue and turning cold; fine cirrus clouds were forming high up above Leah.

"Well, ain't you going to tell me from the start?" Billy said.

He could see the white flag flickering past the black trunks of the spruces, and the black front sight waving again. He told it to Billy from the beginning. When he came to the end and found the deer, the grin fastened itself to his face again.

"There he was!"

"There he is!" Billy said, slapping his knee. "Give me your rifle!"

John handed it over. Billy took his knife and pressed the point into the bottom of the stock, leaving a little triangular dent.

"There you are. You got a witness to prove it."

Finally they began to drag the deer toward Billy's house. When they reached Billy's dooryard they hoisted it into the back of the truck and went inside. John had blisters on both hands.

"You can have him weighed if you want," Billy said, "but I'll tell you right now he weighs a hundred-seventy pounds. I dragged out enough deer in my time. I can tell every time. You take him down to the freezers and have him weighed. You just do that. Hundred-seventy pounds."

"I'll give you a hindquarter, Billy."

"Like hell you will! Never you mind about that. I got more meat picked out right now than I can use."

"You got yours already?"

"Hell, no! Know where it is, though. Keeps better in this warm weather, it ain't dead. Git my buck any day I want, providing some damn' fool don't run on him meanwhile."

"You take the liver."

"Well, O.K., Johnny. I'm kind of sweet on liver. I'll take it."

"How about some backstrap? Peel some off, Billy."

"Nope. Nothing doing. Now, we going to have a snort?"

They were both a little drunk on hard cider when they brought the deer down to Leah and hung it in the Cotter garage. John's father brought beer out to them and they all stood around with the neighbors, admiring, hefting and patting the deer. When Bruce came home he had one thing to say: "I suppose Billy shot it for you."

Franklin sat on the edge of his box, his beer held carefully in both hands, his expression tense and interested. Billy had come to the place where they were dragging the deer out of the woods.

"Heaviest hundred-seventy pound deer I ever dragged out," he said. "I told Johnny. I says, 'That deer weighs a hundred-seventy pounds.' You know what they weighed him down to the freezer lockers?"

Franklin shook his head.

"Hundred-sixty-eight pounds! Now that was next day. See, Frank? He bled and dried out a little that night. I bet my skivvies he weighed one-seventy on the nose, we got him dragged up here. I dragged out enough deer, by God. I can tell every time!"

Franklin shook his head in amazement, and John was startled to see on his face a quick look of amusement.

"How was the liver?" Franklin asked. By his expression he didn't like liver, but the idea of eating the liver out of the deer obviously fascinated him.

"Tender," Billy said. "Tender as all hell, as I recall."

"What's *that?*" Franklin asked, pointing under the table and drawing his feet up.

Jake the raccoon put his pointed nose out into the light, and snarled.

"That's Jake," John said. "He's a friend of Billy's."

"Sometimes he is and sometimes he ain't," Billy said. "He sort of hangs around here."

Franklin watched the raccoon warily.

"He's wild?" he asked.

"He is when he wants to be," Billy said. "The other day I caught him thinking how good one of my chickens would be could he git the feathers off. He could, too. I laid down the law, by God! I put the law on them chickens, far as Jake's concerned. Old Jake, he got kind of riled up in the process and so didn't I. What come of it, he took off and never come back for three days. Figured he never would come back, but I guess he cooled off some. He's a hell of a lush, far as cider's concerned. Can't leave it alone. That's why he's mad now. Got himself a hangover."

The raccoon snarled again and hit Billy's leg with a long arm, claws scratching against the denim.

"You watch it, you goddam drunk!" Billy yelled, leaning over and glaring into Jake's determined eyes. Jake backed away, snarling.

"I always give him some," Billy said resignedly. He took down a jug of amber cider and poured a bowlful. Jake lapped a few times, shivered and backed away, then approached cautiously and began to drink.

"He hates it sometimes, but he can't leave it alone. Let that be a lesson to you, Frank," Billy said.

Franklin was so absorbed in the sight he hardly heard.

"Look at him lick it up!" he said. Jake stopped lapping and gave Franklin a wary glance. "That's O.K.," Franklin said quickly.

"Don't let him scare you, Frank," Billy said. "He knows he gits rough with the guests he'll be nursing a sore hide!" He laughed and stamped his foot. Jake looked suspiciously at the foot, then went back to his cider.

"Did you catch him?" Franklin asked.

"Nope. He just come bumming around. Lazy. Too damn' lazy to catch his own living. Eats some frogs, though, down to the swamp."

"He eats *frogs?*"

"Why, sure. Killed my cat, too. Et ***her***. That damn' coon'll eat anything at all."

"Didn't you get mad when he ate your cat?"

"Well, yes, I did, Frank. But Old Jake's just as good as a cat—maybe better. More company."

"I mean, didn't you *like* the cat?"

"I guess I liked her well enough for most purposes. She didn't particular care for me, howsomever. You know cats. They just don't give a damn."

"I guess that's so," Franklin said. "Not like a dog."

"You damn' well right, Frank." Billy sat for a moment, then jerked his head up and stared at John. "Johnny, you remember Daisy?"

"Sure I do, Billy," John said.

Billy's face evened out; his eyes seemed to grow still and dark. He became as serious as John had ever seen him.

"Atmon shot her. Or Bemis did it. One."

"No, Billy!"

"Yes they did—one. Bragged about it too. . . ." His voice went high and unstable at the end.

"How come?" John asked, half believing it. Billy shook his head jerkily, hunched his shoulders and put his mouth into a hurt, childish line.

"Don't *know,*" he said, his voice rising on the second word. "When I was gone . . . You know, when I was gone . . ."

"Why would they do a thing like that?"

"Said she was running deer. Said she was running deer. . . ." Billy tried to control his voice. He shook himself like a dog and reached for his pipe, set his face but couldn't manage it. He took a long drink, then, too carefully, set his can on the windowsill. "Can you imagine that, Johnny?" he asked.

"Bemis? I didn't think he'd do a thing like that."

"Oh, he would, all right. They was hunting together. Running *deer,* for Christ sake! Daisy *never* run no deer. Be like a squirrel running a God-damn' lousy damn' bastard *horse!"* He looked apologetically at Franklin, then added softly, "For Christ sake. She was just a little bitty rabbit dog. She didn't care for *nothing* but rabbits."

"Nobody took care of her when you were gone?"

"I asked everybody would they take her. Bob Paquette said he would. Now it ain't Bob's fault, I know that. She just come back here looking for me all the time. Bob, he wrote me a letter. Only letter I got when I was away. He told me he just couldn't keep Daisy to home. She come back to Pike Hill looking for me. Bob come and got her back two, three times. Next time she was dead. Bob says he found her out by the road, right next the graveyard there, shot four times through the body. It was Atmon himself told me he and Bemis found her running deer. Wouldn't say which one done it. Maybe he and Bemis both had some fun. . . ."

"I'm sorry," Franklin said.

"I asked the game warden could they do that? He says they ain't supposed to. How do you like that? They ain't *supposed* to! He says you know for sure who done it? Goddam right I know! He says you better git a lawyer and witnesses and habeas corpusses and e pluribus unems and Christallmighty! A man killed my dog, that's all I know! Daisy, she was the sweetest little dog you ever see. She never hurt nobody, except rabbits. She was all hell on rabbits. Shot forty rabbits front of Daisy one year. I damn' near lived on rabbits that year. You ought to heard Daisy on a hot trail. *Ki Yi Yi!* Jesus! Wouldn't she go right out straight? Daisy'd dream about rabbits. Sometimes she'd wake right up out of her sleep a-running and a-yelling! Right after them rabbits, right out of her sleep! You'd see her little legs begin to twitching and her nose to puckering. Didn't she look ashamed to herself when she woke up! She'd look all around pretending they was a rabbit under my bed. I'd look down at her and grin, then she'd look up at me and give a shit-eating grin and go back to sleep. Damnedest dog."

Billy reached over and weighed Franklin's beer in his hand. "You ain't doing too bad, Frank." He opened a couple of cans and handed one to John. "You ever see a beagle, Frank?"

Franklin nodded. "They're nice little dogs. My uncle Jaynis has one."

"Best dog there is, bar none. I aim to git me another come the time I git twenty dollars together. I don't hope to git one nice as Daisy. You don't git one dog like her your whole life." His mouth formed into the crooked line of the hurt child again and his eyes turned darker. They seemed to be sinking deep into his head. The beer can crumpled slightly in his big hand.

"You know what I'd do if I run acrosst them two doing that to Daisy?" He spoke softly. "I'd shoot their legs off, only I don't mean their legs." He looked meaningfully at John. "And I'd leave 'em die slow out in the woods all night laying on the cold ground like Daisy done. A man's got to be *mean* to shoot a little dog like that, Johnny. I can't understand it, he'd have to be so mean." He drank, spilling a few drops on his shirt and overalls.

Franklin watched him, frowning in a tense effort to hide his pity. And it was pity, John felt, not just sympathy, as if Franklin knew better than Billy that people could be that mean. He looked quickly at John, and caught his eye for a moment. The look said clearly, "I can't stand much more of this."

Jake twirled his empty bowl across the floor, then looked out into the cleared space in the middle of the room. He stood splay-footed, breathing deeply, his muzzle slowly moving from side to side. He looked like a drunk in Futzie's looking for an argument.

"Drunk's a coot," Billy said disgustedly. Jake growled. "I give him too much. He's O.K. with a little—gits kind of playful. But he's a ornery old critter gits he too big a bellyful. *Jake!* You mind your P's and Q's now or I'll boot your ass out of here! Mind you don't do no business on the floor. I'll rub your nose in it like I done before." Aside, to John and Franklin: "He kind of loses control of his puckerstring sometimes."

Jake looked from Billy to John, then for a long time at Franklin.

"What's he looking at me for?" Franklin asked plaintively.

"He likes you. The old slob's gitting sentimental now. He won't hurt you none," Billy said. "Let him set on your lap if he wants."

Jake slowly approached.

"I don't know if I want him to," Franklin said. He sat stiffly, waiting. Jake put his paws on the box and looked up at Franklin. When he jumped to Franklin's lap Franklin jumped too, and the box, the spilling beer, Franklin, Jake, and all nearly went over. For a second Jake looked like the man in the circus balancing himself with practiced calm on top of several teetering boxes. It looked as if Jake himself kept the whole business from toppling over. Franklin, shaken by the experience, hardly dared to move his hand as Jake licked it for spilled beer.

"Pet him, Frank. He loves attention," Billy said. "Go on, now; he won't hurt you none. I told you, he *likes* you. Once old Jake makes up his mind he likes you, you could step on his balls and he wouldn't do nothing."

Franklin cautiously put his hand on Jake's head. The raccoon responded like a fat puppy—coy and fawning.

"It's kind of disgusting, ain't it, John?" Billy said. "He gits like that. By the *gee,* he'll hate himself in the morning."

"It's getting pretty late," John said.

"Wait a minute," Billy said. "Listen!" John heard nothing but the wind, now coming back into his consciousness, whistling and sighing past the shack.

"Thought I heard something." Billy cocked his head and closed his eyes. "Thought I heard the fire whistle—wouldn't be too damn' surprised I did." He shook his head. "There! Heard her again!"

"I heard a whistle," Franklin said.

"I did too," John said. The frantic *moo* of the steam whistle on the firehouse came to them clearly in a lull of wind.

"One, two, three," Billy counted, "thirty. Two. Wait a minute.

One, two, three. Now wait . . . Four short. Thirty-two—that's down by the river, from the railroad bridge to the Northlee town line. Four short— Forestry call! We can see that from the height of the land. Come on!"

Jake ran for the corner beneath Billy's bed, and Billy grabbed the beer.

Outside, the sky was bright as clear noon, blue and untroubled, but under the trees darkness seemed to bleed out of the ground and they couldn't see at all. Billy turned the truck around, lights on, and they drove rattling to the Huckins graveyard. The whistle blatted its windy, panicky message through the valley of Leah. The riverbanks were burning orange from the railroad tracks to the woolen mill. Even at this distance the flames danced and flickered and shot in every direction at once. Smoke flowed up the bank and over into Leah, where it slid along streets and around houses, dimming out streetlights and windowlights. A siren was just then winding down, but the whistle repeated its simple statement over and over.

"They can't git the hoses through the fire to the river," Billy said. "Oh, boy! What a dinger! Look at them little ants running around down there!"

They could barely see, along the edges of the long fire, strange energetic shadows—little men.

On the Vermont side of the Connecticut River the men were doing better, with the wind blowing their fire to the water. Little sparks streamed across, some dying in the air, some in the river, but some carrying over the river, over the fire on the Leah side, where they swirled in big arcs over the houses and buildings of the town.

"Your dad's yard is O.K., Johnny. The mill's in the way. It ain't going to burn past the Cascom River, and them brick walls will stop her. Ain't much to burn in the mill yard, neither, but cars. I can see 'em driving the cars away now."

"God help those houses on Poverty Street," John said.

"Thinks I, I'll git me a rock to sit on and watch the show. Let her burn, you little bastards!" Billy shouted. "Yahoo! Lookit, Johnny, she's a-going past the railroad bridge! They can't do nothing!"

"You don't give a damn, do you, Billy?" John said, but Billy didn't hear him.

"Could they git the hoses down to the river, they could stop her, maybe, before she gits to the first houses. If they don't, Johnny boy, they ain't going to have enough hose to save all them houses. Ayuh! Wash them roofs down good and they'd have her stopped. They ain't got the pumps nor the hose for it."

"Maybe they can stop it in the back yards. Not many trees," John said.

"Nope. They ain't *going* to stop her," Billy said.

"You act glad about it," John said.

Billy whirled around and stared fiercely at him.

"You damn' right! You *God*-damn' right! They ain't nobody down there in that town ever done me the common courtesy of *nothing!* Ain't one of 'em I owe squat! Let her burn up!" He finished his beer, threw the empty can on the body of the truck and turned conciliatingly toward John.

"Now you know me, Johnny. I never hurt nobody and I don't figure on starting. Have a beer. Here! How about you, Frank?"

"No, thank you. I haven't finished what I've got," Franklin said. Then, nervously, almost on the edge of panic, "John, is the town going to burn up?"

"I don't know," John said.

"Don't you worry, Frank," Billy said, "even if Leah does burn to hell, you won't git hurt."

"If Leah burns, Pike Hill goes too," John said.

"Ayuh," Billy sighed. "I know that, Johnny. I know I'll have to go down and help. Them little bastards will want me now, all right—for a short while." He scratched his leg and then said, thoughtfully, "If only the town would burn and not the woods. Too bad, ain't it, Johnny?"

CHAPTER 14

Sam Stevens put the telephone back on its hook and turned slowly around in the farm kitchen, kneading his nose with a wide knuckle. "It ain't a question of no fire department, no volunteer fire department, neither." He was obviously imitating the voice he had just heard, carefully pronouncing *dee-partment.*

"Eh?" Aubrey said. Adolf, Mrs. Pettibone and Jane waited. They knew it had been Chief Atmon on the phone.

"Well, sir, Leah is burning up, is all."

"Sam!" Mrs. Pettibone said.

"It ain't quite that bad, now. Don't git your water hot," he said kindly. "Least I hope not. Listen to Atmon, you'd think the world was coming to an end. Why in hell they made him fire chief, too, is beyond me. He'd much rather set down there in the Town Hall playing with his guns and pretending to be this here *Dragnet* fella. One job is enough for most men. Two is twice too many for Atmon."

"You tell us what he said!" Mrs. Pettibone said. She got up, her hands flighting nervously, and poured more water into the stove reservoir.

"They's houses burning down on Poverty Street. Atmon wants me to put that three-hundred-gallon tank on the pickup and come help. Git your coat on, Adolf. Come on, Aubrey."

"One thing," Sam said as the men stamped their feet down into their boots: "I ain't going to use no water from my well. They can fill her down to Leah, by God!"

"I'm going too," Jane said.

"Now Janie, they ain't hardly room in the truck."

"I can squeeze in. Adolf can ride on the back."

Sam thought for a moment.

"I ain't going to ask you *why*."

"That's close to the Spinellis'."

"Too close for comfort," Sam said. "Ayuh. Aubrey, you hear me? You help us git that tank set, then you stay here. Way the woods is, fire could break out anywheres. You hear me?"

"Don't want to go to Leah anyways," Aubrey said.

"How about your sister?" Mrs. Pettibone asked.

"Don't care about her," Aubrey said. He had his coat and boots on, ready to go outside.

By the time Jane was ready the men had backed the truck under the big tank, where it hung in the shed, and chained it on. Sam was making the last inspection, his flashlight moving up and down. Occasionally its beam shot past the truck into the dry stubble where they had cleared brush and grass from around the house and barn.

The tank gonged and rattled as they drove down the gravel driveway and headed toward Leah on the Cascom River Road. The wind definitely smelled of fire now, not merely the fall smell of burning leaves and wood. Tar and rubber were burning, too. As they came nearer they saw the angry red glow of fire reflected in the moving smoke above the town.

In the Spinellis' kitchen Father Desmond sat across from Mrs. Spinelli, drinking a glass of red wine. Jane stood just inside the door, amazed at their calmness as they turned toward her. Two blocks away she had seen a woman run, crying out loud, her arms full of blankets and a saucepan banging against her side. Men ran everywhere, pulling toy wagons full of dishes, splintering furniture in their haste to force it through doorways. On Poverty Street the world was coming to an end, and here they sat drinking wine.

"Hello, Jane," the young priest said. "I haven't seen very much of you lately."

"The town's burning up!" she said. He smiled, and she noticed the specks of soot on his shiny face. His hands, too, were dirty.

"I'm afraid it is," he said, and turned to look meaningfully at Mrs. Spinelli, as if Jane's words supported what he had been telling the old woman.

"No, no, no, no, no!" Mrs. Spinelli said, although her expression hadn't changed at all. She seemed quite calm. She hadn't recognized Jane. In her lap she held the blue-and-gold pillow Mike had sent her from boot camp, and she ran her brown fingers delicately across the embroidered word *Mother*. The priest leaned toward her, his bulky shoulders pushed forward so that the black cloth shone across his back.

"No, no, no, no, no!" Mrs. Spinelli said. Then she looked up, surprised and pleased. "Janie! Where you been?"

The priest turned to Jane, his usual good nature gone. He looked as if he might cry. "I can't explain it to her," he said. "She won't leave the house. She won't believe me."

"Where's Mr. Spinelli?"

"He can't do anything with her, either. So much to do now! Mrs. *Spinelli!*" he said sharply but unconvincingly. The old woman crossed herself and felt around in the folds of her black skirt for her rosary.

Mr. Spinelli came half-running into the room, then stopped short.

"Janie!" he said, taking her hands. "Janie, am I glad to see you! We got trouble. Mama lost her marbles. She won't *hear* nothing about the fire. She just sits with the pillow all day. She's sick to her head, Janie!"

"I don't care what you tell," Mrs. Spinelli said, "I got my kitchen here. I ain't going no place. He took my Mikey." She pointed her rosary-knotted hand at the priest. "Now he wants my house, my kitchen. What I done?"

"Mama! He didn't take Mikey! My God!" Mr. Spinelli crossed himself. "Mama, Mikey got in a accident on his motorcycle, remember?"

"I live a good life. I go see Father Brangelli."

"Mama, Father Brangelli ain't here any more. This is Father Desmond. Father Brangelli, he went to Pittsburgh, Pennsylvania!" He moaned and shook his head. "Five years ago," he said hopelessly.

Jane found herself going toward the old woman, who now looked up into her face, tears sliding easily, as they always had, down the burnished cheeks.

"Janie, you *good* for Mikey. You fix everything, ha?"

"I'll keep her here, in the kitchen," Jane said. "If she has to move I'll take care of her. You go ahead."

"Thank you, Janie. We got so much to do," Mr. Spinelli said. He and the priest stood at the door, knowing that they had to go back to the fires.

"You'll take care of her?" Father Desmond asked, officially relieved of the duty and yet not quite sure.

"You're a good girl, Janie," Mr. Spinelli said. "We'll come right back as soon as we can." They left.

"You stay with me, Janie. You hungry? I get you something to eat. You thirsty? I get you a glass *vino*. I get you." She jumped up, carrying the pillow like a baby against her shoulder, to pour Jane a glass of wine.

CHAPTER 15

William Cotter came back to the office with old Madbury, the yardman. He decided that the yard itself was in no great danger—the fire would have to cross the Cascom River, and the thick brick wall of the woolen mill would keep it even from the river, barring some odd catastrophe.

"I guess I better stay up the rest of the night," Madbury said importantly, "just in case." The fire was a great excitement to him, and as William Cotter looked into the old man's simple eyes he thought of Christmas and birthdays. Madbury said good night and went off through the yard, his flashlight poking here and there through the smoke.

William Cotter mashed a long butt into the tin ash tray on Bruce's desk. "If I smoke one more cigarette I'll get cancer," he said, realizing that he had been saying this over and over to himself all the time he had been making the rounds of the yard. Just one more and he'd get cancer. In that case he'd sealed his fate months ago. No will power at all. John didn't seem to have much, either—

not like Bruce, anyway. He wished he'd had a daughter. He always got along better with women than with men. A daughter like Jenny Lou, only white—he smiled. A daughter like Jenny Lou. He'd have traded both his sons for one like her. He and John had both been wrong about those kids' coming. Gladys would have cracked up, sure as hell, like she almost did when she had the change of life. Of course that was during the war and she was worried about John getting killed. He was never worried about John, though. How could anybody really get worried about John? Nothing ever happened to John. He did get mad, though, when he heard about those kids' coming. Mad as hell. Don't understand Franklin, either. Another one of those damn' polite ones. They look at you calm as hell and don't say anything. Why can't a father have respect? They don't even love me.

Franklin's another one of those damn' polite ones, don't stick their necks out and the next thing you know you've said too goddam much and you feel like an ass, just trying to be nice. Just like the rest of Leah—looking at you. Somebody has to talk, don't they? Somebody has to be friendly, don't they?

His own father had been another one. State senator, mouth shut, made money, worked his ass off, died off his rocker and couldn't even go to the bathroom by himself. He was a hard man and nobody liked him very much, just respected him, feared him. He knew one person feared the old man still. Afraid of him even when he lay in his coffin. Didn't even like to go down to the graveyard.

He still didn't like to go down there, just as he didn't want to go to the hospital to see what was left of Bruce. He was afraid that the eyes, so much like his father's eyes, would open up and look at him. They couldn't, of course. The doctors said they couldn't. He could tell himself over and over and over they couldn't.

He wanted to go home, have himself a shot of bourbon and go to bed. He didn't smoke when he was in bed. But he shouldn't leave the yard. Maybe Madbury *would* stay up all night. Like hell. As soon as he got tired of being the boy on the burning deck he'd go home to bed.

William Cotter reached for the telephone, startled to find another cigarette burning in the ash tray, and called home. Gladys answered.

"Johnny home, Glad? Everything O.K. there?"

"He and Franklin are eating supper. Are you all right, dear? What's happening? Have they saved those houses on Poverty Street? Miss Colchester called for the Red Cross. We're making up food. I'm making macaroni and cheese. Bill, are we all going to be burned out?"

"Take it easy, Glad. I don't know as much as you do, but the yard's O.K. Let me talk to Johnny."

"I saw the fire from Pike Hill," John said. "You want me to come down there with you?"

"Oh, the yard's O.K., I guess. It probably won't cross the Cascom. The mill's in the way, for one thing. No sparks coming over here just now, just smoke all over the place. I think the wind's going down a little. Maybe the fires are changing it a little. You know, making their own wind. I wish you'd come and spell me later, though. Would you, Johnny?"

"Sure. When do you want me?"

"How about around eleven?"

"I'll be there at eleven. I'm going down to the fire and see if I can help."

"Well, take care of yourself, Johnny."

The dirty office seemed to turn. Smoke hung in the drab room. He knew he couldn't work, so he took the bull's-eye lantern and made a tour around the yard. He found where oil from the one-lunger had dripped into sawdust; remembering theories of spontaneous combustion, he kicked the oil-soaked sawdust out onto the dirt. It was something to do, anyway, even though he'd never heard of sawdust bursting into flame right on the ground.

The trucks were all shining and silent in the big garage-shed. The Cascom River, dried to the size of a brook, and dirty as it came through town, hardly seemed to move at all. A frog plopped into the black water and turned around to look at the lantern. Suddenly he saw hundreds of frogs' eyes, all looking at him, all silent. *Thousands* of eyes—the place was infested with frogs. He hurried up and down the short stretch of riverbank bounding the yard and found the river crammed with frogs of all sizes and colors, many of them huge, green-brown bullfrogs. Excitedly he flashed his lantern over this drought-caused bonanza of frogs. *Millions* of frogs, and all of them probably hungry as hell. Their eyes were bright BB's scattered over the water.

He ran off to find Madbury, and came across him in the roofing shed among the tar-black rolls. "Nothin' out of place, I can see," the old man said seriously, duty showing in his dedicated eyes. As he spoke he searched the far corners for sparks.

"You like frogs' legs?" William Cotter asked.

"Huh?" The old eyes narrowed. He pointed his flashlight into William Cotter's face.

"You like frogs' legs, I asked you."

"Ain't et none since I was a kid," Madbury said grudgingly, still wanting to be the brave watchman.

"I said do you like 'em?"

Madbury took time to think. It wasn't a proper question, but it was a straight one. "Us kids used to be crazy for frog legs. I ain't had none since I was a kid."

"How did you fix 'em?"

"Frypan."

"We dipped them in corn meal, then dropped them into hot bacon grease. Remember how they used to kick, right in the pan?"

"Seems I remember that," Madbury said.

"You come with me!" The old man followed, shaking his head but coming right along. When he saw the thousands of copper-bright eyes, he believed.

"Bald-headed Jesus!" he said, and there was no more watchman in him.

"We'll need a burlap bag, for one thing," William Cotter said.

"I got some Number Two, Number One hooks over to my house," Madbury said. "We git us a couple long pieces of furring—maybe one-by-ones, and make us a couple of gigs. Godalmighty! I never seen so many frogs in one place!"

"O.K. You run over and get the hooks. I'll get a pair of pliers out of the sawmill and a couple of one-by-ones, pine."

In the sawmill he found a pair of pliers under the planer, but his most interesting find was a long cane pole rigged for fishing, with a trout hook on a short piece of gut leader. One of the men must have tried some fishing during the lunch half-hour. He took the pole and two long pieces of furring back to the river.

"I'm a fly fisherman," he said excitedly. His hands shook as he unsnarled the line. Looking up the long pole he saw, over the woolen mill, the red glow of the fire. It made the sky fairly bright in that quarter and helped him to see. He cut a piece of red wool from the small end of his necktie and threaded it on the rusty little hook. The pole was quite springy, and the second his fly hit the water he had a frog by the tongue. The frogs mobbed the hook, jumping over and on each other's backs to get it. The river boiled with frogs whenever his fly touched the water.

When the old man came back, out of breath, William Cotter had landed and released a dozen frogs. Madbury had thought to bring a burlap bag, and he strung it over a bush. After sticking himself he got the big hooks straightened out and a gig made on the end of one of the long one-by-ones.

"I'm going to take the barb off this hook," William Cotter said. He'd had to pull a bullfrog's tongue half out, the frog grunting and squirming, before he could get the hook loose. This one he knocked over the head and tossed into the bag. Madbury danced up and down the mucky bank, trying to spear bullfrogs only. It was difficult to miss the hungry leopard and brown frogs, who practically dived into the gig itself.

The frogs kicked and grunted when they were hooked, kept mobbing the piece of red wool even after it grew dark and slimy. They waited on the surface for the darting gig, their little eyes stupid, bright and willing. It seemed as if all the frogs on the river came to see the excitement. The bag filled slowly with big bullfrogs: wounded leopard and brown frogs hopped and crawled brokenly off into the dry brush.

"Goddam!" Madbury yelled, "we going to have that bag full-up in no time! I just stuck one his legs are bigger'n bananas! Goddam drumsticks!"

CHAPTER 16

John knew he'd been smart to leave the car at home. The streets were full of trucks and cars and amateur traffic directors to whom nobody paid any attention. Half the people were watching and half were insanely and erratically busy. One side of Poverty Street was a solid wall of wooden tenements. The other side was an even more solid wall of orange fire. The street itself was empty except for a burning car and discarded furniture, and the asphalt melted and ran down the gutters like watery mud. The car baked and burned, its tires firey wings. From the next street over, Mechanic Street, the town pumper had gone as far as it could into the alley between the houses and tried ineffectually to spray the roofs of the standing tenements. A bucket brigade carried water up the wooden fire escapes, but this seemed hopeless too. Most of the men were still trying to bring out clothes and bedding to the waiting cars and trucks.

The Town Square was filled with women and children, mattresses and television sets. Dogs ran between the cars and people, wagging tails and biting tires. John saw no cats at all: the paranoid creatures, he thought, usually considered any excitement to be a plot, and had left town until things cooled off. Young children, their faces cold and pale, were towed on tottering stiff legs behind their mothers.

He found Chief Atmon among the clutter of tank trucks, some of them fuel-oil carriers, some milk trucks, some farm pickups with tanks chained on—all of them filling at the hydrant, then taking the water to the ravenous pumper. Atmon stood on the flat bed of a pickup and bellowed, pointed and raged. His police uniform was a little too small for him, but his fireman's helmet and his .44 Magnum revolver both seemed a little too big for him. The business of filling the tanks proceeded, and nobody paid much attention to the chief of fire and police.

"You next!" Atmon bellowed, pointing to the next truck in line. "Sam Stevens! You next!" Without quite looking at Atmon, Sam spat. John went over to him.

"Anything I can do to help?" he asked Sam.

"Walll, now, John. Ain't nobody knows what to do. A few more won't hurt none. You can help Adolf on the tank, I suppose."

The brownish hydrant water glugged slowly into the tank. Adolf held the hose, listening to the hollow, slopping splash inside. He nodded to John, flipped his long hair back and grinned, pointing down inside.

"Hurry it up, there!" Atmon shouted.

"I could piss in it," Sam Stevens observed. Adolf laughed, along with the rest of the waiting men, then slapped the side of the tank.

"Kem on, demmit!" Adolf said. One man kicked the hydrant. Atmon turned the other way, still shouting and pointing.

"Wind's changed," Sam said. Everybody laughed. "I don't mean Atmon. I mean the wind!"

Everybody looked up. The fire they could easily see towering above Poverty Street leaned the other way, back toward the river, and the heat began to lessen a little. The smoke, that had made a wild moving ceiling over the town, thinned as it came back the other way. A few stars shone through it.

"The wind's changed!" Atmon shouted.

"If it holds, by God, we might save the other side of Poverty Street," Sam said.

"Maybe," someone said.

" 'Twon't hold long," someone said. John looked down and saw that it was Eightball, a town garbage collector and part-time worker at Cotter & Son; a dimwitted young man with clear bright eyes and straight, glossy black hair growing out at right angles all over his round head. Strangely symmetrical and clean, his rosy, gleeful face betrayed his loyalty: Eightball was on the side of the fire.

"Eightball, we need a parade!" Howard Randolf, limping slightly, a double-bitted ax across his shoulder, stepped over the hose and leaned against Sam's truck. Eightball giggled. "I say we need a parade," Howard said seriously, then pointed his ax handle.

John could see farther than most. He stood on the tank and looked up the street toward the square. Among the trucks, keeping formation, zigzagging back and forth around piled furniture, the white helmet-liners and gleaming gold and blue satin of the Legion Drum and Bugle Corps bobbed and weaved and advanced.

" 'Theirs not to reason why, theirs but to do and die,' " Howard said. "Where in hell's the National Guard?"

"What the hell are you doing with that ax?" Atmon shouted from his perch. So many eyes turned upon Atmon at once—so many eyes filled with such quiet disgust—he turned away.

"I guess our fire chief thinks the only way to put out a fire is to sprinkle water on it," Howard said.

Sam spat.

The Legion arrived, led by the shoe clerk from Endicott Johnson's. In a great unintelligible bass he halted and at-eased his platoon. He nearly saluted Atmon, then evidently thought better of it.

"What do you want us to do?" he asked.

"Put out the fire!" Eightball yelled. Everybody laughed except Atmon and the shoe clerk. Some of the legionnaires smiled. "Put out the fire!" Eightball cackled, trying to repeat his triumph.

"O.K., O.K., Eightball," someone said, smiling and patting him on the head.

"All right," Atmon said. "You take your men and go to the pumper. Find Charlie Bemis. He'll give you something to do."

"Tenn-HUT!" The impossible bass rang out, and the Legion Drum and Bugle Corps forward-marched. Most of the platoon, too embarrassed to march, did a ragged route-step.

Finally the 300-gallon tank was full. As the truck started up, Howard Randolf swung himself up beside John. "The National Guard *is* being mobilized," Howard said. "Now they're getting their armory ready for some of the refugees. I heard you had a preview at Pinckney's barn."

"Not as bad as this one," John said.

"I heard you were quite a hero. But let me tell you something, Johnny Cotter. Everybody's doing all right. The old bags are mobilizing, bobilizing, mobilizing, bless their carnivorous old hearts! Nobody's going to go hungry this night, nor sleep in the cold. There'll be plenty of human kindness spread thick, my boy—as much as there ever was nastiness the rest of the year. More! You know, I kind of love this town, even if I am a twenty-year upstart." He waved his ax toward the square.

"Maybe that's why you like it," John said, "but as for me, you can have it."

"Ah! Of course! You shouldn't be here at all! You don't fit the pattern. You went to college, to war, to school in France—you've been weaned, Johnny. Where are all your friends who did the same? Gone, aren't they?"

"Most of them."

"Of course! How many of them came back here to settle after college? Wait a minute—I don't mean the gutless wonders who want to be their fathers all over again."

"None I can think of."

"Now Leah spawned some pretty bright boys, didn't she? Fruitful Leah. Wasn't there a Rhodes scholar in your class?"

"Henry Blakemore."

"And where is this all-around American boy?"

"New York, I think."

"Gone. All gone away," Howard said dreamily. "Poor Leah! Out of the Eightballs and the Atmons and the Billy Muldrows she somehow manages to produce a few examples of Homo sapiens. And then they leave her. No loyalty, Johnny. None at all."

As they passed an alley leading to the burning houses, the heat hit them a nearly singeing blow. Yet the fire, searingly hot as it was, had turned a darker and less threatening red, like a fireplace embering down. The bucket brigade seemed less useless, and Bemis had put the Legion boys to work on it. For the first time it looked as if the other side of Poverty Street might be saved.

They waited their turn at the pumper, and in a few minutes the tank had been sucked dry. "We're not being too helpful here," Howard said. John followed him over to the town clerk, who seemed to be in charge of everything.

"Howdy, Mr. B.," Howard said.

Mr. Bemis smiled wearily. "All that back-cutting didn't do much good, did it?" he said.

"I can turn in my ax," Howard said, "honorably. I even have a slight wound. I *got* a Purple Heart, so just gimme a aspirn."

Mr. Bemis smiled. "You done a good job, Howard."

"What can we do now. Mr. B.?"

"You done enough, Howard." He saw John. "Hi, John. You been busy?"

"He ain't been kissed yet," Howard said. "How about the bucket brigade?"

"I think we've saved the houses on this side," Mr. Bemis said.

"If the wind stays put . . ."

"Northlee's sending a tank truck and another pumper. We'll be able to run down the street pretty soon, damp the fronts down properly. Takes a good deal of water this way. Slops out."

Joe Beaupre, the young policeman, came to confer with him. The armory was ready, the Red Cross was finding cots and blankets, and the Salvation Army had called from Boston. They were sending canteen trucks.

"From *Boston?*" Mr. Bemis said. "What do you make of that?"

"Said they were on the way. Ought to get here in a few hours. We're pretty famous," Joe Beaupre said. "It ain't often a whole town starts to burn up."

"Newspapers are gitting a little tired of just plain old forest fires," Mr. Bemis said. "Howard, you and John want to help, you go through them tenements and see if they're empty of people. Didn't have no time before. Don't want nobody trapped if they do go. This fire ain't out by a long shot."

In one high-ceilinged kitchen they found a great horned owl in a carrion-stinking wire cage. A pan of fried potatoes had been upset on the floor. The owl stared at them and snapped his beak as they stepped carefully among the potatoes.

"We ought to let him go," Howard said. He sat down on a wooden chair, his feet stretched out, watching the owl.

"They're not protected," John said. "They kill rabbits and stuff."

"So who's protected? You're looking at a fellow carnivore, my dear young friend, a fellow hunter and eater of meat. We've got to stick together or the herbivores will breed us to death. A united front, I say!" He pounded his fist on the oilcloth-covered table. The owl jumped and hissed. "If I didn't think he'd gobble my hand like a bleeding mouse, I'd give him his liberty."

"Come to think of it, they kill skunks, too," John said.

"I rather like skunks." Howard frowned at the owl. "They have the courage of their convictions."

John opened the icebox and found two quarts of warmish beer.

"Anybody who'd leave a poor owl to burn doesn't deserve our honesty," Howard said. "Where's the opener?"

They found a pound of hamburger for the owl, who quickly tore off the paper and stood in the meat, kneading it while he ate.

"Whoever lived in this warren probably learned his manners from the bird. Did you notice the library? A pile of *True Confessions, Real Romances, Confidentials*—you know the stuff: 'I killed my baby with a hammer and now I'm sorry.' "

On the wall, in the light of the bare overhanging bulb, a nude calendar girl smirked through her patina of grease. A crude vagina had been penciled in just below her bellybutton. Howard pointed at it. "And yet there were children gotten here. I saw the inevitable detritus in the bedrooms. And that anatomical inaccuracy is not the work of a child. In spite of its location there is about it a certain knowledgeable accuracy of detail. A man did that, Johnny. Above the kitchen-midden, the magic symbol. Man is distinguished by his art."

They left a dollar on the table to pay for the beer. The owl seemed too involved in the meat to desire escape. They left him and continued through the building, each with a bottle of beer in his hand.

"It's funny to look out other windows," John said. "You get such a different feeling about the town—like it was another town altogether."

They stood in an apartment full of new kitchen furniture; there were chrome-plated legs on all the straight chairs, formica tops on all the tables, whether in the kitchen, dining room or living room. Tiny, shiny pictures hung high against the walls. The waxed floor shone, bare except for the art-square linoleum rug on the kitchen floor.

They went through the incredibly clean apartment to the front bedroom. Even the bed had chrome-plated legs. "The operating room," Howard said. "Completely aseptic, as you can see."

The fire across the street made the room like an oven. The walls were almost too hot to touch. Both pumpers were working down the near side of the street, spraying each other and the buildings. Each had canvas dropcloths strung along one side to protect the men and the tires. The wind still held from the east.

"Feel like Nero watching Rome?" Howard asked.

"No. Do you?"

"I can see how the crazy bastard felt." Howard leaned his elbow on his knee, one foot up on the windowsill, and stared broodily into the flames, his long, gullied face as red as a devil's. The fire was brighter than the electric lights at the head of the bed, and for a long time he stared into it. When he turned around his eyes seemed curiously blind.

They finished their beer and the tour of the tenements. With the fire at least partly under control, the town clerk had changed his headquarters from Mechanic Street to the end of Poverty Street, where he could see down the length of the row of collapsed, embering buildings. John and Howard sat down with him and had some coffee from a Thermos bottle.

"It's a miracle," Mr. Bemis said.

"You done a good job, Charlie," Sam Stevens said. He waited for the pumper to come back and drain his truck-tank.

"Say, Howard," Mr. Bemis said, "you sure done a job of work tonight."

"Now you mention it, I came into town this afternoon to buy groceries. I was drafted. What time is it? My wife will be having the state police after me."

"Ten o'clock," Mr. Bemis said. "Go and call from the firehouse. I'm going back there myself pretty soon. There's three or four forest fires going and I guess I'm the fire department."

"That's no lie. Where's the manly pillar of the law?"

Mr. Bemis smiled, but shook his head disapprovingly. "Chief Atmon's doing a good job, Howard."

"If anybody saved them houses it was you, Charlie," Sam Stevens said deliberately. Coming from the big man the judgment was final and binding. None of the men disputed it by so much as a change of expression.

John and Howard walked back toward the Town Square and the firehouse. Some of the refugees who had found a place to spend the night were coming back to see their houses burn. Those who lived on the east side of the street waited for the fires to die down so they could move back. Already the cars, trucks, and toy wagons were deploying around the back fire escapes. The watching people stood in odd groups and in lines, their faces turned toward the sparking, beam-falling red mounds. All the burned houses had now fallen in upon themselves, and the west side of Poverty Street looked like a range of low, incandescent mountains.

As they were walking along, Howard went out into the street and pulled a derelict mattress up onto the sidewalk. John helped him drape it over a granite post. Howard sat wearily on a horse trough. "I'm an old man. Wait a minute," he said. He seemed suddenly to be completely exhausted. He'd seemed young and spry enough before, but now his dark, lined face was slightly yellow under the streetlight. The lines in his forehead were ropy folds. "Johnny, are you familiar with the emotion of joy? Joy," he said, "is when you realize, for no reason and on no special occasion, that you are happy."

"I've never done that, I guess," John said. "If I was ever really happy it was because of some outside happening. V-J Day, for instance, which most likely saved my life."

"In the First World War I was in the Navy. I can remember no joy whatsoever from that experience, armistice or no armistice. But goddam it! At least recognize its existence once in a while. Joy does exist."

"Even if it does, it doesn't last."

"So what? Why ask it to last forever? You've got to eat your cake to enjoy it."

"I guess you're right," John said.

"You guess I'm right. Oh, well."

"Joy, shmoy, as long as you're healthy," John said.

"So you think I made an ass of myself the other night," Howard said, and looked at John with that shrewd expression that is always deliberately put on. It seemed to John that Howard was really very sad.

"Howard, you have no idea how much I admire you. But you just don't seem very joyful right now, that's all."

"Hell, John," Howard said, grinning, "I ate that cake. Only difference with me is, I know I ate it. I can taste it when I burp." He got slowly to his feet, and they went on toward the firehouse.

The wind seemed to be undecided. It still blew from the east, though occasionally whirls and puffs in the stream of smoke above the town moved in several directions at once. As quickly as it had filled with people and white sheets and the carnival-colored bedding of the town, the turf beneath the tall elms of the Town Square had emptied again. Here and there across the seared grass a piece of fluttering paper, a bottle or can or unwanted cardboard box remained. The homeless people had been absorbed by the town.

In front of the firehouse the Northlee pumper, red enamel and shining brass, dripped water and coughed hollowly as its slowly revolving old engine idled. The Leah pumper alone could now cope with the embers of Poverty Street. The bucket brigade was straggling back, the Legion Drum and Bugle Corps with them, the legionnaires swinging their helmet-liners by the straps and no longer marching.

"We just happened to be practicing," one of them said, and John was surprised to see that it was Keith Joubert, one of Junior Stevens' high-school friends, and a bully. The blue-and-gold uniform was wet and bedraggled, the shiny jump-boots were scuffed and damp, and the imitation *fourragère* of yellow boondoggle had become slightly unstrung. The oversized ribbons—the usual ones, but also the combat infantryman's badge and the European Theater ribbon with three battle stars—shone damply on the wrinkled satin. The other legionnaires turned in their buckets and went home, but to John's continued surprise Keith Joubert sat down on the firemen's bench next to him.

"We just happened to be practicing when they called us," he said apologetically, "so we come all dolled-up like this."

"The First World War finished all that," Howard said, pointing to Keith's uniform.

"Finished what?" Keith looked at Howard with the common expression, the one used in Leah for fools. John wondered if he had ever made his face over that way. He tried it and found it familiar—the small stresses and folds around his mouth formed easily. He had used it on Howard the other night when Howard had gone overboard about the poetic novelist. He guiltily wiped it off with one hand, and held his hand over his face for a moment to make sure it stayed off.

"Finished what? Finished the crippled peacock strut, the crossed white straps which made a perfect target even for an arquebus, the upright method of dying in battle. Soldiers, or their leaders, found that olive drab in the brown-brindle muck was better for morale than the gay crimson or whatever rainbow colors uniforms were. It's generally agreed, and I see you've been in a battle or two so you'll probably agree too, that it's better not to be seen by the enemy. All those bright colors, they used to think, frightened the enemy—filled him with panic. Filled his gunsights is more like it. Everybody's brave enough, but the dead can't help with the fighting."

"We ain't in no combat," Keith said.

"Oh, I know. Not when you march to the drums and bugles. You do make a pretty sight when you do. I admit that. You really do. But didn't I detect a note of apology in your voice when you explained to John, here, that you just happened to be practicing in your finery?"

"Huh?"

"Jesus! I've got to telephone my wife," Howard said, ducked around the men in the door and disappeared inside the firehouse.

"What a crazy bastard!" Keith said. "If that bastard seen as much combat as me he wouldn't shoot his mouth off so much. I ain't seen you for a long while, Johnny. What you been doing with yourself?"

"Not much. Using up the G.I. bill."

"What'd you do in the service, anyway?" Keith sounded more as he used to in high school—as if he were looking down at a small intellectual-type who couldn't get out of his own way. It had always been the same and always would be, John supposed. The unfairness of it welled up in his throat. For a second he looked clearly and steadily at Keith. A great many things had happened since high school. Even in high school he had once had a fair fight with Keith and decisively beaten him—bloodied Keith's nose and pinned him to the ground. That didn't change anything. He could have done it every day for a week, except that Keith was rarely alone and he couldn't beat up Keith Joubert, Donald Ramsey, and Junior Stevens all at once.

"I was in the Army," he said.

"What part of the Army?" Keith asked. John could see visions of typewriters and neat clerks in Keith's eyes.

"First ASTP, then the Infantry, then in Intelligence. I was in three years altogether, one year overseas."

"What the hell's ASTP?"

"Army Specialized Training Program. I was supposed to be an engineer. Then came the Bulge and we were all Infantry."

"You see any combat?" Keith's eyes gleamed—either he was looking for a brother in that mystique, or he knew. Suddenly John had an irresistible desire to smash Keith Joubert. The red, stupid head, the bright aggressive gleam of insensitivity in the eyes, the intense poise of ignorance! He tried the expression himself, with the insane desire to keep it and let it grow. He would be one of them—sure of himself and of his rectitude and virility and strength. He would know nothing and therefore everything. He would *know*. He looked steadily at Keith.

"I killed a man once. I shot him four times, three times in the chest and one time in the face. You should have seen him. Shot him at about one-foot range with the M. 1911 A1 .45 automatic. I've always wanted to do it again. God! it squashed that son of a bitch! Knocked him clear on his ass, blood all over the goddam place. You should have heard them gook women scream. Man, you should of heard 'em! Them big slugs mashed that gook, man!"

"Women?" Keith asked, no disapproval in the question, just curiosity. John looked at him, leering.

"Just gooks. Just Flips. The guy shot at me through the door.

Boy, did I cream that bastard! Four times. *Zug, zug, zug, zug!"* He poked Keith each time with his finger, where the bullets went in. This time Keith began to smell a rat. He drew back disapprovingly.

"You off your rocker?"

"I get that blood lust, is all," John purred at him. *"Zug, zug, zug . . ."* Poking.

"Cut it out!"

"Whatsamatter? I'm just telling you! *Zug! Squish!* Combat, boy!"

Keith drew back farther, then seemed to remember that attack was his prerogative, not John Cotter's. He stood up and leaned forward menacingly.

"Who you trying to snow, Sonny? You're acting kind of unfriendly."

John looked at him some more. The look seemed to have a fine kind of power. Keith couldn't move so long as he looked at him. He waited until Keith was about to speak, then went on in his newfound, lovely, purring voice:

"Aren't you the Keith Joubert I used to go to school with? Seems to me you and Donald Ramsey—he's the coward who works in the Post Office now—and Junior Stevens—it seems I remember the three of you throwing me in the fountain just before the DeMolay dance. That was fun, wasn't it? Then there was the time at the scrape you spent the afternoon ducking me. Remember that? Then there were the times you chased me home, and the times you goosed me in class when the teacher wasn't looking, and the times you jumped me on the way home from school are too many to remember. I didn't have much fun at all because of the three of you. The funny thing was that if I met any of the three of you alone you were nice as pie. Isn't that funny? Alone, you were almost polite. Remember that? Remember the time we had a little fight all by ourselves because anybody could beat up on John Cotter? Remember I gave you a bloody nose and twisted your arm until you said 'Uncle'?"

"You always was a sissy," Keith said.

"I cried, I remember. When I was a junior in high school you and your friends made me cry. A junior in high school. I cried because of the unfairness, and because I was tired after fighting you, and you ganged up on me. You made me cry when I was sixteen years old—much to old to cry. Imagine crying at sixteen, like a girl. Just a sissy."

Keith stood back, his face strangely softening. "That was in high school. We shouldn't of done that." A look of pity. "But you was such a easy one to git all riled up . . ."

"No, I wasn't. I tried to let it go by. I laughed like a coward at your stupid jokes. I never fought until you laid hands on me. I tried to avoid you. I spent most of my time trying to keep away from you. Nothing I did or might have done would have changed it. I could beat you up, alone. Ramsey I could beat up with my left hand, alone. Junior Stevens I couldn't beat up, but alone he never started anything. The three of you or Junior and one other of you—those were the odds. And now you've got the nerve to pity the little sissy! Pity or cruelty, those are the only strong emotions you'll ever have, except the one that fades and comes like a wave, but is always there: Fear, Buster, fear! You're afraid even when you're marching to the drums in your pretty uniform. You're afraid because it's too pretty, or because it isn't pretty enough. You're afraid of women—you always were. You're afraid of men. You're afraid of God!"

"Don't you say nothing about my religion!"

"I'll bet if I called you a son of a bitch you'd say I insulted your mother."

"Don't you say nothing about my mother!"

"How about your father?" John asked.

He watched Keith carefully, gauging the amount of pressure in Keith's increasingly rabbity motions. The object of experiment again assumed the predicted role, came close and leaned menacingly.

"Think you're wise, huh?"

"Compared to you, Buster, I'm the brightest star in all the firmament." He judged that if he used one more word Keith could not understand, or tried to stand up, Keith would have to fight. Several bystanders had caught the meaning of Keith's ceremonial struttings, and now observed.

"You watch your mouth!" Keith said, stuttering, pumping up his rage.

"Don't you remember that you can't beat me up alone?" John asked.

"You little bastard, I ain't taking nothing from you! You don't scare me none!"

"Ayuh," John said, "only I can see you're scared of something. It must be my piercing eyes. I can smell it on you. You stink of fear like a whipped dog."

Ten or more men had gathered now, Howard among them. John tried to make up his mind before his own rage made it up for him. Keith seemed frozen in his menacing stance, but one word could break the spell. If he made the slightest move toward getting up, Keith would swing. If he merely sat still, Keith would think up the worst insult he could—something about yellow—deliver it and go home. This seemed unsatisfactory. Yet a grubby, rolling-around fight would be even worse. He'd just have to end the fight neatly, and he wasn't sure he could. At least he knew what Keith would do first—try to hit him as he stood up. He decided to stand.

Keith was no fighter. His fist came slowly, almost hesitantly. It had always been that way with him. He didn't telegraph his punches; he wrote letters. His bullying had been that way too—weirdly harmless and picky, at first; then savage and cruel.

After the fist passed by, John helped the arm along, turning Keith all the way around. Then he put a simple stranglehold and a hammerlock on him. These carefully applied, he sat down on the bench with Keith completely helpless in his lap. As he expected, he was much stronger than Keith, who cursed in a high, spitty voice. John found that by regulating the pressure of the stranglehold he could make peculiar bagpipe effects with Keith's sounds. Some of the spectators seemed to find these amusing.

When Keith stopped screaming John asked calmly, "You had enough?"

More incoherent curses, stopped this time by pressure on the hammerlock.

"Say 'Uncle' again for old time's sake," John suggested.

"I'll kill you!" Keith screamed.

John had been working one foot up behind Keith's back, balancing Keith on his other knee, the stranglehold exchanged for a double hammerlock. Suddenly he braced his back against the bench and kicked Keith down the driveway. Keith got up slowly, examining a long tear in the knee of his satin pants.

"He tore his pretty pants," John said. He sat calmly on the bench.

"Don't overdo it, Johnny." It was Bob Paquette, who had come out of the firehouse with the others to watch. Junior Stevens stood beside Bob, a fierce, interested smile on his red face.

Keith came slowly and ominously back toward John, who still did not get up. "You want the next lesson?" John asked.

He braced himself as Keith charged, arms flailing. At the last moment Keith shut his eyes and landed sitting down, two dirty footprints on his chest.

"I ought to kick your guts out," John said.

Keith raged as he scrambled away. He was crying, or nearly crying backward. From his bawling, disintegrated face issued a con-
ing backward. From his bawling, disintegrated face issued a continual, hoarse, incoherent blat. It was still audible half a block away.

Howard sat down next to him, a surprising amount of admiration in his eyes. "That was about the most *conclusive* fight I've seen since Louis and Schmeling," he said. Billy Muldrow had been watching, too. He came diffidently through the crowd and put a hand on John's shoulder.

"Oh, Johnny!" he whispered. "You showed that son of a bitch! You did it so beautiful. Cool? You never even got up off your ass, God *damn* it all!"

"What started the fight?" Howard asked.

"I don't know."

"You was cool!" Billy said.

"Cold, I'd say," Howard said.

Bob Paquette hadn't come over, hadn't done more than look at John before turning away. When John met Bob's glance no sign of recognition had passed between them. He had turned back into the firehouse with the others. Inside, the phone rang steadily for a long time and then there was a longer silence, until Mr. Bemis' voice called out, "Where?"

"What's happened?" Howard said, listening.

John got up stiffly, knowing that he must go down to the yard to relieve his father, and nearly bumped into Eightball, who had come running out. "Started up again!" Eightball said, grinning slyly. Billy pushed Eightball back.

"Goddam moron," Billy mumbled.

Bob Paquette ran out ahead of the crowd. "Poverty Street's caught again. The fire crossed over. Don't ask me what they're going to do now!" The men all climbed on the Northlee pumper and chugged off around the square, leaving John alone on the sidewalk. He walked down River Street toward the yard.

He'd let the goddam town of Leah burn to the ground. They made him seem vicious; they disapproved! He wondered if Bob Paquette had disapproved, in high school, when Junior and his buddies tormented John Cotter. Maybe Bob just stood there then with the same expression of superior distaste on his face: the expression of Leah secure in its own rituals. But how did John Cotter, born with a fair amount of brains, the possessor of perhaps a good amount of strength for his size—how did he manage to separate himself from this set of rituals? Nobody had bullied Bob Paquette; nobody bullied some of the flagrantly superior idiots of high school, the apple polishers, the ass kissers. Why John Cotter? Maybe one little incident in some forgotten time at the beginning of memory had begun the irreversible progression—perhaps that time when he was four years old and filled his pants at the playground and smeared the slide. One thing was increasingly certain—the problems of high school could not be solved thirteen years later. He had just picked a fight with and degraded a thirty-two-year-old man, a veteran of his country's wars, the father of three children. It was too late to explain to Leah that the seeds of this harvest of rage had been planted long ago.

He should have fought so hard, so bitterly, so dedicatedly—once upon a time—that they would have had to leave him alone. It could only have happened once: the first time. Instead, he had given up his right to be a fighter and an inviolate person, and the result had been a long education in the ways of sadism. He could see it even in the faces of strangers. One night in Paris an incident had brought him straight back to Leah. It was on the corner of rue du Four and rue des Canettes, by a bakery. A small woman in a bright blue plastic raincoat had come around the corner toward him, and for a moment he thought it was a young girl, because of her light, skipping walk. She turned around to face a man who followed her; and it was then, with a familiar dread, that he saw that she was middle-aged, and that her skipping walk was a taut dance of fear. The man hunched down and made a tearing, growling noise in his throat. She whimpered, but didn't run away—couldn't run. The man turned her with his eyes and she walked back ahead of him—to what room of pain and execution? In spite of a lust so terrible he couldn't speak, the man must take her inside before he hurt her. Sadism picked its scene as rage did not, could not. Perhaps the man needed a certain audience—his children . . . ? As he watched the two of them go down the narrow sidewalk of rue des Canettes he'd been nearly smothered by memories of Leah.

As he crossed the railroad siding on Water Street he picked up a heavy clinker and threw it as hard as he could against a clapboard wall. The loose boards slapped together with the hollow boom of a shotgun, and part of the clinker stuck in the wood and stayed there. His finger began to sting—the sharp edge of the clinker had bruised and cut. A small glob of blood grew alongside his nail, and as he crossed over to the lighted office he wiped it on his dirty shirt.

CHAPTER 17

In the Spinellis' kitchen Jane sipped her wine and heard the indecision of the wind as it changed. No indecision appeared in Mrs. Spinelli's watching eyes. Black in her Indian's face, they moved to inspect the order of her kitchen; pots and pans, the oilcloth on the table, Jane sitting across from her. She still caressed her pillow.

"Father Demon," she said.

"Father Desmond," Jane said, startled. "You know Father Desmond."

"No good." The old woman kneaded her pillow.

"It's all right not to like him, Mother. Lots of people don't like him too much, but he tries to do the right things. Where did you hear that 'Father Demon'?"

"Somebody told me." Then she whispered, "They trick me."

"Who tricks you?"

"Everybody. Not you, Janie. Good girl." She smiled. "You come when I need you. You make that no-good Irish go away and leave me be." She got up and came around the table, patted Jane on the head and took Jane's glass to refill it from the half-gallon bottle on its stand beside the refrigerator. She dropped her rosary and absently scooped it up again. The Virgin's candle guttered low, and she replaced it, lighting the new one from the old and then pushing it firmly into the soft wax in the ruby tumbler. When she settled in her chair again she gave a long, theatrical sigh and tilted her head as if from weariness.

The electric clock in the shape of a teapot buzzed, and the little square eye in it blinked black and white. Jane drank her wine as she waited, the grapy fume of it familiar and nostalgic—everything gone for good was missed in some way. She knew herself to be the kind who never visited just to visit, or even visited out of vague duty. If it hadn't been for the fire she wouldn't have come to the Spinellis' again until one of them died, and she was afraid it would be Cesare Spinelli who died first. The quick and the caring ones died first, not the confused, pottering old women. She would probably be one of the latter herself.

But it was a kind of talent not to be daunted—really daunted—by anything, to do the usual, necessary things day after day in spite of any tragedy; to just plain live. Mrs. Spinelli would not leave her kitchen, she said. But she would if she had to, and her husband would pay for it. He would suffer the grand, satisfying (to the woman) fuss, and after it was over the woman would come back screaming and crying and get a big meal for everyone in sight. Refreshed by it all, she would continue to live on her husband's energy.

Well, if living itself were a kind of simple talent, she herself had better learn to settle down to it. She wondered what would happen to her. Did John Cotter figure in any plan at all? Perhaps she would live on like the old, old people of Cascom Corners, who were so careful that they just dried up and died only when the last little bit of moisture had evaporated out of them. She might live on and on at her grandfather's farm until he died and Mrs. Pettibone died, until Aubrey died and Adolf learned enough English to go to the city, until the farm went all back to wildcats and foxes and woods.

It was eleven o'clock when the steam whistle on the firehouse started screaming again. Mrs. Spinelli didn't seem to hear it. If she did, her only reaction was to nod her head. She was primed and ready for disaster.

"They ain't going to take me away," she said calmly.

Jane had been hoping that Cesare Spinelli, or even the priest, would come back before the old woman changed her mind about being calm, but it was Sam Stevens who crunched the porch boards and pushed open the kitchen door.

"How do, Mrs. Spinelli," he said, standing solidly inside the door. "Your husband's on his way over, so don't git worried. I don't guess you'll have to move for a while now. Janie? How you doing?"

"I just heard the whistle again," she said.

"Oh, I guess we're going to lose the whole of Poverty Street, both sides. But the wind's changed, and we got to git back to Cascom. They's a fire coming round the other side of Cascom Lake. They got the State Police, National Guard, Salvation Army, Red Cross and God knows what-all heading out to save Cascom and Leah from the other side, now. Goddam wind won't make up her mind which way she's going to blow. State Police are taking over so Atmon can't mess things up too bad." He sighed and sat down on a spindly kitchen chair. A glance at Mrs. Spinelli had evidently convinced him that she would not object.

"Did anybody get hurt in the fire?" Jane asked.

"Feller got his leg crushed when a stove fell on him. They kind of think an old couple name of Bouchard—French—never got out. Can't find 'em anywheres. Let's see, now—Keith Joubert got hurt some, too."

"Keith? What happened to him?" She couldn't understand why her grandfather smiled.

"Seems he got into a argument with your boy friend"—he looked quickly at Mrs. Spinelli, saw that she hadn't been listening, and went on—"Johnny Cotter. I never seen nobody took care of in such short order."

"Who got taken care of?"

"Why, Keith Joubert, strange to say. I never would of predicted that. I'll tell you something. You don't want to fool around with John Cotter in a fight. I never seen such a cool feller in a fight."

"John Cotter?"

"Correct. He never even *hit* the other feller. Shot him down the see-ment and tore his pants, kicked him flat on his bee-hind and sent him home quicker'n you can say 'scat.' Damnedest thing I ever did see."

"They had a *fight?*"

"Warn't much of a fight. Keith Joubert run home with his pants tore and his elbows all scraped."

"Why was John fighting?"

"Well, now, Janie, you got me there! Oh, well, thank you, Mrs. Spinelli!" The old woman had brought him a glass of wine.

"This here's what you call 'dago red,' ain't it? I never had none before." He held the glass up between two huge fingers, looked through it at the light and drank it in one gulp. "Damn' good. Kind of sour, though, ain't it?"

Mrs. Spinelli smiled and filled his glass again. "Watch out!" he said, "you're going to git me drunk!"

"Take a lot of wine, get a big man like you drunk," she said, and was laughing as Cesare Spinelli came in. Cesare immediately began to laugh too.

"What's funny?" he asked, smiling and chuckling.

"I swear your wife's trying to git me drunk on this here grape-juice," Sam said.

"That's good! That's good! I'll have a glass myself!" Cesare pulled a chair up to the table and sat smiling at everybody. "I never seen such a fire, Mama," he said hopefully.

"Going to lose the whole of Poverty Street, I reckon," Sam said. This seemed to have a bad effect on Mrs. Spinelli. She began to look around for her pillow.

"She's kind of shook up by it all," Cesare said.

"Can't say as I blame her none. It ain't easy what she's been through."

"I know it," Cesare said, clenching his hands.

Yes, Jane thought. It's the man here who suffers most. But why shouldn't she identify more with the woman, the mother who had been bereaved? She felt that perhaps it was because she herself had never suffered very much in her life. She should at least have had to take her woman's chances with death, the death of someone she really loved.

CHAPTER 18

But the office wasn't empty. Madbury and William Cotter crouched on the floor above a six-foot square of old fiberboard, their bloody hands working amid the ruins, the silvery, twitching ruins, of hundreds of mutilated bullfrogs. Rows of pearly, skinned legs grew on one side and piles of limp skin, like kid gloves turned inside out, grew damply on the other. The pierced frogs quivered legless in a box; the bag of uncleaned frogs oozed and palpitated, its neck held shut by a cinderbrick.

John was too shocked by the first glare of red gore to speak. His father looked up guiltily.

"Frogs' legs, Johnny!" he said.

"Hundreds!" Madbury said, his childish old face screwed up tightly as he tried to kill a frog by repeatedly shoving his knife-point into its head. The frog croaked a little but didn't seem to mind too much.

"Nearly done," William Cotter said, his arm gory to the elbow as he pulled it out of the burlap bag.

"Poverty Street's on fire again. They're going to lose both sides of it," John said.

"Wind's changed, though," Madbury said without looking up. He couldn't kill the frog so he cut off the legs anyway and threw the front part into the box. "Cats'll take care of the mess. We just stick the box out in the shed and we'll have every dang cat in Leah down here."

"There's going to be a lot of hungry cats around, from Poverty Street," John said.

"Lots of hungry people, too," William Cotter said.

"They're mostly all taken care of. They opened the National Guard armory, for one thing. The town's taking them all in somewhere or other. They've even got the Salvation Army up from Boston."

"Well, that's nice," William Cotter said.

"Salvation Army's all right," Madbury said. "Don't care for the Red Cross much."

"That's because he doesn't care much for Mrs. Rutherford," William Cotter said, winking at John.

"Goddam old busybody," Madbury mumbled.

"Red Cross. Fresh Air. She keeps busy, does her best," William Cotter said, grinning.

"So don't everybody. Old bitch."

"Done! Throw the bag away. It stinks," William Cotter said.

"I could use this here piece of fiberboard," Madbury said.

"Take it! What a mess!" William Cotter seemed to be a little tired of frogs. He and Madbury divided the legs and wrapped them in advertising flyers. Madbury took the fiberboard, the box of gore and his frogs' legs, and went home. William Cotter went to the basement washroom to clean up. The office reeked of the half-fishy, half-ammonia odor of frogs. Before his father came back upstairs John opened a couple of sooty windows and let the burned tar stink of the fire mix in with it.

William Cotter came back upstairs rubbing his hands and arms with handfuls of stringy toilet paper. He still looked a little guilty.

"I just had a fight," John said.

"You did!"

"I won, too," John said. His father threw the toilet paper away and sat down to listen, lighting a cigarette quickly and expertly with his Zippo. The gesture was very youthful, like that of a college boy who is proud of his expertness with cigarettes. John told him about the fight. "I looked kind of *mean,*" he said.

"You don't really know how you looked. I mean you just felt that way," William Cotter said quickly.

"No, I've always fought differently. I can generally get a guy down, but I never felt so expert about a fight. This fight *looked* good, you know? I felt sort of professional. It was too easy."

"Keith Joubert's a good-sized boy. . . ."

"Look," John said hesitantly, "you know how I've always felt about Leah. You have, too—felt the same way, I mean. I think you have. . . ." He could tell that his father was becoming excited by this intimacy. A little afraid, perhaps, yet eager. It had never happened before, and for a moment he thought he had better veer off, then went on, "I mean we're both sort of misfits in Leah." He hoped his father would not admit everything for the sake of the moment, and went on without waiting for an answer, "Only, I can take off when it gets bad, and you can't."

"That's right. We're both the same!"

Do you believe it? John wanted to ask. "You're a misfit too," he said carefully.

"Don't I know it!" his father said.

"But do you know what kind? Why?"

"I'm no businessman, Johnny, like Bruce was. Is," he added.

"I don't mean that."

His father looked away, a suggestion of pain on his face. Then, surprisingly, he said, "Seems to me you're still feeling a little mean."

"I could be a businessman."

"I hope you can. I hope you will," William Cotter said.

"But I don't mean that. I mean the way we get along with people. We aren't really treated right. We aren't! They think they know everything and they really don't."

"Maybe they really do, Johnny."

"They don't know anything about *me!* I'm different when I'm not in Leah. I get along fine, like everybody else. In Leah they look down their goddam noses and I can hear them think. That's why I picked a fight with Keith Joubert—because the son of a bitch has had himself convinced for years that he could lick me. Well, he *can't* lick me, but I'll bet he's home right now convincing himself all over that he can. I could *kill* that bastard and he'd still think he could lick me! What the hell can you do?"

"I thought it was Junior Stevens who used to pick on you, Johnny."

"Oh, sure. But he *can* lick me."

"It seems to me," William Cotter said diffidently, with a hesitant sort of respect, "that most people don't always figure whether they can lick somebody else or not."

"They do here; I can see them thinking it. But that isn't what I mean. I don't want to be king of the hill or anything like that, I just want to make them stop *judging* me all the time. I want to be a zero, an unknown quantity."

"You know, Johnny, lots of people go all through their lives without ever having a fight."

"So I feel persecuted. The only thing is, I never feel persecuted unless I'm in this one particular little town. I swear I get along perfectly everyplace else. Nobody ever gave me a hard time—for long—even in the Army. Why the hell should Leah do it to me?"

"You were born here."

"I've thought of that, too. Did you ever think you could go somewhere else and start over with a clean slate?"

"I used to, Johnny. I even thought I could be a businessman, once. I don't believe it any more."

"You believe that saying—that you can't run away from yourself? You know—you get somewhere new and there you are, exactly the same as you were before you took off. I don't. I think maybe *you're* the same, but the place isn't the same and the people don't look at you the same, and that's part of what you are—how the people look at you." He put his feet up on the desk, noticing that his father liked the gesture. He had been a little surprised at his father's attitude. Perhaps a little disappointed that his father hadn't gone along all the way as he thought he would. He hadn't expected any difference of opinion at all.

"I want you to stay here, Johnny. I know you're interested in more than a contracting business. I know you went to Paris and to college and all that. I mean, I went to college too, but not the way you did—to learn all that stuff. Now, I know you know a lot more than I do about a lot of things. But I always wanted you to come back here to Leah. I'll tell you, Johnny. I always liked you better than Bruce. It was hard to like Bruce. I mean I *love* Bruce and all that. You know that, and I'd always do anything I could for you two boys, but what I want to say is that I always got along better with you—not as well as I'd want to, because, as they say, you're a different generation and all that, but you weren't so *mean* as Bruce could be. He was like he was always getting *revenge* for something, and God knows I never did anything to Bruce—I don't know. I gave him a spanking now and then, but I never did it mean. I gave you a few, too, but I was never mean about it, or really mad at you, was I?"

"No. You were always fair."

"See? I was always fair to you boys! I was always fair! So I can't figure it out. What was Bruce so mad about? What did I ever do to Bruce to make him so mean? He could die and never say a good word to me. And his mother, the same to her. God knows *she* never gave him—or you, Johnny—*any*thing but pure one-hundred-percent love. Now I don't give a tinker's damn about the town, Johnny. That don't worry me one little bit. Live and let live. I just want to be a father to you two boys and have you two boys feel I'm your father. Is that so much to ask?" He fooled with a cigarette butt, then decided that it was long enough to light. His hands were trembling.

"It seems to me that it isn't something you can ask for," John said coolly. As he said it the coolness vanished, and he interrupted himself, raising his voice to make it seem that he hadn't finished the sentence: "Like that," he said. "Like that! I mean it's . . . of course I feel you're my father. You've always done anything I wanted—given me anything I wanted—and Bruce, too."

William Cotter slumped back in his chair. "Of course you can't just up and ask for . . . that," he said.

"No! No!" John said desperately. "*You* don't have to ask for it. You can't talk to most fathers. Let me tell you! Nobody ever talks with his father the way I'm talking to you. I'm telling you! There just isn't any communication at all. You don't know. None of my friends ever talk with their fathers. They've got it all figured out what the old man will say already and they're never wrong. They've heard it all before. I mean it!"

"But they . . ." his father said, "But they . . ." and he looked at his wrist watch. "Christ! It's midnight! Gladys will be worried I got burned up. If I call her she'll have a fit before she answers the phone. I'll see you later, Johnny. Can you take it till, say, three? Walk around the yard once in a while and just take a look." He spoke quickly, as if he were out of breath, gathered up his frogs' legs and left, leaving John with a sick welling of pity, a pang of inadequacy so sharp he wanted to bang his head on the desk.

The wind had stopped for the first time since he'd come home to Leah. The silence hummed in his ears and he could clearly make out the cracklings and snappings of Poverty Street, the pumper-engines and occasional shouting. He could see the huge red pillar of smoke climb straight up. Then the whole sky began to fill with smoke, and the stars went out. The air along the ground began to fill, as if the whole sky were crammed with smoke, and the brown haze had nowhere to go except down along the ground. He got down on his knees and looked up along the railroad siding. As he watched, the smoke settled until it held a level about one foot from the ground. The ceiling of Leah had fallen, and a reddish umber glazed all lights and bright surfaces. The streetlights retired inside their bulbs and glowed faintly. The oppressive stink of burned tarpaper and paint mixed with the once-pleasant odor of burning leaves and poisoned it, made it cloying and suffocating. He went back into the office and shut the windows.

He tried to read a circular on the installation of aluminum drain-pipes, then an illustrated manual on the installation of Heatilator fireplaces, then an expensively bound book of samples and specifications of asphalt siding. All of the flyers were grimy, and hundreds more were piled in one corner of the office, beneath the counter. Some were full of pictures of pretty girls, and he pulled them all out to look at the grimy, pretty girls.

None of the symmetrical, characterless smiles were Jane's. None of the famished, angular bodies were hers. He kicked the pile back into the corner. "Hell of a note," he said. Then he tried it a little louder, "Hell of a note! HELL OF A NOTE!" he screamed into the empty office. He began aimlessly pulling out the drawers of Bruce's desk. One was locked. A new Yale doorlock had been installed in it. The desk was oak, but the locked drawer was on the bottom and the bottom of the drawer was flimsy plywood. He pried it out with his knife, and the contents of the drawer fell to the floor. He looked around guiltily, but Bruce was not there. A metal box, not locked, sat on top of a book—a standard account book in red-and-black binding with the word *Record* stamped in gold on the cover. The metal box was heavy. He opened it cautiously and stared for a minute at a dark, angular pistol. Carefully oiled and set into a sheepskin form, the blue pistol waited coldly and silently. It seemed to create its own alien darkness, as if he had stared suddenly into a nest of snakes. He picked it out and worked the slide. A fat round jumped out and rolled on the desk top. He removed the clip and ejected the chambered shell. On the left side of the slide he read the small, delicate stampings: *Ortgies Patent. 7.65 mm.* and a long German word he didn't know, but which seemed in its combining long harshness the perfect comment upon the cruel, beautiful Germanness of the weapon.

He held the pistol until it began to warm in his hand; then unloaded the clip and wiped everything, even the shells, with the sheepskin and put them back in the box with the gun. He opened the record book and read, in Bruce's large round handwriting: "Whoever breaks in here, do not go any farther or I will find out who did it and kill you. I mean it."

He knew that Bruce probably just about did mean it. If Bruce had been—he almost thought, "alive"—if Bruce had been around, up and around, John knew he would have taken many precautions before going any farther. He knew very little about his brother. Bruce never talked honestly or confidingly about himself, and John realized that he had never been very interested in any of Bruce's secrets. Just getting along with him, or away from him, had taken up most of his time.

On the second green, lined page, Bruce had written, "I am writing this all down so I can remember what I thought and what I wanted when I thought it. Bruce Cotter, Oct., 1946."

Eleven years ago. He leafed through the book quickly. It was crammed with words, right over the margins on all the pages, and the last entry was made on the night Bruce went to the hospital. John held it in both hands and found himself shivering. A sentence had jumped out at him: "Nobody gives a good sweet Jesus if I die." He began to read from the beginning: "They are all getting ready for that jerk to come home in triumph from the whorehouses of Manila. I am supposed to welcome our hero with modesty befitting a slacker who just stayed home through this 'glorious living hell,' etc. etc. etc.! and tell the little mama's boy what a hero he is. I hope he has syphilis. Let him try to get along in civilian life and see what a flop he turns out to be! He had better not try to tell me any war stories!

"Five more years if there is no depression and I can take off.

"Figured Minetta Randolf is about 18 yrs. old. One more time and I think she will spread for me.

"My father is not only lazy, he is stupider than anybody. Freddie the Idiot would be more help. Eightball fired—he is stupider than my father, if that is possible."

No secrets there—except about taking off, and Minetta. And yet it still seemed like indecent exposure. Because Bruce seemed so fearful and predatory, he should have been capable of a deadlier hatred, more vindictiveness than the crude, childish words revealed.

"He had better not try to tell me any war stories," seemed so pitifully inadequate, so much like a small boy who could think of nothing to say.

"I would like to see Mrs. Rutherford raped by a buck nigger in front of the Women's Club with the Eastern Stars as guests. Ha. Ha."

That was better for Bruce. But the "Ha. Ha." at the end . . .

He read on. So much poison, so much hatred. John began to skip pages, scanning the repetitious passages of spite. Every once in a while he came upon references to Bruce's "taking off." "Three more years and I can take off . . ." set in the middle of a paragraph, or what would have been a paragraph if Bruce had used indentations. Minetta Randolf was mentioned often, and her father: "Howard Randolf is a stupid loud mouth failure. He didn't even know what we were doing downstairs. Her mother knew, the dirty old bitch. She was enjoying it and her own daughter! I was enjoying it until Minetta started crying and I got the hell out. I didn't think she was the type to cry about it. Says she loves me. I bet."

Bruce hated New England. New England was too cosy, he said. But the subject of Minetta's loving him evidently fascinated him: "Right afterwards she always says she loves me. Sometimes she cries. She gets soft all over. It is funny. All of a sudden she gets as soft as goose down. Her lips get all sticky and soft. She feels like she is going to turn to water and run right out from under me. Maybe that means she means it. Ha! Whore in Montreal said the same thing. Minetta says it all the time lately. She said I just look at her and she melts. Her mother is hinting around we should be engaged. Ha. Ha.

"Pretty soon now and I can go look for the place."

This must have meant the taking-off idea. John skipped through the book looking for it.

"I want to work for it, don't want it to be so easy. I want to climb mountains, get in ambushes, have to kill men for it. I want to ride a horse and carry a pistol, a big pistol right out in the open where everybody does and nobody thinks twice. That is where I want to go. I have to fight and struggle and almost get killed finding it or it does not seem worth anything when I get it. Like in the dream when I was flying the secondhand Kaiser-Frazer, hell of a funny name for an airplane. God I was happy!! It was early in the morning in China, with the Flying Tigers or something. This great big Junkers transport came over with the black crosses on it. It was a hospital plane, only it was a fake hospital plane full of German troops. Machineguns sticking out. I left her in the doorway. I loved her. She waited for me, beautiful, passionate, she loved me. I went out and warmed up the secondhand Kaiser-Frazer and took off after the Junkers transport. I shot it down. They hit my plane, too. I flew back just as the sun came up yellow and clean. Hot steamy morning but cool, sort of. I flew back around the field and the huts and the clean place. I was afraid when I shot down the plane but that made it feel so good and clean when I landed and she was waiting for me and all the congratulations and comradeship of the brave men, too!"

John shut the book with the sudden, real knowledge that if Bruce knew he had read that, Bruce would kill him. Closer to Bruce at that moment than he had ever been, for a fearful second he felt Bruce's presence in the office. He thought of the pistol, made a panicky motion toward it as if to snatch it out of its box. Then he got up and walked around nervously, looking out of the windows. When he first came home, he remembered, his father had looked up, seen his face in the window and been afraid that it was Bruce. He clearly remembered the quick look of fear on his father's face.

But the record book was there, open and defenseless. Bruce must have believed that he would come through the operation or he would have destroyed it. Maybe. Maybe he couldn't do it even if he wanted to. It would be a form of suicide to destroy the only sincere expression of himself, his love, his desire to live.

The fear had gone, and in its place was an unfamiliar emotion toward Bruce he wanted at first to resent, to ward off. His brother, his flesh and blood—the old words out of a past mostly read about, mostly felt but not experienced—now seemed forceful as a blow. He had been too busy escaping the man to be aware of his humanity. He had pitied more any number of tragic strangers, objects of fate and the newspapers. And yet his relationship with Bruce *had* been intensely personal, in a way. It had always been between the two of them alone: no mediators, not his father and mother, surely, had ever entered into it. No judges, no rules—they had fought each other all their lives, guided only by their own wit and strength. No quarter had ever been given, and he had been as guilty as Bruce.

He had never suspected in Bruce a desire for happiness, even in fantasy, and he knew why—he himself was capable of the same destructive, eternal hatred. They both hated Leah and wanted to escape. That much they had in common. Bruce had never made it, though. The scalpels, bludgeons against the infinite complexity of his brain, had left him comatose, permanently deranged. He would most likely die.

They had an attendant for Bruce now, a pale creature of the night in a dead-white uniform who sat at the side of the bed and listened to his breath, turned him over and pressed the feeding tubes through his nose every two hours. Bruce's eyes remained closed and would be closed forever—except for the impersonal brutality of examination, the doctors' purposeful fingering, the eyeball living and bright but insensitive as a grape in the needle of light.

The operation had been unsuccessful but the patient had lived, and was living, and would go on living without his brain, like the decapitated rooster in the newspapers, down whose neck hole they tucked kernels of corn: the rest worked, grinding and dissolving and bulging in and out all the way through. Every day his mother came and sat beside him for a few minutes. . . .

John put his hand around the hot metal lampshade on the desk, then pulled it away burned. She wanted him to go see Bruce, too. Good God! Bruce looked fine, she said, except that he needed to gain some weight. They shaved him every day and turned him over like an egg in an incubator so he wouldn't rot. He had had to learn all about Bruce now, in spite of an almost hysterical desire to hear nothing. When his mother spoke he left the room. If she were not looking he put his fingers in his ears, and yet the deadly small pieces of information burned their way through somehow, through doors, through the bones of his head. They came and grew like maggots until he knew everything. Everything. The doctor's hands—he knew how they wrenched the flesh, how they forced the lump of manlike protoplasm with professional strength. One time in college he had wandered into the wrong building and ended up in an old high room thick with formaldehyde—the air grabbed him like a hand. The body of an old bum lay spread-eagled on a galvanized tray, and the poor old bastard was so skinny he had no buttocks at all. A medical student watched John and as they talked ran his bare hands into a long slit in the bum's belly and pulled out his innards, dry and much handled, fondled them, strung them out on his arms like a snakekeeper, pulled the loops out, squeezed, patted them—all to prove a point that didn't need proving: that to him the contents of a man's belly was so many pieces of strung and lumpy elastic. The strong, show-off hands had been developing, learning.

He snapped the lampshade with his fingernail. He heard a doctor say one time that he had just seen an interesting liver. He wondered if his brother had an interesting brain. He himself had seen brain all over the side of a wall and all over women's shaking black skirts—even on the windows, red and gray, giving a kind of stained-glass effect, and he knew then and would always know that he had been the one and only cause of that splattering of intelligence. Automatically as the memory returned he tried to stop it, first trying to think it away, then shaking his head; but this time it was as if he tensed himself for a recurring pain that didn't come on time. He sat for a moment rigidly waiting, and although the memory was clear and immediate, the old sickness didn't come. It was as if he had not been the one to fire the shots into the old man, as if it had been Nakano or Parsons who had murdered him. Murdered him.

"I am thinking about it," he said out loud, "and I'm not sick. I could even eat meat right now."

But then a terrible upwelling came in his throat. *All right, hello, there you are, old buddy. Now we know where we are again.* But now it was not the old Filipino hanging gored in his mind. Now his mind flirted dangerously with images he tried to keep under control. Bits of food danced by, a piece of red meat, a bowl of brains. He gagged and staggered to the door: Bruce had come, his head open like a bowl, his eyes leaking gray, and he had the body of a hawk. When he turned, Bruce was there, still moving like a mote across his eye that couldn't be blinked away. Bruce leaned forward and the gray gushed out like puke, leaving the cavity of his head bony and reddish, the dura torn ragged around the edges. The eyes were empty. The hawk's body stood on yellow legs and claws and leaned slightly forward as if against an expected bullet.

He swung his head violently, so that his lips and cheeks pulled away from his face. This helped. He did it some more and developed a headache. That was better. He began to repair the drawer of Bruce's desk, then said to hell with it—the plywood would not stay in place. He took the plywood to the door and scaled it out along the railroad tracks. He would take the book and the metal box home with him. No one would ask him what they were. He took the pistol out of the box and started feeding cartridges into the magazine. When the magazine would take no more he put it into the gun and worked the slide, chambering a round, then removed the magazine and added one more round. The safety seemed snug and unlikely to work loose. As the phone rang he slid the pistol into his back pocket.

"Johnny?" his father said, "Charlie Bemis just called. Jesus Christ it looks as if we're going to lose Leah! It looks bad, Johnny!

Take the ton-and-a-half—the Dodge. Keys are on top of my desk. Poor Charlie's about had it. Pick up a load of men at the firehouse and take 'em out to Cascom. You can see the red from here. God! Never mind the yard any more. I don't know what they're going to do now!"

"O.K.," John said. "Now take it easy. The wind's stopped."

"Fire makes its own wind, Johnny."

"Take it easy . . ." He didn't have a name to call his father, and now he needed one. "We'll do what we can. We'll stop it . . ." He almost said *Dad,* but it was as if the muscles of his tongue and jaws had never formed the word before.

"Well, all right, Johnny. I've just got to stay here with your mother and the kids. I've just *got* to. You know how your mother gets." And then, in an urgent, low voice, as if someone had just come into the room, "Johnny, for God's sake be careful!"

"All right, Dad."

His father was struck silent. The word had been as startling as a shot. "I'll be careful," John said.

"All right," his father managed to say, and was silent. John hung up first.

He found the keys to the ton-and-a-half, locked the office and started across the murky yard toward the garage. He could hardly see, and rubbed his eyes until they ached. At the garage doors he stopped, surprised by a peculiar lightness in him, as if gravity had lessened. It had to do with his father, strangely enough, and it was as if the big, amorphous man had gained, as he had gained from the few words they had spoken, stature and strength. He had answered his father, had recognized him, on his own, and only his own, responsibility. But why should he feel some small disloyalty to Bruce?

The ton-and-a-half sighed, popped, and ground into life, jumped backward as he let out the clutch. Naturally it had been left in reverse. He fooled with the gearshift until he found out where all the positions were, then eased out into the smoke, headlights boring redly across sawdust to a red shed wall. The truck waited alive, rocking a little in a pothole, while he locked the garage. As he drove up River Street toward the square, the smoke grew thicker in the headlights, but it no longer seemed a deficiency of his own eyes.

CHAPTER 19

As Jane and Sam came away from the Spinellis' kitchen Adolf jumped out of the truck, in his jerky, eager way, banged his head on the doorframe and stood smiling and rubbing the bump.

"Thank you! Thank you!" Cesare Spinelli called from the doorway.

"Nothing. Nothing atall!" Sam called back.

Jane climbed into the truck and sat in the middle with her feet up on the gearbox, and Adolf slammed the door on his side as if he didn't care whether or not all his hands, feet, arms and fingers were tucked in safely or not. The springs creaked and the seat lowered under Sam Stevens. Slowly, carefully, he turned the truck out of the driveway toward Cascom.

"I don't envy that little feller," he said. "One son, he's dead, and his wife addled. Don't envy him one bit."

"Wow," Adolf said.

"Lucky you ain't got no responsibilities. Eh, Adolf?"

"Sure!" Adolf said.

And here I am, Jane thought, with no responsibilities either. She felt that if she had loved Michael Spinelli enough, maybe she could have saved him from the mailbox—although that would have saved her a portion of those ten blank years, too. He would simply have taken off, and that would have been that. Cesare Spinelli might still have had a son.

"Wow!" Adolf said. He stared over the hills toward the east, where a great, angry glow, a perfect half-circle of bright red, marked the advancing fire. The smoke of Leah's fire had thinned as they left town, and this glow, this upwelling of reflecting smoke, was a hundred times as big. Whole hills were burning.

"That tore it," Sam said. He didn't increase his speed.

A state policeman stepped out into the road and waved them to a stop, came over to Sam's side and leaned in, his face close to Sam's, his wide-brimmed hat bending against the windowframe.

"Where you going?" he asked.

"I'm going home," Sam said.

"O.K." The policeman stepped back to wave down another truck.

"Ain't going to be no goddam sighteers when all the country's burning up," Sam said disgustedly.

The road turned and climbed, leaving the Cascom River. Sam shifted to second on the hill, and the fire came up into their eyes.

"Has it got to the farm?"

"Not yet, Janie." Sam shifted carefully into high at the top of the hill. "I make it close to Cascom Corners, though. They hadn't let all them fine pastures go back, they wouldn't be in trouble. Woods come clear up to the two-holers in Cascom Corners."

The lake reflected the red clouds, here and there even the sharp yellow of burning trees. A hill-farm house and barn across the lake flamed untended and shot a spike of fire straight up into the clouds of smoke.

"Murphy place," Sam said. Nobody lived there. Jane remembered when someone had. Several school-shy boys and one girl, a long time ago, came on the school bus with her into Leah. They had moved away, and the farm had been vacant ever since. Each year less pasture showed on the side of the long hill.

They were going down again into the valley of the river, down into the smoke which flowed slowly between the hills; another river. A convoy of National Guard trucks passed them on the way back to Leah for reinforcements, their headlights appearing as dim orange buttons at first so that it was difficult to tell whether they were headlights or taillights until they were only a few yards away. At the gravel road to the farm a guardsman in full uniform, carrying a rifle, stepped out beside them.

"Can't go up this road," he said, his young voice matter-of-fact and final, as if he expected Sam to turn around immediately.

"Now listen here, son," Sam said.

"Orders," said the guardsman, tapping his front sight against his helmet-liner.

"I live here, sonny. Like as not your orders didn't cover that." Sam seemed to find the situation amusing.

"I got my orders. Nobody, but *nobody,* goes up this here road."

"Well, now. I wouldn't put her quite so strong, I was you," Sam said as he let out his clutch.

"STOP STOP STOP!" The soldier shouted. He jumped back and pointed his rifle at Sam's head. Sam stopped the truck, set the emergency brake, stepped out and faced the soldier squarely as a house, his huge body solid, his legs slightly spread.

"You going to shoot me?" he asked, smiling sternly. Finally the soldier lowered his rifle. "That's better," Sam said. "Now look here, son. This here's my own road, goes to my own farm, nowheres else. I appreciate you boys' help and all—I want to say that. But, son, you got to use your own head. Things is going to happen tonight ain't halfways in your orders. Anybody wants to come up this road tonight, you let 'em, hear? They'll be coming to fight fire, not to see no sights nor to steal. Next your officer comes by you tell him what I said. Sam Stevens is my name."

After a moment of thought, the soldier shifted his rifle, in a deliberately unmilitary way, to the crook of his arm, like a hunter. "I guess you're right," he said. "This ain't no war, Mr. Stevens. You go ahead home."

They climbed the hill in second, coming out of the smoke as if from under water.

"My God!" Jane said. The house looked full of fire, and her hands grew damp all at once; she could feel the beat of her heart. The front windows of the house were furnace doors, a dull, boiling red. As the truck turned, the fires went out—reflections of the valley below. The kitchen lights were on. Mrs. Pettibone came running, her white apron to one side, her face sickly in the shed lights.

"Oh, Janie!" she whimpered, her deep-set eyes wide and wet, "Janie, I'm so glad you're back!"

Adolf wrenched the door handle until it worked, and Jane climbed out after him.

"Janie, the fire!" Mrs. Pettibone cried.

"I know, dear, I know. Everything will be all right." She put her arm around the old woman and straightened her apron, saying gently as they walked up to the house, "All right, all right, don't worry, now; it's going to be all right, you'll see."

At the door she turned to see all at once the cause of Mrs. Pettibone's crying. The farm was all alone above an evil plain of smoke, alone except for the spruce-dark summits of the near hills, tindery and threatening. Deep down in the smoke, by the lake and the river, bright flashes shone upward, surrounding the lake like a huge pincers, visibly advancing. Above the layer of smoke a clear layer of air was broken here and there by pillars of dark red and orange where fierce crowning fires forced up through it, flames threading upward, whirling showers of sparks fountaining up and settling back down again. The fire was too angry, too determined. It seemed that no man could live down there, that their trip from Leah had been impossible, miraculous. The whole world below was red and burning. Far above, in a limbo of clear air filled with cold light from a small, high moon, escaping columns of smoke all turned together at right angles toward the west as a stream of air at that altitude caught them.

Sam came up behind and turned his old face toward the fire, which now gleamed in the shiny skin over his cheekbones as it had in the windows of the house. He pointed upward, his big arm moving slowly.

"See that wind up there, Janie? Now, that wind's near two miles up, I reckon. Well, Janie, if that wind comes down here to us, I figure the Old Feller's pretty goddam mad. If it don't, we got a chance to do some good. The Old Bastard *could* take himself a fine, long leak and solve the problem straight off. That ain't likely. He never done me no goddam favors. I never asked for none. See you can git us men something to eat. Aubrey ain't much good; same as Adolf, his gut's empty."

CHAPTER 20

John parked the truck in line with several others in front of the firehouse. Guardsmen and civilians were unloading shovels and Indian pumps and stacking them against the building. Inside, sooty men just back from the front lines and clean men just arrived leaned on their shovels and added to the babble of noise in the high room. In one corner Red Cross ladies stood behind a trestle table piled with sandwiches. A large chromed coffee-maker, borrowed from the Welkum Diner, steamed and dripped behind them. Squashed paper cups littered the floor. In the center of the room quieter, listening men surrounded tables and a radio. Once in a while the telephone in the center rang, and the noise would stop as they all turned to watch Mr. Bemis, whose withered, pale face and bald head were snow-white against the black receiver. The noise would grow again until Mr. Bemis had to wave his hand up and down, trying to stop it so that he could hear.

John went up to him, ducking under the rope which made the center area more official, and waited for Mr. Bemis to finish his telephone conversation.

"Hi, John," the town clerk said wearily.

"I've got a ton-and-a-half, flat bed, Mr. B. My father called up and said you needed transportation."

"Correct. You wait, will you, John? We're sending men out as soon as we git news and all. It won't be long."

"You look tired," John said.

"So don't you!" The town clerk grinned and cackled, his white fingers kneading his temples.

"What's Atmon doing?"

"He's out to the fire, John."

"He's a man of action, Atmon is," John said. Several of the men at the table laughed, especially the firemen, but Mr. Bemis looked up and shook his head.

"Chief Atmon's keeping busy, John." The phone rang again, and Mr. Bemis sighed as he reached for it.

John ducked under the rope and looked for a place to sit down, then saw Billy Muldrow and Howard Randolf sitting against the wall in the back of the room. As he pushed his way up to them Howard raised his hand, Indian fashion. "How!" he said. "Why there's the very fellow now!"

"I thought you went home to bed," John said.

"It's few men and small who'll be sleeping this night."

"Hi, John," Billy said. "Sit down! Waiting, waiting. Just like the Army, ain't it, John?"

He sat down on the floor next to Billy and leaned back against the brick wall.

Junior Stevens squatted nearby among the black-uniformed Riders. Bob Paquette was there, too. They all seemed to be excited about something as they listened to Junior, who bobbed up and down on his haunches as he spoke. Bob Paquette looked right at John, then turned away without any sign of recognition.

"My old buddy, Bob Paquette," John said.

"He's gone over, Johnny," Billy said.

"He didn't like the way I treated Keith Joubert. You know why?" John asked Howard.

"You *did* rather demolish the idiot."

"It's not that. Somehow it was in bad taste, see? I'd like to give that bastard a bad taste for every time he and his buddies ganged up on me. They're willing to admit I've got a higher I.Q., but not that I can beat Keith Joubert. That's in bad taste. What has the poor bully got left?"

"Oh, he must have *something* left," Howard said, grinning.

"No matter what you're saying, it ain't true," Billy said vehemently. "I match Johnny up against any one of 'em!"

"Well, thanks, Billy," John said. For a moment he was very grateful to Billy, but then, in the face of Howard's amusement he added, "Only don't match me with Junior right now."

"As the mouse said, 'I've been sick.' " Howard said. He reached across Billy's long legs and slapped John on the knee.

Billy poked around in his back pocket and came out with a mashed sandwich. He opened it and looked inside as a man looks in his handkerchief after blowing his nose. It was jam. He began to eat. Howard jumped up, his knees cracking.

"I'll get us some coffee." He pushed toward the Red Cross ladies.

John noticed that Billy was even grimier than usual. The deep cracks in his face were black lines, full of soot. His checkered hunting shirt had lost its red squares and now was a patchwork of gray and black. Above his boots large splotches of dirt stained his long shins. His overalls had turned a shiny black.

"Oh, I been out to Cascom once already," Billy said.

"Where?"

"Up to the Corners. Old Murphy place burnt up. We didn't have no more chance than nothing."

"How about Sam Stevens' place?"

Billy grinned at him. "I reckon she's O.K., Johnny."

"Who?"

"I says I reckon she's O.K." He tried to stop grinning and his face inflated. For a second he looked like a huge chipmunk. "Sam's place is O.K., I reckon."

"Who told you about that?"

"Everybody and his brother knows you been squiring Junior's sister around."

"They think it's too soon after the funeral or something?"

"It ain't that! Everybody knowed Mike Spinelli warn't no match for her. Just a heller, Mike was. Him and his goddam motorcycle.

You want to know something, Johnny?" Billy waited, his eyebrows raised, his eyes bugged out.

"What?"

"I don't see what a wonderful woman like her seen in him."

"Oh, I don't know, Billy."

"Goddam fine woman. Never should of married that guinea in the first place. Ayuh!"

Howard came back with three paper cups of coffee and settled down against the wall again, sighing, his knees again cracking. "I'm going to tell you, John," he said, "I'm an old man. I'm fifty-five years old."

"I'm forty-five, come November," Billy said. "I ain't no spring chicken, neither."

"An old man in a dry month. My bones are drying up like sticks, my loins are withered and sere, I've given up all of youth's frivolities, I'm careful, I'm crotchety, I'm a bag of incipient rot." Howard nodded as he spoke, "And yet I'm enjoying this business. I feel like a kid allowed to stay up late. All the excitement! I hope to hell my house doesn't burn down, of course, but aside from that, I'm enjoying myself."

"Like a war," John said, "I felt that way about the war. But I don't feel much about this."

"It's your home town, not mine. How about you, Billy?" Howard asked.

"Don't ask Billy," John said. "He and Leah aren't speaking."

"Screw Leah," Billy said.

All voices suddenly stopped. Everyone looked toward the center of the room, where a sudden tenseness at the table had gained immediate attention. Junior Stevens bent over Mr. Bemis, and the little town clerk looked up at Junior, a banty rooster facing a big dog.

"I told you three times, no," Mr. Bemis said.

"Why not?" Junior asked. He was on the edge of rage, his big face growing red. Mr. Bemis' high, dry voice carried clear authority.

"There's enough confusion now with everybody running around. You and your motorcycles would just add to it. We git plenty information right now. This ain't no fun-fair you can show off your pretty uniforms at. We got enough trouble right now without you ramming around killing yourselves."

"We just want to help, for Christ sakes!"

"Flying squadron! Be picking your flying squadron out of the ditches. We got enough to worry about."

"Git through traffic—go where nobody else can. . . ."

"Why don't you grow up? Find out them noisy putt-putts ain't good for nothing. All them damn' things is good for is for you never-grew-up kids to ram around on showing off, making a noise nobody can think to! Think everybody admires you, showing off like that? Think you're goddam asses, that's what they think! You killed a boy a while back—your own brother-in-law. Ain't you satisfied yet? You want to help? Take off them fancy uniforms and git set to use a shovel. We got no time for flying squadrons!" It was a long speech for Mr. Bemis. He looked back to the papers on his table.

Junior's shoulders began to shake. His face, marked by little white lines, turned dark and brutal. John had never seen Junior this angry, had never seen his pride injured so badly as Mr. Bemis' dry, authoritarian words had injured it. A windy, croupy noise came from Junior's mouth, half words, half breath: "Wha . . . wha . . . wah . . ." Then he gave the table a violent shove with his thigh. The edge caught the town clerk below his bony chest and shot him up against the back of his chair. His hands fell to his sides, his pencil bounced on the cement floor. He looked up at Junior, trying to catch a breath, his open mouth vividly red in his white face.

After a few seconds of shocked disbelief, Joe Beaupre and two firemen jumped Junior and bulled him to the floor. Hands came up out of the tangle and descended, feet scraped along the cement. Out of the grasping, grunting tangle Junior's scream of rage was as steady as a siren: *Sonsabitchinbastardssonabitchinbastards* . . . Occasionally muffled, but not for long. One of the firemen scrambled away, holding his bitten hand as if it were a baby, in the crook of his arm. He ran to the door and danced up and down, blowing on his bleeding hand and crooning softly. Joe Beaupre and the other fireman couldn't hold Junior down. He rolled out of the pile and on his way to his feet put the fireman out of action with a short, vicious elbow to the chest. It was a blow so swift and expert it brought a concerted, horrified, yet admiring sigh from all the spectators, John among them. It stopped Joe Beaupre, too. With much grasping and jerking and a great amount of embarrassment he pulled his gun from his trick police holster. For a moment he had forgotten how to unlock it.

Junior turned his back on Joe Beaupre and faced the town clerk, who was still out of breath. "You're a no-good little son of a bitch, Bemis! You're the one playing the hero. We offer to help as best we can—" Self-pity broke his voice for a moment. "And you turn us down. We'll help, all right, but no thanks to you!" Rage again began to gather in his face. "So goddam high and mighty! I'll tell you something, you'll git yours some day! The biggest thing about you is your goddam mouth!"

He whirled around and in the same motion slapped the heavy revolver out of Joe Beaupre's hand. It bounced across the floor, everyone jumping aside to let it pass, and stopped in front of John.

"What were you going to do with it, anyway," Junior said to Joe Beaupre, "shoot somebody?" He laughed raucously, but was obviously afraid; he had done a little too well. He was just a little too quick to turn and walk out of the firehouse. The Riders followed him.

Then the town clerk began to scream, "Stop! Stop! Beaupre! Arrest that man! Stop!"

Many wondering eyes focused on the town clerk, including Joe Beaupre's. The town clerk's screaming slowed and stopped, and there was dead silence in the firehouse.

John found himself walking down the narrow lane cleared by the revolver's slide, toward the center table. He held the gun flat in his hand. One side of the cylinder and the end of the barrel were scratched silver through the blue. He handed it to Joe Beaupre and spoke to the town clerk, with a new attitude evident in his voice—one that came to him in a quite new, communal way: he knowingly echoed the sentiments of the men of Leah:

"Now, Mr. B. We have a fire to fight."

He had never seen in any man's eyes such clear hatred, even as the town clerk laughed and reached for the ringing telephone. The pale hand on the receiver quivered, everyone watching it. Wide blue veins deltaed down the hand and along the fingers. The telephone rang again before the town clerk answered it, and then he looked up calmly as he listened. "Ayuh. Ayuh. Ayuh." He hung up and sent two trucks to Cascom, and the crowd in the room was less pressing. A Red Cross lady peeped in, and then another, and they took up their stations again. No one had seen them run away.

"Fire's out of control," Mr. Bemis said, looking at John. "Seems the wind's coming up again. Fire crowned over the state highway, burnt up a National Guard truck. Gitting kind of dangerous out there."

"Better there than here," Joe Beaupre said. He was outwardly calm again, and seemed to want to forget about the fight.

"You take your truck and pick up them full Indian pumps, all the men you can get on," the town clerk said to John.

"O.K., Mr. B." The town clerk didn't smile at him now.

He went outside and moved the truck up to the pile of Indian pumps. Billy and Howard and several others began to load them on. John stood on the truck and piled, jamming shovels into the cracks in the planking to keep the dripping pumps from rolling off. The smoke was leaf-sweet and sickening, and the men wheezed and spat on the sidewalk between bursts of effort. When the pumps were loaded, Howard and Billy got into the cab with John. At the corner the Riders flagged the truck and jumped on; John wondered if they had known it was his truck. In any case they couldn't jump off now. He turned on Bank Street and overdrove his headlights just a bit on the road to Cascom.

"Been me scratched Beaupre's gun up like that he'd most likely shot me dead on the spot," Billy said.

"I'll never figure that one out," Howard said wonderingly.

"Old Mr. B. said some pretty hard things to Junior," John said. "Now what the hell is that?"

A little red dot whirled around and around in the road, and he slowed down and stopped. A state policeman and a flashlight.

"Where you headed?"

"Cascom," John said.

"You ain't going to git through, you know."

Don't riddle me, John thought.

"There's a National Guard truck burning up right square in the road. Looking for a bulldozer to clear it away. You better go on up to the Stevens' place. You know where that is?"

So his wait was going to end. He drove on, faster than before until he felt Howard's leg involuntarily jabbing the floorboards for a brake. Would she be there, though?

They descended into the smoke along the river, then climbed out of it on the big hill above the lake. They would have to go down into it again, but from now on it would be like entering a furnace. All the far hills were fire or embering fire, and flames higher than houses whipped the edges of the lake. He stopped the truck on the summit and went around to the back.

"Anybody not want to go down?" he asked. It seemed a reasonable question. The Riders looked at him stolidly.

"It's your truck, John," one of the men said. In the glare, their sweaty faces made them look like painted Indians. No one decided to stay, so they descended into the murk again, into the cloying stench of burning trees.

He missed the road to Sam Stevens' farm and had to turn around. A National Guardsman, his uniform black with sweat and soot, waved him on up the gravel road. He could see about twenty yards ahead, and followed the lighter color of the gravel as the truck ground up the hill. Then they could see and breathe freely again, and there was the high house among the dark barns and against the black mountain. But the house was not white now; it was pink, and even the spruces of the mountain reflected in a weird, blackish way the colors of the fire below.

The state police had set up headquarters in front of the house, and a Salvation Army canteen truck was parked next to the police cars. All faces kept turning toward the valley, and as they did they flashed pink and the eyes stared and stared—fixed expressions not of fear or of awe, but a steady watchfulness. It was impossible to get used to that fire.

Word was passed that a whole family had died—a wedding party in Cascom. Nobody knew the name of the family. The ladder-rung mill in Cascom had burned, too.

"There won't *be* no more Cascom," somebody said.

John let the others unload the Indian pumps and went straight up to the kitchen door, Junior following him. Several women, two in Salvation Army uniforms, washed dishes and made up sandwiches in the big kitchen. He and Junior stood helplessly on the edge of this efficient uproar. Then Jane came into the room, in dungarees and a faded flannel shirt, carrying a tray of white coffee mugs.

She saw him at once, put the tray down and came up to him empty-handed. In the old clothes she was unbelievably trim and neat. She was completely beautiful to him, and tired, and would be soft if he touched her. She hadn't noticed Junior, only him, and he saw that she had begun to cry as she stood in front of him with her arms hanging down. He put his hands on her shoulders.

"I don't know . . ." Jane said; "I can't stand to look down to the valley."

"It's all right, Janie," he said.

"It's so *mean*. It won't stop."

"No. We'll stop it, all right," he said. She took his arm and pulled him across the kitchen, through the hall and into the sitting room, where the stuffed wildcat glared down from the top of the piano and the deer heads stared rigidly from the walls.

"I wanted you to be here," she said. "I missed you." She wiped her eyes with the back of her hand, and he took her hand away and kissed her. Her lips were soft, almost liquid, and he pulled her up against him, his hands on her shoulderblades. As they came apart he looked into her eyes and saw the iris in them; a dark, ferny green.

"I love you," he said, and she put her face against his neck, her arms tightly wrapped around him—a bear hug—as if she were a little girl who didn't want to be sent away.

"That won't burn up," she mumbled fiercely against his neck. "I love you!" Then she added with an odd little giggle, "John Cotter never burns up, he just fades away."

"I'm through fading away," he said. "I mean it, Janie." He took a handful of her hair and gently pried her head up. Her eyes were coolly open, watching him, and she looked at him for a long time.

"I *mean* it," he said.

"I'm just an old widow. What the hell does it matter?"

"Stop that!" He took her by the waist and shook her. Her head bobbed back and forth loosely and she stopped smiling. A Salvation Army woman looked in and then fled. He went over and shut the door, then pushed her into the Morris chair. "Now listen to me," he said, bending over her, "listen to me!" She sat primly, a little girl again, her hands together under her chin as if she were praying, and looked up at him. "Listen, Janie, I'm sick of being careful; I'm sick of trying to be invisible. From now on they're going to love me or hate me, understand? I'm *in!* God dammit! Do you understand?" She raised her eyebrows slightly, noncommittally.

"Listen!" he said desperately, "I love you! I'm through being nothing! I'm through waiting for something to happen!"

"What good would it do me if I said that?" she asked.

"You don't have to say it now, because I'm making things happen." He picked her up and kissed her again, then set her on her feet. He left her standing there and hurried out into the kitchen, where he grabbed a sandwich and Junior's arm. "Come on, Junior," he said, "we got to fight fire."

With a look of wonder on his face, Junior followed.

They walked single-file down the old logging road toward the front lines, John leading. Howard Randolf, Billy Muldrow and the Riders were strung out behind. Every third man carried an Indian pump, the rest shovels and axes. The state police had given John a geodetic map with a heavy black line drawn across it in crayon. A series of little clearings, most of them connected to each other, were strung across the side of a hill above Switches brook, in which there was still a trickle of water. Their job was to clear a line of all brush and, if possible, wind and water supply allowing, to build a controlled backfire through the clearings. This might possibly slow the fire, but there was little hope of actually putting it out until the weather changed drastically—until it rained.

He stopped, flashing his light along the dry leaves, trying to find the cutoff Sam Stevens had marked for him on the map. It would soon be light enough—would have been then, except for the slowly moving brown smoke that kept the day back. While he searched for signs of the connecting trail among the blackberry bushes, the others waited stolidly. Billy, of all the men, might have been better qualified to find the trail, but he was content to let John make the decision about it. And so were they all.

When he decided which trail to take, they followed him, silent except for the dry crackling of the leaves and sticks under their feet. After a few yards the trail became distinct, and they made steady progress down the hill toward Switches brook. A trickle of water did still run among the stones, and John detailed one of the men to clear stones and dig a hole deep enough so that they could refill the Indian pumps there. It was Slugger Pinckney whose shoulder he patted, and Slugger began immediately to roll the heavy stones aside. No one had as yet disputed his authority, and as he wondered about it he decided that he wanted to keep it.

"Goddam!" Junior said, "I used to catch some fair keepers in Switches brook. Now look at her!"

As he walked up the hill on the other side of the brook to detail the men to their clearing jobs, he was grateful to Junior for this speech, which reinforced his authority in the only possible way. Now the Riders would certainly follow Slugger's example, and Junior would not try to foul things up. By saying nothing, Junior would have left him in doubt. By speaking only of the fish, he had declared himself.

The little clearings were full of berry bushes and spreading circles of ground juniper, the juniper dry as tinder. In between, the surviving hay was brown. Around them, tall pine and hemlock were ominously dark, as if in complete, warmingful contrast to the bright torches they could become. The men worked feverishly, some cutting the juniper and saplings in a ragged line along the hill, others dragging the cut brush down out of the way. The shovelers used the sharpened edges of their shovels as brush scythes on the smaller stalks and branches. They worked without looking to see who worked next to them, sweat running onto their tools and into their boots, blood from thorn scratches running down with the sweat.

As more men came down the trail they were referred to John, who stopped chopping long enough to set them to work. By nine in the morning they had met with other crews on each side, and went back over the ground they had cleared, this time more carefully, until they had a firebreak twenty feet wide cleared of nearly everything that would burn. All the larger trees near the edge had been cut to fall back away from the cleared ground.

"Now we got everything all ready," Junior said, "where in hell's the fire?"

The men came straggling back from their final inspection of the firebreak, dragging their tools, and flopped on the ground around John.

"Two bits it don't come at all," Slugger said.

John examined the broken blisters on the insides of his thumbs, and pulled off a piece of skin as big as a quarter. Howard Randolf lay on his stomach, breathing deeply, as if he were either asleep or sick. Bob Paquette still kept his distance. He hadn't spoken to John at all, but had followed all his suggestions without objection. Now John looked straight at him and said, "You men sure did a job of work."

He expected no answer, but regretted the remark as soon as he said it—they would think of the firehouse business, and the more glamorous job they might have had. But they were too tired to react to that. The only response was a series of sighs and groans as the men tried to get comfortable on the rooty ground.

"We ought to be relieved pretty soon now," John said.

"Just tell 'em not to step on my body," Howard said.

Billy Muldrow rolled over and grinned, his face black and tired. "I could do with some sleep myself," he said.

They heard a loud crack from up the hill toward the fire, then more cracklings and scrapings, then the thud of hoofs. A small buck came floating into sight on the top of a long jump. The deer came bounding down the hill toward them. To the right, several more deer crashed by. The little buck cleared the firebreak easily and landed among the men, then continued down toward the brook in long arcs, his front legs cocked daintily as he soared above the ground.

"Jesus!" Billy Frisch yelled. The hoofs had missed him by a foot. "That dumb bastard damn' near tromped on me!" He put his fingers in the triangular hoofmarks.

"You want to be careful," Junior said. "Them deer are dangerous." They all laughed.

"Fire must be gitting close," Slugger said. "I seen a red fox earlier, going out straight for Leah."

"I seen a wildcat, two bear and a elephant!" Junior said.

"Aw, shut up." Slugger rolled over and groaned into the ground.

Smoke, now a little darker than before, veered over the top of the hill above them. They listened for the sounds of fire, but could hear nothing. Far over to the left another deer crashed down the hill. They saw one flash of its white flag, but heard it all the way down to the brook, where a stone clinked before the deer began to climb the hill on the other side.

"Here come the fresh troops, I do believe," Junior said.

Sam Stevens led a column of men up to the firebreak. "I'd say you used good judgment, John, not to make a backfire. Wind's too tricky. Anyways, they got some food for you boys back to the house. That's a good job." Sam surveyed the cleared ground, nodding.

The Riders got up, slapped dust from their uniforms and started back with the rest of the men who had arrived before dawn. John decided to go up to the top of the hill and see where the fire was. His knees were stiff and his shoulders ached as he stood up. Howard Randolf was in the process of raising his body from the ground, and John stopped to watch.

"One!" Howard said, and pulled up one knee. "Two!" He pulled up the other one. "Don't cry, friends, don't pity an old man." He finally got to his feet and stood shakily. "Where in hell are you going, Captain?" he said to John, who had crossed the firebreak toward the fire.

"I'm going to look at the fire," John said. "From the looks of you, you'd better head for the sack."

"Legs, old legs," Howard said, leaning over and gripping his legs above the knees, "function!"

"I'll see you back at the house," John said.

"No, no! I've got to see it. I've got to see it!"

They climbed over the felled trees and started up the hill toward the smoke, climbing over old stone walls and blowdown. Howard managed to keep up, although he frequently groaned and sometimes had to lift a leg over with both hands.

"I just realized that I was married in these pants," Howard said, leaning against a poplar sapling. The pants were heavy tweed, torn at the knees. "I bought these pants in London in 1928. Damn' good pants." He took a few deep breaths. "I was married in these pants, but I don't hope to die in them."

"Think you'll die with your pants on?" John said.

"Pants on and fly buttoned," Howard said. He grinned painfully, exposing his long yellow teeth.

"You sure you want to try this hill?"

"In spite of anything I may have said, I haven't given up yet," Howard said.

They stood below a ten-foot cliff of stone, a huge boulder set into the side of the hill. Beneath the boulder the ground was slightly damp, and faded water weeds showed that a spring had once run there. As John examined the hole beneath the stone a little green frog looked out at him, then backed inside again.

"Find a hole and crawl in," John said.

"What? I'm not that far gone," Howard said.

"The little frog." John pointed into the damp hole.

"Oh! Sure, Captain. Sure. Draw your own conclusions," Howard said, smiling. "Now let's go see our approaching fate."

They rested again before they reached the vantage point, a rock platform they could see above them, cutting the smoke like the prow of a ship. For the first time they could hear the distant crackling of the fire.

"One minute," Howard said. "Give an old man a minute." He half-fell to the pine needles and rolled over on his back. "I could sleep for a week. Right here."

"You'd be nicely broiled."

"That doesn't appeal. But listen, Captain . . ."

"Why the 'Captain' business?"

"I admired—I really did—the way you took over that. . . ." He waved a slack hand down the hill. "Indeed I did. The circumstances were difficult, but you made no mistakes. You're a leader."

"Like hell."

"No, you are. When something *has* to be done, you do it."

"Come on, let's go."

"Old Sam Stevens knows," Howard said. " 'That's a good job,' the old patriarch said. You heard him. That old man knows. He's got bright eyes."

"We'd better be moving along," John said. "The fire's just over the hill. We may have to run back down, Howard. Do you think you ought to try it?"

"I try anything."

Howard got up, groaning, and followed John up the last hundred yards. They climbed on hands and knees over the last ledge onto the stone promontory, into the driving stream of thin smoke.

The fire was there.

"Jesus God," Howard said softly. They stood on the edge of a volcano, seared by the rising heat from a valley of oily flame. The coals of trees blinked behind the advancing wall that was white-orange at its base, growing into red, weaving into a dirty black shot with dull red before it rose above the trees with a whoosh, throwing large twigs, leaves and small branches straight up, burning them into nothing before they fell back to the ground. Just below, a green balsam, a perfect fifty-foot Christmas tree, turned brown all at once and in the next second burst into light, each branch, each needle afire at once. They both crouched back, arms in front of their faces.

"Captain, I suggest we retreat!" Howard yelled over the roar of the burning tree. "In fact, I suggest we run like hell!"

They turned and ran, jumping, sliding down the ledge, pushing through the wiry brush that was a fuse leading the fire up and over the hill. Howard shot by on a slide of needles, scrabbling to get hold of something, and rolled over before he came to rest on his back against a stump. He lay there hugging himself, his face grayish with pain, breathing in deliberately short gasps. "Unh, unh!" he said. "I . . . broke . . . some . . . thing."

"Can you walk?" John climbed down to him and put his hand on Howard's chest. Howard moved his arm to push John's hand away.

"Hurts . . . to . . . breathe."

"Move your legs." Howard moved his legs, his bony knees showing through the torn pants. "Good," John said. He looked up and saw wisps of fire flowing through the smoke above the ledge. "O.K., you've most likely broken a rib or two. Let's go."

"No. . . . Don't . . . have . . . energy . . . anyway."

"Get up!"

"All done . . . been . . . fun."

"You'd rather die than stand a little pain?" John felt anger begin to rise in him.

Howard's eyes were pleading. "Go . . . on. Don't . . . give . . . a . . . damn."

"I do, so get the hell up!" He reached out and pulled Howard's arms loose. Howard opened his mouth, his tongue protruding, his lips pulled away from his long teeth, and screamed. The fire crackled and the wind pushed over the hill; a hot, eating wind that took John's breath. He pulled Howard out from his niche beside the stump, grabbed his rigid arms and sledded him down the hill. Flame poured through the brush where they had been, and the green blackberries hissed and dropped. Howard's arms went limp, and John had to get a new hold on him. He took one arm and bent it at the elbow, put his own arm through the crook and pulled. This worked until they reached a small depression in the ground. Howard slid into it and stayed. John couldn't pull him out.

"Get up! Get up!" he yelled into Howard's face. Howard's lips bubbled as he breathed, and a little spray of spit hissed up each time he exhaled. "Wake up! You son of a bitch, wake up!" Howard breathed on, and now he was taking long breaths—slow, irregular breaths, but long ones. It convinced John that he was legitimately unconscious. By squatting down and partly burrowing underneath Howard, he managed to get a fireman's carry on him, but just barely staggered to his feet with the limp body over his shoulders, took three steps and tripped over a ground juniper branch. He fell heavily into the junipers with Howard on top of him. His mouth pressed against the needles and the stink of the juniper berries rose sharp as gin in his nose. He felt as if he were drowning in the dark bush, and scrambled out from under, only to fall again. Above, the fire's approach seemed vicious and personal, and a long salient of the red flame reached down toward him. He stood up, and his knees were weak and shaky. "Wait a minute," he said. "Wait one minute, John. Damn it, Howard, why do you weigh so much? O.K. now. O.K." He rolled Howard over and pulled off Howard's belt, then looped it around the limp wrists and drew it tight, forced the tongue of the buckle through the leather, then rolled Howard over onto his belly again. "It better work, John," he said out loud. He squatted down and got the arms over his head, held the belt down on his chest and got up, Howard draped over his back. "Damn it all, now, Howard," he said, "why did you have to grow so long?" Howard's knees rested on the ground, but this way John could move shakily forward, providing he picked his way carefully. He knew that if he had to duck very low to go beneath blowdown, he would fall again.

He managed to drag Howard a hundred yards this way, until he came to a long, rotten white birch fallen across the way. He didn't think he had enough strength to push Howard through the branches, or even to lift him over the trunk, so he stood gasping, then sank unwillingly to his knees. His knees would not hold, no matter how he commanded them. Sweat nearly blinded him; his hands on the belt were numb and cramped into claws. For the first time, as he sat staring at his boots, Howard's long-breathing body relaxed beside him, he wondered if he would make it. In his exhaustion—and he knew it was because of exhaustion—the matter didn't seem very important. But the fire kept coming. A spark settled beside him, another landed on Howard's cheek and must have burned the flesh before John made himself brush it off. Howard was still unconscious. Another spark burned John's head like a bee sting, and he smelled burning hair. "God damn you, Howard," he said weakly. He didn't want to turn around to look at the fire, and he knew that this, too, was partly due to exhaustion. It hardly seemed worth the effort. He could hear it singing up through the trees, could feel its heat against the back of his head.

"Got to!" he said, and as he got to his feet he was surprised that the short rest had done so much for him. He draped Howard over his shoulder again and moved on. The birch was rotten, and he walked right through it, only having to kick the bark away. The little black branches were as unsubstantial as spider webs.

His breath came out of his mouth in little groans, and he listened to the absurd sounds with, he thought, a great deal of disinterested speculation. Had his vocal cords sprung or something? At one point he was quite sure that Howard had bitten him on the shoulder-blade. He clearly felt the long teeth, and stopped to look at Howard's lolling head, his slack jaw and protruding tongue. To his right, through sweat, surrounded by little rainbows, the advance feelers of the fire passed him, and real fear gave him sudden energy. He ran, a heavy, stabbing run that quickly nauseated him. He retched and kept on, bounded from a slim sapling and would have fallen except that another sapling supported him and pushed him on again. He fell several times, once kicked a pretty shower of sparks from a burning bush, tried while running to spit on a spark that seared his hand. He had no spit. He seemed to have been running for days, and Howard's weight became a part of the fire, or the dream of escaping through molasses.

When he saw the first man across the firebreak he thought it was a bear, a fellow victim, and didn't shout for help until he started to fall, and kept on falling, turning and turning over in the air. Below him was a pretty little lake, blue and cool. and as he fell he wondered why he didn't enter the water—he fell toward the lake and yet never hit. And then his own shouting came into his ears, "HELP HELP HELP!" and they were dragging him, Howard still attached, through the branches and across the rooty ground.

When he reached the house he was staggering, and his feet seemed prepared to meet the ground before the ground was there. He stood swaying, watching while Howard was inserted into the police car. Then, when the car sirened off down the road, he turned toward the kitchen. Two men took his arms and helped him up the steps. "Boy, am I pooped," he remembered saying over and over, and when he sat at the kitchen table, with a cup of hot chocolate in his black hands, he couldn't remember who the men were who had helped him up the hill. The crew he had come with had all gone back to Leah.

"Why, Jane!" he said, "are you still up?" A silly question—she sat across the table from him, her tired eyes looking intently into his.

"You're the one who shouldn't still be up," she said softly. "I called your father and told him you were all right. I told him you'd stay here."

"Good." He looked around the big room. "Now there's a spot would be perfect," he said, pointing to a far corner. "Just let me sack out over there." He could feel his bones crumpling wonderfully into the corner. It seemed the nicest and most comfortable corner he had ever seen.

"No corner," Jane said. "You need some sleep. You need a bath."

"Too pooped," he said. His eyes closed and he let his head float off—a lovely, weightless feeling—and then Jane had a firm hold on his arm and he was walking.

"Up the stairs," she ordered.

"O.K., O.K.," he kept saying. All the way up the stairs he couldn't feel his legs at all, but they did keep working. Finally he leaned against the bathroom doorframe thinking how wonderful the running water sounded.

"I guess we can spare a few gallons of water," Jane said. She bent over the big tub and swirled the water around, then got him a towel from the cupboard. "Here." She pushed the towel into his hands. "Get some of that soot off and then you can sleep. I've got a bed made up for you." She went out and shut the door.

The next horrible interruption of his lovely weightlessness was a knocking on the door. "Come in," he said, and Jane came in, strangely angry.

"Look at you, sitting there!" she said, "Why don't you take a bath and get it over with? You don't want to sit there all day!" He thought he *had* taken a bath—remembered very well taking his clothes off and sliding into the nice water. But there he was, still in the torn, cruddy clothes, sitting on the toilet seat.

"I'll be damned, Janie," he said. "I'll be damned!" Suddenly he thought the whole situation was terribly funny, and he began to laugh. Jane began to unlace his boots, and suddenly it was very sad. "Janie, Janie," he said sadly, "don't do that. Let me do that."

"You don't seem to be able to do it," she said. After the boots came the streaked, wet socks, then his shirt. "You're the dirtiest man I ever saw," she said, and it was still sad to him.

"Yes, you know," he said, "I'm the filthiest man there is. Oh, that's so true. I'm a dirty son of a bitch, Janie."

"Don't get maudlin," she said, put her arm around him, lifted him up and slipped off his pants. She helped him into the bathtub and he lay in the warm water, one leg twitching, the spasm traveling up and down his thigh like a wave.

"I've still got my shorts on," he said. "Crazy damn' thing take a bath with shorts on. Feels like a little kid wet his pants or something, you know? Doesn't seem right, somehow."

"It's my Puritan modesty," she said.

"My shorts. *My* Puritan modesty," and the blue waves of nothing closed in again, happily, happily. . . .

CHAPTER 21

He was asleep in the shallow water, his knees up in the air, and she scrubbed him clean. There were raw places on his head where hair and all had been burned away, and he didn't wake up even when she scrubbed the raw spots, just slept quietly, breathing deeply, an expression of calm happiness on his face she had never seen there before. His dark face had smoothed, looked terribly young and pure. When he was reasonably clean and the water black, she took off his shorts and washed him there, and then let the water out and rinsed him off with clean water. He slept on, but somehow even in his sleep cooperated when she raised him up and walked him into the small bedroom under the eaves. He sighed at the touch of the cool sheets, and lay relaxed on the old, sloping hammock of a bed. Before she covered him she stood and admired the smooth body, the graceful curve of muscle on his thighs—now no longer in spasm—the silky black hair curling from his armpits and over his chest, the muscular ridges of his belly. Then she pulled the sheet over him and lay down beside him. Just for a moment, she told herself, and then back to clean up the bathroom.

She ran her hand down the sheet over him, the image of the hard body erotic in her mind, and she thought of children—of babies—of babies and the primal reason for sex, of all women and all men, of the couplings and the need and the continuity of things. She herself was meant to open and need, to receive this man. She wanted to shake him, to hit him awake. Her thighs rubbed easily together. He slept on, relaxed, oblivious. She leaned over and kissed him on the lips, and he slept on. I could wake him, she thought, but I know that if he woke and wanted me, I would refuse him. Refuse him because I want him so badly, so permanently. That's not honest, but I'm too old to be honest. His arm came over her and still he slept, his square hand on her waist, and she meant to go clean up the bathroom, had to get right up and go clean up the bathroom. . . .

A late afternoon sun, nearly horizontal, shone through the small window and made the sheets and pillowcases gold. The first thing she saw was the face of Mrs. Pettibone, the sallow face smiling with a kind of fierce joy, and then John's arm across her breast, each little hair on his arm reddish in the sunlight. He still slept.

"Why didn't you wake me up?" she said to Mrs. Pettibone, who stood over the bed.

"Janie, I looked in earlier, but you was sleeping so nice, so peaceful."

"I never meant to go to sleep," she said. "I just lay down for a second."

"Oh, you was so cozy, so nice. I just didn't have the heart to wake you up," Mrs. Pettibone said, tilting her head as if she were looking at a child in bed. Jane got up and smoothed her clothes.

"He fell asleep and I had to help him to bed."

"Don't you go feeling embarrassed, Janie. I didn't mean no harm looking in on you like this." Mrs. Pettibone was close to crying, and Janie put an arm around her.

"It's all right," she said. "It's all right, dear. I know you didn't mean anything."

Mrs. Pettibone wiped her eyes with the back of her hand, then whispered, "You was so nice, so nice there." They both looked down upon the sleeping man, upon his strong arms and the presence of him picked out in the warm light of the late sun. He sighed in his sleep and his arm moved slowly across the sheet, then moved slowly back again. Suddenly Mrs. Pettibone kissed Jane on the cheek, lowered her head and left the room.

Jane was about to follow her when John's sleeping face screwed up into an expression of intense sorrow, and tears rolled from his closed eyes.

"Bruce," he said clearly—as clearly as if he had been awake and had spoken to his brother. His chest jerked with an occasional explosive hiccup; the voiceless sob of a child.

A shy tapping at the door. Mrs. Pettibone called softly: "Janie, I meant to tell you. Mr. Randolf has two broken ribs and heat something—prostation? And they're holding the fire at the firebreak, they think. He'll be all right, the policeman said." And she padded back down the stairs.

"Bruce," John said again. He lay on his back as if he were paralyzed, his arms spread out, his palms up and fingers slack.

Do I dare touch him? She wondered. The green window shade scraped the frame; the round pull twirled slowly in the sunlight. Motes of dust turned and glinted. It seemed too calm and ordinary an afternoon, here in the old-fashioned room, for such sorrow.

"Bruce." His mouth opened, his teeth were exposed, and he made an agonizing sound with an intake of air: "Huh-huh-huh-huh . . ."

"John!" she said sharply. She couldn't stand to hear it, yet couldn't leave. Her own eyes had begun to burn, her throat to hurt in an effort not to share his sobs. "John!" She didn't dare touch him, knowing as she did his odd, inimical relationship with his brother. What swift, frightening reaction might come from the touch of her hand?

His face softened, he stretched his arms, then his trunk and legs arched beneath the sheet, and he came awake looking straight into her eyes. For a moment his expression was totally blank—watchful—then he smiled and reached for her arm. He pulled her down on top of him and kissed her. His face was like fine sandpaper, the whiskers dry and hard.

"What a pleasant surprise!" he said. "For a minute I thought I was home in bed, but the window wasn't in the right place." He hiccuped again, and felt his chest, surprised. Then he noticed that his face was wet, and he looked at her, the question in his eyes.

"You were crying in your sleep," she said.

"Me?"

"You were crying hard."

"Probably trying to get Howard off that goddam hill. What's happened? How long have I been sleeping? How's Howard?"

"He's all right. The state police said he had some broken ribs, and heat 'prostation' according to Mrs. Pettibone. They think they've stopped the fire for a while at your firebreak."

"Nothing but good news. I can stop crying?"

"You weren't crying about the fire."

"You mean I talked in my sleep?" He smiled worriedly. "What did I say? Jesus! You'll learn all my secrets."

"I will?" she asked.

"Yes, you will." He looked steadily into her eyes. "If you want to—if I can think of any to tell you."

"You said, 'Bruce.'" As she said the word he shivered slightly, and his face assumed the blank, watchful look again. He was completely still.

"I did?" He seemed to be trying to remember. "All right. First, would you bring me my clothes? I want to show you something in my pants' pocket." His face was deliberately calm, deliberately expressionless. She brought the torn and sooty clothes and he took a small pistol from the back pocket of his dungarees. He examined it and put it on the bedside table.

"That"—he had trouble getting a breath, then went on—"belongs to Bruce. It's loaded. It's dangerous, like Bruce. I've been carrying it around in my back pocket. I found it in the office, and I found—" His eyes searched the corner of the room, nervous and entirely unlike his usually steady eyes. "So I was crying? I found a book of Bruce's—sort of a diary, all locked up in a drawer with this gun to guard it. Secret! Listen. He's my *brother,* and I never knew how he felt. I never bothered to know how he felt. I didn't know he hated me quite so much. I never *bothered* to know how much he hated me, hated our father. But he had it all locked up in the box and I read it. The thing is, there's nothing *there*. It doesn't come together.

It doesn't *make* anything. It's just loose hate rattling around in the box. Like Bruce. Nothing there to hold the whole thing together at all. I don't know what happened to make him like that. You know, you've got to find a reason or you can't steady your mind. I don't know my own brother! How can I know anybody?"

"Nobody knew Bruce," she said gently. She wanted again to offer him the comfort of her flesh, and put one arm along his cheek.

"It wasn't anybody else's responsibility to know. I was nearest. It was my responsibility."

"Not your father's?"

"No, he doesn't count," he said, shaking his head impatiently.

"Poor man. He doesn't count."

"Poor man," John said softly. "Poor man. He's poor in sons."

"No, you're wrong."

"I never bothered to pity anyone in Leah, much less my own father, or my own brother. Now, Christ! The poor guy's *dying*. It's killing my father, too. He dies right in front of my eyes. And my mother fiddles around wanting somebody to hug, and nobody will let her."

He threw himself over against the wall, and put his hand flat against the wallpaper. "Jesus Christ, Janie, what the hell is the matter with us? You aren't like that. What do you do to be different? Anybody can look at you and see how generous you are. Everybody knows it."

"I'm not."

"You are! And there's someone else like that. Jenny Lou's like that, and she's kept my mother from coming all apart. That's all it takes."

"You mean the little Negro girl?"

"Yes, Jenny Lou. Maybe you're born with it—with all that affection to give, and it never runs out—and the rest of us sit around worrying about ourselves so much we can't give anything."

"Maybe that's it," she said, "only I've always wondered why you should worry. What do you worry about? You're John Cotter, and your family's always been pretty well off. It isn't as bad as you say it is, either. I mean, it's bad that you and Bruce never got along, but don't you know that every family has troubles like that? Worse ones. What if you were John Prescott, and your father was so mean

—not even drunk—that your mother had to call the sheriff to protect you? What if he was so mean he cut the tails off his cows and beat his wife and his horse with a bamboo pole?"

"Ah, Janie. All our little problems seem big to us, but maybe if my father were more of a tail cutter it would have cleared the air long ago. Maybe Bruce and I would have found a common enemy, and that might have been better for both of us. Maybe we both love him, but we want him to be our father more. Maybe a man wants to respect his father more than love him, and then if he and his father can come to an understanding someday, well, it might seem more valuable. Bruce wrote in his hate-book that he wanted to work, to fight—for some crazy foreign-place happiness he kept wanting—or else it didn't seem valuable. But who was he trying to impress with all the work he did? Maybe he wanted somebody who was hard to impress, not our poor father. All he did was grind the man down, and every time he got a chance he hurt him. God! Bruce could be mean!"

It seemed to her that there was some admiration in his voice, yet she still saw, beneath his quick words, a real despair—something that threatened her, too. The wounds of his brother, or the wounds his brother had given him (what was the difference?) must be healed before she could end this limbo of the farm—this meaningless calm between the two parts of her life. The fire, too, had been stopped for a while, and now she thought of it almost as an ally. Why couldn't it burn up everything—Leah, Bruce, the farm, the Spinellis; burn out all the old places and people and leave her free, burn this futile despair out of the man she wanted?

"What to do?" John said, tossing the pistol in his hand. "Shoot myself with it? Did Bruce deliberately leave me that box—a sort of booby trap?" He tried to smile.

"You'd better stop trying to fool me," she said, "I love you, but that doesn't make me blind. I can love and see, both."

"How do you know it's love, then, Janie?"

"I'm gambling," she said, and for a moment she was frightened.

"I'm a good poker player," he said, "or else I'm awfully lucky." He pulled her down against him and held her rigidly against his chest, his hands tight on her arms.

She was still frightened, not of her love for him—that was no gamble—but of her vision of life with him. Was it a qualification of her love that she wanted him whole and permanent? When the time came, if it ever did, she knew she would never marry another defective; he must at least match her in his ability to live. Her heart made itself felt as it had when she thought the reflection of the fire in the farmhouse windows was real, dark fire; each beat was strong, and between each thudding beat there was a long and wearisome pause, as if her heart were reluctant to beat again. John's trouble was real—she must believe that. It was real, and he was eaten by it. He could not be cured by a slap or a shock—not even by the hottest fire. I must remember that, she said to herself, *I must remember that.*

"I should have gone up to him," John said, his hands tighter around her arms. "I should have shoved them all out into the hall and gone up to him and held out my hands, palms up, and said, 'Gentle, gentle, I give you everything.' I should have done it before they cut his mind out of his head."

She began to cry, not wanting to, partly because he hurt her arms. It was as if she felt some of his pain. The back of her throat hurt worse than her arms, and she knew her tears were sliding against his face. He put his arms around her and slid her off his chest so that her face was against his neck.

"Janie, Janie," he said gently, "what a self-pitying slob of an actor I am, making you cry. It doesn't bother me, really. I've just got to impress you somehow."

"Don't try to lie to me. Don't have good motives with me, you bastard," she said, and bit him on the neck. He jumped, but with a certain precision. He pulled the sheet out from under her and put it over her so that she was underneath it with him, his hands coming up her legs, his body insistent against hers.

"My motives toward you are dark and strong," he said in a dry, husky voice. His hands worked at her clothes and she tried automatically to resist them. His breath was warm, humid and alive in her ear. "I look at you and talk to you," he said urgently, "and then all of a sudden I say to myself, 'My God, John Cotter! She's not only honest and generous, she can listen to my weeping and cry! She's not only beautiful, she's as spare and trim as a deer—but she's soft and warm and nervous. Listen to her tremble! She's not only all these things, but she's here. I *got* her!' "

"Yes, you got me," she whispered, and as she let herself stop resisting, as his hands prepared her for him, the walls of the room, even the glass of the window, seemed to become round; each surface part of a sphere with her body the center of it. Then the sphere became opaque, transfixed, revolving slowly as her arms slid around his covering body. Again the mind blunted, and the sphere, the live center of her, turned. . . .

CHAPTER 22

William Cotter saw Franklin standing by the stairwell, stiff and black, one small hand grasping the railing. His solemn black face, so black it seemed to gather light, to absorb it, was, in the familiar hallway, a point of focus where all certainty—the daily unnoticed comforts of Gladys Cotter's decorating instinct—faded into dark; and in the deep, dark hole there lurked, perhaps, some frightening small animal, an animal that might bite you out of nothing more than fear. Every other object, every other color bore the touch of Gladys Cotter, from the hung tin trays with their fragmentary gold-leaf shepherdesses, whose awkward hands were stuck on black, whose heads had just separated from shoulders and were ever about to collide with borders of fleurs-de-lis, to the bronzed doorstops in the shape of butting goats, screwed by their tails to the summer-party wallpaper.

No reassurance, however, could he find in that ten-year-old African face. Those big brown eyes whose color had seemed to leak over into the whites, those wide white teeth, were always about to draw his startled eyes. All faces were strange to William Cotter, beginning with his own. And the more he studied faces, the more they reflected darkness; the more he peered nervously into them, suspecting that there must be a way he didn't know to get down past the mask of expression.

"Mr. Cotter," Franklin said in his high, shy, boy's voice.

"What can I do for you, Frank?" He cursed himself for a hale and hearty fool. Franklin was about to cry, and his hand trembled at his mouth.

"It's Mrs. Cotter. She's sick or something. She's crying on the davenport!"

William Cotter quickly considered: was it something he'd done? Had she had news of Bruce from the hospital? No. He'd have heard the telephone. John? No. Nothing ever happened to John. Fire or not, John wouldn't burn. Someone might have come to the door during the time he'd run his electric razor. Let it be something! Let it please not be the culmination of this summer, the addition of all the blows poor Gladys had suffered! He put his hand over the little boy's sharp wingbones.

"Come on, we'll see," he said to Franklin, who looked up, expressionless, yet followed him down the stairs.

They both peered reluctantly around the corner of the living-room arch. The sobbing had been just audible from the stairs; now it was rythmical and phlegmy, with a ghastly bubbling in it, and he thought how talented his wife was. No matter how many times he heard her cry, had been the one to do fumbling comfort in the presence of her grief, each new time she was able to tear him in the throat. And it was her crying itself, not necessarily the cause of her grief, even though it might be his grief too, that always worked upon him.

This time, however, he saw with a sense of guilty relief the slight, yet vivid figure of Jenny Lou leaning over the body of his wife. Black pigtails brushed Gladys' washed-out hair, one shiny black arm moved gently over the lank back and collapsed shoulders. Jenny Lou did not cry, but with a gravity of expression that seemed terribly old, terribly wise, crooned into Gladys' ear, over and over, a kind of meaningless lullaby: "Now it's all, *all* right, and the day will come. Now it's all, *all* right, and the day will come," as if, instead of a thin seven years, she possessed a great black mammy's fund of worldliness and warmth.

Gladys Cotter shrugged and gasped, her body full of bones, her long shanks twitching beneath her cotton summer dress. For a long time he and Franklin stood watching—for such a long time, minutes, that he felt himself to be part of the scene, and Franklin too; part of the conscious artistry of some stage director, as if they all belonged, had been assigned there, and were not temporarily and by chance arranged to witness sorrow. My wife, he thought, This poor old dame is my wife. And what specific thing did she now cry about? What now? Some thing or some time—what caused it? Whatever it was, he agreed with her, was tortured into agreeing. It was terrible, godawful, and he could cry too. For a moment, considering the most obvious reason, he was overcome by a vision of Bruce's incomplete, vegetable body: not by the injustice of Bruce's fate, but by the sharp horror of the knife against comatose flesh. Was Bruce's fate unjust? No more than any man's. The horror was that he half believed that Bruce deserved some kind of punishment. *My son, my flesh!* Had Bruce's cruelness turned his tissues rotten, corrupted his brain? There was the horror! God or Fate or whatever should never work such neat sums out.

And how unnatural, how prone to work some havoc on the tender flesh of his own body, that he feared his own son! Feared even to visit the unconscious wreck of his son in the hospital. Knowing this, no wonder Gladys cried! His son—could he remember?—whom he once held up to pee, his hands gentle on the warm little body, whom he had taught such joyful disciplines as how to tie his shoes, and how to tell the right shoe from the left, and how to button buttons.

Why this family had disintegrated neither he nor Gladys knew. It was the fact her woman's mind seized and mourned. No wonder she cried; and let her.

He stepped back, right on Franklin's toe. The little boy winced, but made no sound, and they looked at each other, understanding the need for retreat. He motioned for Franklin to follow him into the kitchen, where they sat hiding in the breakfast nook with a Pepsi-Cola and a can of beer he had opened as silently as possible.

"Do you know what she's crying about, Frank?" he asked. Franklin sat across from him with, as near as he could tell, a sympathetic yet remote expression on his face; Franklin wasn't about to let himself become too much involved.

"I think she's crying mainly because Jenny Lou has to go home," Franklin said. "I mean that sort of started it."

"She sure took to Jenny Lou. She always did want a little girl."

Franklin was noncommittal, as if he considered such problems beyond comment at his age. "It's too bad," he said, and stuck his finger into the bottle of Pepsi-Cola.

"We've both had a wonderful time with you kids," William Cotter said. Jenny Lou's song of comfort, and an undertone of sobs which now was not so desperately gaspy, came insistently into the kitchen. "Your little sister," he went on, staring worriedly at Franklin and knowing the nakedness of his expression, "has been awfully good for Mrs. Cotter."

"Yes," Franklin said.

"Frank, I'm awfully sorry we couldn't show you a better time up here!"

"Oh, I had a good time," Franklin said earnestly, "I had an awfully good time."

"Thank you for saying so, Frank," William Cotter said. The sobs were slowly dying away, and Jenny Lou's voice had fallen to a gentle murmur.

"I mean it, Mr. Cotter," Franklin said.

"But all this . . ." William Cotter gestured toward the living room with a hand that held beer can and cigarette.

"John told me about that—about Bruce and all that."

"He did!"

"Sure he did. He told me a lot. I like him very much. I like you too, Mr. Cotter."

"Why, for God's sake?" William Cotter said, and then gasped involuntarily, having somehow been shocked right out of breath. "I'm sorry, Frank," he said, then breathed long and purposefully in order to recharge his lungs, to let the shock of such a bald statement of affection drain away. As the boy watched him closely he again tried to speak, but could only listen helplessly to the sounds from the living room. And his inability to throw off the sudden, helpless feeling—self-pity, he must call it, the one emotion that had the power to paralyze his voice—made him scowl. Franklin watched warily, though not obviously surprised, and certainly not afraid. John, his own dear son, could not say, as this visiting ten-year-old could, "I like you." Period. His own son, on the telephone last night, had been tongue-tied, spastic in the mouth trying to say, "Dad." And what words were difficult and twisted the mouth? Lies. Neither of his sons found it easy to lie; Bruce refused to. That was a virtue, wasn't it? Such a cruel virtue! And so they condemned their mother, too, whenever she found it necessary, in the cause of happiness, to lie. *Liar,* they would think, and tell her that no end could justify such means, not even love.

And he, William Cotter, after mastering his self-pity, would now successfully change the subject. He would be prepared to go down to the office as soon as possible. Sneak out. Run. Run with self-disgust. Elope with it. Maybe, for once, he would stay and face a situation he knew only time could cure. No. No. Time didn't cure anything; it just treated symptoms, like aspirin. Gladys would stop crying, eventually, and Jenny Lou would never miss her gift of sympathy. Franklin was young and could take it. (Why should he have to, though?) Never mind, the fact was, he could. (Why couldn't William Cotter?) Because he didn't have to, that was why. He could escape to the office, a good excuse to everybody but himself.

Gladys now appeared in the doorway, Jenny Lou beside her, holding her hand and looking up at the tall woman, the little black head tilted back to look almost straight up, the commiserating eyes half closed. William Cotter was somewhat relieved to see that his problems had come to him: one dishonorable decision, at least, had been averted.

"Bill," Gladys quavered, making no attempt to hold anything back. She never had. Tears had wet her high cheeks, dampened the soft, chamois-like skin around her mouth, reddened the shiny rims around her eyes. The blue eyes stared just over precariously balanced sills of water which bulged from side to side as she made her characteristic shrug of hopelessness.

"Bill!"

He made the comforting words which were no comfort. He knew her well enough not to despise her theatrical entrance. (Who was he to condemn anyone?) That she truly grieved, that she had reason, he knew. It made no difference that these tears had been touched off by the thought of Jenny Lou's inevitable, and sensible, return home. Everything had always gone away from her, as he supposed his own love for her had gone a long time ago. Understanding and pity were pretty good substitutes, he supposed; something worse might have come in love's place. But with such weak medicine he could not help her.

It seemed to him that there must be people in the world who burned so brightly—had more watts in them or something—that they loved and burned all the time, that they were full of passion. Such people would not have felt that stinking, lousy, tiny bit of *relief* when disease cost a difficult son the use of his mind! Such people—such *real* people—would never yearn for relief, for peaceful adjustment at all costs. Such people were run by *honor,* had *virtues, morals,* stuff like that. They were proud inside and out.

Gladys Cotter swayed toward him, pretending to gain support from the little hand of Jenny Lou. Tall, her lean legs as unsteady as stilts, her breasts flat against her big ribcage, she passed the porcelain worktable just as a siren blatted past on Bank Street. He winced as the high scream of emergency, of disorder, flew down his own calm Maple Street and hit his ears. Still his wife came on, wrapped in her own drama, completely unaware of his panic.

He jumped up, cracking his knee against the crowding edge of the breakfast nook table. "God damn it!" he said. Caught already, he knew, by this invention of hers, he would not get away. She had always devised nooks, traps where her family must cuddle and be cozy. The tall, gawky woman wanted to be close and comfy—always! It was like having an affectionate giraffe after him. There must have been a time when he desired her leanness. Yes, and how the memory of old passion could sicken him! He once schemed for those absurdly long legs, pleased and planned her into letting him get between them. He had kissed those now wrecked lips and said loving things into those now hair-entangled long ears as he humped and groaned upon her bones. And for this old debt she now demanded him, all of him, demanded him unto disintegration.

"Now, Glad," he said warningly as she forced him to sit down again, "let's not make the kids go through this." Oh, what an easy liar he was! He found himself watching Franklin's small hand; like a little black house mouse, it nibbled at Franklin's mouth, twitchy as a nervous animal. If Franklin suffered, Jenny Lou did not. She stroked Gladys' arm and tried to pull her away from the breakfast nook where she leaned beseechingly toward William Cotter.

"Come on, Gladys," Jenny Lou purred. "Come on and lie down, Gladys. You don't feel so good."

Gladys allowed herself to be cajoled, but would stay and prolong the scene. No one could take this away from her. He wondered, on the verge of panic, what he could possibly do to stop this. He might rise, with all his strength in affected wrath, scream Stop! and wreck the breakfast nook, break the birch slab and wrench loose the joinings all around, all the time bellowing. Or maybe several peals of gigantic laughter, this time outdoing at least in volume any hysterical fit he'd ever seen Gladys produce, might free him—free him to the extent that tense silence would replace loose despair. Yes, and hurt poor Franklin more. No. His sins were sins of omission: the cruelest under time.

"Oh, Bill! The Fresh Air Lady called!"

"You knew the kids had to go home, Glad," he said carefully.

"Home?" she sang in a breaking voice. "Home to what? The slums?"

Poor Glad, he thought. Both Franklin and Jenny Lou now listened with a new intensity.

"What have they got to go home to? Those awful slums!"

He almost said: Don't pretend that it's their need. Obviously they don't need anything at all. Obviously they have more to give than you.

"Glad, Franklin and Jenny Lou have a fine home of their own, and fine parents of their own."

"Think of what we could give them, Bill!"

To Jenny Lou, who had withdrawn a little, who now watched Gladys with a colder eye, he wanted to say: Please stretch your pity over this inadequacy of truth! Can't you pity a liar as well as an honest beggar?

But how could Jenny Lou know the limits of her own strength, her own rights? At seven years the little girl might think these rich, and white, people could steal her from her mother and father with no trouble at all, if they took the notion. Franklin, too, in spite of his astounding and disconcerting maturity, might grow desperate at the thought of that basic nightmare of childhood. He could think of no way to tell them of their safety.

"Gladys," Jenny Lou said accusingly.

"What, dear?" Gladys Cotter had reeled against the sink cabinet, and stood as if on a tilting deck, facing a sea of cruel and unreasonable opposition.

"We have a fine home of our own, and fine parents of our own."

"Of course you do, dear! Of course you do!" Gladys Cotter moved a supplicating arm toward Jenny Lou, who did not touch it. Gladys wanted some more of that comfort—wanted another good portion, at least, before admitting defeat. Her mouth rounded, her eyes blurred again and she turned her blind face toward William Cotter. "Oh, Bill! I don't want them to go home!"

She had admitted home. She had admitted need. Poor woman! He could not trust her yet. He had seen lies born before, whole and hairy, on the very edge of confession.

A tangle of distant sirens turned the square, downstreet, and busied off, one falling like a long sigh. Perhaps the wind had risen, and the fire again fed on toward Leah. He listened, but heard no whistle or moan of wind at the windows. Protected by the maples, his street would hear it last, and softly.

"You don't want anything!" she said, and began to sob, not bothering to shield him with her hands. She aimed her face at him and bawled nakedly, making him see the tears well up, making him suffer the wanderings of her chin and the rags of drool that grew upon her lips.

"Glad, I know how you feel!" he said, rising as far as he could in the cramped breakfast nook to reach for her arm. This was her next move; that poor last offense that reveals the lie, that leaves no way for retreat. Jenny Lou hadn't moved, and now watched with bright, yet noncommittal eyes. Franklin had crammed himself into the farthest corner of the bench. With his head low and his finger stuck firmly into the Pepsi-Cola bottle, he waited it out.

"You don't care how I feel!" she cried, and hit his hand away. The blow must have hurt her arm very badly—he saw her wince, and her face grew cold and stern for a moment as the pain struck her. Out of dramatic gesture she became, as always, and in every way, genuinely wounded.

"You *bitch!*" she screamed at him, and turned to stagger tragically, blushing, across the kitchen toward the door to the dining room. She disappeared around the corner, he and Franklin and Jenny Lou gaping after. Then he managed, at last, to escape the breakfast nook, and walked unsteadily across to the refrigerator, his mind upon another morning beer—almost, but not quite, fixing upon the two inches of bourbon he knew to be in the liquor cabinet. No, he decided, not the bourbon. He was too tired. The children must be watching him now, unless they were looking into each other's frightened eyes and agreeing upon the horror of this house.

A large red bowl covered with aluminum foil caught his eye, and seemed familiar. Upon the bottom shelf of the refrigerator, the clean sheen of aluminum winked like a cracked mirror, and with a hand he was not surprised to find unsteady he peeled the crinkly stuff away.

The froglegs, pink-white as human skin, as in disaster piled in kicking and swimming attitudes in a gelatin of their own exudate; just the legs, amputated, bodiless, eyeless—the naked product of his play at slaughter. His chest contracted, his mouth filled with waterbrash and he nearly vomited. And again. His ears popped, his jaw locked open and he half fell back, slamming the door too hard. A tinkle of glass falling upon the cold bars came from inside. It was the bottle of Spanish olives that was always falling over—but busy and roiling in there, something called with a cold, connective voice; called his throat into desperate contractions, as if the copper-eyed amphibians he had dismembered alive demanded him to come, to look and drown.

When his nausea at last came under control he sat weakly on a straight-backed chair, his hands on his face, ashamed to look at the children. All he saw was the red darkness, the misty borders of his protecting fingers as they cupped his face.

Jenny Lou had gone after Gladys, and from the living room her high croon of comfort sounded again. Again! And the little girl had been concerned, frightened—who could blame her? Yet even out of such terrible risk as hers, when she had seen Gladys lie in devious ways and must know better than to trust her, she could offer sympathy.

"How we are found out!" he said out loud, and opened his hands to find the dark and compassionate face of Franklin before him.

Soft black, as black as the furry rime upon a burned tree, the little boy's face gathered light and William Cotter's eyes as if all light poured into and grew lost upon that dark and growing continent. Franklin's pink-palmed hand flashed and fell lightly upon his shoulder, and the little fingers gripped him—but with such strength!

And now, he thought, I must—we must—receive the infinite pity of children. "Franklin," he managed to say, "Aren't you afraid at all?"

"No, sir," Franklin said, "not of you."

CHAPTER 23

"No one will bother us here," Jane said, "Mrs. Pettibone will see to that."

"She knows?" John said, feeling a little ashamed of his sudden timidity now that they lay beside each other, apart by the smallest fraction of an inch. He didn't yet want to move away, knowing in spite of the weight of fulfillment that he wanted her. Just wanted her, now, then, any and all times, and would want her. It was relief: the smooth and confident feeling of the end of search. "I love you," he said. They lay, now naked, side by side, and she reached over for his hand and held it firmly for a long time as the sun, dark yellow, left the small under-eave window.

The wind had died away altogether, and from the yard the voices of the men were confidently level, where before short yells and curses had been distorted by emergency. They could hear the chink of coffee mugs being washed and stacked in the kitchen. The stagnant air was sweet and heavy with the smell of fire, and as he moved his hand slowly over her soft thighs and belly another heady sweetness gathered and pressed, grew in him as if the incense of the burning trees, her liquid readiness, the ominous respite of the wind, all worked his blood to urgent heat. She moved, lovely and alive, to welcome him.

Later they heard, as they lay quietly together, the hurried sounds of disorder and pursuit—a car being over-revved, gravel whicking tinny fenders, a scraping crash below in the yard, shouts, and another car, siren whining, coming up the hill after.

John went to the window, and as he recognized Junior's salt-rotted old car, now jammed against Sam's pickup, he heard Junior's voice below, in the house. Chief Atmon and Joe Beaupre jumped from the Leah police car, guns in their hands, and ran across the yard toward the kitchen.

"What is it?" Jane asked as she hurriedly dressed.

"Atmon and Beaupre chasing Junior."

"Oh, my God! What's he done now?"

Junior's hoarse roar came from the foot of the stairs. "Janie! Janie!" a desperate, yet irritated yell. *"Janie!"* and they heard him running heavily up the stairs, out of breath and sobbing hoarsely. "God damn it!" He opened and slammed several doors until he found the right one, then stood silent, struck motionless by the instantly understandable scene: Jane slipping her bra around after hooking it, John with one leg in his pants and his chest bare, the rumpled bed suggestively behind them. For a moment, as this interesting evidence went through Junior's mind, he stood with a reflective cast to his big red face, his immediate problems forced into the background—even though Atmon's brutal and righteous bellow at Mrs. Pettibone in the downstairs hall hung in the air: *"Where did he hide?"*

"Yeah!" Joe Beaupre yelled. "Never mind what he done! Where is he?"

Junior stepped inside and shut the door. "What are you doing here?" he asked John ominously.

"What are you doing here, is more like it," Jane said. More screams from downstairs as Atmon and Beaupre found Mrs. Pettibone intractable.

"Get dressed!" Junior said to Jane, who was obviously getting dressed. John, who fought with an annoying and nearly uncontrollable desire to laugh, had reached a hard knot in his bootlace. He gave it up and reached for his sooty shirt.

"I ought to . . ." Junior began with exaggerated iciness. Jane took one step and slapped him across the face. He nearly fell down.

"Now let's mind your business," she said. "You're in trouble and you came to me for help."

And as if Junior's try at being the protector of his sister's purity had been a kind of hysteria, her slap shocked him out of it. He sat dispiritedly on the bed (but with one purposeful hand pulled the spread up over its revealing disarray), put his head in his hands and asked, "Is everybody going nuts?" in an exhausted voice. Jane put a comforting hand on the back of his neck.

John held back his laughter for a grave and admiring moment. What a woman! He was struck sober by a somewhat frightening, yet strangely erotic, sense of her great value. Now he would scheme for permanence and availability, do his best to lose his freedom in the pursuit of happiness. He sat down against the wall and laughed out loud.

"What's so goddam funny?" Junior asked.

"I just had to be convinced, Janie," John said. "Oh, dear! Oh! Oh!" He laughed and laughed as they watched him. "I'm sorry," he said finally. "I'm sorry, Junior. Is it about your fight in the firehouse?"

"You had to be convinced?" Jane asked. At this, Junior looked hurt—jealous—and John could not blame him. Junior's plight seemed the most pressing thing at the moment. The heavy feet of the law marched up the stairs.

"That I won't ever run away from you, Janie."

"No!" Junior yelled. "They say I killed Bemis, for Christ's sake!" Now, having said it, and having thus invited Atmon and Beaupre into the room, Junior was terribly afraid. He stood up and backed against the far wall, his big hands limp at his sides, his face turned away from the door.

Joe Beaupre burst in, ran across the room and struck Junior on the face with the barrel of his revolver. Blood appeared, rich and dark. Junior didn't raise his arms. Beaupre struck again, and Atmon came for his share. He punched Junior in the chest.

"O.K.!" John found himself shouting at the busy backs of the police. They crowded each other, trying to get in the best licks, but Junior wouldn't go down.

"That's enough!" John shouted. They wouldn't hear him. Their breath hissed, they grunted and worked. He thought of boars, brute and powerful, mounted in maniac lust upon the backs of pummeled sows. They would not stop. They would not stop. Jane tried to pull Atmon away, but he shrugged her off and went on pounding. She slipped and went down on her knees. Seeing her there, helpless as is frail love in the presence of brute force, John felt his arms grow strong and willed himself berserk.

Willed himself, but the blue cloth of authority stretched with an invincible sheen across those bulky shoulders. He would as soon attack a priest as violate this bluer cloth. It was not in his character to do what it would be necessary to do, and this character he had defined over the years spoke only flight and disappearance to him. In order to fight them he would have to assume the authority of his burning town.

He never knew what decided for him—the necessity of one unavoidable action, Jane upon her knees crying, "Stop!" or the soft *smack smack* of fists and metal against Junior's flesh. He searched for a weapon, and a measure of his control was that he did not choose Bruce's pistol, but the narrow bed table. He forced himself between their arms and Junior, held the table defensively against their blows and raged at them, his voice bloated, megaphonic in his own ears: DO YOU KNOW WHO I AM?

Their lustful faces showed no recognition. They tried to move him aside, but he pushed the table edge hard against their faces until it hurt them. Joe Beaupre cracked his hand against the wood and dropped his revolver. As he bent to pick it up John kicked it under the bed.

As if he had been awakened from deep sleep, Chief Atmon showed surprise. "Hey!" he said sternly, and then was even more surprised. Sam Stevens' big arms circled him and held him still.

"Git his gun, John," Sam said. As John took Atmon's big revolver from its holster, Junior fainted. His wrecked face, jaw distended, torn by the sharp front sight of Beaupre's gun, pressed gently against Atmon's chest and left a nest of blood there as he fell.

"What the hell do you think you're doing?" Atmon said. Joe Beaupre was out of it. With a vacant expression on his pale, sweaty young face, he waited. The doorway was full of other waiting faces—Salvation Army women and men just back from the fireline. Jane and Mrs. Pettibone knelt and put their hands to Junior's wounds.

Sam nodded to John, his blue eyes cold and tired.

"Give me back that gun!" Atmon demanded.

"You're under arrest," John said.

"*You're* under arrest!" Atmon shouted.

"No, you are."

"Junior Stevens is under arrest! You're *all* under arrest!" But a nervous shifting of his eyes—Sam still held him absolutely in place—showed that a fearful reorganization was taking place in Chief Atmon's scheme of things. John took the shiny handcuffs from the holder on Atmon's belt and fastened Atmon's right hand to Joe Beaupre's apathetic left one.

"Who the hell do you think you are?" Atmon said, rubbing his imprisoned wrist. John had forced his hand into the cuff, and this surprising strength in John Cotter had further unnerved the chief.

"I asked you that," John said calmly, "but I'll tell you. I'm the man who just arrested the chief of police. In fact I just arrested the whole goddam police force."

"You can't do that!"

"Don't you feel that you're under arrest? Try to get out of here."

Atmon was silent. He looked desperately around the room—as far around as Sam would let him turn—but everyone watched John Cotter. No one met Atmon's eye. John saw this, and evidently Sam did, too. He released Atmon and went to Junior.

"Stand over there," John said, and it was still amazing to him that the two policemen did as they were told. A familiar fear came over him: the descent of responsibility upon his unready shoulders. It seemed to him that everyone waited for the chance to shift responsibility upon him. *Quis custodiet ipsos custodes?* The words were learned at a time in his life when the custodians could damn' well solve their own problems. Well, *Quis custodiet ipsos custodes?* John *Cotter?*

Sam Stevens picked up Junior and placed him gently on the bed. Junior breathed wetly through his mouth. Little bubbles of blood formed at his lips and ran down one side of his chin in a slow, forked stream. His nose was bent and plugged. Women were running for water and clean cloth.

Sam came back to Atmon and bent over to look him in the face. After a time he said: "I knew you was a fool, Atmon. I knew you was a nasty fool. But I figured you wouldn't do no harm since nothing much ever happened in Leah anyways. I was wrong." He grabbed Atmon's arm and pulled him violently toward the bed, dragging Joe Beaupre along too. "Look what you done," Sam said, forcing Atmon down toward Junior's mangled face.

"You don't know it, but you're headed for big trouble," Atmon mumbled.

"Don't hurt him, Sam," John said. Sam gave him a narrow glance, then pushed the police away.

"Reckon there's been enough butchering done," Sam said, "but I'm going to see you in jail, both of you. You can't get away with what you done in Leah! Where in God's name did you think you was, you goddam fools? On television? Ain't you from *Leah?* You think we're going to let anybody git by with being that lousy mean in *Leah?"* The old man's anger filled the room; in the presence of his gigantic wrath the legality of Atmon's and Beaupre's arrest would not be questioned.

"He's having trouble breathing. We'd better get him to a doctor," Jane said. Mrs. Pettibone ran for the telephone.

"Sam, I guess we better get the state police in on this," John said. "I'm not too sure what a citizen has to do to arrest a policeman."

"We'll make it good and legal," Sam said, staring meaningfully at Atmon.

"You're going to be in big trouble," Atmon said.

"WHAT?" Sam crowded Atmon to the wall and raised his huge arms over Atmon's head. "WHAT?"

"I ain't scared of you," Atmon said unconvincingly.

"Don't hurt him, Sam," John said.

Sam watched Atmon closely, then nodded, apparently satisfied. "The hell you ain't," he said, and turned to Joe Beaupre. "I always thought you was a decent boy, Joe," he said sadly. "Now what got into you, anyways?"

"I don't know, Mr. Stevens. He was running away."

"What for?"

Joe looked up with new, though faint, hope in his eyes. "He killed Charlie Bemis and tried to burn down the Town Hall, that's what he done."

Sam thought this over. "Maybe he did. Maybe he didn't. That don't change nothing in your case, though, Joe. You was just beating on him for the fun of it."

"He was running away," Joe said.

"We got eleventeen witnesses to say he wasn't, Joe. You better set on that one. He just run home, Joe, and you know that. He just run home. He didn't aim to run nowheres. You know he used to live here, and the minute you see him turn up my road you knew damn' well he wan't going anywheres."

Junior began to moan. Jane dabbed at a white lump as big as half an egg on his forehead. The watchers stood about the bed, their hands waving as if to help her, or to keep her fingers from touching the most painful parts.

John went downstairs and found Mrs. Pettibone, her connection made, stuttering and sobbing incoherently into the telephone. He took it from her and found that she had called a wrong number.

"They won't come!" she cried, her sallow face translucent about the brown hollows of her eyes, her maloccluded teeth grinding on brown lips. He led her to the kitchen and sat her down, hoping that among her dishes she might find her night meaningful again.

"We'll take him to the hospital in Northlee, Mrs. Pettibone. He'll be fine. Don't you worry, now."

"Oh, John Cotter!"

"It's all right now, Mrs. Pettibone."

She tried to smile, and even tried to hide her teeth from him. "They beat him so!" she said, and then bent down to cry again. "He's such a baby." Her rough hands circled her forehead as if to shade her eyes from strong light. He knew she shaded her unfortunate face from his eyes. "You never liked him anyways," she said. "But you saved him. I see you. You got right in between them and him and saved him. You done it."

I done it, all right, he thought. The state police had come back, and he went out to meet them. Two troopers he didn't know stood in the light from their car's headlights and spotlight, examining

Junior's car. Their brightly trimmed green uniforms, always able to make him a little more alert, a little more nervous, now made him hesitant. He didn't stop, however. It was too late for that.

"Did they get him?" one of the troopers asked.

"They got him, all right. We're going to take him to the hospital. We've got Atmon and Beaupre," John said.

"You what?" Both of the tall young men turned and examined him closely.

"We've disarmed them and arrested them. Right now they're under citizen's arrest."

"What the hell is that?" one asked.

"Oh, Christ, you know," the other said. "What did Atmon do now?"

"Junior Stevens wasn't offering any resistance, but they cornered him and nearly beat him to death. We had to arrest them to stop it," John said. He tried to fill his voice with as much calm authority as he could find.

"Can they do that?" one trooper asked.

"Yeah. It's in the goddam Constitution," the other said.

"You mean some lousy civilian could arrest *me?*"

"That's what it says."

"Damn."

They started toward the house and met Sam Stevens and the others halfway. He handed the two guns to the troopers and made his formal complaint.

"I don't care whether them two goes to jail tonight or not—they will soon enough. I just don't want to see them strutting around with no guns."

In the motionless air the big white house rose up behind them, the black mountain behind it. From the valley of the fire only a dull red glow lay ominously on the smaller hills.

"You better call the selectmen, John," Sam said. "Next time we'll git us a policeman ain't so fond of television."

"What about the sheriff, Sam?"

"Oh, him. He's on his ass up at the county seat. Where'd you expect?" Sam looked out at the embers of the near hills. "We got to git my grandson to the hospital, John. What I can't figure is, what with the fire and all, them two felt like killing a man. Jesus, I don't.

Do you, John?" In the burnished, wide old face that had been wrathful as God's there was now an honest perplexity. He stood with his legs apart, as he always did, ready for any upheaval in his universe and perhaps expecting it.

"He didn't do it," Jane said. "He was there. They saw him run out of the town clerk's office—right into their arms—but he says he was going for help. I believe him."

"If you do, then I do too," John said. They had spent most of the night at the hospital and now drove east from Leah Town Square toward the farm, having picked up Bruce's car. They had left the ton-and-a-half truck parked on Maple Street in front of the dark Cotter house. It was dawn, and above the brown smudge of the fire the sky was white, yet the hills were still dark as night. The fire still burned, now not advancing against the firebreaks and the lines of men. As long as there was no wind the fire could be held, but only rain could put it out for good, and there was no sign of rain. The dry woods-soil burned deep, stumps were emberred to the small roots, and even a small breeze might start the fire's advance again.

"If Junior didn't do it, Atmon and Beaupre have had it," John said.

"They've had it anyway," Jane said. "They're through in Leah, no matter what happens. Nobody liked Junior very much, but nobody liked Atmon, either."

"It's been some night," he said, glancing over at her. In the eastern light she was pale and seemed very fragile. Her clear skin was nearly as white as new snow, it seemed to him, and her hair, drawn back from her forehead, was nearly as light—fine and seemingly brittle, as if she had been carefully carved from ivory, like a cameo. He found it difficult to believe that this slight girl had made such animal moans beneath him, had been so strong with lust the afternoon before. Now he wanted to hold her and comfort her with infinite gentleness, to make her forget the violence she had seen last night; violence he knew she had as much strength to take as he. He reached for her hand, found it cold, and brought her over against him. She leaned lightly against his shoulder, one hand on his chest.

"If he'd done it, he wouldn't have come to me," she said. "He only came to me when he felt he'd been cheated, when it wasn't his fault. I don't know why, but that's always been the way. He's older than I am, but I've always been the one he came to. Not Sam or Mrs. Pettibone or anybody else. It's been that way as long as I can remember, even before our father and mother died. I know he didn't do it, Johnny."

"I know it," he said.

"You've got to know it!"

"Why?"

She moved away to look at him with a startled, doubtful expression. "Johnny, I've got to know you. You've got to be *here*. You've got to take charge. You've got to do everything."

"Janie, I'm not going to run away from you. Even when you say frightening things like that!" He smiled at her, but she didn't seem to be reassured. "As a matter of fact I might be in a lot of trouble. I don't know too much about this 'citizen's arrest' business. Don't know if it applies to duly appointed police officers or not. The state police look at it with a disapproving eye. Any police would, I suppose."

While he had waited for Jane in the hospital waiting room, a captain of state police came over to view this presumptuous civilian. The captain of police had stood for a long time in front of him, looking quite stern in spite of his wonderment. At that moment John nervously went over his relationship with the law, and remembered that it had been two years since he'd renewed his permit to carry a loaded pistol or revolver. Bruce's Ortgies was then beneath his handkerchief in his back pocket. A minor crime, since he was neither an alien or a felon, but he didn't want to be at the mercy of the police—not in the smallest way. He felt himself to be a bad, a very bad, example in their eyes. And the selectmen he called—the two who were not on the firelines—were also quite disturbed. They admitted no love for Atmon and Beaupre, but felt that Junior Stevens probably deserved what he'd got. "He may lose an eye," John had told them. This had made the selectmen more careful. "I didn't know you were in Leah," one had said. "You going to stay home now, John?" The similarity of their pointed questions about his staying home struck him: who was to cope with these odd problems? They nominated John Cotter.

"I'm not going to run away, Janie," he said again.

"Did you see Bruce?" she asked.

"No. Why?" He knew why.

"Because he's your brother." She still held herself away from him so that she could watch his face.

"I thought of it. You know I did. But I can't do it. Maybe it wasn't visiting hours."

"Bruce is in a private room."

"Look," he said, suddenly irritated, "let me take care of Bruce. You take care of your brother and I'll take care of mine."

She didn't answer, just closed her eyes and let her head fall back against the seatback.

"Janie . . ." he said, and found that he had nothing to say. She was honest, and would be honest. She had declared her connection to him, yet now imperiled it out of honesty. Testing? Testing? No. In spite of anything she might find out about him, she was his, and she needed him. So many things to find out! How brave, how responsible he thought he had been until, sitting in the wicker chair in the waiting room, he remembered that his only brother lay empty and waiting in another room! It was then that he became afraid of the police, afraid of his poor mother and father, afraid of the fire, afraid of Jane, afraid to move for fear of breaking his suddenly brittle, fragile bones. Germs from the sinks of the hospital crawled toward him with their object his blind death. The cigarette he smoked was giving him cancer at that very moment. He closed his eyes and saw fluttery yellow lights, the aura of a brain tumor. He could taste the bitter copper of his own last choke. When Jane came, finally, from Junior's bedside, he had nearly recovered, and although he had sweat and was still shivering slightly, he was fairly sure she hadn't found him out.

"Janie," he said again. Tired, showing her age in the brighter light, she watched the black road and wouldn't answer him. For a moment he was extremely angry, perhaps because he, too, was overtired. Then, as suddenly, he was calm again. Did he really want, as Bruce had, according to his diary, someone he *deserved?* Someone he had to earn? Or was that too much for a coward to cope with, and he'd better go back to a French girl with her built-in respect for a hard-on? Or Minetta Randolf, who wasn't so very different, in most ways. She just happened to have her way of taking the measure of a man. Literally. Or the little mimeograph girls of his college-radical days, who did everything they could for the cause and the causers of the cause. The hell with it.

Bruce wanted to ride a white horse into danger, to shoot his way to happiness while the bodies of villains fell lightly into dust; even to receive wounds in that magical spot on the shoulder. Who wouldn't? What simple problems at sundown on the desert street where total honor hung in the balance of a gun! And what lovely finality as the villain (fear) died and was hauled off to Boot Hill (nostalgia). The memory of some fears could be beautiful—the fears that you were not afraid to remember. The fear the Riders deliberately courted (a cylinder is a kind of gun; a piston is a kind of bullet) was such a fear, and he could not blame them for seeking. The gnawing of installment payments, the march of days till rent-is-due, the mysterious stealth of interest, the infinite boredom of manual work—these were the hard ones to remember. Much better to flirt with simple death on a windy road at night.

The black road turned in the headlights now dimming in the light of a clear day, and Jane said, "You missed the turn."

As he watched for a place to turn around he said, "Janie, I used to think if I didn't hurt anyone I was being a good man."

"Then be dead," she said, "and leave nothing."

He turned in a woods road and then, coming back, watched carefully for the farm road. Leave no issue and no issues. Only the dead stayed neatly in the indices of stones where you could always look them up. They never batted an eyelash at anybody.

"What I meant to say was, I know a lot about the sins of omission."

She would not answer. But he did know much about the sins of omission; the sins of emission without emotion. He'd been practicing them for a long time. Sadly he thought: John Cotter, perhaps you were meant to be thus, a man of cheap and sudden gestures, meant to do and run away. What talents you have been given! You can kill. You can hurt. You can please. You can work upon others the sickness of needful love.

"Janie, I love you."

"I don't know," she said.

As they turned up the long gravel road to the farm he glanced at her and found that she had slumped down in the seat. She watched the tops of the hemlocks move by in the smoke they had now entered. Her hands were open, palms up, on her lap.

Mrs. Pettibone had breakfast ready. Adolf and Aubrey, who had just come back from the firelines, ate their pancakes slowly but surely, their hands and faces black except for startling white lines across their foreheads where their caps had been. Soot and exhaustion made them look almost alike. Sam Stevens had slept some, yet he seemed more tired than anyone. He was not talking. Jane didn't mention Junior's hurt eye to Mrs. Pettibone: there was the possibility that it would be all right. She would not look at John, and wanted no breakfast. He saw her last at the stairs, where she thought she couldn't be seen. He was at the kitchen sink washing his face and hands and could just see her through the front hallway. She raised one foot to the first step, then turned and put her face to the wall, arms at her sides, and leaned her forehead against the wallpaper.

She must truly love her brother, he thought. She must believe that he is innocent, and that even so he is doomed. He watched her as she turned again to the stairs, trim and lovely in her dungarees and man's shirt. She climbed slowly out of sight. What lesson in love could she give him? Could she love that hulking bully for the accident of brotherhood, for his imperfections, for his love for her; for all of these things?

He poured maple syrup, and the wedges of white butter floated slowly across his pancake. Mrs. Pettibone came up behind his chair and put her hands on his shoulders. "She's just awful tired, John," Mrs. Pettibone whispered, her teeth clicking, her warm breath conspiratorial in his ear. "Don't you pay it too much attention."

Sam spoke, his voice harsh: "Raddio says we may git wind. No rain, as per usual. Wind."

Forks clinked upon china. Adolf grinned whitely and shook his black head. Aubrey ate on.

"Too damn' much to git one thing at a time. Fire, and now Junior," Sam said. "What next?"

"But I thought they was doing better," Mrs. Pettibone quavered. "They moved the headquarters and all. . . ."

"They'll most likely have to bring it back," Sam said.

"I prayed—"

"Prayed! 'Sprayed' be more of a help. Next time maybe they won't even stop here—set her up in Leah square, by God!" The old man set his chin and stood up. "I ain't asking for nothing. I see Cascom Mountain burn like a pine knot once. Hull goddam mountain. That was in the fall of 1885. I reckon Aubrey see that one pretty close, too. Lost his father's house and barn. It ain't the first time, nor the last." He stepped heavily into his overshoes and went outside.

John followed him. There was no sign of wind yet. The valley of Cascom Lake was full of brown smoke, but the lake and the unnaturally wide strip of dried shoreline were visible. The burned hills were dark beneath the brown smoke: A wind would pull off the layer of carbon and reveal acres of bright coals.

"They could be wrong about the wind," John said.

"Better be," Sam said. "They just damn' well better be, John. I ain't got the poop I used to, for one." Then he looked down at John, shrewd wrinkles radiating from his pale blue eyes; a hint of amusement in those black birds' feet. "Jane, she went to bed," he said, and went off to the barn.

On the way home Bob Paquette came up behind John on his motorcycle and flagged him down. Bob left his motorcycle idling and got into the car.

"Christ, John!" he said. "What the hell happened with Atmon and Beaupre?" His wide red face was round; his hair seemed to bristle with his admiring curiosity. Evidently the time of his disapproval had passed. John told him about the fight and Junior's wounds.

"Citizen's arrest? Man! What a sea lawyer you turned out to be! Would I give my left nut to of seen that? That bastard Atmon!"

"Joe Beaupre did the worst, with his gun barrel."

"I never did trust that Beaupre. Junior made a fool out of him in the firehouse when he couldn't git his gun out. I figured he'd be looking for a chance to git back at old Junior, but Jesus! Beat his eye out!" Bob shook his head, his eyes staring.

"Did Junior kill Bemis?"

"What? Well, John, I don't know. Junior's more or less a friend of mine. Where d'you stand?"

"Nowhere."

"Well, I guess old Junior did, more or less. It sure looked like it from where I stood."

"You saw him do it?"

"No! Now don't go gitting any ideas I did! No, sir. Nobody see Junior do it. We just see him come out right after. Then we went in and found old Bemis croaked. Junior must of smashed his head in with old Bemis' own telephone, the way it looked. Damn' office was on fire, too. Don't blame Junior a hell of a lot."

"Who was there?"

"Oh, everybody. All the Riders. Then there was Atmon, Beaupre, Eightball, Keith Joubert, some firemen, Billy Muldrow—Christ-all! With the fire died down a little, Bemis moved over to his own office. We set around out in the lobby. Junior went in and then after a minute he come running out, and there you have it. That's all I know. Who else could of done it?"

"Somebody could have come in through Mrs. Box's office."

"Well, I guess so, John. But it don't seem likely, after Junior's fight with Bemis and all. I mean, Junior was still highly pissed-off."

"Jane doesn't think he did it."

Bob shrugged, meaning: Of course, she's his sister.

"Did you see Junior go into the office? I mean, did you see him open the door?"

"Nobody did. We was having fun with Eightball or something. We see him come out, though."

"Maybe the place was already burning. What was it, waste-baskets?"

"Ayuh. Beside the desk. Burned up papers, burned the telephone a little, burned Charlie Bemis' arm. That was before we got over the excitement and thought to put out the fire. Atmon see Junior come running out and tried to grab him. We could see the fire inside. Well, Junior kicked Atmon in the family jewels and goddam, he dropped like a wet turd! Junior run right over him and got away. Joe Beaupre had his gun out this time but he dasn't shoot. Old Billy Muldrow come in a-yelling 'Shoot the bastard!' but they was too many standing around with their faces hanging out."

"What about the telephone? Was Bemis talking to anybody?"

"That's the funny part—I mean it was all funny as hell, but Mabel

Hinckley was on the line! Honest to God! Bemis just picked up the phone, I suppose, to call somebody up. Mabel says she heard this dull, sickening thud. That's what she said. Said she knew who done it!" Bob said this and waited, his eyebrows raised, holding back a smile.

"All right, Bob."

"State police went over to the telephone office to see her, they having got the very same ideas as you. She says Charlie Bemis said, 'Daisy?' like that, just before she heard this dull, sickening thud. She says Daisy done it. Daisy made that there dull, sickening thud! Only thing is, the only Daisy we could think of, anybody, was Daisy Colchester. Nobody called her Daisy since 1898! No matter. Mabel Hinckley says Daisy done it!"

But it was not the ridiculous image of Miss Colchester, blunt instrument in hand, that John saw. It was Billy Muldrow, under the prod of inspiration, trying to kill two birds with one stone. "Shoot the bastard!" It really wasn't too stupid a suggestion, and in that situation the woodsman could act quickly. Billy Muldrow was far from stupid. *Daisy done it!* A Daisy Bob Paquette had known well. He saw that he would not even be allowed the slightest reasonable doubt; that Leah in her grasping of John Cotter could ask for further union. Now it seemed quite possible that he must sacrifice his friend for Leah's truth.

CHAPTER 24

He sat on the granite cornerstone of the little Huckins graveyard, his father's bottle of bourbon between his legs, and turned the bottle grittily on the stone. "Go ahead and have a drink," he said out loud. "That's what you brought it for, your father's guilty bourbon." But he couldn't drink.

The tall pines did not move; the maples raised palisades of green leaves that were as immobile as rock. Nothing moved in the amber air of noon. Through smoke the leaves touched by the dull sun were green, yet old, as if they were the leaves of generations past.

He had left Bruce's car at the bottom of Pike Hill, and now waited for a sign, or catastrophe, or his luck to solve the problem of the coming interview.

He hadn't had to come. A few words to Bob Paquette, and wouldn't the town of Leah have gladly snapped poor Billy up! "Daisy was a dog, remember?" And happy logic—the conclusion beautiful for all of Leah—would be quick. He wouldn't have had to go to the police, to the sheriff, or to the selectmen. Just one little bee in Bob Paquette's bonnet, and it would have been out of John

Cotter's hands. It would have finished Atmon and Beaupre, too, and he would have been free of that legal worry.

He didn't say the words to Bob, and when they came downstreet, Bob leading on his motorcycle, Mrs. Box came running breastily out of the Town Hall to tell Bob that the Paquette barn was on fire, and he'd better go home. Bob turned without answering, his footrest scraping, and burned rubber as he raised his front wheel off the ground and the hot engine roared. He took the wrong way around the one-way traffic circle, headlong back toward Cascom Corners.

No one was home at the Cotter house, thank God. A note on the kitchen worktable: *Johnny we have gone to the hospital Bruce worse love Dad.*

Bruce worse love Dad. Worse love, Dad—Bruce. Now he sat with the bourbon warm between his legs and couldn't drink it. The word for father and son; the synthesis of that painful love seemed to him to lie in the repetition of that word: "Worse, worse, worse, worse," but the child's trick of lost meaning wouldn't work. Neither time nor repetition could always kill a lively pain.

In Manila he had killed a man in a situation that was so classic an example of self-defense that no investigation was felt necessary. He had even received in his knee the best of evidence, a spent bullet. And yet that guiltless crime had never let him be for very long. Red meat grew in the mouth; to think of the fragile brain—the semiliquid complexity of brain—was taboo.

Whether Billy Muldrow went to jail or to the old New Hampshire noose, it would be the same. His woods-quick brain could not comprehend a cage. Neither could it comprehend a padded cell in Concord. "Tight's a drum, and cozy," Billy had said of his new little house, but that coziness presupposed an icy wind from the clean, deep woods; it was the coziness of a bear's den in a ledge. The question was, would Billy understand the nature of his move against Leah? As final as would have been the "adambomb" he wanted to roll down Pike Hill, his extermination of Charlie Bemis meant that if he lost, he died. This choice might, or might not, be a conscious part of the gamble he had taken. John did know that Billy could run amok, and that might be the last defense of any cornered animal.

So he was going to tell Billy of Billy's death. When, in Manila, he had crept down toward the bullet-holed door, he didn't know. Now he did. There was no choice, in either case, but to go on and see the destruction at the end. No choice now, because he knew the weight of omission could be greater than the sight of his friend caught and struggling: he could not sneak, his problems solved, and live himself. The only action signifying what love, what dignity there was between friends, must occur in the confrontation to come, whether it was the pity asked for by a child or the hatred in the eyes of a wounded hawk.

He turned to look down upon the town. It, too, looked old through the brown lens of the smoke. The sun was gentle, and shone through the smoke as if through ancient glass, as if through bourbon in a bottle. He held the bottle up to his eyes: Leah preserved.

Before him the graveyard on its tilted ground had been planned for more permanent human occupancy than Leah. The big center-stone dominated the little square, a point of order in a wilderness of advancing trees. The deertrail and the boneless fingers of the birch-bark hand suggested the pleasing asymmetry of the rivers of Leah. Zacharia Calvin Huckins had preferred a tiny stone—one he could have tossed easily upon a wall. Florrie Stonebridge Huckins lay below a slate thin as a knife:

Her load was heavy.
Her back was slim.
Her heart was merry.
Rest her with Him.

And here were the dead children, all the dead children who had missed, among the stones, the living tit of Leah. "Rough," he said, trying to smile. Perhaps he did smile—he felt his mouth. "Not being blind," he said as he got up from his stone, "I know not when I smile." He put the bottle behind Florrie's slate.

Billy's truck was parked beside the yellow shack that had NEW HAMPSHIRE HIGHWAY DEPARTMENT stenciled on the side. Red hens hopped in and out of the old wood-silver shack that lay on its side next to the new one. Billy, with his great strength, had simply tipped it off the cellarhole and rolled the new one on. Hens teetered on beer cans and hens scratched with horny yellow claws the pressed earth of Billy's dooryard. Half wild, they ran silently for cover as John approached.

He deliberately suppressed his inclination to stalk the yellow shack. Movement was visibility, with animal or man, and the need for invisibility was almost unbearable in him. He made himself walk straight to the door. "Billy!" he called. One did not knock on the door of a house in the wilderness.

No answer. He called again before going to the tiny window. All he could see in the darkness was the tiny window opposite, the dark glass looped with dust-strung cobwebs. Around at the front, the door's padlock was open on the open latch, and he opened the door the maximum tactful inch and called, "Hey, Billy?"

The shack felt occupied. Warmth, or perhaps the slight humidity of breath, moved past his face. The animal smell of Billy, though not unpleasant, was lively in the moving air.

"Billy?"

Cot springs squeaked, and the voice pretended to come, surprised, from sleep: "Ayuh. Who's there?" Pretending not to know.

"John Cotter." Your friend, John thought, Come to tell you the news.

"Hi, John!" Billy said. "Come on in and set down."

John entered, and removed a bowl of nuts and bolts from the chair. "Your breakfast, Billy?" he asked. Billy rolled over, his brown underwear buttoned up to his neck. He dropped his big feet to the floor and felt with his toes for his boots.

"Ain't had no breakfast, John. I don't feel too good today." Billy's long face, in the semidark, shone on the cheekbones and forehead with the burnished sheen of rubbed and permanent grime. He hadn't washed since the fire, and his forehead was the color of polished apple wood. He put a black, muscular finger along his brown teeth. "Tastes like a mouse died in my mouth," he said.

John's eyes were opening to the dark. Billy bent over to thread the laces of his boots, and as he bent to the usual task, his wide shoulders moving to the small demands of the everyday gesture, his hair black and curly upon his creased and brawny neck, John saw him straight and painfully as the man he was—living, capable of all the common, hurtful fears, alive to the necessity of having his boots tied, his life calm, his nerves in order, his guts not tied by worry: a man, now, not the tool of Principle, not a friend or an enemy.

"Let's have a little light on the subject," Billy said, and snapped a wooden match with his thumbnail. He took the kerosene lamp and swished the oil around in it, testing, then pushed the chimney up and lit the wick. The smooth yellow light flowed across the wick and grew in the glass chimney. Billy's big hand made delicate adjustments with the tiny knob, and the light steadied, yellow and gentle upon the cluttered table and upon Billy's ugly, lonely face.

"Well, Johnny, what's the news about the fire?" Billy's brown eyes moved in their hollows, unshining. They might have been part of his skin except for movement. He selected a pipe from the table, dumped a small brass washer out of the bowl and gouged tobacco from a round can.

"Paquette's barn is burning. No wind, though. We've got the fire held back for a time, anyway."

"You done a good job out there at Stevens' farm, John, with that firebreak and all." Billy turned his head away as he lit his pipe—as if, in the glare of the match, he were struck by sudden modesty.

The man had committed murder with the same hands he used to light his pipe. The same eyes that now implored shy friendship had aimed to murder. Or just to kill . . . No. Billy Muldrow was not a simple animal; he was of Leah. The social horror of the deed might be stronger in him than in John himself, separated as John had been, for a time, from Leah's simple values. Thou Shalt Not Kill, having become Thou Shalt Not Hurt, had lost the directness of biblical command—had become ethical and personal and thus weak. There were so many formal systems of behavior to weigh and test—out in the world. Back again, he was caught again: Thou Shalt Avenge the Breaking of Leah's Rules. Thou Art Executioner.

Billy's knowledge of his sin would be strong, now that his passion for revenge was spent in action, and Billy, too, must hear those words ringing in the pines. Who would be executioner?

Who had, at the age of thirteen, written *Billy Muldrow eats it* upon the wall of the Town Hall men's room? Who had stood upon the drippy urinal to write big, giggling out of luscious guilt? He hadn't been the leader of that campaign of assassination. Even worse, he had followed Junior and Keith Joubert and the rest, trying to pacify them with the wickedness of his ideas: *Billy Muldrow defenestrates himself.* "What the hell is that?" "That's what so good about it, see? Nobody'll know, but it sounds awful." And for this inspiriation he was unhit, ungoosed, not chased home on a boring summer night. Like all immunity bought with dishonor, it was temporary. He could not tell them that the word had meaning. They would not want it to have a meaning they did not know, and to him it was a further debasement of his honor that, slyly, he did not tell them what it meant.

Guilty or not of Billy Muldrow's unhappiness, he must make no more deception for the sake of temporary peace. It didn't work.

Billy smiled shyly. "Johnny, I'm awful glad you come to see me. You know I'm always glad to see you, Johnny, and I ain't been feeling good."

"That's too bad, Billy."

"I ain't et nothing since yesterday forenoon."

"What's the matter?"—not wanting to hear the reason. He fought with a nearly overpowering quickness of the brain to find a way out. It seemed that with no effort at all on his part an incredible lucidity, as his mind listed and sifted ways and compromises, illuminated all choices, all questions. Could he prove Junior innocent without pointing to Billy? Would Billy's guilt force him to confess? Was Junior really guilty? No to all of them. Why not let Junior pay anyway? God knew he deserved some kind of punishment. (What sins against Junior must someone else then pay for?) No, to all of them.

"Billy . . ." he began, knowing that his face mourned the words to come, and that Billy, seeing it, grew afraid.

Billy's eyes slipped craftily to the side, his long teeth appeared and he cried, "How about some cider, Johnny? Clear the smoke outa your Adam's apple!" He kicked the trapdoor with his heel and caught it on the bounce. Before John could answer—caught again in the grip of procrastination—Billy climbed down out of sight.

The eager brain suggested: Why not hate Billy? Wasn't there a reason somewhere? Bruce hated toads because he once killed them; hated them for the liquid *squish* of their breaking bodies. If Bruce could hate for his cruelty, why couldn't John Cotter? He'd hurt

Billy once, and he must now hurt Billy again—why not enjoy it? Once he'd shot a sitting hawk, *thunk* through the body, and the hawk flew down to die, but he didn't hate hawks for the death of one.

He might lean forward over the trapdoor and softly tell. The glug of cider into the jug would stop, and Billy, who couldn't quite yet dare to know, would know. . . .

"Yo, Johnny. Coming up!" Billy's dirty hand, thumb in the jug's round handle, appeared. He climbed out slowly, placed the amber jug on the table without meeting John's eyes, and felt for tumblers on a narrow shelf between two-by-fours. "Funny old Jake ain't been around. Ain't seen him since the fire started, but I figure come something like fire, all them critters turn back to wild. It's every critter for himself, come fire. Ayuh!" He poured two tumblers of the pale cider and looked straight at John for a second over the one he offered. "Jesus, John! Let me tell you about the buck I seen the other day! What a rack on him! Ten points, anyways. Two-hundred-fifty, three-hundred pounds. Neck like a barrel. I'm going to git him come deer season, Johnny! I know where he hangs out!"

Billy's eyes shone, now, desperately hopeful as he looked into a different future. "You ought to of seen his tracks, Johnny. Damn' near big's a heifer's, they was. Pressed 'way down in so far I had to take near two handfuls of pine needles out to git to the bottom! Big? Biggest buck I ever see. I just got to git that buck, John!"

"Billy, did Junior kill Charlie Bemis?" John asked. The words sounded flat and impolite.

" 'Course he done it," Billy said quickly. "Now let me tell you where I see that buck, Johnny. Just you let me tell you. Maybe you can git a crack at him. . . ."

"Jane doesn't think he did. Billy, I don't either."

Billy pretended to be greatly irked at the interruption. "Ain't you *interested?* God dammit, John, seems I recall the first deer you ever got. You was interested then! Damn' nice little buck, too. Hundred-seventy pounds. Why the hell don't you have no expression on your face? 'Course Junior done it, if that's what's up your nose."

"Billy, you remember when Junior and Keith Joubert and Ramsey and the rest used to pick on you? You'd give them beer and treat them all nice and they'd let the air out of your tires and tip over your outhouse and write your name on the men's room walls? I did that, too, Billy. I hung around so they'd leave me alone and did the same dirty things to you, Billy."

"No you never!" On the big face, on the wide mouth appeared that parody of a smile that is the lips' twist against plain crying.

"Yes, I did."

"You shit you never!"

"Yes, I did, Billy. I'm a dirty bastard like the rest, so don't trust me, Billy."

"No you ain't, Johnny!"

Billy put both black hands over his face, his head appearing in the lamplight and then rocking back into darkness as he bent from the waist, in and out of the cot's dark alcove. The long, dirty hands were wet when he held them out into the yellow light, the strong wrists long from sleeves that had worked back into permanent folds and wrinkles.

"You're just saying that, Johnny. It ain't true," Billy said in the tight voice of a child. High, as brittle as bone, the voice was a triumph against self-pity, and *would* be clear and dry.

John's chest became hollow, as if the lungs and heart and diaphragm had gone out of him, leaving in their place nothing but cold air and a sharp, peripheral pain, as if those organs had been wrenched, bleeding, from the cavity walls. The pain was real enough—the nearest approximation his sympathy could make of Billy's fear.

"Christ. What the hell," Billy said weakly, his voice losing to the stronger force of pity. John tried to breathe, his mouth open, his eyes upon his surrendering victim. If Billy lost to pity, his was not the first caught voice to cry, "Who is on my side? Who?" knowing the inevitable fact of loneliness.

"I ain't asking for nothing. I never asked nobody for nothing."

"That's right, Billy," John said. "You don't owe me or anybody anything." As if he were falling, he had breath but seemed not to. He wanted to do the only instinctive act in the face of such helplessness: to gather the man become infant in his arms, to rock him, to do whatever medicine occurred between comforter and child. Billy sniffled in his dark corner, snuffed up the liquid in his nose as unselfconsciously, as messily as a child, yet without a child's sure call to pity, without much of the innocence that hides death from a child. Billy knew the purpose of the visit, and when he got around to taking his hands away and bringing his poor face back into the light, as he must, John would surely see Billy's death working there, growing like cancer upon the familiar face.

"I didn't want to, Billy," he called across the circle of light, "I never wanted to hurt you, Billy." Out of the darkness Billy's long legs, in blackened overalls, lay splayed apart, the hairless shins skeined with dirt dried into small, curving lines like patterns of sand on a beach. His big boots rested on their heels, toes canted outward.

"Why'd you go and tell me, then?" Billy mumbled through his hands.

"I'm not going to lie any more. I want to be your friend, Billy, honest to God I do! Nobody knows but me, and I had to tell you first."

"Tell me what!" Billy cried, knowing. "I knowed the minute I heard you call my name," he said after a while. "It ain't that about Bemis, Johnny, but what you said you done before. Why'd you tell me that?"

"Just because it's true. So you don't owe anybody anything. I didn't think you'd want to."

Billy still hid in the shadow. "You damn' right," he said, his voice steadying, then growing exultant as he grasped the offered picture of himself. "That why I live up here where I can't even *smell* them little farts down there, you know that? Pay cash for everything! Don't owe nothing, don't ask for nothing!" He sat forward into the light, and the face belied the comforting image of himself as a hard and independent man. The face still cried pity, but it was changing.

"Sure, Johnny, sure! Let the little bastards come and git me! They ain't never seen a man like me before!" He reached over and took his big rifle from against the wall, jacked a cartridge into the chamber and let the hammer down, lightly, upon it. "Me and Old Bungaloo," he said, smiling grimly into the famous scene of resistance against insuperable odds.

It was this that finally brought John to tears. The cold little things passed down his face and wet his neck. His throat hurt. Tears were the most unhelpful response of all: they could do nothing for Billy. He could not stop his tears—no one could do that—and Billy needed help of a different kind if he were to gain the only comfort left to him.

"You said you was the only one knows?" Billy asked. The worn steel barrel-end of Old Bungaloo, and Billy's face—now made up into the smile that meant, "I don't mean it, *maybe*," pointed straight at John. "How come you ain't afraid of me, John, since you know?"

"I don't know why, Billy."

Billy opened the action of the rifle, took out the cartridge and slid it back into the magazine before he put the rifle back against the wall. "I ain't that kind of a man," he said proudly.

"I know that, Billy."

"I just ain't that kind of a man."

"That's why I knew I could tell you, Billy." John kept his face back in the shadow. Tears must not show. This must be a scene between brave men. Billy stood up and took a deep, heroic breath. The light reached his face from below and struck black, angular shadows across it. The nose jutted; the brow was straight above the carved hollows of his eyes; the chin was square and strong. As if conscious of this effect, he took his glass and held it out.

"Drink up!" he said, "and screw 'em all, eh, John? You want to be my friend? Be my friend!"

"Thank you, Billy," John said, with the feeling that these might be his last clear words and that he must get away before he gave himself away. And yet the tears he hid in shadow were tears, also, of admiration for the bravery with which a man could grasp the fact of death and then go further to see, at least, a way to die. Even if temporary, the memory of such a proud and defiant moment might illuminate the last cold one.

"Drink!" Billy said.

John leaned forward to reach for his glass, and as he did his face came into the light, tears dishonorable upon it; more tears where those tears came from.

"John," Billy said, and that didn't help. The tone was kind and concerned. Billy put his hand on John's shoulder. "Johnny, you don't have to do that! Goddam! I forgive you, Johnny. I know how Junior and them used to pick on you. I know why you done it."

Kind, comforting voice! *I forgive you.* Where was the carefully constructed artificial bravery, the act of pride, he had schemed for Billy? Billy pulled him to his feet and held him out at arms' length.

"You're my friend, John. They ain't nothing holds you back from being my friend. Don't you worry none, John. Don't you cry." The dirty, creased face had become paternal and responsible; the brown eyes were dry and worried for Billy Muldrow's friend.

At the Huckins graveyard John stopped to stretch his aching throat and to look high into the silent pines. Smoke filtered the afternoon sun, and the green had an amber, softening sheen upon it. Even the cloudless sky was another shade of rich amber, as if the world had become the cured and woodsy shade of Billy Muldrow and everything of Billy's. He watched the rigid gravestones. No, stones that moved on the earth with a slower rhythm than he could now perceive.

How cheap he had considered the man to be! Billy did not need a vision of resistance in order to consider himself a man. And John had not forgotten, as he watched Billy, that he could be afraid of him. He had been aware of Bruce's loaded pistol, hard in his back pocket. Now he took it out and looked at it. How cheap, how ridiculously toy-like it seemed now! The little machine could work no change upon a man except to kill him, and that change could be worked upon a grasshopper or a toad with exactly the same idiot implications.

He had the urge to throw the pistol deep into the woods, but he did not. If he had lost faith in its strength, Bruce had not, and it belonged to Bruce.

There was no wind at all. Leah stood deep in the tall trees of its valley, houses and steeples all old and golden in the strange light.

CHAPTER 25

Junior spoke with a tongue made careful by the pain of his wired jaw. He said, "I din doot," until she told him she knew he didn't do it, and that he didn't have to say it any more. "Nobody believe it," he said.

"I believe it."

"Ow! Christ it hurts." He moved his head from side to side, both eyes bandaged although only one was injured, and she felt that the negative motion was more of pain and wonderment than of negation. His lips were thick and cracked, as if they had been burned, and had a bluish-yellow cast to them that never, in spite of a rule she remembered about mixing colors, approached green. He hadn't been told about the danger to his eye. For a reason she could not explain she felt that this might be more damaging to his state of mind than the charge of murder.

His bandages and visible bruises no longer excited an extra measure of pity in her; he had always been bruised—had to act out his hurt in anger. What that basic hurt was she did not know any more than John knew the forces that had caused Bruce to be the kind of man he was. She and John were both observers of those with violent needs, and they were both helpless to the extent that they did not know the causes of the need. Neither of them was helpless to treat symptoms, however, as she had (not always) done with Junior. To find the cause might, perhaps, as they said of cancer, let in the air and stimulate its growth; it might be better to let the deep places alone—let the disease either cure itself or more slowly kill its host. She knew that she could never ask Junior *why* he lived the way he did. It would be a breach of dignity she would never let herself commit. To tell Junior that he acted like an ass—that was all right, and signified a certain equality. But let the man be keeper of his own depths and causes.

"Don't feel good, Janie. Think I'm going to upchuck."

She held the basin for him, one hand on the back of his thick neck to guide his experimental retchings. She hadn't heard the childhood word for vomit for many years. Certainly Junior would never use it if he weren't so sick and worried. Puke was his word, and if he were drunk and puking it could even be a virile, boasted act. Poor Junior; in trouble he seemed to show some need for the babyhood he despised.

He gasped and sobbed over the basin, then fell back against the canted bed. A string of drool had been forced between his fixed teeth, and she gently wiped it off. As she did he kissed her hand.

Later in the afternoon, after Junior had gone to sleep, she had coffee in the cafeteria with Charlotte Paquette, who told her that the Paquette house and barn had burned. Evidently someone had thrown a cigarette out of a car and started a grassfire in the adjoining field.

"Bob just called me," Charlotte said. Her round, pretty face was framed by her family's thick black hair. "He said there wasn't anything I could do—they don't even have much left to help move. Ma and Pa and the rest are going into Leah to stay with Aunt May and Uncle Albert." She seemed quite sad and old. "It was such a nice big old house," she said mournfully.

She was staying at the hospital nurses' residence, and hadn't lost her things, anyway. "We had insurance. I don't know what we'll lose—you always do—but it's not so bad except we always lived in that old house. Pa'll build another, only it won't have to be so big. We had three bedrooms we never used except for company. Ma always wanted a new house—they're so easy to keep clean—and an electric stove. I don't blame her, I guess. With all of us working except Timmy and Jean, we'll have enough money. It's not so bad, Janie. You don't have to feel sorry at all. Not with your troubles."

"I liked you all in that big house," Jane said.

"So did I. But we never seem to do very well by ourselves. It isn't the same outside."

"Don't you want to get married?"

"Sometimes . . . I guess I do, Janie. Dick's going to, and he's the first one to get away—I don't mean that—but to make his own family. Maybe we were all too happy and loving together. It was more fun than going to the movies."

When Charlotte had to go back on duty Jane went outside, intending to drive back to the farm, and sat, exhausted, in Junior's scraped and dented old car. She didn't know if she should wait for him to wake up or not. He would want her to be there to say goodbye for the night in a formal way, so that his life could at least have the order of visiting hours imposed upon it. That might help a little.

She pressed the button on the dash compartment panel, not really intending to open it, and the thing fell open with a crash. A flashlight rolled out and fell to the floor. As she put it back her eyes automatically went over the contents of the compartment: a greasy road map, several folders of paper matches, a screwdriver, a pair of pliers, one cigarette half empty of tobacco, a box of condoms. Yes, of course, a box of condoms; the child was a man in that sense, and no doubt used the rubber things here on the grimy seats, wrastling with one of Leah's available women. Poor Junior! In that love she felt that there could be nothing but indifference, even dislike, except for the hot flash of orgasm. No love for Junior in this slum of a car, drunk and giggly, his brutish hands in willing rape of a woman possibly more brutish than himself. Perhaps she was unfair—yet she knew that to certain men sex could be defined by the four-letter-word and contained in the four-letter-word, and that word was synonymous with disgust and related to filth. Therefore the shield, the antiseptic, the garbage bag.

When Junior came running into the room and found her with John, even though he ran from the police, he stopped to disapprove. How deep had his disapproval been? Maybe so deep he courted that beating. Maybe that was why he didn't even raise his hands to protect his face.

She would go no further. She was most likely wrong, anyway. She would give her brother the pity he demanded and the love she had for him. Let him be the keeper of his depths and causes.

She closed the dash compartment upon its odds and ends, walked back across the lawn to the hospital and sat on the iron bench outside the main door. She didn't want to meet the composed faces of the other visitors, to have to guess the secrets of faces made sickly by the consciousness of pain.

On the dried grass of the lawn a woman walked hand in hand with a little girl who limped, who dragged her travesty of a right shoe, a shiny black block. Leaning over the little girl, who pointed at the trees and at the sky, the woman walked slowly. Attentive, kind, yet by a quick movement of her head toward the little girl's sky, by a too long look into that uncluttered space above the trees, she made her boredom plain.

Even here in Northlee the air was sweet with smoke. At least the wind hadn't started up again. If only it would rain! It had been so long since rain she had grown used to the blank sky, and expected no more of each day but an orange, smoky sun. Nothing new in heaven, but here on earth things happened with a quick and disconcerting rhythm. She had been in love—was still in love—but now she was tired. It was as if her exhaustion destroyed both memory and desire, and neither could stir her senses back alive again. Now she must go into the hospital to comfort her wounded brother.

CHAPTER 26

They were home. The big Buick stood in the driveway like a fat sentinel, telling him that his family was home and unhappy. Franklin met him in the kitchen.

"John!" Franklin said. He seemed nothing but pleased and happy to see him home again. "Did you fight the fire?"

"Sure did, Frank." Fire, police and the destructive fever of my ego, he thought, and I've just played messenger for that bitter hugger, Mortality. Some fun.

He took the little boy by the upper arms, lifted him up and looked straight into his eyes. Pleased, Franklin smiled shyly and looked down. The top of his head was knit into a million tight black curlicues. When he looked up, grinning, his broad teeth dazed the eye; his amusement jollied the soul.

"You're a damned good boy," John said. "If one can call you a boy. I think you're a midget in boy's skin. Not only are you a midget, you're a wizard midget, and your sister is an even midgeter wizardess."

Franklin laughed delightedly, surprised into a high, bubbling giggle that brought Jenny Lou running. She stopped short, her eyes wide—the white-circled target eyes of caricature.

"Jenny Lou!" Franklin said. "You're a midgeter wizardess!"

"I'm not either!"

John put Franklin on his feet and picked up Jenny Lou in the same way.

"It's good!" Franklin said. "It's good to be one!"

Jenny Lou then consented to smile. "O.K., John," she said, "I am one, then."

He kissed her on the forehead. "Really," he said, "you should be doing that to me." She did. "Now you have wizardessed me. You are the wizardess of Fresh Air, which is a good thing." He put her down. "Now, where are my mother and father?"

Franklin frowned. "They went upstairs to lay down for a minute, John. They were both kind of sick when we got home from the hospital."

"But Bruce is still the same. I just called the hospital."

"They had an argument," Franklin whispered.

"William wouldn't go inside," Jenny Lou whispered, "and Gladys *cried.*"

"In that case will you kids stay down here and amuse yourselves for a while? I'm sorry you had to see the argument. I'm sure it wasn't much fun."

Franklin shook his head in agreement.

"That wasn't *anything* compared to yesterday," Jenny Lou said proudly.

The door was closed. He stopped in the hall outside and listened, hearing the low mumbles of the famous and most fearsome room in hell; better some honest yells of pain. As he opened the door they were silent and the room was dark. The shades were drawn down to the sills. The long bodies of his mother and father lay tensely parallel upon the double bed.

As he walked straight to the window it seemed that this walk had started when he first approached Billy Muldrow's house, that he hadn't yet stopped, or even been sidetracked, from a purposeful journey. He raised the shades on the golden light of late afternoon.

They watched him, surely amazed that he would deliberately enter a room in which emotion was so tangible.

"I think I know what happened," he said, "you went to Northlee for different purposes. What did you want, Mother?"

"Oh, Johnny!" she cried, and showed him her tears.

He turned to his father, "Did she lie to you? Did she try to scheme you in to Bruce?"

"I couldn't go in, Johnny. Sometimes I can, sometimes I can't, that's all. This time I couldn't." William Cotter pleaded his weakness for pardon. His handsome, oversized head was propped, as if he were a dying king, against the headboard of the big bed.

"I stopped downstreet and called the hospital. There's been no change in Bruce. Mother, Mother," John said sadly, "did you want them together so badly you had to invent Bruce's death?"

"Anh, hanh," she cried, her hands at her neck, her sharp elbows winging out. She seemed to be choking herself, and he went to her and pulled her hands away. She reached for him and he let her hug him; even knelt down so that she could better loop him in with her long and bony arms. Her hair was wiry against his face, her skin was oversoft and toneless. With surprise and pity he found that she was smaller and weaker than he had thought her to be, and that the energy of her embrace was nowhere near as violent, as aggressive, as false memory had made it out to be.

Had he been afraid of this? For as long as he could remember he had been unable to give her such simple comfort as the pressure of his cheek. She had taken, demanded, the cool kiss of parting and of return. But she had received no gifts. She had bought (and paid for) the ceremonial touch of lips, and that was all. He kissed her on the forehead and tried to stand up, but of course she wouldn't let him.

"Johnny, Johnny, Johnny," she cried softly, her hand moving to the back of his head as if she steadied the limp spine of an infant: as an infant he had last given, had last willingly received.

Then she did let him go—another surprise. Perhaps she might know what to do with a gift, no matter how she squandered her demanded signs. How could he know, who had never given?

He chose not to stand, although her arms signaled his release, if he wanted it. "Mother, do you really want us to see Bruce?"

"Yes!"

"He can't see us or hear us," he said, knowing that she did not mean Bruce to hear or see. She had given him painful medicine before, "For your own good."

"Dad," he said, the word easy in emergency.

"I can't, Johnny. I don't want to!"

"I don't want to either," John said, and his mother pushed him up: he should get busy. She watched, bright-eyed.

John walked around the bed and stood over his father, over the big man who had conceived him upon the same bed in which he now tried to hide. His arms lay at his sides, palms up, in the pose of exaggerated fatigue. He shook his handsome head—a slow, continuous no.

"Come on, Dad," John said kindly, "we can do this, anyway."

"No, I can't. You go on, Johnny."

"We can do it, all right," John insisted. His father's face, canted upon the headboard, was imperious and afraid. NO, NO, NO, NO, the motion said, as if an axis of rotation pierced his head from chin to gray cowlick. His shirt was snowy white. His necktie, in small collegiate stripes, ran straight and narrow to his belt. John took one of the limp hands and had it snatched away.

William Cotter's voice was hollow, weak with surprise. "Stop it! What the hell do you care? Are you going to be another son-of-a-bitching *Bruce?*"

"Oh, oh," Glady Cotter said, but when John looked she was not crying. She did not mind a tangle of love—it was indifference that had always haunted her. She was alarmed; she was worried about the outcome, but she would thrive upon the scene.

"No, no. I'm not Bruce," John said. "I want you to come and help me. Don't you think I feel as bad about Bruce as you do? What do you think you're guilty of? Don't you think I feel that way too?" He knew his father's strength was lost to fear, yet felt a great need not to pity the man. There must be another way.

"I love you," he said.

His father rolled violently to his feet. He crouched over his son, one hand held as if to strike him, his face fiercely red with anger. His mouth, when he shouted, seemed to crack along wrong and unfamiliar lines: *"You liar! You don't love me!"*

"But I do," John said, and found that he did. For proof he had a sudden vision of his father dying, his father in Bruce's place before the operation, facing those terrible odds; his father gone. Who would so gently ply himself with guilty bourbon, who could be so shyly kind? He knew his father could not hit him, and now, out of the painful birth of love, would not demand that his father try it.

Gladys Cotter, with a shrill yelp that was perhaps joyful, threw herself between them. She dramatically hung herself upon William Cotter's threatening arm—a measure of her fine instinct in matters of passion—and lied for the scene she must celebrate with hosannas: "Don't hit him, Bill!" she cried.

John admired her very much at that moment. The only useful lies were those never taken, nor given, for truth. Over a shoulder she had tilted with the craft of an actress, he met his father's eye. It was too serious a moment for the smile they both reserved—for the tolerance they shared.

The big Buick seemed to float on toward Northlee, its interior artfully like a cocktail lounge—overcomfortable and slightly suggestive of intoxication—a startling contrast against the wild hills and the dry-brown fields outside. The intimate gleam of softly bent plastic and silver, the cosy mold of the compartment, flattered and relaxed them. Dials indicated, clock ticked, knobs were ready to be pulled or turned for every pleasure, music in soft overbass humbumbled from somewhere. No wonder his father had chosen not to leave this gentle egg for the square room in which Bruce lay dying.

Now, with a tension between them that was affection unexpressed, understanding not quite understood, they drove toward Bruce. His father had suddenly capitulated. With sacrifice he had tried to hide—really tried to hide—he said yes, they must go see Bruce. But now he could not make himself drive fast. They went at exactly the speed limit, and he saw his father watch the dial, and felt him correct their speed.

"You haven't seen him since before the operation, Johnny," he said, obviously trying to keep the statement from being an accusation.

"I am now," John said.

"What got into you, anyway? I mean why do you want to go?"

"I'm doing all the things I don't want to do."

"Yes, you kissed your mother."

"Why didn't she come too?" John asked wonderingly.

"Maybe it was because we didn't ask her not to," William Cotter said.

John wondered again, as he had in the bedroom when she did not hold him with her arms, about the few and trifling gifts she'd ever had from him. Perhaps she was no spendthrift. No, he saw this act begin: she saw her men off on a quest of her own devising. She was a woman, wasn't she? And somehow women always seemed a little closer to the fact of death. What she had seen in the bedroom had no doubt convinced her that the rest of her family survived and loved: as a woman she might, with swift logic, be even quicker than they to bury the dead. She would wait for the survivors.

"We don't know Bruce," John said. "You're his father and I'm his brother, and we never knew him at all, ever. Why not?"

"It's too late to find out now, Johnny."

John had a quick, shaking flap that surged up from his bowels and ran out to the ends of his fingers and toes. "What does he look like? I don't want to be too surprised."

"He's thin, and his hair's growing back in."

"Christ."

"He's all healed up. Healed up very well."

"He's just a man," John said.

"They feed him through a tube, Johnny. There's a tube in him all the time. You'll see that."

"I don't want to see them feed him."

"All right," his father said.

"What do they feed him, some goddam chemicals?"

"No, it's stuff like eggs and vegetables and meat—very nourishing stuff—but it's all like soup. Has to go down the tube."

"How do they do it?" John asked, and asked himself how to stop asking.

"They put it in a thing like a grease gun and pump it down."

"Oh, God."

"Why do you have to know, Johnny?"

"I never had to know anything about Bruce. I never gave a damn about Bruce."

"Johnny," his father said, turning his head for one swift, worried look into John's eyes. "Johnny, I want to tell you something. When Bruce went to the hospital I was glad." He turned his face again, and John saw upon it anguish, as if it were illumined by a flash of red light.

"I felt nothing," John said, "except that I didn't want to come home."

"I felt glad my own son was sick."

"Well, Jesus Christ who could blame you? Let's face it. Bruce was a mean, lousy son of a bitch. Why should that bastard make us guilty? What claim has he got on us?"

"Blood, I guess, Johnny."

"Is there any of his blood on my hands?"

"I've been too busy washing my own, Johnny. I don't know."

They passed Northlee Square and the old dormitories, empty and barnlike among the tall elms. At the hospital parking lot William Cotter brought the Buick into a diagonal parking place as gently and carefully as if it were an ocean liner under the care of ministering tugs. He turned the key and everything stopped except the tick of the inset, reminding clock.

Low and squatty, spreading like a crab, the old hospital ejected a little pulse of steam from its laundry vent. "We better keep going," John said, and they both emerged from the car feeling naked without its comforting shell around them.

They walked side by side, almost touching arms, with the unsteady dignity of fear overcome—or nearly overcome—by resolution. They walked straight through the lobby and entered the long, cream-colored hall with all the doors that opened upon the high white beds of the sick. As they came to the men's ward they stopped to let a nurse push a cartful of medications through the wide doors.

"Cotter and Son," a dry voice called. Howard Randolf beckoned them in with a hand as slow and as lacking in inward energy as a weed waving under water. They entered the ward and came, pushed by the nightmare's end at the end of the hall, pulled by a welcome respite in that journey, to Howard's bed. "*This* is where you eventually see everyone you know, isn't it, John?" Howard said. His lined, gullied face looked terribly clean, as if the hospital had washed and sterilized half the life out of it.

"How are you, Howard?" John asked.

"Why, I'm fine and dying, of course, like all the rest."

"They said you had heat prostration and some broken ribs."

"Yes, and a slight dying of the heart, they tell me."

William Cotter seemed not to hear. He cast quick, apprehensive glances at the sick men down the line, and John wondered if he looked for his own face, washed and faded, on one of the hospital pillows.

His father leaned toward him and said in an apologetic voice, "I've got to go to the bathroom," then turned and walked out, tall and springy, the picture of handsome health. Panic lent him strength this time.

"Well, aren't you a little frightened too?" Howard asked. "All you healthy bastards feel guilty in here." He chuckled painfully and tapped his ribs through the faded hospital pajamas. Only the eyes, deep yet unsurrounded, moved as if on stalks and showed fire. "You haven't been to see Bruce yet, have you?" he said, looking shrewd. "Well, he's had his visitors all right, and I've had the same, grim and vulturine both. Listen, John, don't write and you won't get ileitis of the semicolon. Don't ever make your peace with God, either. Bruce knew better and so don't I. I've had the same buzzards measuring me with their twitchy beaks, and I'd prefer to be Bruce. He can't hear them! Every time he breathes they know the words that wind would carry if it could!"

"Howard . . ."

"What?"

"I thought you were a sanguine sort of guy."

"Man, that *sang* ain't gwine so good no more, don't you know? I've got a dead spot big as a walnut in my heart. Look at Bruce now. That's what you're going to do and you don't like it, do you? You'll be looking at an optimist! He always thought that someday he might get away with his own sins. Can you imagine that? He couldn't keep a sin or a secret or a secret sin from himself, but the poor bastard thought someday he could! If you can't keep a secret from yourself, who the hell *can* you keep it from?" His eyes twitched on the optic nerves, his chest heaved and hesitated in pain.

"He made no treaties, did he," John said.

"He was not only brave, Johnny; he was fierce. 'Why should

men love a wolf more than a lamb or dove?' asked Henry Vaughan, and I might add that women find wolves attractive, too. Oh, well, goodbye, John! Goodbye, goodbye! You want to know something? You may be as fierce as Bruce." Howard put out a weak hand and shook John's. "If you weren't such a shit you'd be a good man. *Goodbye!"*

And so, John thought as he entered the hall again, the descent into the nightmare progresses: first one confronts the milder beasts, the mammals, who are not too distant relatives and haven't the force of terror; then the reptilian bird, the essence of ferocity. That's at the end of the hall, in the dark, feathery place where the talons wait and you deserve it.

The angles of the hall's perspective grew acute, and although he walked slowly, the distance to the door grew small at the rate of the dream in which he was pulled. His mouth dried, his hands sweat, the clean clothes he had put on for the hospital seemed insubstantial and full of windy gaps. The door approached; painted steel, it was too small, gummy at the edges and partly open. He passed right on through, eyes shy and staring, to meet the half-man dying on the white bed.

In the cold light the closed face could have been, for purposes of cruel identification, Bruce's. The forehead was a band of dead white; the shut eyes beneath it were deeply sunken, the dark lids red as fresh bruises. The cheekbones, above the blue swath of shaven beard, were as pearly and ovoid as eggs in waterglass. The expected thin tube entered the left nostril, where it was taped in place, and led the mind down to an inspirated, cruel hook, as would a taut line in the mouth of a fish, no hookeye visible. The wasted face and neck were somehow fungus-like and ripe, as if pale life burgeoned underneath in place of bone, and might split through. The nose was sharp and lean, the untaped nostril black and deep—as deep as the end of the tube's push into Bruce. His mouth was slightly open, and a noisy suck of air, a windy, whistled parody of surprise, repeated and repeated upon the sleeping lips. Through the bristly new hair, a youthful, unmeant crewcut, John followed on the pale scalp the deep red crosshatchings of the stitched-down flaps. Through there the burr holes had been augered and the saw inserted: *See-saw,* and the bonemeal had come shedding out.

John's own scalp crawled as if in response to glittering tools, and his hair, in a design identical to the design trenched upon his brother's head, seemed to stand on end. If he did not love his brother, still the connection had been made in raped bone; in the violation of the most private part of a private man, his brain, brother perceived the shadow of brother's wounds.

The chair beside the bed was empty, as was the low chair in the corner of the room. Beneath the half-pulled green windowshade the golden light of dusk shone weakly, whitened and sterilized at the sill by the fluorescent bar above the bed. Upon the metal bedtable a glass ash tray, centered upon a doily that was itself perfectly centered, remained and would remain innocent of Bruce's nervously stubbed long butts and scattered ash. The time for bad habits—the property of anxious brain—had passed. This thing he had become, lax-armed upon a bed, fingers in the slight bend of coma, was the vegetable of whispers, the fascinating horror all men whispered of.

John stood beside the bed, his hand close to Bruce's white one. Black hairs curled in crisp design upon the backs of the tapering fingers, and the white hand on its narrow wrist emerged as if from a sleeve of soft, woven black. The hand that he had always feared for its unthinking strength in rage, the hand he had found disturbingly weak when he helped Bruce into his last conscious bath, had now in absolute immobility regained its steel. It lay as if waiting for a trump of action—as if, instead of the machine it was, severed forever from its source of power, it saved and bided.

He moved a few inches away, to a point beyond the radius from the elbow to the arc of potent fingers, and only then recognized the distance for what it exactly was. If there had only been a time, if he could only conjure up a time to soften the fear that had grown into reflex! Bruce's touch was as much to be avoided, had always been, as the kiss of red-hot iron; his flesh leaped back from it as if that separation were ruled by the spinal cord itself.

"I want a memory," he said out loud, and the wind on Bruce's lips answered *surprise,* repeated, lost the strength of that suggestion and repeated itself out of meaning into air.

No one could add a thousand little things committed in the course of life, nor, adding just a few, gain the comfort of reason; there *had* to have been a choice, a point where lines diverged like rays from the sunburst of love killed or born, and if he could find that point in time he might at least create a brother in his mind—make Bruce the actor in a play of dignity and worth.

Thunder: above Leah blue-black thunderheads climb in gigantic billows to the height of the Universe, stretch the sky upward beyond a ten-year-old boy's conception of the depth of deep blue. The sound is so loud it is a vacuum in all sound, and shuts the eyes as well as the ears. CRACK in the electric air, and the houses are miraculously standing, the misty hills more or less where they were—or maybe not. Tame bushes in the yard roll white in maniac gusts; the arching maples lash thick branches with willowy irresponsibility, as if, in panic, they have lost their comforting strength. On the back porch two boys, one ten and one seventeen, scream back at the storm how brave they are and face the sting of rain that flings itself through the screen. They are alone in the house, and have run upstairs and down closing windows. They have battened the hatches of the ship their home and now face the storm that is a typhoon; that has transformed Leah into a foreign sea. The lawn and driveway are suddenly water, pebbled by moving sheets of rain. The air is suddenly cold. Stunning thunder crumps dents in the blue-black sky, and lightning spits chimes, a jagged crack, then crackle and BLAM! the hills rock in the violent mist. The boys scream back, their screams lost and joyful in the higher clamor of weather. Along the sill below the billowing screen a row of pint cream bottles rock and tinkle. Seeing that they are about to fall the younger boy runs to save them, slips on the wet porch boards, skids into bottles, sill and screen and falls among the glass. Then he sits to watch his right arm gush, watches the rain mix with the red, wash blood and rain together to the boards and out the scuppers of the porch. The slice in his arm is like a crack in a dam, and he sees himself pouring out. He is the fluid clear or red that is flowing out into the storm. Boy overboard! In a terror of dilution he sees himself for the first time dying, and believes, as he will always believe, that death is precisely such a random flow. As he begins to faint he hears his voice cry HELP, and sees, as if through a dark lens, the white face of his brother. "All right, I've got you," he hears. Like an iron valve a strong hand closes the hole. He knows then that some of him, at least, is left, and that it is his brother's hand saving him, holding his life inside. Thunder would prepare, lightning split, rain wash him into the swallowing ground—but for the one strong hand that holds him inside of himself.

Bruce's tapered hand lay slightly curled against the sheet. Blood pulsed, yet the pale hand never moved. *There* was a memory of rain and brotherhood! Alone, brother saved brother's life. Headline in the Leah *Free Press:* Boy Saves Brother's Life.

I will give him that memory, John thought, give him the memory and take the scar. And with cold surmise he reached for Bruce's hand. He gathered the fingers that were as random as tassels into his own live ones, lifted the hand and turned the hairy arm. There ran the white ridge of the scar, from dark border of hair to dark border of hair—livid across the white as white as a toad's belly.

If Bruce hated the objects of his cruelty, as he had the mangled toads, might he also hate those who helped him? Gratitude was the most unstable of emotions, and there was no plan, no angle of incidence, no physics in that dark mirror. He held the warm hand, and could not let it go. The memory was as inverted as the brain could wishfully make it; the scar could neither be transferred nor erased.

"Bruce," he called to the body of his brother. In the hand a slight pulse ticked—perhaps it was his own. The wind of breath sucked on; the plasm idled. His hand, in the limp one, seemed to separate from his body altogether, and he stared down upon it and upon the one that was held, or held his. A hawk's talon cruelly hidden in a mouse's back: even to witness such a sight meant connection, as if the line of vision itself were palpable as flesh. Held by the long-nailed fingers, their moons covered by untended cuticle, he waited for a sign. "All right," he said, "I give you my hand in payment. Cut it off."

And then cried in terror, for the hand closed upon his.

—Gently, with the hesitation, almost the tenderness, of consciousness. Would he look up along the scarred arm, up the body to the face, his eyes darting closer to the horror he might find there? If the eyes now opened—were now open—charged with the sudden power of sense, signaling the glee of vegetable turned animal . . . Perhaps they smiled at him! He snatched his hand away. No, the face was still and closed; the thin tube still proclaimed Bruce lump. But the hand still moved upon the sheet, slowly clenching and unclenching with the idiot disconnectedness of the claw of a dying bird.

He made himself take the hand again, and suffered the weak clenchings of it. It hadn't hurt him. It hadn't had the strength. Moved by some stray circuit of the infinite, now disorganized, geometry of sense, the hand in spasm merely flexed. If he could forgive, or be forgiven, the same two hands must do their meeting sent by mind, strong in circuit, aimed by eyes. He could remember when he ran from a Bruce who may not have chased to hurt him. Younger, weaker, he had learned to run and disappear as a mouse evades a hawk. Older, no longer mouse, the pattern was still in force: to break it he must willfully give himself.

No sunburst of love born or hate ended, but in his hand the hand of his brother grew familiar. There was no past time, as there never is, no memory of tentative, shared possibilities. So he must be crying out of pity for the death of pride, out of sadness for love unborn.

He had never heard his father cry before, but now he recognized that tortured noise as the expected progression of his father's deep and virile voice. As he turned to add the strength of his arms to the weakness of his father in sorrow, he heard his own smooth, involuntary moans. Smooth in the resolution of indifference, in the loss of hate, this music seemed to become the pure and simple mourning of love that heals and cleans like rain.

CHAPTER 27

Jane waited beside the little graveyard, where he had mysteriously told her to wait. The order had been calm and stern—she hadn't thought to question it. Now she waited with a quiet confidence she could not, although she tried, disturb. God knew there were reasons for anxiety. What had been settled, except that she had admitted need beyond reason or restriction? He had found her in the hospital, and with an inner certainty she could not question said that now he was fit. He'd been to see his brother, and said: "I saw Bruce. He's sick and dying, but there's nothing I can do."

Darkness was coming up Pike Hill, moving up from the valley where Cascom and Connecticut joined as if Leah, as her lights went on, pushed night up into the wild, higher places. In the west the sun had gone out of an orange sky. No wind at all moved the great black pines behind the graveyard, and no animals moved in the new darkness; that shade of night had come when even the red squirrels left talking for fear of silent owls.

Leah smoldered in the east, burned without flame. Only the thin smoke hovered and stayed for warning.

She heard him coming through the trees, his steps soft and precise even in the dry brush. Then he stood quietly beside her. "I didn't want to tell you sooner," he said with difficulty. "It wasn't my move. I didn't mean to let you worry longer than you had to." He lit a match and held it over a piece of paper so that she could read:

DEAR JOHN,

I know you was going to turn me in. I do not blame you John. A man never ought to be punised for what he never done even Junior Stevens. I figured out you would come told me first so I figured you would get this. I have got to close now as I am going out to the woods and I will never be comeing back alive. I hereby deed you my fram and truck approx. 100 acres all there on the deed. Do not let them gip you John G.I. $1000 exempton covers all the taxs. Rember all those good times we have had. You was my only friend John.

Sincerely yours,
WILLIAM HUCKINS MULDROW

P.S. They will not ever find me, W. H. M.

"He's gone, of course," John said. "He means it, I can tell you that. You can call Junior when we get back to the house. I don't want to show this to the police until tomorrow. Give Billy a chance to get himself set. He likes privacy."

"I'm sorry, John," she said.

"I knew it before. I went to see him, and he told me not to worry. His rifle's gone, too. That's how he's going to do it."

She put her arms around his waist, her head under his chin. Above her head his eyes would be fiercely blue, staring, as she had seen them stare, with the power to burn lines in the air; as if they were electrodes aimed—this time back into the deep, absorbent woods.

After a while he turned her toward Leah, and they looked down upon the busy constellation of windows, signs and lights winked by rising heat, masked gently by Leah's pillaring trees. "We've got to go down," he said, and as if in warning answer a parched wind moved like dust against their faces. A dull, continuing fear surged against her and was stopped by his strong arm. Burning and the threat of it constantly hovered, sometimes hardly felt: the deaths of friends and husbands, hills black and dead, rooms ashes of wood or of love . . .

"Will it ever rain?" she asked.

"I suppose it will, Janie, but that's no excuse for waiting." He turned her around again and stared into her eyes. She looked straight into his and received a nearly blinding charge of that fierce energy.

"I forgot," he said, and whirled around. "My father's guilty bourbon!" He went to a thin gravestone, his hand running gently over the edge of it, then bent and pulled up a bottle. "O bourbon," he said, "I know a stronger medicine than you!" With that he threw the bottle through the trees, where it was silently received.

"Wasn't much in it, anyway," he said.

As they walked down again, toward Leah and the things of life, she knew herself to be, again, a part of that purposeful, complicated moil. As they descended into the neighborhood of lights, into the wide tunnel of maples, it seemed to her that the craggy, fertile arms of Leah—threatening or threatened—arched and touched over their heads.

ABOUT THE AUTHOR

THOMAS WILLIAMS was born in Duluth, Minnesota, in 1926, went to New Hampshire when he entered high school and—except for Army service in Japan and graduate work at the universities of Chicago, Iowa and Paris—has been living there ever since. His short stories have appeared in *Esquire, The New Yorker,* and *The Saturady Evening Post.* One was awarded an O. Henry Prize; others have been included in *Best American Short Stories.* His novel *Town Burning* was nominated for the National Book Award in 1960, and his volume of short stories *A High New House* received the Dial Fellowship for Fiction in 1963. He has also been a Guggenheim fellow and was awarded a Rockefeller grant for 1968–69. His novel *Whipple's Castle* was published in 1969. He now lives in Durham, New Hampshire, with his wife and two children and is at work on a new novel, *The Hair of Harold Roux.*